She could not look at him without wanting to kiss him.

"About the night of the ball," Evelyn started.

"Are you worried I won't be discreet about what happened between us?" he asked, and her eyes shot to his, read the knowing look.

"I wasn't thinking that at all!" she protested, then hesitated. "You are discreet, aren't you?"

"A footman could dine out for a month on a tale like that. If, of course, anyone cared to invite a mere servant to dinner."

"Dinner?" she parroted.

"Yes," he said, taking a step toward her. "Footmen eat. We sleep. We even—" He was toe-to-toe with her now, and she had to tip her head back to hold his gaze. She clenched her hands against her skirts to keep from touching him.

"Kiss?" she finished breathlessly, hopefully.

For a long moment he stood very still, staring down at her, his jaw tight, as if he were calculating a complex problem in his head.

It seemed to take forever for him to decide.

Finally, he swore softly, and she was in his arms.

Romances by Lecia Cornwall

THE PRICE OF TEMPTATION
SECRETS OF A PROPER COUNTESS

LECIA CORNWALL

THE Price OF Temptation

AVON
An Imprint of HarperCollinsPublishers

AVON BOOKS
An Imprint of HarperCollins*Publishers*
10 East 53rd Street
New York, New York 10022-5299

First Avon Books mass market printing: January 2012

"Stop, *madame*," the man ordered, his weapon leveled at her.

Panic made her do the opposite. She drummed her heels against the mare's sides, but it was futile. She felt the big horse's breath on her cheek as the rider grabbed her reins and dragged her to a halt.

Evelyn screamed, but the fog caught and held the sound. She raised her riding crop and lashed out, hearing a satisfying thwack as it landed across his shoulder. He cursed but didn't let go. He jerked harder on the mare's reins and looped them around his wrist to cut off any hope of escape. The mare sidestepped, whinnying her own terror, and Evelyn clung to the pommel with one hand as she raised the crop for a second blow, but he tore it from her grip and tossed it away.

He grabbed her collar in a leather fist and dragged her toward him, tearing the delicate lace. She screamed again and clutched his wrist with both hands, fighting his choking grip, digging her nails into the skin above his glove.

The chill of metal under her chin stilled her instantly. She looked into his malevolent eyes, now only inches from her own as he cocked the pistol, the click like thunder against her ear.

"I am not carrying any money or wearing jewels!" she gasped. She had only her wedding ring, and he could have that if he wished.

His laugh was harsh, his breath a sour miasma of stale wine and garlic. The pistol jabbed deeper into her flesh, and his hand tightened on her throat, the leather of his glove squeaking.

"You think *I'm* a thief?" he asked in French. "You are the thief, *madame*. You and your accursed husband."

The hair on the back of her neck rose. "Did Philip send

Both his horse and his clothing were black, casting a sinister silhouette against the silver fog.

Though his face was hidden and only his eyes were visible between his upturned collar and the low brim of his hat, she was certain now that she didn't know him. She caught a panicked gasp between her teeth, swallowed it. She tightened her grip on the reins, ready to bolt, yet still hoping he might pass by, ride on.

But he drew closer and she read cold speculation in his eyes.

She kicked her mare to a gallop, and the horseman did likewise, following her. Fear knotted Evelyn's stomach. Her mount was no match for the powerful stallion. She could feel the rider's eyes boring into her, and she leaned over the mare's neck, trying to coax a little more speed from her, racing for safety.

She'd foolishly left her groom at the gate, wanting just a few minutes of privacy. Terror slowed everything to a crawl, except her pursuer. He closed the distance between them effortlessly, rode beside her. She looked across at him.

He didn't look like the men they usually sent to follow her. *They* remained at a discreet distance and did not approach her.

Nor did they point pistols at her.

Her spine melted at the sight of the gun. Was he a highwayman or a thief? Surely there was too little traffic to draw a thief to Hyde Park at dawn.

But she was here, wasn't she? And all alone.

The mist that had seemed a benevolent veil against prying eyes became a shroud, suffocating and dangerous. It closed in around her, catching at her skirts, slowing the mare's legs, hiding landmarks and guideposts. Her moment of freedom had become a deadly trap.

especially since his abandoned wife remained in London to bear the brunt of his shame.

Evelyn had no idea where her husband was. He could be walking the earth somewhere, hale and healthy, or he could be rotting under it. She smoothed her hand over the violet velvet of her fashionable riding habit. Perhaps she should wear black, but she doubted the appearance of widowhood would win her any sympathy or stop wagging tongues.

Evelyn was tired of gossip, tired of being watched by the Crown and the curious, and scorned by those who thought themselves better than the wife of a traitor. But she'd been ordered to stay in Town. She was not even allowed the dignity and privacy of retiring to the country. Wherever she went, someone was watching her, waiting for her to slip up, to reveal her husband's hiding place, or hoping she'd show herself to be as much of a traitor as he was.

There was nothing for it but to take her exercise alone at dawn, smile bravely at the few social events she was still invited to, and to behave with as much grace as possible until this was over.

She heard hoofbeats behind her and glanced back. There was a horseman riding toward her on a huge stallion. Her mouth dried. Did she know him? Strangers made her nervous.

She turned away, hiding behind the feathers of her bonnet for fear *he* knew *her* and would want to stop and talk about Philip. She guided the mare to the side of the track, leaving room for the big horse to pass by unimpeded, but her heart climbed into her throat and lodged there.

She slowed her horse to a walk, straightened her spine and tried to appear calm and dignified as she waited for the other rider to go by.

Instead, the hoofbeats slowed.

Evelyn looked back. The rider was right behind her now.

Chapter 1

As a rule, only duelists frequented Hyde Park at dawn.
Lady Evelyn Renshaw knew she might be flying
in the face of convention, but if she wanted fresh air, and an
outing untainted by scandal and shame, then this was the
hour to come. It was barely light, and the morning mist was
as thick as new milk, the air sweet as honey, and Evelyn was
blissfully alone.

The sharp-eyed ladies of the *ton* had yet to rise for the
day, to call out their carriages and unsheath their claws. If
they'd gotten out of bed early and driven through the park,
they would have found Evelyn riding alone, and had the
pleasure of tearing her to shreds over tea that afternoon.

It was even too early for the gentlemen who usually
exercised their stallions on Rotten Row while the crowds
were thin and there was space to let their animals run.
They'd not have the chance to ride alongside Evelyn, at-
tempting to coax sufficient proof out of her to win the lucrative bet at White's as to whether Lady Renshaw was
wife or widow.

It had been nearly seven months since anyone had last
seen Lord Philip Renshaw, but the charges of treason
against him ensured the gossip hadn't even begun to slow,

THE Price OF Temptation

To Donna, Pamela, and Sherile
This book wouldn't be possible without your wit,
wisdom, and friendship!
And to Frank, truest heart and dearest companion—
you are very much missed.

you?" she asked, swallowing the bile that came with the words.

A smile pleated his sallow face but left his eyes cold. He had the eyes of a snake, she thought, half expecting him to flick out a forked tongue. "*Non, madame. I come from a much higher authority than that.*"

For a moment she thought Philip must be dead after all, and he'd sent a devil to drag her down to his side in hell.

The man laughed again, heartless in the face of her fear. "No, not *God*, my lady," he mocked. "Higher than that even. Napoleon. Your husband stole something that belongs to France, and the Emperor wants it back."

"What?" It was hard to talk—or breathe—with his fist clenched around her neck, impossible to think with the gun pressing into her flesh.

He gritted his teeth impatiently. "I was told you speak fluent French. Did you not understand me? I can repeat it in English. Your husband is a thief, *madame*. He stole a sacred battle flag from France, and his treachery has cost thousands of braver, better men their lives."

"Is he—" She swallowed. "Is Philip alive?"

His eyes bored into hers. "He has betrayed everyone, both English and French. Do you think he deserves to live?"

She lowered her eyes, refusing to answer that, even in her own mind.

"If the Gonfalon de Charlemagne is returned, then l'Empereur may forgive him and send him back to England. The English will hang him, or course, so whether he still breathes or not, Lord Philip is a dead man, *n'est ce pas*? I assure you, *madame*, you should be more worried about your own life at the moment. I have shot ladies before."

He smiled as if it was a happy memory for him, and Evelyn's skin crawled.

"So tell me, where is the banner? We have searched Lord Philip's estates in Gloucestershire. The only place left is his London home, but it is impossible to get inside if not invited, isn't it? Every eye in London is trained on your door, day and night."

He raised the gun in front of her face when she did not immediately answer, and she stared into the soulless black eye of the barrel, fear choking off words. She could only shake her head.

"You refuse to cooperate?" Quick as a snake, he coiled his arm around her neck, trying to drag her onto his horse. She felt the mare sliding out from under her, but her boot was caught in the stirrup and her leg twisted painfully. She screamed again, and he hit her across the temple with the gun. The mist dissolved to stars. "Return the gonfalon, and I'll let you live," he growled in her ear as she fought to stay conscious.

"I can't—" she panted, dizzy.

"Or you won't?" he demanded. He twisted her arm behind her back and she opened her mouth to scream again, sure now that he would kill her.

"Let her go."

The voice was deep and calm, cutting through the fog like a knife. The Frenchman's grip loosened for a moment as he spun to face the interruption, but he did not release her. She tried to take advantage of the distraction and push away, but her captor renewed his hold and twisted her arm harder. She gritted her teeth at the pain.

"Go on your way. This is not your affair," the Frenchman snarled.

The newcomer's face swam before Evelyn's eyes as hot needles of pain bit deep. She blinked and looked into the man's face, wordlessly pleading for help.

She realized that he looked more impatient than concerned or afraid, as if she were inconveniencing him by needing to be rescued. Her heart skipped a beat.

He *was* here to rescue her, wasn't he?

She cast a glance over the lean length of his body. He hardly looked the part of a knight in shining armor. He wore a faded army tunic, needed barbering and a haircut, and there were shadows of exhaustion under his eyes.

Still, his hand rested on the sword belted to his hip, as if he were prepared to draw the weapon and use it if he had to. She met his eyes again, hope surging.

He had the audacity to smile at her, a charming, heart-stopping grin, as if they were meeting in a drawing room and he found her amusing. Did he mean to reassure her? The flirtatious wink did nothing of the kind.

"Please—" she managed to croak, but the Frenchman wrung her arm again, cutting off further speech. She bit back a cry, unwilling to give her captor the satisfaction of making her scream in front of her rescuer. She watched the soldier's eyes darken, saw his jaw tighten, and every trace of merriment disappeared from his face.

"The lady hardly looks pleased to be in your company, so I can only conclude that her predicament is indeed my concern. I must insist you release her at once." He said this lightly, but she heard the hard edge of warning in his tone.

The Frenchman swore, the sound guttural and ugly. "Who the devil do you think you are, Robin Hood?" he demanded.

The soldier's lips quirked but his eyes remained as cold as the fog surrounding them. "If you wish, but since I have other injustices to right this morning and I'm pressed for time, I'll thank you to speed things along and let the lady go."

The Frenchman laughed as if it was a joke between the two men, but Evelyn felt him tense, the movement of his muscles sudden as he lifted the pistol and aimed it in a single fluid motion.

"No!" The warning tore itself from her raw throat.

But the Frenchman's finger was already curling on the trigger.

The gunshot was loud in Evelyn's ear. She watched in horror as her rescuer dove for the rusty dirt of the track with a grunt of pain.

"You shot him!" she gasped.

The Frenchman shrugged as he shoved the empty gun into his belt, meeting her eyes with a smug look of satisfaction that told her he liked to kill, and was good at it.

"And you're next, *chérie*," he whispered.

The soldier's sword flashed before Evelyn's eyes, a sudden whir of silver, sound, and air that narrowly missed her cheek. Her cry of surprise was drowned by the Frenchman's scream.

Blood spurted, colored the fog for an instant, and sprayed over her face.

Her captor shoved her away and clasped a hand to his cheek. Blood spilled between his fingers, crimson on black leather.

His stallion reared at the scent of blood, its eye rolling in panic for an instant before it bolted, careering wildly down the track with the wounded Frenchman bouncing in the saddle.

Evelyn's boot was still caught in her own stirrup, and she fell as the stallion's escape knocked her off balance, dangling awkwardly against the heaving side of her frightened horse.

Strong hands lifted her back into the saddle, and she

righted her bonnet and looked down at him in surprise, her thanks ready on her lips. The ice in his eyes rendered her dumb.

"Run," the soldier advised her. "He might come back if he can still reload."

He slapped the mare's rump, and Evelyn felt her spring ahead, as eager as her rider to get away.

She cast a desperate glance over her shoulder. Was the Frenchman following her?

There was no one there but her rescuer, tall and brave with his sword still in his hand, staring down the track after her. Then the mist swallowed him, and her hero disappeared as quickly as he'd arrived.

Tears blurred her vision as she rode on and the gate loomed out of the fog. Philip was alive. She was still married to the greatest traitor in England, and apparently France as well. She scrubbed at her eyes, soaking her glove. She had stayed out of his affairs, hoping ignorance would keep her safe.

But ignorance was not going to satisfy them now. Philip's enemies were more ruthless than she'd imagined. His sins required payment in blood.

And the debt had fallen to her.

Chapter 2

Captain Sinjon Rutherford watched until the last hoof-beats faded in the fog. He glanced down at the bloody sleeve of his tunic, now sporting a hole in the scarlet cloth big enough to put his finger through. The Frenchman's bullet had grazed the flesh, but the lady's warning had saved him from far worse.

Still, it was his sword arm, and he had a duel to fight, one he was late for, thanks to the unexpected encounter. He smiled grimly as he wiped his sword on the grass, cleaning away what he could of the Frenchman's blood. *He* would have a far more substantial souvenir than a scratched arm, likely an ugly scar that would keep him from accosting une-scorted females in the future. The blood stuck to the deep engravings that covered the sword, but it hardly mattered. In a few minutes the blade would be stained with more.

English blood this time.

And very appropriate that would be, since the sword had been a gift of thanks for the rescue of another lady, one facing a similar fate to the woman in purple, and at the very hands of the man he was going to kill this morning.

"Gonfalon of Charlemagne," he muttered, wondering what a Frenchman was doing in Hyde Park at dawn, bellowing about a French battle flag. He'd heard of it, of course. Legend had it that every time the French carried the gonfalon into battle, they won. But the gonfalon had disappeared and the French armies had begun to lose at last.

Sinjon frowned. Even if the stories about the flag were true, they were not tales a London lady was likely to know. He remembered the stark terror in her green eyes. If she'd known what her captor was talking about, she'd hidden it well.

Out of habit, Sinjon reached for his watch, then realized he'd pawned it days ago, on his arrival in London, to pay for food and lodging. His second would know the time. The man was probably looking at his own watch at that very moment, wondering if he was going to put in an appearance. He pictured the men waiting for him on the field of honor—Creighton, the two seconds, and of course there would be a surgeon on hand to tend the loser. Maybe he'd have the man look at the graze on his arm while the seconds were sending for an undertaker for Creighton.

He sheathed his sword and started walking.

"Captain Sinjon Rutherford?"

He spun, drawing his sword again, cursing the fog and the complacency that came from being in England. They wouldn't have crept up on him so easily in Spain. Five men appeared out of the mist. Four were big, hard fellows with pistols pointed at him, but the fifth man wore an elegant blue coat and was armed only with an icy stare that swept disdainfully over his ragged appearance.

Sinjon tensed. Footpads, perhaps? Odd that they'd know his name, but the park was full of unsavory characters this morning. Unfortunately, the mist was already lifting, and there was nowhere to run. Wits were his only option.

The toff's mouth tightened in speculation, as if he were

reading Sinjon's thoughts and had wits of his own to bring to bear in the contest.

Sinjon held his sword loosely in his hand, letting the light flash on the blade as he regarded the gentleman with a look of cool amusement.

"Is this about the lady? She rode off that way, frightened but unharmed." He pointed in the wrong direction, but no one bothered to look. Every eye was fixed on him, sober and wary.

The toff drew off his gloves and pointed the way she'd actually gone, his expression bland. "Her servant is waiting at the gate. She's quite safe now."

Sinjon hadn't expected thanks for his good deed, and he saw that obviously he wasn't going to get any.

"Then if this is about my appointment with Lord Creighton, I assure you I'm merely late. I still intend to make good on my challenge."

The gent's mouth quirked. It could have been disgust or humor. Sinjon couldn't tell. If he'd had another few minutes, he could figure out exactly what the gentleman was thinking and know how to play him, but the stranger renewed his unreadable expression.

"You aren't merely going to be late for your duel, Captain—which is, by the way, illegal in England. You aren't going at all." Then he smiled a cold, superior little grin without any humor or warmth to it at all, and Sinjon felt his gut tighten.

"You're under arrest."

Was he caught already? He'd barely been back in England a week, hadn't found any trace of O'Neill. Sinjon knew that without O'Neill, he faced the hangman's noose and Creighton won. He felt the skin of his neck prickle as the toughs stepped forward to pin his arms. They were big men and there was little point in resisting. One took his pistol and another reached for the sword.

"Careful with that," Sinjon warned.

"French, in't it?" the man asked, turning the blade in his thick hands, cautious as a plowman holding a lady.

"Yes. So's the blood on it." It wouldn't do to have them think it was English blood, considering what the charges against him suggested.

"That will do, Mr. Gibbs," the gentleman said calmly, and the man unbuckled the belt at Sinjon's hip, the sword sighing as it slid back into its scabbard.

Sinjon played his last card. "You could let me fight the duel," he said to the toff. "I intend to force Creighton to admit the truth, and that would make arresting me quite unnecessary."

He read a touch of admiration in the man's eyes, but it was gone in the same instant.

"Hardly. The duel is a trap. Creighton's men are waiting, and they have orders to kill you." The gent's bland tone was at odds with the hard speculation in his eyes.

Shock leapt along Sinjon's limbs, and he tensed, clenching his fists. "Are you here to see it done, then?" he growled, trying to jerk out of his captors' grip, but they held him as if he were a kitten. "Go on. Try," he said, keeping his eyes on the toff.

The man smiled, and tilted his head, genuinely amused. "I'm here to save your life, Captain, not end it."

"What do you want?" Sinjon demanded.

"This is hardly the place for such a discussion. Have you breakfasted? No, I suppose you haven't. Soldiers probably don't eat before battle, and men don't dine before a duel, do they?" He didn't wait for an answer. "Bring him along," he ordered, as if the thugs were children and Sinjon was a stray puppy they'd found in the dust. Willing or not, there was nothing to do but follow or be dragged to whatever fate— and the toff—had in store for him.

Chapter 3

"**M**y lady!" Evelyn's butler cried as she appeared at the kitchen door. He began issuing orders at once. "Get Lady Evelyn's maid, and fetch the doctor!"

Evelyn held up her hand, though it still shook.

"I'm fine, Starling. The blood isn't mine. I met with a mishap in the park." She winced at the pain in her arm as she raised it to brush a gore-stiffened lock of hair out of her eyes.

Starling's face was pinched with disbelief as he held out a towel to her, but she concentrated on wiping her face. Her stomach rolled at the brownish smear that came off her skin.

If not for the soldier who happened past, things might have ended differently.

She had not even thanked him for his kindness, and he'd risked his life to save hers.

It was more than Philip would have done for her.

"Is my sister awake yet?" she asked.

"No, my lady. Shall I send her maid up to get her?"

"No," Evelyn said quickly, relieved. She'd come through the kitchen specifically to avoid Charlotte. If her sister caught sight of her torn and bloody riding habit, her bruised throat and mussed hair, Charlotte would swoon, and as there was blood involved, she would probably keep on swooning until the smelling salts ran out. Then she'd fly into a tizzy and send for Eloisa and Lucy at once, and Evelyn knew she would find herself henpecked half to death by all three of her sisters before the clock struck noon.

It seemed she could still avoid the worst, since even Charlotte's sharp-eyed, gossipy maid didn't appear to be downstairs yet.

"Send a bath up to my room," she ordered as she folded the bloody towel into a neat square and tucked it into her pocket. She held tight to her composure, behaving as if this sort of thing happened every day in Hyde Park and had not upset her in the least. She ignored the pity in her loyal butler's eyes, left the kitchen and walked slowly up the main stairs.

In the privacy of her bedroom, Evelyn could not get out of her bloodied garments fast enough. She tore them off, not bothering with buttons or fastenings, and flung them into a corner. A fat teardrop flew off her smeared cheek and pattered onto the white cover of her bed, leaving a rusty splash. She stared at it for a moment before she shuddered, snatched up the coverlet and tossed it away too. She looked around for any other spots of blood, not wanting a single reminder of the attack, or the man's threats.

There was nothing. Her room was as clean and stark as always, not a thing—save the pile in the corner—out of place. She swallowed, trying to stem the fear that there might even be worse to come.

Philip wasn't dead, and he was a thief as well as a traitor.

She crossed to the basin and scrubbed at her cheeks until they stung, not daring to look in the mirror until her skin was clean again. She dropped the washcloth onto the bloody pile.

When her maid knocked on the door, Evelyn was sitting at her desk, serenely composing a letter.

She ignored the curious servants and listened to the sound of the water singing against the sides of the copper tub as they filled it.

"You may go," she said without looking up, including her maid in the order, waiting for everyone to depart before she locked the door. She dropped her robe and stood before the mirror. There were dark bruises on the white skin of her throat, on her arms and legs, as if the darkness was slowly overwhelming her at last. Before today the bruises had been on the inside, hidden away from prying eyes, and now each mark was a visible testament to the horror.

Philip was alive.

Evelyn sank into the soothing sanctuary of the tub and shut her eyes. She half expected to see her attacker's burning eyes and feral snarl as he made his demands, but it was the soldier's face that came to mind, his gray eyes filled with uncompromising courage as he assessed her situation and then had the audacity to *grin* at her. She shifted in the tub, and water sloshed over her breasts, a warm caress.

In another time and place that roguish grin might have charmed her, made her heart flutter. He'd most definitely been handsome as well as brave. She shifted again, sinking into the water until her knees rose like white islands.

Of course, when a lady found herself in such peril, any rescuer would seem like the handsomest man in the world.

And if he'd known who she was, who her husband was, would he still have come to her aid?

She tightened her mouth at the bitter answer to that, and pushed the thought away. Perhaps there were still people who did not know her sordid tale, hadn't judged her yet. She clung to that faint hope, but it was as slippery as the small bar of rose-scented soap in her hand.

When Evelyn joined Charlotte for breakfast an hour later, she wore a high-necked morning gown with long sleeves, and a cashmere shawl. Josephine, the former Empress of France, had made the shawls fashionable throughout Europe. No one wore them now that Napoleon had divorced her and married an Austrian princess instead. Josephine had been discarded and abandoned by her husband, just like her, Evelyn thought. She wore the shawl as a reminder, and because it was soft on her skin, and beautiful.

Charlotte eyed the plain blue gown. "Good heavens, Evie, what are you wearing? You look like a widow!" She dropped her fork on her plate with a clatter, spilling the plump bite of kidney that adorned it. "Have you had news? *Is* Philip dead?" she asked hopefully.

Evelyn waited while Starling poured tea for her. "No, Charlotte, there's been no news. I daresay you'd know before I would, since your husband is keeping a close watch for such information."

Charlotte frowned as she held out her own cup. Starling refilled it with fragrant chocolate. "There's no cause to take that tone, Evelyn. Somerson has your best interests at heart. As a peer of the realm, it is his duty to see that Philip is caught and hanged for treason. As your brother-in-law, he wants what's best for you. He'd be mortified if even a penny of your dowry were confiscated along with Philip's fortune."

Evelyn hid a bitter twist of her lips behind her teacup. The esteemed Earl of Somerson was indeed doing his best to distance his wife's sister from her traitorous husband. In fact, all three of her powerful brothers-in-law were ready to step in and take control once the fate of Philip's vast wealth was decided. They said they would protect her, but she knew if they had their way, their disgraced sister-by-marriage would end her days hidden away in a small suite of rooms on someone's remote country estate, forgotten by her family and polite society.

Evelyn kept her expression bland as Charlotte grumbled at her lack of gratitude and then turned to family news.

"Eloisa and Wilton arrived in Town yesterday, but Lucy and Frayne have been delayed because one of their sons has a cold. Eloisa will visit you today if she has time, but she'll want to see her modiste at once, of course. Fashion must come first in light of our current disgrace." She paused only long enough to drain her chocolate and signal for more. "Eloisa says she can face anything, so long as she is properly attired in the latest style, and I must agree with her." Charlotte cast another baleful look at Evelyn's clothing. "You'd do well to prepare for the coming battle by getting yourself up in something smart and elegant too."

Evelyn stared at the untouched toast on her plate.

The coming battle indeed.

Another Season was starting, and the *ton* was about to pour into Town like hordes of well-dressed invaders. With new ears to hear it and new lips to spread it, the gossip about Philip Renshaw was about to begin all over again.

Unlike her sisters, Evelyn didn't care what she wore as people stared at her and whispered behind their fans. She clasped her fingers in her lap, hoping inner strength would be armor enough against the slights and insults.

Starling served Charlotte a large sausage and another kidney from a silver dish, and she licked her lips.

"You must be anxious to see to the opening of Somerson House, Charlotte." Evelyn said hopefully.

Propriety demanded that Evelyn needed a chaperone in her husband's absence, and her sisters had vowed to take turns staying with her, ignoring Evelyn's objections. Having one of her sisters constantly by her side was supposed to give society the favorable idea that Evelyn was a respectable widow, despite Philip's treason. Who could believe her guilty of any complicity in her husband's crimes with the esteemed Countesses of Somerson and Frayne and the Viscountess Wilton by her side?

Except for the fact that her sisters were the three silliest women in England.

"Will the children be coming to Town this year?" she asked, hoping the need to organize home and nursery would draw her sister away.

Charlotte shoved a forkful of food into her mouth. Evelyn's stomach gave a queasy shrug. "I employ dozens of maids and footmen to open the house, and a veritable army of nursemaids to see to the children." She stabbed the sausage and bit off the end. "Speaking of servants, my maid told me this morning that your last footman has quit, Evie. Joined the army, gone for a soldier."

Evelyn glanced at Starling, who nodded apologetically. Her heart dropped to her slippers. It was difficult to find servants who would work for the wife of a traitor. Now, her last footman had decided he'd prefer the peril of French guns and the hardships of army life to a well-paid post at Renshaw House. He had not even said good-bye.

Evelyn thought of her own soldier again. Even if his coat was faded, he'd been every inch a hero. She hoped her footman would be as brave.

"Come and stay at Somerson House," Charlotte coaxed through another mouthful of food. "There's too much work in this house for so few servants."

There was indeed more work with Charlotte in residence. The cook alone was busy day and night.

"I couldn't impose," Evelyn said firmly. "I shall simply hire a new footman."

Charlotte snorted. "Who would want to work here?" She had the grace to blush. "Oh, sorry, Evie, but *really.*"

Evelyn raised her chin. "I'd only be underfoot, Charlotte. I'm sure you'll be very busy planning your annual ball."

Charlotte swallowed the rest of her sausage in one gulp so she could reply. "It's only weeks away, and Somerson says we mustn't allow family misfortune to change our plans. He has instructed me to carry on as if nothing was amiss, and so I shall, with Eloisa and Lucy's help. And yours as well, of course, in the background. We are the daughters of the Earl of Tilby, and we'll not be sneered at by anyone."

Evelyn swallowed a smile. Unfortunately, the Earl of Tilby had *only* had daughters, and the title had died with him, though Somerson was petitioning to revive it, and have it added to his own string of titles.

While no one would dare to actually *sneer* at the late earl's three eldest daughters, there was a good deal of mocking laughter behind gloved hands and fluttering fans while Evelyn's sisters stormed through society in complete ignorance of popular opinion.

Evelyn had been born late in her parents' lives, and was only a child when her sisters catapulted onto the bosom of society like a troupe of acrobats. Tilby's title and their own good looks had made them popular debutantes, and each in turn claimed her Season's most eligible lord as husband. It appeared that a vast dowry could blind a suitor to any fault.

Even in the schoolroom, Evelyn had heard the gossip about her sisters, and the tales of their vanity, gluttony, and indelicate behavior. It had taught her to act with dignity, to listen more than she spoke, and to use her head for more than a place to display the latest in fashionable hats.

"If you won't come and stay at Somerson House, Evie, then at least come with me to the modiste's today. A new wardrobe is just the thing to drive away melancholy and guilt. Somerson says you're to be invited to our ball despite everything, so you will need a gown."

Evelyn shifted in her seat, and felt every one of her bruises. "Not today."

"But if that hideous thing you're wearing is the best outfit you can come up with, I'd say it's *urgent*!"

Evelyn drew the lovely shawl around her shoulders. "All the same, I have other plans for the day."

Charlotte sighed, and a kidney-scented gust of wind filled the room. "Visiting that foundling home again, I suppose. If you had children of your own, you wouldn't need to—"

She stopped when Evelyn's head came up, and colored anew, every fold of her face turning scarlet. "Oh, sorry," she mumbled. "But you could accompany my girls to the park with their nurses if you wish to spend time with children, or go and see Eloisa's boys. You look like a breath of fresh air would do you good."

Evelyn's stomach clenched at the mention of the park. She imagined blood and watching eyes. This time, *he* wouldn't be there to rescue her. "Perhaps tomorrow," she said, rising. "If you'll excuse me, Charlotte, I have some letters to write."

"To whom?" Charlotte demanded, as if it were her business. As if Somerson wouldn't tell her exactly what mail Evelyn sent if she asked him.

"To Kitty Dacey."

Charlotte made a face. "Good heavens, why are you writing to *her*? She was your governess, wasn't she?"

Evelyn smiled. "Yes, she lives by the sea now, with her husband, father's old valet. I had promised to visit, but that's impossible now."

"And a good thing too! You can't be seen *visiting servants*." Charlotte rolled her eyes. "As if doting on worthless orphans wasn't bad enough. You have eight lovely nieces and nephews—"

Evelyn refused to be drawn. "Enjoy the modiste, Charlotte."

Charlotte set her fork down at last. "I most certainly will, but I warn you, Eloisa will *insist* you see her modiste at once when she catches sight of you. I can't understand why you're being so stubborn. I look forward to the new styles each year." She sighed and patted her rounded belly, filled to capacity with kidneys, bacon, and sausage, and sloshing with chocolate. "I must be breeding again, since nothing from last Season fits. I need a whole new wardrobe, so I won't be back until supper." She turned to Starling. "Have the cook bake some quince pies. I have a craving for them."

Evelyn retreated to the quiet of the library, and let Charlotte's demands occupy the few servants she had left.

She needed a new footman. She looked at the unopened copy of *The Times* sitting on the desk. She couldn't bear to read it, to see the caricatures and comments about Philip's—her—scandal. Advertising for a new servant would only add to the gossip. She sighed.

She didn't just need a footman. She needed a miracle.

Chapter 4

Sinjon was escorted to an elegant library and pushed into a leather chair.

"Not much of a prison," he quipped as the sailors laid his sword on the wide mahogany desk.

The room reminded him of his father's study. Only the family portraits differed. He looked up at the sober strangers glaring down at him as they silently judged his guilt.

He'd spent much of his childhood standing before the sour faces of his own ancestors as his father lectured him on duty and responsibility. Perhaps if he'd paid the slightest attention, or done as his father wished and joined the Church, he wouldn't be sitting here now, facing charges of treason and a hangman's noose, but they'd both known that despite his saintly name, he was hardly cut out to be a man of the cloth.

"It's not a prison, Captain. This is my home," the toff said. "I thought this would be more comfortable than a cell at Horse Guards, and more private."

"Private?" Sinjon asked, his brows climbing into his hairline. What the hell did that mean? Suddenly, the elegant room felt more dangerous than the dankest dungeon. He looked at the burly sailors, but at a curt nod, they silently retreated and shut the door behind them.

"Let's start with introductions before we go on to explanations. I'm Adam De Courcey, Earl of Westlake."

An earl? Since when did earls invite renegade army officers into their homes for private chats? Since Westlake already knew who he was, Sinjon didn't bother to reply. He crossed his legs and waited for the promised explanation.

Westlake's mouth rippled at Sinjon's failure to observe the niceties of social introduction, and he turned to pull the bell.

Sinjon waited to see who would come through the door. Creighton, perhaps, or the earl's thugs, or maybe a detachment of redcoats would drag him away to a real prison for failing to be polite, but it turned out to be nothing more terrifying than a dour butler in impeccable morning dress.

"Good morning, Northcott. Captain Rutherford will be my guest for breakfast. We'll have it here in the library." He took his place behind the desk and looked at Sinjon. "Do you prefer coffee or tea?"

"I prefer whisky," Sinjon replied.

Westlake folded his fingers into a steeple and regarded him over the top of them, like God presiding over the universe. Sinjon held his stare, still waiting to find out why he was here, and unwilling to let his guard down until he did.

"Coffee, then, Northcott," Westlake said, dismissing the butler.

The earl looked at the weapon on the desk, lying amid crystal inkwells, embossed stationery, and leather-bound books. "A very fine sword for a disgraced army captain with little fortune," he said speculatively. "It's French, isn't it?"

"It is," Sinjon said pleasantly. "Either you have a knowledge of weapons, or the French inscription on the blade gave it away."

The earl's brows rose at the rebuke, and he unsheathed

the sword and ran a manicured finger along the blade. "Ah, yes. 'Fortitude, Strength, Courage,'" he translated. "Beautiful work, and the finest steel. Probably a family heirloom." He met Sinjon's gaze. "A sword fit for a French colonel, I'd say."

Sinjon's gut clenched. It was indeed. And it was nearly impossible to believe an enemy officer had made him such a gift, but Westlake didn't understand just how grateful the French colonel had been for the kindness he had done him.

He wondered how much more Westlake knew, but the earl's face was cool and unreadable. He got to his feet and crossed to the window, his back to Sinjon.

He left the sword on his desk, unsheathed, close enough for Sinjon to grab it if he were so inclined. A test perhaps. Sinjon pitied him. Westlake had no way to know that he never did the expected. He was curious, and he assumed the thugs were still within shouting distance and fast on their feet, so he sat back and waited.

"How did you know Creighton planned to murder me?" he asked.

Westlake turned. "Is that your way of saying thank you? I know because I have men watching him. And you. It was rash of you to challenge him, alone as you are in London. You didn't even know the man who volunteered to be your second."

Sinjon frowned. "He introduced himself as Bassett."

"He's in Creighton's employ."

An uneasy feeling prickled Sinjon's neck for the second time that morning, like a noose slowly drawing in against his skin. "What does this have to do with you?" he asked. "If you wished to warn me, then consider me warned and I'll be on my way." He reached for the sword, but Westlake shook his head.

"It's not as simple as that."

"What isn't?" Sinjon asked, leaving his hand on the sword. The hilt warmed under his palm, a familiar friend.

His only friend.

"You're a wanted man. An outlaw," Westlake said. His eyes roamed over Sinjon's uniform, pausing pointedly at the loose threads and telltale patches where his epaulettes and badges of rank had been torn away.

He'd worn them proudly until the day he returned from patrol to find soldiers waiting to arrest him. The major's sword had flashed in the harsh Spanish sunlight as he stripped him of his rank before commanding his own sergeant to bind his hands. The major had to bellow that order twice before it was obeyed. Creighton, damn him, had stood by and watched, waiting until his hands were bound before he dared to step forward and strike him. Sinjon fingered the small scar on his jaw as he faced Westlake.

"You were arrested for treason in Spain, ordered to appear before a court-martial, accused of spying for the French," Westlake continued.

Actually, Creighton had demanded that Sinjon be hanged at once, without waiting for a trial. He'd even chosen the tree, and had the rope ready. Fortunately for Sinjon, the major liked protocol, and wouldn't hear of it. Nor would he listen to Sinjon's side of things.

"But," Westlake went on, "you escaped custody before your court-martial—I assume you had help—and you got yourself aboard a ship bound for England. Since you did not go to France or America, I can only imagine that means you believe yourself innocent of the charges, and you've come home to prove it."

The muscles in Sinjon's jaw tightened. He made a mental note never to play cards with Lord Westlake. The man spoke without a hint of emotion in face or voice. There was no way for him to tell if he was about to hang or be offered a drink in celebration of his adventure.

The same sergeant who had been ordered to bind his wrists had unbound them again later, in the dark, with the help of Sinjon's guards. His men had taken up a collection, coins they could hardly spare, to help him escape. They brought him his sword and the tunic of a dead private to wear over his own uniform. They wound a linen bandage around his brow, and that was all the disguise he needed to get aboard a casualty ship.

Westlake paced, his polished boots silent on the thick carpet, his eyes never leaving Sinjon's. "Unfortunately, your accuser, Major Lord Creighton, has also returned to England, not to see you brought to justice, but to kill you." He paused, and Sinjon waited. Not that he didn't know the tale, but he was fascinated that Westlake had managed to get so near the truth.

"There's a part of this I can't quite understand," the earl said, frowning. "If you were afraid of execution, you'd be in hiding, not confronting Creighton on St. James's street in full view of dozens of Horse Guards officers and gentlemen of the *ton*. Your story is not unknown in London."

Still Sinjon said nothing. Yes, it had been foolish, but he was frustrated and angry. Creighton's lies had destroyed his reputation and his career, and there was only one other soldier who knew the truth—well, one *English* soldier, anyway—and he'd disappeared before anyone could question him. Sinjon assumed that Creighton had paid him. Or killed him.

Westlake ignored Sinjon's stubborn silence. "Since your arrival in England, you've been looking for a wounded sergeant named Patrick O'Neill."

"You've been following me," Sinjon said blandly.

"Of course. I assume O'Neill can help you in some way?"

Sinjon grinned with gritted teeth. "I'm merely in London because the Season is starting and I want to dance at Almack's," he drawled, but there wasn't a hint of appreciation in Westlake's eyes for the jest. They both knew that a disgraced and fortuneless army captain would never be allowed within the hallowed confines of Almack's. He simply wasn't suitable marriage material for the virginal and well-dowered daughters of earls and dukes, despite the fact that his ancestry was every bit as pedigreed as theirs. Of course, Westlake didn't know that.

"I believe you have family connections in the north of England. You might have gone there."

Sinjon's smile faded as the game took yet another turn in the earl's favor. He shifted in his seat. This was one hand he couldn't afford to lose. Losing meant a long rope and a short, uncomfortable drop. Would a bluff work, force Westlake to show his hand?

"Do you know where O'Neill is?" Sinjon asked, testing the idea.

"No," Westlake replied. "How well do you know Evelyn Renshaw?" he countered, trumping a knave with a queen.

"Who?" Sinjon asked, still wondering who held the ace.

"The lady you rescued in the park this morning. Lord Philip Renshaw's wife."

Renshaw. King of Spades, and all things sinister. The stakes rose.

Sinjon's eyes narrowed at the infamous name. He'd heard of him, of course, but he hadn't known the man had a wife. Everything he had read suggested that Renshaw was an old man, craven and greedy, but the lady had been young and beautiful, even with fear in her eyes. His chest tightened.

Being associated with a traitor's wife was a complication he didn't need.

"I've never seen the lady before today. She needed help, so I helped her." He recalled the look of terror in her green eyes, the dark smear of grease on her cheek where the gun had sullied her perfect skin. She reminded him of another lady, in similar circumstances, in Spain. Rescuing the French colonel's pretty wife had been the start of his troubles. How ironic yet another damsel in distress would end them, since assisting the lovely Lady Evelyn had gotten him arrested, and that might still prove to be the death of him.

"And Lord Philip?" Westlake prompted. "Do you know him?"

"The only Philip I know is a footman in my father's service. He taught me how to skip rocks on the pond at—" He paused, closed his mouth.

"Yes, you're the Earl of Halliwell's son, aren't you?" Westlake said as he crossed to the desk and opened a file and glanced at the contents. "Third born." He looked up, awaiting confirmation, but Sinjon let the information stand uncontested, since it was true enough, though Westlake had missed the fact that his father had disowned him.

"Shall I read on?" Sinjon could almost see the ace sticking out of the earl's monogrammed cuff. "Your father wished you to enter the Church, but you bought a military commission instead, with money you won at the tables. I hear it added up to a small fortune. Was it skill or just luck?"

"A captain's commission is damned expensive. Especially if you want a decent horse and a properly tailored uniform," Sinjon drawled, smoothing his hand over his ragged coat, but Westlake ignored that joke too.

"You were only in Spain for eight months before you were accused of spying for the enemy. A number of the men under your command spoke on your behalf even before the trial, and many of your peers describe you as an excellent officer. You acquitted yourself honorably in battle, so the accusations are difficult to credit." Westlake looked him over without a hint of admiration or censure.

"Did you know the tales of your escape are legendary, Captain? One account says you fought your way out of camp with this very sword. You're a hero to many, just for getting away."

Sinjon remembered the two guards who had assisted the sergeant in freeing him, even cheerfully agreeing to being knocked *lightly* on the head for effect. "They're good lads." He hoped they weren't flogged for letting him escape.

"They say the same about you. A good officer. That's about the highest possible praise a ranker can give a commander, isn't it? You have the kind of reputation that's hard to live up to, and almost impossible to best."

He shut the file and sat down again, looking at the sword. Sinjon followed his gaze. The naked blade gleamed seductively in the morning sunlight pouring through the window, a lovely, thoroughly dangerous creature. Evelyn Renshaw sprang to mind in comparison.

"You, the accused spy, are a hero, yet Major Lord Creighton, the officer who did his duty and exposed your treachery, has been cast as the villain of the piece, at least in Spain. He's a hero in London, since the *ton* has only heard his side of the story," Westlake said conversationally. "It seems logical that he should be the hero, don't you think? But he isn't. You are. Why is Creighton so unpopular?"

Sinjon's jaw tightened. Because Creighton was the traitor, a would-be rapist, and a cheat. He was the kind of officer who got men killed on a whim, and had the gall to enjoy a hearty dinner before doing it again the next morning. He let his disdain show in his eyes but remained stubbornly silent.

Westlake fished a folded sheet of parchment out of the file and held it up. "You really should take this seriously, Rutherford. This is a royal warrant. Innocent or not, you've been declared a fugitive from the law, and I have orders to find you."

The hangman's knot tightened against his Adam's apple and made it impossible to swallow. Sinjon met Westlake's eyes coldly. "Will I get a trial before you hang me? Is there time to have my coat pressed, or is there a private and comfortable gibbet awaiting me in your back garden?"

Westlake tilted his head, amused at last. "I have no intention of hanging you. In fact, I wish to help you."

The ace had been played at last.

Sinjon narrowed his eyes. "Now why would you do that?"

Westlake's features shifted into an icy smile that offered very little in the way of reassurance. "We'll get to that. Tell me, did you happen to overhear the conversation between Lady Evelyn and her attacker?"

There'd been the nonsense about a mythical flag, but it was the lady's soft, desperate cry that caught his attention, the single word "please," spoken on a sigh as she'd met his eyes. Had the bastard broken her arm? His own injured limb ached for hers.

"I heard her scream," he said. "When I reached her, her captor was insisting she had something he wanted. I assumed it was the usual thing women possess that men desire."

Westlake pursed his lips, looking as prudish as an old maid. "Not in this case. The man was a French spy, here to question Lady Evelyn about an important piece of treasure that's gone missing. He thinks she's keeping it safely hidden away on her husband's behalf."

Sinjon gave him a slow, roguish grin. "Ah, then it is the usual thing a man desires."

Westlake shifted in his chair, frosty with matronly disapproval. "Have you ever heard of the Gonfalon of Charlemagne, Captain?"

"Of course. It's a legend, a trick to get men to fight, to make them believe that bullets and swords have no power against flesh so long as they stand beneath a scrap of magical cloth tied to a pole."

"Ah, but imagine if *we* were holding that pole instead of the French. It could end the war sooner, and in our favor," Westlake mused, his eyes glowing.

"Do you truly think that's all it would take? One look at Charlemagne's flag in British hands and Napoleon's crack troops would cut and run, too terrified to fight us?" Sinjon asked.

"Isn't that how magic works?"

Sinjon wondered if the earl might be simple. Good birth didn't always mean good sense. Usually, it guaranteed against it. "They might just fight all the harder to get it back."

He got to his feet and hooked his thumb under the tattered and empty place where his insignia used to be and met Westlake's eyes. "What's any of this got to do with me? I'm out of the army, remember?"

Before Westlake could answer, the door opened and a butler and two footmen entered, bearing trays. The fragrance of crisp bacon, fresh bread, and hot coffee filled the room, making Sinjon's mouth water.

"Thank you, Northcott," Westlake said brightly as a pair of footmen laid a white linen cloth on a table near the window and set out plates and cutlery with crisp efficiency.

"Shall I pour the coffee, my lord?" the butler asked, and

Westlake nodded. Steam curled invitingly over the rim of two china cups. The earl crossed to the table.

"Do come and eat, Captain Rutherford. Your friends call you Sin, don't they? You'll find this much better fare than you've been living on at the lodgings you've taken. I understand you've had nothing but cold pies and stale bread for the five days you've been back in London."

There didn't seem to be anything Westlake didn't know. The thought kept Sinjon stubbornly on the opposite side of the room, though the meal looked delicious, and the earl was right about his diet.

"You still haven't told me what you want," he said, not willing to be bought for so cheap a price as a cup of coffee and a rasher of bacon, even if it was cooked to perfection.

Westlake sat down at the table and unfurled his napkin with a flourish, as if it was the gonfalon and did indeed have magical powers to make men do as he wished.

"Truly, I meant what I said about wanting to help you. It's my job to look for men who will be useful to the Crown, men who can provide certain discreet services, uncover the kind of secrets that might fester and become dangerous to England. Do you understand?"

"Not at all," Sinjon said.

Westlake picked up a pitcher of cream, thick and yellow, and poured it over a bowl of ruby strawberries. Sinjon's mouth watered.

"Well, it appears you have a talent for gambling. You earn a decent living that way, don't you? You're willing to take risks, play for high stakes. The last man I knew who could do that had a talent for reading faces. He was good at getting people to reveal their darkest secrets. Ladies in particular. Do sit down."

"What happened to him?" Sinjon asked.

"He got married," Westlake replied, as if it were the worst fate a man could suffer.

He filled a plate with sausage, bacon, eggs, and fried bread and held it out, and Sinjon took the indicated chair at last, too curious and too hungry to resist the lure of food and information.

"I need a replacement for him," Westlake said. "And you need a place to lie low until we can find a way to prove you innocent of the charges against you. Creighton is a dangerous enemy, and you are without funds or friends. I can help you find Sergeant O'Neill, for example, encourage him that it would be worth his while to help you if he knows the truth."

Another ace. Westlake held them all, plus a few extras, it appeared.

It was quite an offer.

Warning bells chimed in Sinjon's brain, and he set his fork down carefully, sat back and folded his arms. "What would I have to do in return?" he asked. "There's always a price."

Lord Westlake spooned a strawberry into his mouth and leaned across the table, smiling like a cat with prey in its claws.

Sinjon swallowed the uneasy feeling that crept into his throat and hoped this meal wouldn't prove to be his last.

Chapter 5

Evelyn Renshaw stared out the window of her sitting room. There were two men watching the house today from the small park across the street.

"I can see you," she muttered through the glass, glaring at them. They would probably report that she'd gone mad and had begun talking to herself. What then? Would the wolves close in, come to question her again, imagining her more biddable after weeks of scrutiny?

She rubbed her arm, still bruised and sore from the French madman's assault three days earlier, and wondered if there were other, more subtle spies she couldn't see, waiting for her to emerge from this house so they could pounce. She hadn't been out since the attack in the park, and her only visitors were her sisters.

She glowered at the ordinary people strolling along the street and shivered. Everyone was starting to look suspicious.

There was a polite tap on the door, and Evelyn turned to stare at the closed panels. It couldn't be Charlotte, since she wouldn't have bothered to knock. It might be Lucy or Eloisa, though, since they liked to wait for Starling to announce them. They came whenever there was more gossip to report, or if Eloisa had a swatch of fabric or a pattern book she wanted Evelyn to see.

"Come," she called, bracing herself as Starling entered. No, it couldn't be one of her sisters after all. Starling was smiling.

"There's a lad outside who wishes to apply for the post of footman, my lady. I took the liberty of interviewing him myself first, and he seems quite suitable. He says he can start at once, and I thought you might like to see him, if it's convenient."

Evelyn's chest tightened.

Just like that? One footman leaves and another appears to take his place? The wolves were growing bold indeed if they were coming right to the door.

She opened her mouth to tell Starling she wouldn't see the man, didn't wish to hire anyone new, but shut it again. Her desperate lack of servants gave her sisters more fuel for their argument that she should quit this house and stay with one of them. Charlotte had informed her this morning that they had decided to draw straws. The sister who chose the shortest straw would take Evelyn as a houseguest for the Season.

The clock ticked off the seconds, and Starling shifted.

"He seems reliable, my lady. Willing to work hard, and he's clean and mannerly."

Evelyn pursed her lips. How silly. She'd hired servants before. Every member of her staff was hardworking, reliable, clean, and mannerly. She had interviewed each of them in this very room, asked the necessary questions, read them the rules of the house, and hired them. Surely she would know at once if this "footman" was one of the sharp-eyed agents of the Crown, or a cheeky gawker come to stare at the traitor's wife just to say he'd done it. If that proved to be the case, she would make him regret he'd dared to set foot in her salon.

"Show him in, Starling."

She sat down on the settee, arranged her skirts and smoothed her face into authoritative lines.

Then *he* walked into the room, and Evelyn leapt to her feet with a gasp.

It was the soldier from the park. For a long moment she gaped at him, hoping she was mistaken. She'd dreamt of him every night since the attack, a bold hero with a rascal's grin riding to her rescue. She blinked. Perhaps she was seeing things, truly losing her wits.

He was dressed in a plain brown coat and tan breeches, the tattered scarlet tunic gone, but his gray eyes were as keen on her now as they'd been in the park, and his smile was unmistakable. It still made her heart turn over, even now, when she doubted his motives.

Dismay warred with fear. He'd come for a reward, or worse, he'd come to blackmail her, realizing how lucrative such a story could be to a poor soldier. She forced herself to stand her ground as he advanced into the room. He didn't stop until he reached the very center of the Turkey carpet.

He bowed properly enough, but his gaze was direct, bold, not deferential and downcast, as befit a servant or a man looking for a job.

He filled the whole room, and took all the air.

Warning bells sounded in her head, and she looked around for a weapon. There was a Chinese vase on the table near the door, but it was too far away, as was the fireplace poker. Unfortunately there was nothing more deadly close to hand than the feather cushions on the settee.

She settled for a glare of haughty disapproval. "What do you want?" she demanded.

The cocky familiarity faded. "Why, I've come for a job, my lady. Did Mr. Starling not tell you?"

Anger kindled at his boldness. The hero who had rescued her was nothing but an adventurer, a fortune hunter. "Truly? That's all? You haven't come to ask for a reward, or to—" She stopped short of saying the word "blackmail," and raised her chin instead, met his eyes. "How much do you expect?"

He had the nerve to grin. "A fair wage for my work would do."

She didn't have the patience to play games. "Mr. Starling will show you out." She moved toward the bell, but he held up a hand.

"Wait, my lady. I appear to have given entirely the wrong impression. I truly am here because I want honest work, nothing more. What occurred in the park is done. You needed help, and I was fortunate enough to be nearby. I have no thought of reward. Or blackmail."

Blackmail. He'd said the ugly word aloud, and she swallowed.

He took a step forward and Evelyn forced herself to stay where she was, meaning to be master of this situation. She met his eyes, and felt her stomach drop. There was no greed, no curiosity. He looked earnest, almost gentle. It was the same look that assured her he would rescue her, see her safe.

It took her breath away.

"I have knocked at every kitchen door in Mayfair looking for a job. Is there a position open here or not?" he asked, without anger or disappointment.

She examined him again. He was tall and lean, but broad shouldered. His dark hair was tied in a neat queue, and he was freshly shaven. He should have looked ordinary, nothing more than a typical and harmless servant, but he was the kind of man a woman couldn't ignore. Even without his uniform, she could feel the strength emanating from him.

His face was open, his gaze honest, as if he'd rescue her again if she needed him to. It felt like a warm blanket. She pushed the false sense of security away.

"I thought you were a soldier." She made it an accusation.

"I was wounded and sent home."

She trailed a glance over him. He looked whole, perfect, a fine specimen of—

"Where?" she asked, breathless.

"In Spain, my lady," he said flatly, and the spark in his eyes and the tight set of his jaw told her he had purposely misinterpreted her query. The location and circumstances of his injury were his own affair. She could understand that well enough. She put a hand to the lace collar that hid her bruises.

"And before the army? Whose service were you in?"

He fixed his eyes on the wall behind her. "The Earl of Halliwell's, my lady, at Chelton Hall, in Northumberland."

"Have you references?"

He met her eyes, his sharp expression without apology. "Unfortunately no. I left to join the army, and did not take proper leave of his lordship."

"I see," she murmured, on her guard again. "No references."

"I've got a strong sword arm, true aim with a pistol or a rifle, and I can polish boots, fetch firewood, serve at table, or do whatever else the job requires."

She held his gaze. He was bold and strong. He had come to her rescue in the park, defeated the Frenchman. Was that not enough? He stood as his own reference.

For the first time in weeks she felt safe.

"Then I trust you were not—injured—at the park?" she asked.

"I assure you I am fit and ready to start work at once."

She shook her head. "Oh no, you've mistaken me. I can see, that is, I assume, you are fit to do the job." She clasped her hands together, trying to still the nervous butterflies circling her stomach. "I—I only wished to ensure you did not suffer any harm on my account," she explained quickly.

Unexpected tears stung her eyes at the memory of the attack, and she crossed to the window and looked out at the men in the park. They blatantly stared back, not even bothering to be subtle anymore.

She swallowed the bitter taste in her mouth. "There are a few matters to address before you start your duties," she said stiffly, not looking at him. Perhaps if there was a new footman in the house, a tall, muscular fellow, the wolves wouldn't be quite so bold. If he stayed, she might feel safe all the time.

She turned to look at her new footman. "I've neglected to ask you your name."

Sinjon wondered if Evelyn Renshaw could spot a lie. His tongue knotted itself around his tonsils. "Sam Carr," he managed, the unfamiliar name tripping over his teeth on the way out.

She nodded, her green eyes softening. He liked the way the soft gray light of the afternoon touched her face, but he hadn't missed the glitter of tears before she quickly blinked them away, or the shadowy bruises under the lacy edge of her collar. If her spine were any straighter, the delicate lines of her jaw any tighter, she'd crack like porcelain.

His heart lurched. Westlake said she was stiff and cool and formal. She never showed emotion and rarely smiled. He suddenly had a desire to see her relax, watch a smile light her eyes. She was prettier than he remembered. He let his gaze trace her delicate profile, noted the pallor of her skin, the fragility of her slender body. The Frenchman could have broken her in half, but she'd fought him as best she could. If he hadn't appeared, then. . .

"Sam Carr," she repeated, as if trying to fix the name in her mind.

He hated lying to her, but he had no choice. It was Westlake's price.

She raised her chin, and the afternoon light streamed over the stubborn little point. "I'm sure Mr. Starling described your duties, but there are rules I need to make clear before you start."

Sinjon came to attention automatically, a soldier, and the son of a stern father.

She hesitated, raising her eyebrows, and he realized he was looking at her directly. He resisted the urge to wince. Westlake and his butler had spent the past three days teaching him to keep his eyes downcast, since a servant did not look at his betters.

It was difficult with Evelyn. He *wanted* to look at her, even if Sam Carr was forbidden to. She was beautiful. If he'd kept his eyes on the path three mornings earlier, she might be injured or dead by now, instead of dressing him down with a haughty glare. He stared at the toes of his boots.

"I insist on the utmost discretion," she said. "Whatever you hear or see in this house must remain private, do you understand?"

"Perfectly, my lady."

"You will not drink spirits on duty. A pot of ale is served with meals, and a glass of wine on Saturdays."

He nodded crisply, but hid a smile.

"*Do* you drink spirits?"

"Not to excess, my lady. You remind me of my father,

though. He issued the same orders to his—" He stopped, wanted to bite his tongue. Playing this role was more difficult than he'd thought it would be.

"To his what?"

"To his staff. He was head footman at Chelton Hall," he managed.

"I see." Fortunately, she accepted his word for it and went on. "There is to be no—interference—with the female servants in this house, or in the neighborhood, for that matter." A scarlet blush accompanied her warning, blooming over her cheeks like a rose garden, making her prettier still by lending color to her pallid complexion. He hid another grin, imagining in a most unservantly way of interfering with *her*.

"Do you have a sweetheart?" she asked casually. Too casually.

"No, my lady." It was likely true enough. Caroline had probably given up waiting by now, and married someone else.

She blinked at him as if she could not quite believe it. It was flattering, coming from her, given what he'd heard about her strict morals. She didn't look strict. She looked fragile. He noted how the light from the window lit the soft highlights of gold and copper in her brown hair.

"Is that all, my lady?" he asked. He couldn't afford to be distracted. He was too used to flirting with beautiful ladies, charming them, but he could not give in to the temptation to toy with her. There was a vast difference between the lady of the house and her lowest footman.

"You will have Sunday mornings off to attend services if you are so inclined, and Wednesday afternoons are your own. Your quarters are off the kitchen, and—"

"May I ask if you have recovered from your misadventure in the park the other day, my lady?" he interrupted. She looked so brittle, so utterly vulnerable, that he couldn't help but wonder.

She swallowed. "I am perfectly well, thank you," she said stiffly. Then her gaze softened. "I owe you my thanks for coming to my aid."

He crossed to her side at the window, and she held his eyes as he traversed the room. He pointed to her neck, resisting the urge to brush her collar aside. "You're still bruised."

She gathered the lace around her throat with long delicate fingers. "But no worse than that," she murmured, and turned to look out the window.

He followed her gaze to the two men in the little square across the street, carrion crows among the peacocks and popinjays of Mayfair. Westlake was subtle, so they could hardly be his men. *He* was Westlake's man. He wondered how well he blended in, an earl's son, a soldier, trying to pass himself off as a footman. He looked at the frustration on Evelyn Renshaw's face, felt it himself.

"Are they always here?" he asked.

Her jaw tightened, and for a moment her expression was haughty, a lady about to dress down an impertinent servant, but he kept his eyes on hers and waited for an answer. She looked back at the watchers, her scorn all for them now.

"Every moment of every day," she muttered.

He could feel her fear like another body in the room. She was as afraid as she'd been in the park, and she was angry too, a spring coiled too tight, ready to break.

"It's a warm day. Perhaps they're former soldiers like myself, and in need of refreshments. Look at the one on the left watching that lad eating the apple."

She looked at him in surprise, her green eyes wide and

clear, but he wanted more. He wanted to see her smile. He grinned at her, but she did not smile in return.

"Charity is a kindness, don't you think?" He didn't wait for her to answer. Instead, he picked up the tea tray and balanced it on his shoulder.

She looked baffled, but the fear had left her eyes for the moment. He strode down the hall with the tea cups rattling. He marched down the front steps and crossed the street.

"'Morning, lads. Fancy a cup of tea?" he asked, lowering the tray before the first agent, keeping his eyes on the second.

"What's this?" the man growled, eyeing Sinjon suspiciously.

"Compliments of the lady inside. She thought you looked thirsty." Sinjon leaned closer and caught the stale fug of cheap gin on the first spy's breath. "Perhaps she's wrong."

"Clear off!" The second man took a menacing step toward Sinjon, his fist curling. He stopped at the look in Sinjon's eyes. He might be holding a tea tray, but he was an officer, a gentleman, and socially superior to either of the inept louts before him.

"Who do you work for?" the first one demanded.

Sinjon held the man's gaze without replying, letting him draw his own conclusions, make up his own name.

The spy dropped his eyes. He jerked his head at his companion and they slunk away down the street.

With a grin, Sinjon turned toward Evelyn Renshaw's window and bowed.

The lady was smiling, and he'd wager it was the first time in months for that.

Chapter 6

Sinjon had grown up in a house with two hundred servants, but he had never considered what the staff actually *did* in the world belowstairs. Until now he'd had no reason to.

He looked around the kitchen of Renshaw House with a twinge of guilt.

The blond kitchen maid called Annie was polishing copper pans, using salt and lemon that made her hands as red as her runny nose. Cook, a jolly ball of a woman named Mrs. Cooper, was peeling the last of the winter apples for pie. She presided over the process with all the consequence of a queen signing a declaration, and the room smelled deliciously of cinnamon and fruit. His mouth watered. At Chelton Hall, he'd often visited the kitchen to charm tarts from the cook, but as mere footman at Renshaw House, he didn't dare steal one.

Sal, the maid of all work, was ironing table linens in a cloud of steam, her hair frizzing in the heat.

John the Coachman, who also served as groom, stood inside the back door on the excuse that he was waiting for the apple parings and cores for the horses, but in truth he was making sweet eyes at Annie, who blushed at every wink.

Sinjon was trying to remember the instructions Westlake's footman had given him for polishing silver. His hands ached from rubbing, and still the metal refused to shine.

He straightened his legs under the table. The knee breeches and the formal blue and gray coat of his livery were old fashioned and ridiculous, and the powdered wig was itchy and hot, but in the uniform of a servant, he was quite invisible.

Until he went out.

On the street his footman's garb marked him as a member of Lady Evelyn's staff, and he was accosted by strangers who wanted to know what *she* was like, and if there'd been any sign of the traitor.

The upper classes did not deign to speak to him directly, of course. The people he'd once danced and ridden and gamed with as Sinjon did not even glance at Sam. Instead, they sent their servants to make bold inquiries. Once the maid had gotten the details on her mistress's behalf, the lady would serve up every salacious morsel to the *ton*'s most notorious gossips.

He developed a new respect for servants, if only because they knew the secrets that could raise or ruin their masters. If lords and ladies suspected, they might treat their maids and footmen better, be more careful about what they said and did in front of them. But to most of his class, the humble folks who saw to their every need were completely invisible.

He continued to polish, wondering if his hands would look like Annie's by the end of his time here. Weeks, Westlake had predicted, possibly less, if he found what they wanted quickly. So far, he hadn't discovered anything but sore muscles and blisters.

The kitchen door opened and Evelyn's lady's maid came in and poured herself a cup of tea.

"What kind of mood is her ladyship in today, Mary?" Mrs. Cooper asked.

Mary rolled her eyes. "Same, of course. Never a hair out of place, never a complaint or a harsh word." She threw herself into a chair. "Downright boring, it is. What's the point of working for the wife of a traitor if there's never anything to tell when someone asks?"

"Lady Charlotte's maid knows plenty," Annie said. "And she's happy to tell anyone who'll listen."

Mary sniffed. "Half of it isn't true. She hears things from Lady Eloisa's lady's maid, who learns it from Lady Frayne's butler. Lady Evelyn's sisters are better informed than she is about her own husband. Or better liars."

"Is her ladyship going out today?" Sal asked, setting the iron in the fire.

"No. She's writing letters." Mary sighed. "Yesterday, it was reading, and the day before that she was sorting linens for the Foundling Hospital. She hasn't been out in four days. What am I to do? She puts on a morning gown and leaves it on until tea. Why change into a walking dress or a riding habit if you never leave the house? There's no requirement for evening gowns either, since she's never invited anywhere, or any need to dress her hair. My skills are growing as stale as yesterday's bread."

Annie sighed. "Poor lady. *Could* she go out for the evening, even if she wanted to? I heard from Lady Charlotte's coachman that Lord Philip took all her jewels."

"She has a few good pieces left," Mary said. "There's a string of pearls with a ruby clasp, and a locket with an emerald in it."

The green stone would match her eyes, Sinjon thought, picturing her at a ball, the locket around her slender neck, glittering in the candlelight as she laughed. Speaking of glittering, he could see a shiny spot on the silver platter now, and felt an unexpected surge of accomplishment. It fizzled when he looked at the pile of unpolished pitchers and serving spoons piled up beside him.

"Any callers expected today?" Cook asked. "There's no point working my fingers to the bone baking scones or tarts. She won't eat 'em, and she should. She's too thin."

"Too thin! A lady can never be too thin!" Mary countered. "You're looking at her next to Lady Charlotte, and *she's* too fat!" Everyone laughed.

The merriment ceased abruptly when Mr. Starling entered the room. "That will do, if you please. Mrs. Cooper, try making strawberry tarts. They're her favorites. Mary, I understand she's been invited to the opera tomorrow night. Best make sure everything is ready if she decides to accept." He looked at the clock. "Sam, the post is due to arrive. You may go up and wait for it."

Sinjon got to his feet and wiped the polish off his hands, and Mary grinned. "No wonder she hired you. You fill your stockings well, don't you?"

"Mary!" Mr. Starling warned.

Mary blinked innocently. "What? When I worked for Lady Trimble, she hired *her* footmen on the basis of how well they looked in livery. They had to be handsome, of a particular height, and with a fine leg. She had twenty-four of them, all identical, like a set of lead soldiers. Once they had their wigs on, you could scarcely tell one from the others. They called them all 'James' for simplicity." She cast an appreciative eye over Sinjon once more. "Since Lady Evelyn only has one man about the place, it's a good thing you're pleasant to look at."

"What about John Coachman and Mr. Starling?" Annie asked. The other women frowned at her, then looked back at Sinjon, their eyes softening.

He missed his boots and his army uniform. He missed the dignity and deference he was used to, and he needed a graceful exit.

He gave them a dazzling smile, the kind that made debutantes and dowagers swoon. It appeared to have the same effect in the kitchen as it did in the salon. "Excuse me," he said, bowing low.

Giggles followed him up the stairs, and so did Mr. Starling.

"Don't open the front door unless you're certain it's the post, Sam," he instructed. "And you're not to answer any impertinent questions from passersby or stand about gossiping on the step."

"Why doesn't Lady Evelyn go out?" Sinjon asked. He knew the answer, of course, but perhaps Mr. Starling knew things he didn't.

For a moment the butler's mouth tightened stubbornly, but Sinjon held his eyes and made his curiosity look like concern. Truth to tell, it was. He hadn't seen Evelyn outside the library since he arrived here.

Starling sighed. "You seem like a good lad, Sam. You're quiet, unlike those hens downstairs. I'd never tell *them*, of course, but we're men, and she needs a man's protection. I'm glad she hired you. I'm hardly likely to deter trouble at my advanced age."

"Has there been trouble?" Sinjon asked. Surely she was safe enough in her own home. He doubted the Frenchman from the park was bold enough to come pounding on her door.

"Yes. They came and searched the house after they arrested Lord Philip's partner in crime, Charles Maitland. They come back to ask her questions every so often too, and always the same questions. There's some that watch the house, but they keep their distance for the most part. But the other day, Sam . . . I don't know what happened." Starling's face creased with concern. "Something happened in the park, though she wouldn't say what it was. All I know is that she came home with blood on her clothes."

"She must have been hysterical," Sinjon said. Hysterical ladies babbled, and said things they weren't even aware of. His cousin had fallen into a pond once, and came out crying and confessing to stealing a biscuit, as if the two things were connected.

Starling shook his head. "She wasn't upset at all, and that's part of the trouble. She doesn't talk, or scream, or cry." He leaned close. "She must be beside herself, poor lady. She stands to lose everything. The Crown could take Lord Philip's lands and this house and every penny he has. She'd be left with nothing."

Sinjon's mouth tightened. "Is she guilty?"

Starling glared at him. "Of course not! She's a lady to her fingertips. I've been in her service since her marriage to Lord Philip. She's kind, charitable, and gentle. She doesn't have a single sin on her conscience. She doesn't even gossip!"

"But she's afraid," Sinjon said, recalling the fear in her green eyes the day he arrived, and how she'd tried to hide it.

"Yes, terribly afraid, every day, though she'd hate that any of us knew," Starling said. "She gave us a brave speech after Lord Philip disappeared, about how she'd see we kept our jobs and would make sure we were safe. Us! We're the ones who should be protecting her."

They reached the upper hall that led to the front door.

Lady Charlotte's maid stood there, also waiting for the post, an outgoing letter in her hand. Starling's features stiffened into a butler's formal hauteur. "I trust you'll remember I've told you this in confidence, Sam," he said, his eyes on the maid. "There's to be no gossip about her. Not outside or inside this house."

Sinjon nodded to the maid and took her letter. Was she watching Evelyn, reporting what she saw to Lord Somerson? Guilt twisted his stomach. Was there anyone who wasn't watching Evelyn Renshaw?

The lady was under siege, and it was only a matter of time before the walls she'd built to protect herself would crumble around her. It was no wonder she guarded every word, every look, every emotion, even here in her own home.

It would be a harsh blow, losing everything, even if she were guilty, as Westlake suspected.

Sinjon opened the front door and blinked at the spring sunshine. He wasn't here to get involved. He had his own innocence to prove, his own neck to save. He didn't have the time to fall under the spell of Philip Renshaw's pretty wife.

The warm breeze brushed his face like a caress, and he frowned.

If Evelyn was innocent, then why was she so afraid?

Chapter 7

Evelyn watched her new footman open the door to admit her eldest sister. He stood to attention as Eloisa swept in, his military bearing evident, even in livery.

She was so busy staring at Sam that she took no notice of her sister at all until Eloisa stopped in the middle of the room and shrieked.

Sam was instantly on alert, reaching for the sword that wasn't there, and Evelyn hid a smile as he colored. He shot Eloisa in the back with a killing look as he straightened his wig and resumed his post inside the door, close at hand in case Evelyn or her guest should need anything.

Eloisa didn't even notice the alarm she'd caused. She was staring at Evelyn. "Good heavens, Evie, what are you wearing? Charlotte told me your wardrobe was a dog's breakfast, but I thought she was exaggerating, or hungry, but she was perfectly right. Is that *last year's* gown?"

Evelyn watched Sam's eyes flick over her, and felt her skin heat more under his scrutiny than Eloisa's. She covered her confusion by smoothing her hand over her muslin skirt.

"Yes, but the ribbons are new." Green now, instead of pink, for a touch of maturity and soberness.

"Has it truly come to that?" Eloisa squawked. "Making over your old gowns? Can't you afford new ones?"

"I am hardly walking the street in rags." Evelyn looked at her sister's outfit. Eloisa was smartly turned out in yellow from the feathers in her hat right down to her half boots. It felt as if the sun had risen in the room, and Evelyn tried not to squint in the glare. "You look as lovely as always," she said, knowing Eloisa was waiting for the compliment.

"Of course I look lovely. I make the effort. It is exhausting, but it is my duty to set an example." She patted the glittering gold frogs on her spencer and smiled. "A shining example."

Her lips pursed in dismay as she looked at Evelyn's gown again. "Evelyn, it won't do to have you going around town dressed as if you didn't know any better, or don't care what people think. It reflects badly on me. *Do* you have money? Is it as bad as that? Have *all* the modistes closed their doors to you?"

Starling brought in the tea tray and set it on the table, and Evelyn took her place behind the teapot. She was hardly penniless, but economies had to be made in case the worst happened.

She forced herself to smile. "All is well. I simply don't have the kind of social commitments this year that warrant the expense of a new wardrobe." What *was* the accepted etiquette when a traitor's wife appeared in public? she wondered. Did fine gowns make what her husband did less terrible? Of course, if anyone might know the rules of fashion for such a situation, it would be Eloisa.

Eloisa tossed her yellow gloves on the table as if laying down a challenge. "That's all the more reason to dress well." Her expression sharpened. "Unless you know something, you sly creature. Don't keep me in suspense. Have you heard from Philip?"

"No, I haven't. Tea?" Evelyn tried cutting her sister off, but should have known better. Eloisa ignored the offer and slumped on the settee, crushed.

"How disappointing you are this morning! I came here with such high hopes. My friends are no longer amused by the old stories about Philip. I need something new to tell." She laid a hand on her cheek. "And my modiste, Evie! I was her favorite client. I didn't even need an appointment. She hung on every *on dit* I could tell about Philip. But no more. My stories are out of date. Now I must wait for her attention like everyone else."

Evelyn laughed. "Poor Eloisa! What will you do?"

"I shall be forced to make something up!" She sent her sister a look of entreaty. "Help me think of something, Evie. Do you have a lover?"

Evelyn glanced over her sister's shoulder at Sam. Somehow, he wasn't as invisible as he should have been. In fact, he looked as keen to hear the answer as Eloisa. Evelyn felt a blush rise over her face. "I am still a married woman!"

Eloisa made a rude noise. "So is Lucy, but that doesn't stop her!"

Evelyn's eyes widened. "Does Frayne know?"

"What difference does it make if he does? She's given him an heir and two girls. I doubt he's still expecting another boy off her."

"You make her sound like a mare," Evelyn murmured. "Tea?" she offered again.

Eloisa took the cup only to set it down with a thump. "You've done it again, haven't you, managed to change the subject? You're very slippery, Evelyn. We were talking about you, not Lucy! And Philip, of course."

"You brought Lucy into the conversation, not I," Evelyn protested.

"Only because I think you should follow her example. Why be loyal to Philip now? Who knows what he's up to wherever he is? Teach him a lesson, I say. Come and stay at Wilton House, and we'll find you some cheerful company. Oh, Evie! I hear your name everywhere. How can you bear to be tied to that monster?"

Evelyn fixed her sister with a hard stare. "It was *your* husband who arranged the match."

Eloisa's eyes widened. "You were Wilton's ward after father died. It was his duty to see you respectably married. I doubt he expected you'd take your vows so literally! It wasn't a love match. Philip wanted the land you'd inherited from father, and he was willing to marry you to get it, and why not? Linwood is a valuable estate. Wilton couldn't think of any reason why the marriage would be unsuitable. I know Philip is old, and a traitor, but he's very wealthy. At least for the moment, wherever he is."

The perfect match indeed. She had merely been tossed in as part of a contract entirely based on money and land, something that came with Linwood, like furniture or livestock. Philip had been pleased she was pretty, of course, but from the start there were other things on his mind, plans she was not part of, and she was too innocent, and too afraid of her new husband, to pry. She knew now she should have asked questions. Lots of them.

Evelyn couldn't look at her sister without making a biting comment, so she searched the room, looking for somewhere to put her eyes, to give her time to calm down. Her glance brushed Sam, and she frowned. Was that sympathy in his gray eyes? She wanted no one's pity. She sent him a hard glare, but his eyes were soft, deep, and warm, a haven.

Her stomach curled, and she took a breath, forced herself

to look away, but she could still feel his eyes on her like a soothing caress.

She had no idea what to do next. Perhaps she should send Sam out of the room for his impertinence, but that would make Eloisa notice him, wonder what he'd done. Eloisa would insist he be dismissed and tell her she was incapable of hiring good help. Eloisa would bring Charlotte and Lucy into the argument when she refused to fire him, and then she would have another battle on her hands.

Evelyn turned away from Sam and changed the subject. "Is that a new bonnet?"

Eloisa grinned. "I've been waiting for you to notice it. Do you like it?"

The confection on her head was so covered with feathers, twigs, and flowers that it was more like a funeral pyre for a game bird than a hat.

"It's lovely," Evelyn said. Behind her sister's back, Sam rolled his eyes dramatically. He had the audacity to grin at her, just like he had that day in the park, and shake his head.

The park.

It was a frightening memory, but with Sam here, standing by, it didn't seem so terrifying. And it was true that Eloisa's hat was dreadful. Evelyn quickly raised her teacup to hide a smile. Eloisa crossed to the nearest mirror to admire her reflection.

"Madame Estelle makes the most divine hats. I gave her one or two ideas, of course, to set the trend. In a few weeks everyone will be wearing a bonnet like mine. I haven't decided if it's to be known as the Wilton Hat or the Eloisa Bonnet." She turned to Evelyn, her eyes glowing. "I have decided, however, that yellow shall be *the* color of the Season. I've ordered my entire wardrobe in shades of lemon, cream, champagne, and butter."

Evelyn watched Sam's lips quirk, and she brushed her fingers across her own mouth to still a smile. "Sounds delicious."

"Doesn't it? It was Charlotte's idea to give the colors delectable names. Every lady with any style at all will be wearing butter and cream this Season. I have ordered the most divine gown for Charlotte's ball, in custard brocade." Eloisa looked archly at her sister. "It's only a fortnight off, and you'll need a gown too. Mustard, perhaps, with an over-skirt of buttermilk . . ."

Sam grimaced. He stood perfectly still, properly at attention, his hands behind his back, his chin high. Only his face reflected his thoughts as he played with her, mocked her sister. She knew she should have been shocked, but she was enjoying herself. Had she ever admitted that at tea with one of her sisters before?

Still, she'd have a sharp word with her new footman later, and let him know that decorum was to be strictly—

"Evie! I've asked you twice what you're going to wear to Charlotte's ball. It's important you look your best."

Evelyn swallowed. She could wear silk or sackcloth and it would make no difference. She pictured herself walking through Charlotte's ballroom, followed by a thousand whispers as she pretended not to notice the scornful way eyebrows climbed in horror at her presence, or how a hundred fans snapped open to hide mockery or pity or hatred as she passed.

"I've decided not to attend Charlotte's ball this year," she said. "I can't see why my being there will be of any importance one way or the other."

"You must come! People will think you have something to be ashamed of if you stay home!" Eloisa spluttered. "There are at least a dozen people who would stand by you."

Evelyn tilted her head. "A dozen? Out of Charlotte's usual three hundred guests? Hardly encouraging, especially when six of them will be my own family."

"Well, better to have six people by your side than no one at all! But that's why you need the protection of an influential lover, a gentleman with a title, a fortune, and a taste for notorious ladies." Eloisa smiled. "I will put a word in Wilton's ear. He is not without influence. Nor is Somerson, or even Frayne. They're bound to know someone right for you."

Was it her imagination, or had Sam looked shocked for a fleeting instant? His expression was bland and unreadable now, and she frowned, wondering if she'd been mistaken. Why would he care?

"Not Frayne!" Evelyn quipped in mock horror, and laid a dramatic hand on her heart.

Sam's eyebrows rose a fraction of an inch, and a muscle twitched in his jaw in appreciation, and Evelyn felt warmed by it.

The Earl of Frayne was notorious for his scandalous affairs. It was no wonder Lucy had decided that what was good for the gander would suit her as well.

And if there ever was a goose, it was Lucy.

Eloisa didn't laugh. "Oh, Evie, you must take this seriously! Come to the modiste with me tomorrow. We'll use my name, and you can wear a veil. They can hardly refuse to serve you if I'm standing behind you. We'll get Lucy and Charlotte to come with us. The four of us will make a formidable force against insult."

"I have a perfectly suitable gown upstairs," Evelyn said.

"What color is it?" Eloisa demanded.

"Green," Evelyn replied. She glanced at Sam, and his lips spread in a warm smile, as if he approved. Her heart leapt, and she pursed her lips. It didn't matter one whit what he thought. "Or blue," she said. His smile faded.

"No one is wearing green or blue this year!" Eloisa cried. "You will stand out, no, you will *stick* out! Charlotte and Lucy will be horrified!"

"Then I shall stay home."

"No! No, that won't do either," Eloisa said, reversing herself. "You will stick out all the more if you are absent from your own sister's annual ball! It is one of the most important events of the Season."

Evelyn kept her expression flat, letting her sister know how little she cared.

Eloisa wasn't deterred. "I'll make an appointment with my modiste for tomorrow anyway, and my shoemaker." She stood up and pulled on her gloves. "I'll come early, and we can take a turn through the park first. You look like you could do with some fresh air."

"Not the park!" Evelyn blurted before she could stop herself. Eloisa raised her eyebrows. "I hear it's going to rain tomorrow. My cook's elbow aches when the weather is about to change."

Eloisa sniffed. "Excuses. I suppose there's a reason why you cannot visit the modiste either. A plague of locusts on Bond Street, perhaps, predicted by your butler's bunions." She turned to go. "I despair of you, Evelyn. I am going to consult with Charlotte, see which suitable gentlemen might be on her guest list."

"No one lower than a marquess, or perhaps a prince, if one of them is between mistresses," Evelyn quipped, meaning to quell her sister. But Eloisa smiled. So did Sam. A lazy, appreciative grin that made her heart take a slow turn in her chest.

Eloisa pecked Evelyn's cheek. "That's the spirit! I shall

ask Lucy which prince is currently unattached. She'll know, if anyone will."

"It was a joke," Evelyn protested, but Sam was opening the door for Eloisa. A yellow feather floated out of her hat as she passed, and he caught it and tucked it into his wig with a roguish grin.

Evelyn snatched it out again and gave him a look of censure. He followed Eloisa down the hall and let her out.

Evelyn went to the window to watch her sister get into her coach, newly painted a deep golden yellow. Even her horses had golden coats, and yellow feathers on their heads.

"You have no reason to avoid the park, my lady."

Evelyn turned to find Sam in the doorway.

"If you wish to go riding, I will escort you, and I promise no harm will come to you."

She read the truth of that in his eyes. Deep, soft, gray eyes, trustworthy and stalwart.

"I—" she began, suddenly finding herself breathless. She straightened at once. "I really must speak to you about your behavior during my sister's visit," she began sternly, but he grinned, tying her tongue in a knot.

"It was good to see you smile."

Her heart skipped a beat. "Still, it was bad of you to mock Viscountess Wilton."

His lips thinned in contrition, but failed to dim the light in his eyes.

"I assume you weren't serious about Mrs. Cooper's elbow," he said, not bothering with an apology. "There isn't a cloud in the sky. I checked when I let Elo—er, Viscountess Wilton—out." He pointed to the sunlight pouring through the window to pool at Evelyn's feet. "You can't stay inside forever. Your sister is right about that, at least. Don't hide yourself away, my lady. Step outside. Fight the battle."

Evelyn's heart melted. Her soldier. Her hero. He had kept her safe before, and she so desperately wanted exercise, fresh air, and freedom. He'd promised to keep her safe.

She believed him.

"Thank you, Sam. If it will not interfere with your other duties, you will accompany me tomorrow. I'll have John Coachman pick a suitable horse for you. I assume you ride?"

"Er, yes, my lady. I was in a cavalry regiment."

She imagined him on a horse, sword drawn, charging across a foreign battlefield toward the enemy. Her breath caught in her throat again. He didn't seem to notice. He was regarding her politely, as if the idea had been hers all along.

"I will be ready to ride out at six. You may inform Mr. Starling, and see that John Coachman has the horses ready."

"Yes, my lady."

She caught a glimpse of that rogue's smile of his, and knew if he stayed any longer, she'd be tempted to smile back.

"That will be all," she said stiffly.

The view from behind, she noted as he walked away, was almost as inspiring as the one from the front. She dropped her gaze at once.

What had gotten into her? She was every bit as bad as Lucy. But she felt a little of the fear lift from her shoulders. Perhaps a ride in the park would not be so bad after all.

And with Sam by her side, she'd feel safe again.

Chapter 8

Sleepy shadows stretched across the kitchen the next morning when Sinjon glanced at the clock on his way to the stable. He was fifteen minutes early for his appointment with Evelyn Renshaw.

He corrected himself. Footmen did not make appointments with ladies. They obeyed commands. He grinned. This morning's ride had been his idea, and his command.

Not that Evelyn Renshaw was a woman who took orders. If he'd been in a position to wager on it, he'd bet every lady in London would be wearing yellow within a week.

Except Evelyn.

He frowned, and wondered if she would find it so easy to resist Eloisa's plan to find her a lover.

Sinjon swallowed, and ran a finger under his cravat. Evelyn Renshaw was young, beautiful, and ripe for seduction, and if *he* could coax a smile from her, a blush, then she wasn't immune to masculine charm. Her husband had been gone a long time.

If she took a lover, it wouldn't be him. Another gentleman would have the pleasure of sharing Evelyn's bed. He had no idea why that bothered him so much.

He barely knew the lady, but he recognized beauty, and

knew that tightly controlled emotions often hid deep passions. She was an intriguing woman, one he might have taken the chance to seduce himself if the situation had been different and he wasn't playing her servant.

Perhaps it wasn't lust, but his protective inclinations toward damsels in distress. The Earl of Frayne frequented the lowest brothels, attended the most scandalous parties, and there wasn't an actress in London he hadn't bedded. He could imagine the type of lover Frayne would suggest for Evelyn. And Frayne's countess was nearly as bad as her husband. Mothers warned their sons to stay away from Lewd Lucy. His own father had done so with him when he first came to London. Not by name, of course, but she'd been included in the general category of "women of high breeding and low reputation."

The Fraynes would probably sell Evelyn's favors to the highest bidder. His skin crawled, and he shook the sensation off. It wasn't any of his business. But Evelyn Renshaw needed *someone* to keep her safe, a man who could protect her from treason, scandal, penury, and dangerous Frenchmen roaming Hyde Park. He'd have to be a gentleman, honorable and upstanding, good with a sword, and with enough fortune to keep her.

He'd have to be as unlike Philip Renshaw or Frayne as possible.

Sinjon's brother William came unbidden to mind. William was handsome, rich, the heir to his father's earldom, and he had never done a single dishonorable thing in all his life. Or an interesting one. He'd be the perfect man for Evelyn.

Sinjon felt an irrational surge of jealousy and forced it down. Will was more likely to look down his nose at Evelyn than to accept an invitation to become her protector. William would miss the sparkle of diamonds in a coal heap, since he never saw the potential in anything. Evelyn was a gem, despite the taint of her husband's treason. It hardly mattered. William was probably tucked away in the country, married to a dull heiress by now, and had likely never heard of the Renshaw scandal. Sinjon let out a long breath, glad Evelyn's lover wouldn't be William, at least.

"Good morning."

He turned at the sound of her voice. She was wearing a brown velvet riding habit with a pink silk cravat. She looked fresh, pretty, and vulnerable, someone who would never consider taking men like Frayne or even William to her bed. Sinjon stopped when he realized he'd taken a step toward her and was about to offer his arm like a gentleman. He lowered it, clasped his hands behind his back.

"You aren't wearing yellow," he said, retreating to the safety of teasing her, but she blushed as pink as her scarf. His heart skipped another beat. When was the last time he'd seen a woman blush when he teased her? "Not that you should. Or shouldn't. It's just that you look—" He shut his mouth, realizing he was babbling like an idiot.

She appeared to be waiting for the rest of the description, her eyes fixed on him expectantly, her lips parted. But it wasn't his place to tell her she looked beautiful.

The groom appeared, leading the saddled horses, and she turned her attention to mounting. Sinjon cupped his hands for her booted foot and boosted her into the saddle. He caught a flash of trim ankles, a teasing whiff of a subtle perfume, and found himself tempted to sniff her skirt, to identify the tantalizing fragrance.

He made himself turn away and mount his own horse, his stomach knotted. He glanced at her again. She was arranging her skirts, settling herself on the sidesaddle. She looked up at him, and his heart lurched.

No, he decided, William definitely wouldn't do, and he hoped she had the good sense to refuse Frayne too, if her brother-in-law came sniffing around her skirts. He'd find a way, somehow, to protect her from that danger as well. His hands tightened on the reins in frustration. A lady was hardly likely to seek her footman's advice on love.

He scanned the street as they rode out of the mews, looking for more pressing threats than eager lovers. Only a chimney sweep, the milk cart, and a sleepy tradesman carrying a heavy box of tools marred the silence of the morning, but Evelyn was nervous. He read it in her shoulders and in the tight grip she had on the reins. Her mare's ears twitched as she sensed her mistress's distress. If anyone dared to bid Evelyn good morning or tip his cap to her, she'd probably bolt down the street in a wild panic.

"Are you armed?" she asked tightly.

He smiled at her, his grin carefree, confident and reassuring. "I borrowed Mrs. Cooper's largest kitchen knife, though I'm certain we won't have need of it. At least I hope not. Cook said she'd whip me if I didn't return it in the same pristine state it was in when I took it," he quipped, and watched her shoulders relax a little as she smiled.

He also had a pistol tucked into small of his back, but he didn't tell her that. She might smile at the knife, but a gun would probably terrify her.

She surprised him by making a joke of her own. "Then we shall be careful indeed. I daresay Mrs. Cooper can best even the bravest soldier."

He glanced at her sharply, wondering if she'd meant it as a compliment or an insult. She blushed and looked away. "I mean, even the Duke of Wellington himself would be hard-pressed in hand-to-hand combat with Mrs. Cooper."

He sent her an appreciative grin.

"Did you ever see His Grace while you were in Spain?" she asked.

He'd dined with Wellington and his officers. The great man had spoken briefly to him of horses and the quality of the claret. But privates did not sup with generals, so Private Sam Carr bit his cheek and played his role.

"Oh, I saw him riding by at a distance a time or two. I cheered him with the rest of the lads," he told her. Every soldier of any rank cheered when Wellington rode past.

"And you are content to give up the glory of war for a dull post in London?" she asked, reminding him that he was not a soldier now, but only a servant, and not her equal.

"War isn't glorious. It's bloody and dangerous and a waste of life," he said, barely remembering to add, "my lady."

She lowered her gaze to her hands. "I know a group of ladies, all mothers and wives of officers and common soldiers, who knit and sew for the men fighting abroad. They are desperate to believe that there is glory in it, especially if the worst comes to pass, and their son or husband falls in battle. Glory gives them hope, you see, makes it bearable."

He understood. How could he not? Glory came from behaving with honor, even in the most inhuman circumstances. There was shame in the army too, in the accepted practices of flogging, pillaging, and rape, and in allowing brutal and incompetent officers to command good men. Officers like Creighton.

He wondered what she'd say if she knew his story, his shame. Suddenly it mattered all the more that he prove his innocence. He'd been a good officer, and the role of a subservient footman did not come easily to him. He was polishing boots while other men fought.

Of course, he couldn't imagine the elegant Evelyn Renshaw in a sewing circle of soldiers' wives and mothers either. She would be as out of place there as on a battlefield. Or would she? She had more inner strength and bravery than some of the men he'd commanded. He looked away. He didn't want to admire her, but it seemed he could do nothing else. It was a foolish game. Inner strength protected deep secrets, and bravery hid fear.

"What a surprise to see you this morning!"

Sinjon froze at the sound of Creighton's voice, every muscle tightening, ready for battle. He reached for the pistol at his back and pressed his horse forward before he realized Creighton wasn't looking at him.

He was staring at Evelyn.

To Sinjon's astonishment, she was *smiling* at the black-guard. He stopped where he was, baffled. She looked delighted by the chance meeting, as if she knew Creighton well, and liked him.

Creighton was smiling back at her, a frightening sight. His eyes roamed over the curves beneath Evelyn's riding habit, and Sinjon's gut tightened with indignation. He reached again for the pistol, ready to draw it if he had to, or to grab her reins and get her away from Creighton if he moved to touch her, but she rode forward eagerly, toward the major and away from his protection.

"Good morning, my lord! It is indeed a pleasant surprise to find you in the park so early." She was actually flushed with pleasure, Sinjon realized in horror. He must have made some small noise, because she looked back at him briefly and gave an imperious, damning little wave, ordering him to fall back and ride behind as Creighton pulled his stallion alongside her mare.

Sinjon's nostrils flared as he glared at Creighton's broad back. The vile major wore an expensively tailored army tunic, so new it glowed in the morning sun. Sinjon doubted it had seen battle, or ever would. The man almost shone, the perfect image of a brave, noble officer. His splendor was reflected in Evelyn's adoring eyes, and Sinjon's mouth twisted. The clothing of honor couldn't hide the maggot underneath. He stood where he was as Evelyn and Creighton rode on, too stunned and disgusted to kick his horse forward. Evelyn was gazing up at Creighton, smiling.

And he'd thought she only smiled for him.

He waited for her to notice that he hadn't moved, willed her to look at him, to read the warning in his eyes, but she rode on, oblivious.

He was just a footman, and she thought Creighton was a gentleman.

The image of Creighton's hands on the French colonel's wife filled his mind. Above her torn bodice and bloodied lips, there had been terror in the lady's eyes, but there was no fear on Evelyn's face. She felt herself safe with an officer and a gentleman of her own class. Sinjon's hands tightened on the reins. If she knew what Creighton was capable of, she would be very afraid indeed.

Evelyn laughed, and the sound carried on the breeze like birdsong. He kicked the gelding to a trot, catching up, but remaining a respectful, servile, three paces behind, out of earshot but still within easy reach if there were orders to be given.

The high collar of his livery throttled him. He wanted to tear it off, ride forward and punch Creighton out of the saddle and pound his grinning face into the dust.

He touched the pistol again, started to draw it out. One shot. That's all it would take to avenge dozens, hundreds, of wrongs.

"Ahem."

Sinjon met the Earl of Westlake's icy gaze. He was riding the opposite way along the track. He didn't stop, or speak, just warned Sinjon with a glare.

Sinjon stared back, letting every bit of fury and frustration show in his eyes. Westlake's expression didn't change. In fact, he looked bored. He rode on, his eyes sliding past, as if Sinjon truly was nothing more than a footman.

Sinjon swore under his breath. Westlake's reminder had been clear. He had work to do, and it didn't include shooting Creighton in the back. Nor did it include deciding whom Evelyn could ride with, or sleep with. Without Westlake's help, he could still hang for treason, and Creighton would go free.

His anger simmered. It appeared that Philip Renshaw wasn't the only traitor the lady was acquainted with. He wondered whom else—what else—she knew that could get her hanged alongside her husband. She laughed again, and he gritted his teeth.

A true traitor's wife indeed.

Chapter 9

Evelyn set down her pen and blotted the letter carefully. She was writing to a school for orphaned girls in Lincolnshire, sending a generous donation of Philip's money while she still had access to it. She'd sent a dozen such letters over the past months.

Her husband's gold would do more good if it were used to feed and educate poor children than it would if the Crown confiscated it.

The Prince Regent and rich lords like Somerson or Wilton or Frayne had grand enough fortunes.

Trusted friends had helped her distribute her gifts. Isobel, the Marchioness of Blackwood, had taken the jewelry Philip had given Evelyn and sold it for her. Those funds had gone to the Foundling Hospital as a very large and anonymous donation.

Marianne, the Countess of Westlake, had helped her sell several valuable paintings from Philip's collection. It had been a particular joy to sell off the portrait of his favorite mistress, portrayed in nude glory as the Greek goddess of love. The proceeds of that sale had gone to war widows, the donor's name undisclosed.

There were other works of art, books, and furnishings

to be sold as well, but slowly, carefully, so the Crown didn't notice.

She folded the letter with a smirk of satisfaction. Lord Creighton had offered to help her in her charitable pursuits after seeing the painting she had sold and recognizing it as Philip's. He mentioned he would be traveling to Lincolnshire in the next few days, and offered to deliver her unsigned letter and the generous donation of funds to the orphan school there. He was a true officer and gentleman, and she knew no other soldier with such kindness, such honor.

Well, perhaps one.

If Sam Carr had sufficient class and fortune to purchase a commission, she was sure he would make as fine an officer as Major Lord Creighton.

She trusted Lord Creighton as she trusted Sam. Creighton treated her with the kind of courtesy she used to enjoy as an esteemed lady, a peer's daughter. He did not ask about Philip.

He traveled often, and had offered to carry any letters she wished to send. She had no need to worry about the money falling into the wrong hands.

She had met Lord Creighton through one of the ladies who belonged to the charitable sewing circle. Miss Anne O'Neill had a brother who had served as a sergeant in Creighton's regiment. Major Creighton paid Anne a visit to tell her that her dear brother had been wounded and was missing.

While the ladies could do no more than to stitch prayers for Sergeant Patrick O'Neill's safe return into every garment, Major Lord Creighton could do so much more.

He had offered to make inquiries at Horse Guards, and the queries of an esteemed major would garner a better response than the pleas of a mere sergeant's sister. Anne was exceedingly grateful for his lordship's kindness, and the other ladies in the sewing circle were equally smitten with the gallant officer.

Unfortunately for Evelyn, after Philip's treason was made public, the ladies of the sewing circle decided that it would be quite impossible to allow the wife of a traitor to work in their midst. They had cut off all contact with her, snubbing even her donations of knitting wool, as if her offerings were tainted by Philip's sins and might somehow harm their men.

She'd been dismayed until Major Lord Creighton had come to call, mentioned seeing Philip's painting at a recent sale, and kindly offered to take her donations and turn them over to the ladies as his own.

Evelyn tickled her lips with the end of the quill pen. It had been a wonderful morning. If it hadn't been for Sam, she would not have gone riding at all, and would not have chanced upon Lord Creighton.

She wondered now if Sam had known the major, or at least known *of* him, in Spain. Or perhaps he'd known Sergeant O'Neill. She would ask when she saw him next.

She frowned, and realized she hadn't seen him all afternoon. He'd been stiff and formal as he helped her dismount after the ride, for once the perfect servant, even bowing as he took his leave of her, unsmiling. He hadn't been the same Sam she rode out with.

The door opened and Starling entered the room. "There's a note for you, my lady," he said, and held out a letter on a silver tray.

For a moment she considered the tray. It might fetch enough for a donation to another deserving charity, but Starling was waiting, and she could hardly snatch it out of his hand and send it off to the pawnshop.

"Thank you, Starling." She took the letter and turned it over to look at the wax seal. "Would you send Sam to me, please?"

"He's not here at present, my lady. Today is his half day off."

Irrational disappointment twisted her heart. The thought of Sam not being in the house, even for just the afternoon, made it dark and frightening again. She looked up to see Starling watching her sympathetically, and smoothed her expression.

"Of course. I'd forgotten. That will be all."

Starling hesitated. "Is there anything *I* can do, my lady?"

She forced a smile. "It's nothing. I merely had a question for Sam. It can wait."

She turned to the letter and opened it, and her smile became genuine.

It was an invitation from Major Lord Creighton to ride with him again tomorrow morning.

Chapter 10

Sinjon slipped inside Lord Philip's chamber and stood leaning against the door for a long moment, his heart pounding. He wasn't used to creeping into other people's private spaces like a thief.

He had crept *out* of numerous bedchambers, of course, silently picking up his clothes and leaving his lover of the moment naked, satisfied, and fast asleep in her bed. Surely this was the same, but in reverse, and without the pleasure.

The room was hot, and he took off his wig and tossed the hated thing into a chair, and wondered where to begin.

It was his half day off, and he had things to do outside Renshaw House, but first he planned to find whatever it was that Westlake thought was hidden here, get it over with. The sooner he could leave this house, the better.

The vague fragrance of French cologne, popular among the dandies at Napoleon's court, haunted the chamber. Highborn French army officers wore similar scents, and it reminded Sinjon of war and enemies and treachery. He was instantly alert, his senses keen, the way they had been in Spain. He forced himself to relax. There were no perfumed French patrols lurking behind the bed curtains.

Of course, a fortnight ago he would have sworn that there were no French spies in Hyde Park either.

He hesitated a moment more, listening for sounds in the hall, his ears pricked, a bead of nervous sweat slipping between his shoulder blades, but the house was silent around him, a place of secrets and mystery, the quiet home of a somber lady.

Sinjon opened the drapes, and sunlight crept nervously into the room. He unbuttoned the top collar of his uniform so he could breathe.

The furniture was dark, masculine, and imposing. There wasn't a hint of Evelyn's presence. He wondered if she had ever come here to lie in the huge bed with Philip, or if her husband had gone to her when the need arose.

Sinjon ran his palms along the sides of his breeches and forced himself to concentrate on his task. Westlake had told him they had searched the entire house. The Crown's best men had rifled Philip's desk, looked under beds and inside cupboards, carried away his letters and personal papers, and found nothing.

They had also searched Evelyn's rooms. There wasn't a single love letter, or even a terse note from Philip among her papers. The only jewels they found were her own family heirlooms. Other than her wedding band, there were no gifts, no tokens of love or esteem from her husband.

That in itself seemed most suspicious to Westlake. A lady might destroy or hide the sentimental mementoes of courtship and marriage, but not jewelry. A man as wealthy as Renshaw could easily afford to cover his wife with expensive gems. His mistresses had flaunted the eye-popping jewels he gave *them*. What had Evelyn done with hers?

Of course, a woman like Evelyn had no need of jewels to

be beautiful, Sinjon thought. Nor was she the type to compete with her husband's whores.

He pursed his lips, dismissing the honorable reasons. Even a woman like Evelyn—especially a clever woman like Evelyn—would hide her valuables if she were guilty, or was afraid they might be taken from her.

Perhaps that's what he was meant to find. The lady's treasure horde, put by for the future, once the Crown stripped her of her land and Philip's money. That would hardly prove her guilty of treason. Of course, with a husband like Renshaw and friends like Creighton, what additional proof did anyone need that the lady was also a traitor?

From Westlake's brief lessons, Sinjon knew checking for hidden compartments was the first order of business.

He opened the bureau and found nothing unusual. Renshaw's cravats and handkerchiefs lay in orderly rows in the drawers, pristine and untouched, ready for his immediate use should he ever return. He bought the best, Sinjon noted, running his hands over the finest linen, the richest silk, the softest, most expensive woolens. There was nothing under the folded garments.

He crossed to the wardrobe and opened it. Several coats still hung inside, but there were no secret panels behind them. Likewise, a dozen pairs of Lord Philip's boots and shoes were neatly lined up in the wardrobe, but the floor beneath them was solid, the boots themselves empty.

Sinjon frowned. Where else could he possibly search that the Crown's agents hadn't already looked?

Quick footsteps came down the hall, and he froze.

Evelyn?

He imagined confronting her here, in the intimacy of her husband's bedroom. He swallowed and tried to think up an excuse for his presence here. He could plead that he was merely curious, but that would still get him dismissed.

His heart stopped as the footsteps paused outside the door and the latch began to lift. What would Westlake do if his newest agent were caught?

He'd hang him.

Sinjon swore under his breath as he dove into the wardrobe. The coats flew from the hangers to attack him as the door opened and someone entered the room. He peered out through the crack.

Sal. He let out a silent breath.

The maid set her bucket on the floor and took out a cloth, flicking it open with a crack like a pistol shot. Humming, she began to dust, a mere wafting of the rag over the furniture. Dust motes gathered, filled the air, and swirled like an angry mob in the beam of sunlight that streamed through the half-open curtains before settling again.

Sinjon's eyes widened as he caught sight of his wig, still sitting on the chair near the window.

It looked like a stray cat, napping where it shouldn't, and he waited for Sal to notice it.

She walked right past it.

She dusted the table beside it, firmly shut the curtains behind it, and gave the rest of the room a shrug before she left.

He almost sagged in relief as the door clicked shut behind her and her footsteps echoed back down the corridor.

He kicked open the wardrobe and fought off the embrace of Renshaw's coats. His heart was pounding and his shirt stuck to his skin. He sat down on the carpet to catch his breath. How did real spies manage? Wellington's observing officers braved danger and gunfire to gather information without a moment's trepidation, while a maid with a dust cloth made *him* shake in his shoes.

He'd found nothing at all, and that wouldn't do. Westlake expected more, and he had to admit that he'd grown curious himself about the Renshaws' scandals.

Especially Evelyn's role.

He got to his feet and picked up the coats. Something glittered as it fell from an inside pocket. He caught it. It was a cameo locket, a portrait of a laughing lady, exquisitely carved, with diamonds and rubies set in her hair. She was naked to the waist, looking out at him with a saucy glint in her finely crafted eyes.

It opened with the twist of a thumbnail and he found a note, folded small around a frizzy red curl that almost certainly did not come from the lady's head.

Come to me soon, it read.

It was signed, *Lucy.*

Sinjon's eyebrows shot up. Lewd Lucy and Philip Renshaw?

Now that was a scandal Eloisa Wilton could dine out on for at least a month. He wondered if Evelyn knew. He slipped the token into his own pocket and hung up the coats, doing a poor job of brushing out the creases.

He shut the wardrobe and smiled. He'd found something the Crown's agents had missed after all.

He looked around the room again as he reached the door, and his eyes fell on his wig. He'd almost forgotten it.

How on earth did Sal walk right past it without seeing it?

But how did people he'd known for years walk right past him as a footman without recognizing him?

Secrets, it seemed, hid best in the most obvious places.

Chapter 11

Sinjon spent the rest of his half day searching the dockside taverns for Patrick O'Neill. Many of the wounded soldiers sent home from the war simply stumbled off the ship and into the nearest tavern, and there they remained until their money ran out, or they found the courage to go home. He'd hoped it would be that simple with O'Neill.

Men in tattered uniforms watched him suspiciously as he passed. No one knew Sergeant O'Neill, but they were willing to tell their own tale for a pot of ale, or offer an account of the latest battles, which Sinjon craved nearly as much as news of O'Neill. Wellington was winning at last.

Sinjon wished he'd been at Cuidad Rodrigo and Badajoz. He would have been if not for Creighton.

He asked the sharp-eyed dockside whores, who turned a pretty penny on a soldier's misery, but they did not know their customers by name, nor did anyone recall a sergeant with a saber wound on his jaw.

Discouraged, he watched the newest ships come in, disgorging their cargo of wounded and maimed, the debtors of Wellington's victories. O'Neill was not here either.

Sinjon was beginning to think that the sergeant had died

of his wounds on the way home from Spain, or that Creighton had killed him the moment he arrived in London.

He roamed the streets, letting his anger at Creighton simmer. He wondered what he would do once he was exonerated of the charges against him and Creighton was proven guilty, and if that would ever happen at all.

He supposed he could go back to war, since it didn't look like the fighting would end anytime soon. Or he could settle down, marry, perhaps.

He sighed. He'd had the chance to marry Caroline, who came with a fine dowry and a piece of land, but he'd bolted, run away to war. That life was as wrong for him as a career in the Church.

At the very least, when this was over he'd go north, make peace with his father, try to explain things to Caroline. After that, the rest of his life loomed before him, a blank page.

It was dark by the time he found himself on St James's Street, walking past the gentlemen's clubs he'd once frequented as a member. As a servant, he could not even stand in the doorways.

It was here in front of White's that he'd challenged Creighton to the duel that hadn't happened. Westlake was right. It was a rash, stupid thing to do. He realized that now, but he'd felt helpless, desperate. He still did, caught in Westlake's web of intrigue. The earl held his life in his hands, and he doubted Lucy Frayne's naughty locket was going to fulfill Westlake's expectations.

Standing in the shadows, he watched the gentlemen arrive for the evening. Harry Tipton strode up the steps and Sinjon smiled bitterly. Tipton owed him money, and probably thought he needn't repay it, since he was in disgrace.

He made a note to visit Tipton first once he won free of the charges against him.

Frayne and Wilton entered together, their heads close, discussing something. Probably Evelyn, and which of their disreputable friends might make a suitable lover for her. His glare burned into their evening coats, but they walked on, oblivious.

Then Creighton's coach pulled up and the major went up the steps with one hand in his pocket, his pace insouciant, as if he hadn't a care in the world.

Creighton hadn't so much as glanced at him this morning, and he didn't look into the shadows now. Was Creighton so certain that he was gone? Sinjon's mouth twisted.

Creighton's coachman jumped down to lean on the side of the vehicle to wait. Sinjon crossed the street.

"Cold night," he said, and pulled a flask from his pocket.

The coachman regarded him suspiciously for a moment before taking it. "Rum," he said. "I expected cheap gin. You a soldier?"

"Was," Sinjon replied. "I'm out of the army and I'm looking for work. You know anyone looking for a groom or a stable hand? Your master, perhaps? This is a fine rig he's got. Must be wealthy."

"Was," the coachman parroted. "He's been selling paintings, and his mother's jewels as well, or so the maids say. They're always the first to notice when family heirlooms disappear."

Sinjon pretended to take another swig. "Is his title an old one?"

The coachman shrugged. "He has rich relatives, an earl on his father's side and a viscount on his mother's, but he's a soldier like you, a cavalry major." He looked Sinjon over. "You seem a likely chap for stable work, but the major hasn't hired anybody new for some months, though we could do with the help."

"Hires soldiers, does he? I've been looking for an old friend named O'Neill. He was my sergeant. Know anyone by that name?"

The coachman reached for the flask again. "We have an O'Donnell, but he's straight in from the countryside. Don't think he'd make a good sergeant, if you know what I mean." He twirled his finger next to his ear.

There was a scuffle on the steps of the club, and they turned to watch.

"Pay me what you owe me, damn you!" Tipton cried, grabbing Creighton's sleeve, knocking his hat down the steps.

"I haven't got it, Harry, I swear! I only came here tonight to see someone about a vowel he owes *me*."

"You've been back in England for weeks, damn you. You promised to pay me when you got home. You said you had an inheritance coming!"

Creighton pulled his lapels loose from Tipton's grip. "Then you misunderstood me. It is not so much an inheritance as a dividend on an investment. It hasn't paid out yet."

"You risked my money in some foolish scheme?" Tipton growled.

Creighton smiled, his teeth long and yellow. "Not foolish at all, old chap. In fact, it's a sure thing."

"Oh, and how's that? Where is this fortune coming from?"

Creighton spoke so low that Sinjon had to prick his ears to hear his reply. It echoed off the stone facade of the building.

"Lincolnshire," he whispered.

"What in hell does that mean? What's in bloody Lincolnshire?" Tipton demanded, but Creighton slipped out of his hands and hurried down the steps, like the coward and cheat he was.

Sinjon bent and picked up his hat. "Yours, *sir*?" he asked, holding it out, his other hand on the pistol under his coat. He wasn't wearing his livery now. If—when—Creighton recognized him, he could shoot him if Creighton drew first. It would be honorable enough even for Westlake.

But Creighton didn't spare him a glance. He simply snatched the hat from Sinjon's hand and got into his coach.

Sinjon watched him drive away, disappointment gnawing at him.

Lincolnshire? Creighton's family came from Devon, not Lincolnshire, and O'Neill was from London.

He walked away, his footsteps echoing on the cobbles, and wondered if he'd ever be free.

Starling was still up when he returned, nursing a cup of tea at the kitchen table. He handed Sinjon the keys and a lantern. "Go and check the doors for me, lad, and save my old bones the trip up the stairs."

Sinjon prowled through the silent house. He checked the windows and the front door, and peered out across the square at the park. Somewhere in the dark, someone was watching the house. Poor bastard. It was a cool night, and the starless sky promised rain before morning.

The door opened as he passed the library, and Evelyn stood there.

She gave a strangled cry, surprise perhaps, and he caught her elbow.

"It's me, my lady," he said. "Sam."

She wore a lace robe tied tight over her nightgown, and her hair hung down her back in a simple braid. She looked like a girl, freshly scrubbed and very young. Her cheeks were flushed and her eyes were wide, shimmering in the light of his lamp.

"You're back!" She sounded surprised.

Standing so close, he could smell her perfume. Her face was inches from his, and he could feel her breath on his cheek. He was tempted to kiss her. His mouth watered and he couldn't seem to tear his eyes from the lush softness of her mouth. He felt a tremor run through her body, but couldn't tell if it was an answering desire or fear.

He let her go and stepped back. "Just making sure everything is locked up, my lady," he said formally.

She blinked at him.

"Did you enjoy your time out?" She held up a hand before he could answer. "No, I shouldn't have asked. It's not my business where you went or what you did."

He could see it mattered to her, suspected that she'd been waiting for him, just like Starling. "I went to look for an old friend from my regiment," he said softly. "Nothing more."

Her shoulders relaxed. "Oh." She licked her lips, and the moisture shone in the lantern light, tempting him anew.

"Is there anything you need, my lady?" he asked. He couldn't stand in the hall, not with her wearing her night-clothes, looking at him like that. He clutched the lantern tighter, fighting the temptation to reach for her.

"I wasn't waiting up for you, if that's what you think," she said, looking him over. "I was finishing a letter, and getting a book to read."

She held neither in her hands. Her long fingers were clutching the high collar of her nightgown to her throat, a sign that she was nervous. It would be so simple to pull her into his arms, tell her he knew she was lying before his mouth descended on hers. He smiled at her instead, tilting his head, letting her know that despite her protest, he knew she'd been waiting for him.

"Shall I escort you upstairs? You haven't got a candle. Or

a book." He was rewarded with a very becoming blush. Was her skin hot to the touch? His palm tingled.

She turned and went back into the room, picking up a book from the desk, a candle, and a letter. She held his gaze as she returned, her eyes glittering with the flame, angry and beautiful, passion replacing her usual control.

"There, you see? I can take myself upstairs, thank you. Go about your duties, if you please," she snapped. She thrust the letter into his hand. "You may leave this by the front door. Someone will call for it tomorrow morning."

He bowed as she turned and walked away, a ghostly white figure moving silently up the stairs.

Sinjon waited until her light had disappeared around the bend in the staircase, then went back toward the front hall to leave her letter on the table. He glanced at the address, and paused. His mouth went dry.

"Lincolnshire," he muttered.

He swore under his breath and put the letter into his pocket. In the kitchen, the kettle was still hot. He opened Mary's sewing basket and took out a needle and thread. Carefully, he softened the wax seal, slipped the thread behind it and loosened it without breaking it, opening the letter like a hardened spy. Where did a gentleman like Westlake learn these tricks? There was a sum of money wrapped in a letter, and he counted the notes. One hundred pounds.

The letter was brief, and unsigned. The money was an anonymous donation to a school for orphaned girls in Lincolnshire. He frowned.

What was Creighton's connection to all this? He was hardly the charitable type. The only organization for females he was likely to support was a brothel.

But Evelyn gave to the needy. She supported the Foundling Hospital, and the ladies' sewing circle. Perhaps she had other causes as well that he didn't know about. His skin prickled.

Was Evelyn using Creighton to send money out of London? Perhaps she was planning to run away with Creighton, once they'd stolen Renshaw's fortune. The letter did not seem outwardly suspicious, and the scheme would put Philip's money out of reach of the authorities. "Clever girl," he muttered.

Or was Creighton swindling the traitor's wife? He needed money, or so the coachman had said. He was hardly the type to wait patiently to amass a fortune, or to help a woman in need. In Spain, he'd broken a young lieutenant's jaw because the man owed him twenty pounds and couldn't pay. A hundred pounds wouldn't go far at the tables. One bet and Creighton could lose it all. But he might win.

Sinjon resealed the letter without the money.

In the library, he found another envelope and put the money inside, carefully considering his choices before tucking the packet into a book of poetry.

He put the letter on the hall table and stood at the foot of the stairs, looking up into the darkness above, wondering if Evelyn was asleep.

Was she dreaming of Creighton?

He headed for his own bed with a grim smile. All he had to do now was wait and see what Creighton—and Evelyn—did next.

Chapter 12

Creighton prowled through the corridors of his aunt's town house, searching for something else to sell, something as valuable as the Gainsborough painting he'd already taken. If his family found out, he'd be disowned, but how else was he to survive?

He passed the ormolu clock in her private sitting room and glared at it. Above it, his aunt's portrait glared back, an ugly thing that wouldn't fetch tuppence. It was nearly ten o'clock. Where the hell was Bassett? It shouldn't take this long to fetch a letter from three streets away.

He poked at a small landscape in a gilt frame, a view of the family estates in Devon. He hadn't been there in years. The place meant nothing to him, but the painting might fetch enough to pay for a night's wagering at White's. His current losing streak couldn't last forever.

He snatched the picture off the wall and tossed it on the settee. How he hated living this way, but he had little choice. His gut clenched as he considered the gravity of his situation.

He had to find Rutherford, and kill him.

He was here in London, somewhere, possibly watching him at this very moment. Creighton opened the door to his aunt's bedchamber, knowing he was the first man to enter her private sanctum in forty years. He crossed to the window and checked the street. There was no sign of Rutherford, or Bassett either, for that matter. He turned to the massive jewelry chest that squatted in the corner and forced the lock, cursing Rutherford as he did so. He was reduced to this, stealing from his own family.

Sinjon Rutherford was the worst of fools, an honorable man, despite the fact that he had neither fortune nor title. Rutherford stood ready to right the world's wrongs, save damsels in distress, and win the admiration of men of all classes. *He* would never stoop to pilfering an old lady's heirlooms. Creighton hated him.

He remembered the day he met the good captain in Spain. Rutherford won a fortune at cards from him, money he didn't have. He'd been forced to sign a vowel in front of a dozen witnesses.

He'd planned to cancel the debt, as he usually did, with a bullet between the captain's shoulder blades. In war, men died every day, which was one of the things Creighton liked best about Spain. There were always new officers to game with, wet lads fresh out of England that he could cheat until they got themselves killed. But Rutherford managed to return from every fight unscathed, and covered in glory.

The day the vowel came due, Creighton was unable to pay it. He'd gone on patrol hating the man.

He ignored the neat rows of pearls and the garnet earrings, and pulled up the velvet lining of the drawer, searching for the key he knew must be there. Dust flew up at him, choking him.

It had been very dusty that day in Spain too, on the remote mountain road where he'd happened upon the pretty wife of a French officer, her coach crippled by a broken wheel. She'd faced her enemies with admirable bravery. Her husband was a wealthy colonel, she said, and would pay handsomely for her safe return.

Creighton had seen the possibilities at once, financial and otherwise. He let her write a note and send her driver running to her husband with it.

Then he'd given her maid to his men to keep them busy while he took his pleasure with the lady.

Sinjon Rutherford had found him in a most dishonorable position when he arrived, with his breeches around his ankles as he knelt between the lady's naked thighs.

The woman started screaming, pleading with Rutherford in French, begging for help. Rutherford had sent him sprawling with a single punch, disgust clear in his eyes. With his breeches down, he couldn't fight back, or defend himself. Now was that honorable?

By the time he got to his feet and found his sword, Rutherford had given the woman his coat to cover her torn bodice, and had her behind him, under his protection. The captain's sword was pointed at his throat.

"Don't be a prude, Rutherford," Creighton murmured to the silence of his aunt's chamber, recalling what he'd said then. "She's the enemy." He ripped the velvet lining out of the drawer and tossed it aside.

"She's a woman, not a soldier, Creighton," Rutherford had replied.

Creighton had tried playing the superior officer card. "Why are you here, away from camp, Captain?"

"I've come to collect my money. I wanted to be first in line, since you owe so much to so many others."

Creighton had smiled, thinking luck was on his side after all. They were alone, except for the lady. A quick sword thrust was all it would take to cancel the debt.

"Please, Captain," the woman pleaded. "I have sent a note to my husband. He is Colonel Jean-Pierre d'Agramant. He will come for me, pay for my safe return." She didn't look so pretty now, Creighton had thought, with her mouth bloodied by his fist, but she'd fought like a tigress, and he was still aroused. Once he killed Rutherford, he'd take her next to his corpse.

"You see, Rutherford? She's about to be ransomed. An afternoon's sport won't harm her. When her husband arrives, he'll pay me, and I'll pay you." He reached for the flask in his pocket and held it out. "Let's have a drink while we wait. It will be some while before her husband gets here. We might as well pass the time pleasantly. I'll even let you go first."

As long as he lived, Creighton knew he would never forget the way Rutherford's face twisted with revulsion.

He tore open yet another drawer in the damned Chinese puzzle of a jewel box, and scattered the contents.

"We'll wait for the Colonel, Creighton, without harming the lady," Rutherford had said.

For a moment after that, things began to look up. His men emerged from the bushes, fastening their flies. They assessed the situation—and their own guilt—and chose to side with him. They took Rutherford's sword, held him at musket point.

Creighton stripped Rutherford's coat from the French-woman and began to drag her away for a little privacy.

"I've heard d'Agramant is the best swordsman in France," Rutherford called after him. "Rape his wife, and he's more likely to kill you than pay you. Is an afternoon's sport worth your life?"

That had certainly shriveled any hope of enjoying the lady's favors, and his men started to mutter among themselves.

"We vote that the lady remains unharmed," his sergeant spoke up.

He'd twisted her arm behind her back until she screamed. "This is not America!" he shouted. "You don't get a say in this. The woman is mine!" He raised his pistol, and the nearest man went down with a cry, clutching his leg. The French bitch began screaming again, a shrill, earsplitting sound. He hit her to make her stop, knocking her unconscious, just as her husband arrived with a troop of French Guards.

There'd been murder in d'Agramant's eyes when he saw his wife. Creighton remembered the burn of fear in his belly. He'd dragged the woman against his chest and held his knife at her throat. "I'll kill her," he warned.

Now, he picked up a letter opener from his aunt's desk and threatened the back of the cabinet, looking for a secret compartment.

"And I'll shoot your men, one by one, until you let her go," the colonel had replied, imagining that he cared about their sodding lives.

It made him laugh even now. He pressed the letter opener into a promising crack in the jewelry chest's mahogany frame the same way he'd pushed the knife against her breast.

"Throw down the ransom and go, *monsieur*. I will send her to you when you are out of shooting range."

The colonel's expression didn't change. At his nod, one of his men shot the first British soldier. Rutherford threw himself in front of the rest of the cowering redcoats.

He faced the Frenchman without a trace of fear in his eyes. "They're innocent."

The colonel gave Rutherford the cold, sour, superior French smile usually reserved for English visitors to Paris. He pointed his pistol at Rutherford's heart.

"*Et vous, monsieur?* Are you innocent as well?"

Rutherford hadn't answered, didn't plead for his life. Creighton would have, if there'd been time, but d'Agramant didn't wait. He glanced at his wife's battered face, her torn dress, and gave the command to fire.

In the deafening volley, every man on the road was running, screaming, dying in the hot yellow dust. Rutherford dropped and rolled. He landed next to Creighton and the woman. He actually *stood* in front of her, Creighton recalled, protecting her even then.

Did the fool think he was impervious to death? When the firing stopped and the air was filled with the acrid stink of burnt powder, d'Agramant dismounted and stalked toward them, his eyes locked with Rutherford's. Creighton flinched as the colonel's sword dimpled the skin of Rutherford's throat.

"Your wife is unharmed, *monsieur*. Take her and go," Rutherford said, his voice steady.

"Unharmed?" the colonel hissed. "You think I can allow you to get away with this?"

"Do it," Creighton encouraged as the Frenchman's sword pressed deeper into Rutherford's flesh.

He used the letter opener to destroy another drawer, imagining it was Rutherford.

The Frenchwoman woke and began to scream at her husband in rapid French, explaining everything. Creighton would have hit her again, or stabbed her, but Rutherford turned on him like a wolf, moving even before the colonel could put up his sword. D'Agramant's blade carved a long deep gash in the captain's neck, and hot blood splashed across Creighton's face as Rutherford wrenched the knife out of his hand. His only thought then had been of escape.

Creighton could tell by the look in d'Agramant's eyes that he knew the truth. He shoved the woman at Rutherford and ran, leaving the honorable fools to see to her.

He hadn't gone more than a mile in the hot Spanish sun, with Rutherford's blood drying on his face, before he began to have doubts. If the Frenchman let Rutherford go, or he escaped, what then? Wellington hanged men for rape. It was his word against the captain's. Creighton had ridden hard for headquarters.

He'd told them how he found Rutherford selling secrets to the French. His men were all dead, killed by Captain Sinjon Rutherford.

When Rutherford returned, he was conveniently in possession of an expensive French sword.

Creighton had insisted they hang him at once, but the officer in charge, yet another honorable fool, had insisted on a proper court-martial.

Then O'Neill stumbled into camp, wounded but alive. At least the sergeant had a saber slash to the jaw that rendered him mute.

Creighton sent Private Bassett to finish both Rutherford and O'Neill, but he was too late. Both men escaped.

Who knew Rutherford had so many friends? Officers who liked the captain demanded immediate payment of the gambling vowels Creighton held, and refused to play cards or even share meals with him. Lord Wellington decided it was best if he returned to England.

Creighton stared at the wreck of the priceless chinoiserie cabinet littering the floor of his aunt's bedroom. There had to be a key to the safe where she kept the real jewels, but it wasn't here.

He ran a shaking hand through his hair. He needed money. He couldn't hide like a rat in this house forever. The plain gold chains and silver lockets mocked him, an old lady's sentimental treasures, all worthless. He kicked at them with a curse that sullied the spinster's chamber. He sank to the floor and rubbed a hand across his mouth, wanting a drink.

Perhaps he was safe. He hadn't actually *seen* Rutherford since the day the captain, ragged and hollow-eyed, accosted him on the street and foolishly challenged him to a duel. Rutherford hadn't turned up for the dawn meeting, but he was here somewhere, an outlaw with a price on his head, waiting for his chance.

He'd hoped Rutherford would do the honorable thing and walk into Horse Guards. They'd hang him on sight, of course.

Invisible, hidden, Rutherford was even more dangerous. He still had the French sword, and Creighton feared it would end up buried in his back on some dark night, unless he found Rutherford—and O'Neill—first.

He heard familiar heavy footsteps on the stairs and got to his feet. Bassett was back at last. Creighton employed the burly ex-soldier to keep an eye out for trouble, guarding his life, running his errands. He went into the sitting room and closed the door on the bedroom, so Bassett wouldn't see the mess and suspect there was a greater gain than he was offering. Straightening his coat, Creighton waited for the man to deliver Evelyn Renshaw's very welcome letter into his hand.

It had been an incredible stroke of luck to discover that Evelyn Renshaw was selling off her husband's treasures. By chance, an infamous portrait of Renshaw's mistress was being offered at the same auction where he'd sold his aunt's Gainsborough. The portrait was the tamest part of Lord Philip's collection of erotic art and books. It was being sold under a false name, and after the sale Creighton followed the man who collected the proceeds, hoping he would lead straight to Renshaw, so he could claim a reward or possibly blackmail the traitor.

Remarkably, since Renshaw was the least charitable man in England, the seller had delivered the bulging purse to the Foundling Hospital. There were rumors that someone was making large anonymous donations to charitable institutions. The betting books held that it was the Earl of Darlington, a potty old fellow who'd vowed to give away every penny of his fortune before he'd leave it to his hated relatives.

It hadn't been hard for Creighton to see that the gifts were coming from Evelyn Renshaw as she sold off her husband's collection. It had pained him to see Renshaw's fortune wasted on orphans and widows.

He'd been wondering if he could blackmail the traitor's wife when, quite by chance, he met her when he went to visit Anne O'Neill, in hopes that she had news of her dear brother.

He'd held Anne's hand as she cried over Patrick's unknown fate, and it had been easy to convince Evelyn that he was a great believer in charity. He let it slip that he was on his way to Devon, to endow an orphanage near his family home. As he'd hoped she would, Lady Evelyn graciously provided a gift of her own to accompany his.

Two hundred pounds.

The use to which he put her money was charitable enough. He'd needed a new uniform and boots. He could hardly go around London looking like he had something to hide. He dressed like a hero, and people believed he was. Evelyn's money had bought the best, and he hadn't felt a moment's guilt, knowing she was keenly interested in keeping warm clothing on the backs of British soldiers.

He smirked. He already had plans for whatever generous gift she thought she was sending to the orphans in Lincolnshire.

He needed new evening clothes for the Somerson ball. If the amount was generous enough, he'd treat himself to a visit to Mrs. Beaumont's. The expensive bawd and her talented girls must be feeling the pinch since Renshaw stopped visiting. Creighton was certain they'd appreciate seeing some of the traitor's money again. After a few days underground, he'd pay a visit to Evelyn, describe the gratitude in the eyes of the orphans, and gallantly offer his services again.

"I'm back," Bassett growled from the doorway.

Creighton snatched the letter from the soldier's hand and tore it open. The enclosed note was brief, and suggested the headmistress use the enclosed funds for books and warm clothes for her pupils. As usual, it was unsigned.

He grinned as he reached back into the envelope. It was empty.

He looked suspiciously at Bassett. "Is there another letter?"

"No, my lord."

Creighton's rage exploded like an artillery barrage. Cursing, he tore the letter to shreds with his teeth, then threw a vase against the wall. He realized Bassett was watching his tantrum with amusement.

"Go!" he screamed. "Get out of my sight!"

Now he had something else to fear.

Had Evelyn Renshaw forgotten to enclose the money, or was she on to him?

Chapter 13

Evelyn sat in the library, looking out over the rain-washed garden. She usually liked the rain. It kept her sisters indoors, and away from Renshaw House. The complement of watchers diminished as well in the wet. She could sit in the window and not be gawked at.

But the rain had kept her from her morning rides for two days, and she was bored. She had written all the letters that needed writing, and she was trying to read a book, but the lines blurred.

Rain seemed much nicer in the country. It made the earth smell sweet and the wildflowers bloom. It dripped from the eaves like music.

In London, rain turned everything a glowering gray, and made all that was miserable about the city worse. The cobbles turned slick and greasy, and the black sky scowled at the houses that squatted under the deluge.

If she were at her estate at Linwood, away from London and prying eyes, she'd walk out into the wet woods, listen to the sound of raindrops on the leaves, and revel in the feeling of cool moisture against her skin, a delightful counterpoint to the summer heat.

Such an outing was out of the question in London. Ladies

who walked in the rain were considered odd, and Evelyn didn't need any further speculation on her sanity.

She *was* safer indoors. She had not heard from the Frenchman again, and she credited Sam with that small victory. Philip was still out there somewhere, alive, still tied to her by marriage. Surely it was only a matter of time until she heard from him.

She wrapped her shawl more tightly around her shoulders, scanning the wet garden, wondering if there might be someone out there after all.

A knock at the door made her jump. She let go of the indrawn gasp of breath slowly, knowing she was being ridiculous.

"Come." Her voice shook a little, and she cleared her throat and sat up, straightening herself to a more dignified posture.

Her heart leapt when Sam entered, carrying a tea tray. She could see the steam rising from the pot, smell the buttery, fruity aroma of freshly baked tarts. His expression was slightly wary as he approached her, and that put her on edge all over again.

He set the tray down. "I have orders from Mrs. Cooper not to leave this room until you've eaten at least three strawberry tarts. She said you hardly touched your breakfast."

He forgot to bow, she noted, or to say "my lady." He was studying her as if searching for some clue to ill health he could report to the cook, or was trying to see inside her head and read her thoughts. She looked away, staring at the tea tray.

What had changed? He was obviously not here to make her smile today. There was no teasing in his eyes, no clever quip on his tight lips. She missed it, especially now, with rain drowning the city.

It had been three days since their ride, and their meeting in the hall in the middle of the night. Not that she was counting, of course. She raised her chin and met his eyes, forcing down the ridiculous idea that she'd missed him. Ladies did not miss their footmen, no matter how attractive and amusing they were, or brave, or impertinent.

She *had* been waiting for him to return that night, but only because she'd been afraid he wouldn't come back, another servant gone. She'd paced the floor as the hour grew late, struggling to convince herself she was being foolish, that Sam would not quit without notice.

He'd had time to hear the stories by now, to know Philip was guilty of treason. Surely to a soldier who'd faced the French in the field, been wounded, seen the horrors of war, Sam was likely to find Philip's treachery all the more despicable.

She had felt such a sense of relief when she heard footsteps in the hall that she'd run to the door of the library and flung it open. She'd barely restrained herself from bursting into tears and throwing her arms around him when she found him standing there in the dark.

She'd never felt such an impulse with any other servant. When Sal had received news that her uncle died, Evelyn had patted her shoulder and bought her a ticket home for the burial. Mary took a fortnight's leave to tend a sick relative in the country, but Evelyn hadn't feared she wouldn't return, or dreaded a future without her.

How silly she was being with Sam, acting like a green girl with a crush on the gardener's son. Why did the most inappropriate men hold the greatest appeal?

He stood waiting, his expression solemn and correct, not in the least affected by her haughty lady-of-the-manor stare.

She forced her eyes away from him and looked at the plate of tarts.

"There are at least a dozen tarts here! I thought you said three."

He smiled as if she'd caught him out, and her heart turned over. Ladies swooned over much lesser smiles, she'd heard.

She was not the type to do so.

"I think Mrs. Cooper is hopeful that you will exceed three. She sent to a cousin in Kent for the strawberries. She swears they grow the finest berries in England."

She caught something in his eyes. "You don't agree?"

"I happen to know the best strawberries grow in Northumberland."

He picked up the silver tongs, placed a single tart on a plate and held it out to her. "You may judge the quality of the berries from Kent for yourself, of course."

Her mouth watered as she bit into the tart, aware that he was watching her. The sweet tang exploded on her tongue. Sam's throat bobbed and his mouth tightened as he watched.

"Delicious," she said truthfully. "But I believe the sweetest strawberries come from my estate in Dorset." She glanced out the window. "In fact, they are best picked in the rain." *That's* what she would be doing if she were at Linwood today.

"My brother and I liked to fish in the rain," he said. "There's a slow pool in the river where the fish gather in wet weather."

It was the first time he'd spoken about his home since she interviewed him for his post. There was a soft, wistful look in his eyes, and she could almost see the boy he'd been. "You miss it."

He met her eyes, and his expression hardened. He put

another tart on her plate and handed it to her, and she took it with a frown, realizing the subject was closed. Obviously a change of topic was in order. Or she could let the conversation lapse, and sit in stony silence while he watched her eat.

"Did you know of Major Lord Creighton in Spain?"

His eyes narrowed, and she read cold suspicion in the glittering gray depths for an instant before he looked away. He fixed his stare on the wall behind her, every line of his body stiff.

"Yes," he said, his jaw tight. "I knew him. Will that be all, my lady?" he said, waiting to be dismissed.

Evelyn bristled. Yet another topic he wasn't willing to discuss. The man was a deeper mystery than Philip had been. She'd learned to hate secrets. She wanted to open Sam up, lay him bare and find out what he did not want her to know.

Perhaps it was simply that he disliked officers in general. Many soldiers distrusted their superiors, even a good one like Major Creighton. Sam was bold and outspoken, and she knew he did not take orders well. It was a dreadful flaw for a servant, or a soldier. She ignored his request to leave.

"I have a friend who is looking for news of her brother, a sergeant. His name was—is—Patrick O'Neill. Did you know him as well?" she asked.

His jaw dropped as he met her eyes. She drew back, stunned by his surprise, and began to babble.

"Anne, my friend, is most concerned for her brother. She hasn't had a letter from him in months, and when Major Creighton brought her news that he'd been seriously wounded, she was quite beside herself."

"Creighton went to see her?" Sam asked, his tone dark and tense.

It put her on her guard.

"He wished to see for himself that Sergeant O'Neill was safe at home. Is that an unusual thing for an officer to do?"

"It is if it's Creighton," he said, his voice knife-edged.

She raised her chin. "Lord Creighton is a kind man, and a noble officer. Surely his concern for the men under his command is proof of that."

There was anger in his eyes now, a dangerous silver spark like lightning in a stormy sky. "Is that all my lady? I have work to do."

"Do men think it shameful to be wounded?" she asked, goading him, angry at his stubbornness. "I mean, perhaps Sergeant O'Neill doesn't wish to come home if he's . . ." She paused, imagining the worst, a man disfigured, horrific to look at.

"If he's what? Scarred, missing a limb?" he growled. "War changes men on the inside as well as the outside. Men bear scars you can't even see. They worry that their loved ones won't understand, will fear them or hate them because of those scars. It takes courage to go home," he said, glaring at her as if she were at fault.

His audacity made her angry as well. She got to her feet.

"Is that the kind of wounds you have, Sam? On the inside? Is that why you chose to stay in London rather than go home?"

His eyes held a warning that she was trespassing in dangerous territory, but she walked toward him, caught in the maelstrom of his gaze, wanting to know. She was lady of this house, and he was a servant. She had the right to question him. She desperately needed a reason at this moment to see him as just a servant. She didn't want to wonder what it might be like if he were someone other than her footman, if he was a gentleman of her own class.

In the anger in his expression, she read a touch of uncertainty, and that sparked her own anger at *everything*, made her bold. She didn't need this man, or any man. She reached out to touch a tiny scar on his jaw, a white line that stood out against the tan of his skin.

"Poor Sam," she said, holding his eyes, filling hers with mocking pity, the same look people regarded her with.

He caught her hand and held it away, glaring at her. His grip was firm, but surprisingly gentle. Her own anger melted, and she felt excitement race through her veins at the physical contact between them.

"Don't pity me, my lady. I'm not a charity case."

"Then tell me. Was there a woman, someone you lost because of your wounds?" she asked.

He looked away. "I lost her before I left for war. She was one of the reasons why I went."

She felt a flicker of jealousy. Her fingers curled into her palm, her hand still caught in his.

"Did you love her?" she asked.

His smile was heartless. A dimple appeared beside his mouth, one she hadn't noticed before, near the upper end of the little scar. "That was the trouble," he said, his voice low.

"What? Loving her?" This close, his eyelashes were long and soft and dark, his eyes heavy lidded as he looked down at her. She could read banked fires there, something that stirred a most ungirlish longing in her.

"*Not* loving her," he murmured.

Was that relief that flooded her? "And since? Have you been in love?"

He searched her face. "I've come close."

She had no idea what that meant. He was near enough to kiss her, if he just lowered his head a few inches, or if she stood on tiptoe to reach him. Her mouth watered, wanting it.

He didn't move, didn't speak. Their hands were still

joined, and she squeezed his, giving him permission. He stared down at her, and the gray of his eyes disappeared into blackness. He drew a sharp breath and his mouth softened. She let her eyes drift shut, anticipating his lips on hers.

He stepped away so suddenly that she had to steady herself against the back of the settee. She opened her eyes in surprise, her flesh cold where his breath had warmed her, her hand empty.

He was a safe distance away, out of reach, breathing hard, his skin flushed, as affected as she yet resisting the desire she could not.

A hero and a gentleman, despite his birth.

She felt a blush heat her skin from toes to hairline.

Once again he had come to her rescue, this time saving her from herself. The difference in their positions yawned between them like a canyon. Sam was not a friend, or an equal. He was her servant, and he could not be more. Ever. She tightened her shawl, pulling her dignity together. "That will be all."

"Thank you, my lady." His tone was cool, correct, untainted by even the hint of desire or regret. It was lowering in the extreme.

"Sam?" she stopped him as he reached the door. He turned. "The Somerson ball is tomorrow night. I realize it is your usual time off, but I will have need of you." It felt good to remind them both of his status as a servant, emphasize her right to command him.

He bowed and inclined his head, as if he were a gentleman doing a lady a favor only he could grant, acquiescing to her wishes as an equal. It was not the subservient reaction she'd hoped for.

"Shall I order the coach for nine?" he asked with a half

smile playing on his lips. Lips she'd almost kissed. She swallowed the renewed burst of desire and raised her chin.

"Nine-thirty would suit me better. Now you may go."

That devil's grin deepened, and he met her eyes, tossing her dismissal back at her, and she wondered what game they were playing.

Whatever it was, it was dangerous, and without knowing the rules, she was completely out of her depth.

Chapter 14

Sinjon sat up as Evelyn sauntered toward his bed, wearing a lace nightgown that was more suggestion than substance.

She was beautiful, her limbs white against the darkness, her hair loose around her shoulders. He held out a hand to her, hard and ready. This time he wouldn't do the gentlemanly thing and stop before her lips met his. He wanted Evelyn as he'd never wanted any woman before.

"Evelyn," he muttered, wishing she'd hurry, and she smiled, a teasing, seductive twist of lush lips that made him harder still.

Suddenly, Creighton was there, catching her hand, pulling her against his chest, pressing his cruel mouth to hers. Sinjon watched her eyes drift shut as she sank into the kiss.

"No!" he yelled, raising his sword, and she turned in Creighton's arms and laughed. Suddenly it wasn't Evelyn, but Caroline, then he heard a scream and she was d'Agramant's wife, fighting Creighton as he tore at the lace gown. Sinjon leapt toward them, only to find himself tangled in his bedsheets.

He woke in the darkness of his little room off the kitchen, his heart pounding, his naked body sheened with sweat. He threw off the suffocating linens and lay back, listening to the steady beat of the rain outside.

Damn Evelyn. He needed sleep, but he couldn't get her out of his mind, remembering the way she'd looked in the salon, standing in front of him with her eyes closed, her lips parted for his kiss. For a crazy moment he'd wondered if the settee was going to be strong enough to hold them both in the throes of passion. It had been all he could do to step away from her.

Evelyn Renshaw was far too dangerous for a casual afternoon tumble.

He'd embarrassed her, made her angry, but it had been the right thing to do. He rubbed a hand over his face. Sometimes being noble was damned inconvenient. He rolled over, crushing the insistent jut of his erection into the mattress.

Her face filled his mind when he shut his eyes again, her soft lips parted, waiting—

He shifted again, turning onto his side. Still, he could see her eyes in the dark corner of the room, shiny with desire, seductive green pools a man could drown in. Even now he heard the call of the siren that lived in those emerald depths. He pulled the pillow over his head.

She was Philip Renshaw's wife, and Creighton's . . . what? Friend? Admirer? *Lover?* The idea turned his stomach.

He needed to tell Westlake that Evelyn was giving Creighton money. Or was the wily major simply fleecing the traitor's wife, the way he'd cheated so many others? Sinjon had been over and over it in his mind. He couldn't see Evelyn as the villain, and he was beginning to fear his attraction to her was clouding his judgment.

Unfortunately, a servant's time was not his own, and it was tricky to get away, run errands, visit spymasters. And this week he wouldn't even get his half day. Evelyn needed him as an escort to the Somerson ball.

He knew from past years, when he had attended the event as a guest, that everyone of importance would be there, along with a great many who managed to wheedle or buy invitations. He'd won his first invitation to the annual party in a game of faro.

A thought crept into his lust-fogged brain, giving him hope that he was still capable of sane, rational thought. Westlake would be at the ball, wouldn't he?

The earl was probably one of the first names on the list of invitees, since his countess was the granddaughter of a duke, and sister to a marquess. Not to mention that the Westlakes had long been companions to the king and advisors to the Prince Regent.

Sinjon got up and dressed, and went to the library. He scrawled a quick note and tucked it into his pocket. It was sure to bring Westlake running.

Chapter 15

Evelyn's maid swept her hair up into an elegant nest of curls and began to thread a yellow ribbon into the coiffure.

"No, not yellow," Evelyn said firmly.

Mary's jaw dropped. "But it's the latest fashion, my lady! Lady Charlotte's maid gave me half a dozen ribbons for your hair tonight, each in a different shade of yellow." She held them up. "This one is custard, and this one is butter, and this one is—" She paused, frowning. "Well, I can't recall the exact name, but it reminds me of roast chicken."

Evelyn resisted a smile. "I'll wear my pearl earrings as usual, Mary, and forgo the ribbons." She took the earrings out of the jewel box and passed them to her maid, tilting her head so Mary could fasten them. She didn't miss the disappointed twist of her mouth.

She gave the maid a brilliant smile. "I don't think my hair has ever looked nicer. The curls are lovely." Mary blushed with delight, instantly over her pout.

"Thank you, my lady." Mary looked at the ribbons again, wistfully. "Perhaps a ribbon of butter under your bodice?"

Evelyn shook her head. "Green tonight." The color complimented her eyes, made her skin glow, and gave her confidence, though she knew her sisters would hardly approve. Eloisa had sent a yellow silk gown. Charlotte had sent dancing slippers to match. Lucy had sent lace gloves, dyed marigold yellow, and a fan with a lively lady in lemon being chased through a garden of yellow roses by a golden-skinned satyr.

She drew on her gloves and gave her gown a final pat. Surely what she wore should be her own prerogative. She looked in the mirror yet again, knowing she was putting off leaving, caught sight of Mary's sympathetic expression and straightened her shoulders at once.

"Don't wait up, Mary. I plan to dance the night away," she said with forced gaiety as she swept out of the room.

Starling and Sam were waiting at the bottom of the steps. Starling looked proud, almost fatherly, but the look in Sam's eyes took her breath away.

His gaze moved over her like a touch, intimate and warm, heating her skin. She read bold masculine appreciation in his expression, and her stomach flipped. She paused on the steps without even realizing, caught in the silver glitter of his eyes, trapped by an emotion she'd never felt before. She was not Philip Renshaw's wife, or Tilby's youngest daughter, or the sister of two countesses and a viscountess. She was Evelyn, and she was beautiful in this man's eyes.

"My lady?" Mary asked. "Is anything amiss?"

Sam held out his hand, ready to escort her down the rest of the stairs. She took a breath, then a step, and laid her fingers in his palm, felt his close around them.

Even gloved she felt the spark that flowed between them. It gave her strength to float down the rest of the steps. At the bottom he turned and offered his arm, and she laid a hand on his sleeve and let him escort her out to the coach, as if he were a gentleman and she a debutante.

He settled her in the coach and stepped back, closing the door, and she felt as though a candle had been snuffed, leaving her in darkness. She put her hand to her nose, as if her glove might still hold some hint of him. There was nothing but the faint tang of vinegar polish.

Why was it she couldn't see Sam as just a servant, no matter how hard she tried? She'd known him as her rescuer first. He hadn't been a servant then, and wasn't it right that a lady should be appreciative of such a service and such a man?

He was still rescuing her, even if it was from nothing more than Eloisa's barbs, or her own foolish desire to kiss a footman.

She clasped her hands together, and the satin of her gloves warmed instantly. It was most unlike her to behave so indelicately. She was known—*had* been known—for her grace, her dignity, her adherence to good manners in all situations. Perhaps the strain of the past few months was finally telling. She shut her eyes.

Tonight of all nights she wanted that calm poise back.

As a start, she would control her emotions, turn her thoughts away from Sam and the way he made her knees shake.

But he was riding on the back of the coach. She could feel him there. If she turned, she would see his shadow through the oval window. She forced herself not to look to see if the admiration for her was still shining in his eyes.

As she neared Charlotte's palatial town house, her nerves gathered themselves in her stomach, tightening into a knot. The whole of good society would be here tonight. She hoped they would be so busy looking at each other that they would fail to notice her. Surely by now there was newer gossip, fresher scandals to feed on.

The coach pulled up under the lighted portico, the torches

glancing off the white stone facade, and she waited for Sam to open the door.

She pasted a smile on her face in preparation.

She would climb the imposing front steps of Somerson House, present her invitation, and hear her name called.

She would find one of her sisters in the crowd, fix her eyes upon her, and walk in with her head held high.

There would be a shocked hush at the mention of Renshaw's name. She'd ignore the whispers and the people who turned their backs on her.

She'd take her place among the matrons and dowagers, if they allowed her to do so. Otherwise, she would stand alone and watch the crowds.

She would not hide in a corner or allow anyone to chase her into the lonely sanctuary of an unoccupied room.

She was an invited guest, and she had done nothing wrong.

Evelyn felt a rush of fury. Philip was a coward as well as a traitor, leaving her to face his shame, but she would be brave, like Sam. He'd faced Napoleon's guns, and the hardships of war.

She had her own war to fight, and she meant to face down her enemies tonight and emerge triumphant.

Sam opened the door and let down the steps. She took his hand and climbed out.

"You look beautiful tonight, my lady," he murmured. "When the other ladies see you, green will become the new color of the Season, even if it is just envy." He gave her hand a quick squeeze before he released her and bowed.

She blinked at the top of his head for a moment in surprise. Good heavens, did she appear so nervous that he felt he had to reassure her? Her stomach fluttered with butterflies, but she lifted her chin and climbed the steps, forcing herself to smile graciously, as if nothing at all was amiss.

Chapter 16

Adam Westlake scanned the Somerson ballroom, identifying the people he knew. It was a game he played to keep himself amused at dull parties. He knew almost everyone, either by name, face, or reputation. He had thick dossiers on some, noting everything from misdeeds to outright crimes. He kept his expression bland, as he nodded to acquaintances and mentally listed their sins.

Countess Charlotte swept past, and he squinted at her gown. She shone like the noonday sun in acres of shimmering yellow silk.

Marianne slipped her arm through her husband's and leaned in close. "What a crush. There must be two hundred people here!"

"More, I'd say," Adam murmured.

"Look, Evelyn is arriving. How brave of her to come!" Marianne gushed. "Oh, dear, she's not wearing yellow."

"Neither are you," Adam said to his wife as he watched Evelyn. His file on her was nearly empty, but there was a possibility that her secrets could surpass everyone else's, depending on what Sinjon Rutherford discovered. Evelyn's placid face was free from any hint of treachery or deceit. She kept her head high, her pace graceful, and met the baleful glares of the worst *ton* gossips without the slightest glimmer of guilt. He felt a surge of grudging admiration.

Marianne smoothed a hand over her pale blue skirt. "I bought this gown because I thought you liked blue!"

"And so I do," Adam said, tearing his eyes away from Evelyn. "But why comment that Evelyn is not following fashion when you are also at fault?"

Her eyes instantly lit at the gentle rebuke, and Adam felt the familiar pull of lust for his wife. Goading her had become a game, a trick to set her unruly passions alight. She would make him pay for his remark later, and keep him merrily dancing to her tune all night long. He smiled, already looking forward to getting her alone. She read the message in his gaze perfectly, and slid her eyes away, blushing.

Her expression changed to angry indignation.

"Look at Lady Dalrymple's face! How rude of her to frown at Evelyn like that! Evelyn hasn't done anything wrong! And Mrs. Cox, too. I happen to know that she—"

Adam squeezed her arm to silence her, but Marianne sighed as someone else caught her interest.

"Major Lord Creighton is smiling at Evelyn. How gallant he is!" Adam frowned at the major's scarlet tunic. The gold braid complemented the yellow the ladies wore, but Creighton hardly deserved to be standing in an earl's ballroom, wearing a uniform he'd disgraced.

Unfortunately, it wasn't easy to topple a popular man, especially one who presented himself as a military hero who'd ferreted out a traitor in the field. Adam resisted the urge to frown. If Rutherford could prove his claims against Creighton, then he himself would find it a pleasure to see the major hanged in his elaborate dress uniform.

Evelyn gifted Creighton with a warm and lovely smile that matched the one she'd worn in the park the morning he'd chanced upon them riding together. Adam swallowed a grim smile. The fury on poor Rutherford's face had been almost comical by comparison.

Although they'd seemed quite companionable in the park, Evelyn spoke only a few words to Creighton now before she moved on. She plunged into the turbulent sea of yellow-clad females, their sour faces matching their gowns as they glared at her. Evelyn looked like she was drowning in a bowl of pease porridge, but she was doing it with admirable grace.

"Your pardon, my lord. I have a note for you."

Adam turned to find Somerson's butler holding a folded scrap of paper on a silver tray. He scanned the room for the sender, someone watching him, waiting for him to read the message, but he saw no one. He took it, and dismissed the servant with a crisp nod.

"Who would be sending you a note here?" Marianne demanded.

"I shall have to read it to find out," he said. He waited for her to step back, to give him a few scant inches of privacy in the crush, but Marianne was the most curious woman on earth. She leaned over his shoulder and waited to read it along with him. He had no choice but to open it, knowing if he did not, it would only make her more suspicious.

Meet me at the postern gate before supper is served.

Adam felt his stomach drop into his shoes as Marianne stiffened. The message could be from anyone, and might mean anything. "Meet you at the postern gate? In the dark? Who sent it, Adam?"

He met the simmering speculation in her eyes.

"It isn't signed," he said, keeping his tone bland. "Perhaps our coachman sent it. Maybe one of the horses went lame."

She tilted her head in disbelief. "He's perfectly capable of dealing with such a trifling matter on his own, and *he* would have signed it."

She snatched the note out of his hand and held it close to her nose, like a hardened spy, or a jealous wife.

"No perfume . . ." she said, "and the handwriting doesn't look feminine." She returned it. "Do you intend to go?"

He raised his eyebrows at her deft investigation. "I suppose I must. You're not going to let me rest until you know who it's from, are you?"

She smiled sweetly. "I suppose you aren't going to let me come with you."

"Not a chance. Why don't you go and find Evelyn? I'm sure she could use a loyal friend by her side, and no one would dare to sneer at *you*."

"Thank you, my love. I will indeed. Oh, she's being henpecked half to death by her dreadful sisters!" she said, and hurried away to rescue her beleaguered friend.

The night was moonless, and the garden path was pitch-black. Adam wished he'd brought a pistol with him, but he wasn't expecting this meeting, and Marianne would have easily found the gun under his tight-fitting evening coat. Likewise, his silk stockings and elegant patent-leather dancing shoes did not allow for any concealed weapons.

If trouble arose, he'd have only his wits and his heavy gold pocket watch to protect him. He took out the watch and swung it on the end of the chain experimentally, satisfied it would deter an assailant for a moment or two if it hit him in the right spot.

Someone was waiting by the gate. He saw the white wig

in the darkness, and guessed who it was. He put his watch away.

"Good evening, Captain Rutherford. My wife takes exception to my receiving unsigned notes at parties," he scolded. "In future, perhaps you could send word to my butler if you wish to see me. Northcott always knows where to find me. Or you could come to my shipping office at the docks next time you're in that part of Town."

"So you know I was at the docks on my last half day, do you?" Rutherford asked, his voice dark.

"Yes, of course. Did you find anything?"

"Not at the docks."

Adam couldn't read Sinjon's expression in the dark. "Is this about Creighton?"

Rutherford hesitated before replying. "Evelyn mentioned he's looking for O'Neill. He went to see O'Neill's sister, but she hasn't heard from Patrick in months."

Adam already knew that. "Anything else to report? Word of the gonfalon, for example, or evidence that Philip Renshaw is hiding under his wife's bed?"

"No, but apparently he was hiding under Lucy Frayne's bed at some point."

Adam's eyebrows rose in the dark. *Evelyn's own sister?* He swallowed his surprise. Perhaps Rutherford might prove useful after all. No one else had discovered that little family secret. "Well, who hasn't?" he quipped.

Rutherford didn't laugh. Adam heard him shift his feet in the dark, as if considering what to say next, working up to something. He frowned. There was something the captain wasn't telling him, something important. He waited, knowing silence drew confessions out to fill the empty air, encouraged men to blurt out their sins.

But Sinjon Rutherford didn't say a word.

"Are you still there, Captain?" Adam asked.

"Yes."

"And is there anything else?" he prompted. "How are things between you and Lady Evelyn? Does she find you a credible footman?"

Another telling hesitation. Now what might that mean? Adam felt annoyance ignite, burn along his nerves. "I trust you're not here to tell me you're quitting. There is no possibility of that. Think of this as a military mission, do or die. We need Renshaw and the flag."

"And I need O'Neill," Sinjon snapped.

"So you do," Adam said. "With so many people looking for him, hopefully someone will turn him up." He paused. "If he fails to appear, you'll need something else, something important—in place of his testimony—to save you." *Renshaw would do. Hell, not only would finding Renshaw save him, Rutherford would probably earn a knighthood for capturing the traitor. All other sins would be forgiven.*

But the silence was icy now, stubborn. Rutherford had decided to keep what he knew to himself. The frill of irritation filled Adam again.

"I'll bid you good night, Captain. My wife is waiting for me, and I have to come up with a story about who I met out here, and why."

"Tell her it was someone who owes you a debt," Rutherford said bitterly.

"Which remains unpaid," Adam replied. He turned and walked back through the dark garden.

What was it about Renshaw House that bred treason and unspeakable secrets? Rutherford might not trust *him*, but he had faith in the captain. Rutherford was an honorable man.

But did Sinjon Rutherford's loyalty lie with the Crown or with the lovely Evelyn Renshaw?

Chapter 17

Evelyn should have worn yellow after all.

Every eye in the room was fixed on her, and there wasn't a single friendly face in sight, not one welcoming smile. In green, she stuck out like a moorhen among canaries.

She raised her chin as her name was announced and the first shocked hush fell over the room. She read mockery, outrage, curiosity, and even amusement on the faces of Charlotte's guests as they stared at her.

Then came the indignant crack of fans snapping open, like the opening volley of a battle. She squeezed her own fan and walked forward.

The buzz of whispered comments rose, as if a swarm of hornets had suddenly been unleashed around her.

She looked for her sisters in the crowd, but they were of little comfort. Eloisa's mouth hung open, and her eyes bulged in horror as she regarded Evelyn's gown. Charlotte's eyes were filled with the tears of that most pitiful of creatures, the hostess who realizes her ball will not be a success after all. Lucy, wearing a daringly low-cut yellow gown, was ignoring her, her gaze fixed on the gentleman by her side.

Evelyn made her curtsy to her sister and brother-in-law. Somerson's eyes roamed over her meager jewels, assessing the value. She held her smile. He'd find them lacking, given the tales of Philip's vast fortune, but these were her own, and she was proud to wear them.

"There was a wager as to whether you'd dare to come tonight," her brother-in-law said.

"Did you win, my lord?" Evelyn asked sweetly, bristling inside.

His lips pinched. "Unfortunately not, but I'm sure your sisters are delighted you're here." He turned to Charlotte. "I think it's time we started the dancing before the evening is a complete disaster."

Charlotte blinked at Evelyn, her eyes glistening. "Oh, if only you'd worn yellow!" she warbled as she followed her husband.

The orchestra struck up the first notes, and most people turned away from Evelyn at last, focusing their attention on the dancers crowding the floor. She breathed a sigh of relief.

"Good evening, Lady Evelyn." She turned to find Lord Creighton by her side. He bowed gallantly. "May I look forward to the pleasure of dancing with you this evening?"

Evelyn's stomach tightened. She hadn't planned to dance. It would make her even more the center of attention and speculation. If widows could not dance, surely a traitor's wife should avoid the merry pursuit.

But the whole object of coming was to show the world that she had nothing to be ashamed of. How better to accomplish that than to enjoy the ball to the fullest? At the very least, she could *look* like she was enjoying herself. What a canny actress she'd become.

"I would be happy to dance, my lord," she said to the major. It *was* kind of him to ask her, since no one else was likely to do so. "Perhaps the next set? My sisters are headed this way, and I assume they want a word with me."

"Of course," he said with a toothy grin, and stepped out of the way as Eloisa and Lucy sailed toward her like attacking frigates. Eloisa's dark expression was a declaration of impending hostilities, and Evelyn braced herself.

"Oh, Evie, how could you? That dress is simply—" Her mouth worked, searching for the right word.

"Too prim?" Lucy offered.

"Too *green*!" Eloisa growled.

"It does match my eyes better than yellow," Evelyn said, noting the golden glaze of fury in her sister's hazel eyes, but Eloisa was too incensed to notice the set-down, and it likewise soared over the yellow feathers that adorned Lucy's empty head.

"Was that Lord Creighton I saw you speaking with?" Lucy asked. "How I'd like to see what's under that scarlet tunic of his! What lady could resist such a hero! They say he captured a dangerous spy in Spain, single-handed, and saved the lives of a thousand men!"

Eloisa tsked. "Don't change the subject, Lucy. We're discussing the fact that Evie—our own sister—has come to the most important ball of the season practically dressed in *rags*."

Evelyn raised her chin. She remembered the look in Sam's eyes as she'd descended the stairs. She wished he were here now, standing behind Eloisa, teasing her, taking the sting out of her sister's comments, but Sam was outside where he belonged, waiting for her. That offered a little comfort.

Eloisa took hold of one of her arms, Lucy the other. "Come to the ladies' withdrawing room. I'll find a yellow ribbon, or at least some gloves. It isn't too late."

"I fear it is," Evelyn said, disentangling herself with as

much grace as possible. "Everyone has seen me by now. It would look most odd if I suddenly changed my clothes."

"It would look like you've come to your senses!" Eloisa pleaded. "It won't do for you to stand here all night—*standing out*!"

"You really do, Evie," Lucy drawled. "Perhaps we could loosen your bodice a little, or plump up your bosoms to better advantage. If people want to stare, give them something to stare at, I always say."

"Evelyn!" Marianne pushed through the crowd to reach her, her warm smile like a lifeline.

Evelyn's own smile was genuine for the first time all evening.

"How lovely you look tonight! That particular shade of green is so cool and refreshing," Marianne said pointedly. She was wearing pale blue silk, with a magnificent necklace of diamonds, amethysts, and sapphires around her neck. She looked like a countess to be reckoned with.

Evelyn noted that Eloisa and Lucy gaped at Marianne, but they didn't dare say anything against *her* gown.

"Hello, Eloisa, Lucy. How nice you both look as well," Marianne said. "I hear each shade of yellow has a particular name this Season. What is the color of your gown called?"

Eloisa preened. "My gloves and shoes are 'caramel,' and my gown is 'almond.' The ribbon at my bodice is 'orgeat.'"

Evelyn tilted her head. "Orgeat? Like the drink they serve at Almack's?"

"Just so," Eloisa said stiffly.

Marianne turned to Lucy. "And you, Countess Frayne? What do they call the color of your gown?"

But Lucy was ogling the gentlemen on the dance floor, and Eloisa had to jab her with an elbow and repeat the question.

"Oh. I believe it's called 'toasted crumpet,'" Lucy replied.

Marianne's porcelain complexion flushed with the effort of not laughing, and Evelyn hid her own smile behind her gloved palm.

"Ooh, look! Here comes Lord Creighton again," Lucy gushed, and tugged her bodice a half inch lower in preparation. The major, however, only had eyes for Evelyn.

"I believe this is our dance," he said, bowing politely and extending a hand to her.

Evelyn hesitated a moment, then put her hand in his and let him lead her onto the dance floor. Odd, when Sam touched her, she felt breathless, dizzy. But with Lord Creighton she felt nothing. Actually, his touch made her want to pull away.

"How was your visit to Lincolnshire, sir?" she asked politely as the music began and they moved down the line of couples.

He frowned, and Evelyn glanced at him in concern, trying to concentrate on the steps.

"Did you by chance forget something when you wrote your note, Lady Evelyn?"

Evelyn stumbled, but his hand under her elbow instantly righted her. "What do you mean, sir?" she asked. Had she signed her name to the letter by mistake, or smudged the ink?

He looked regretful. "There were no funds enclosed with your kind letter. The headmistress was quite baffled."

She stopped dancing. "But I remember putting—"

He led her off the floor to a quiet corner. "I'm sure it was just an oversight. You have much on your mind of late. It's of no matter. I gave the school a generous donation from my own purse. You may simply reimburse me at your convenience."

Evelyn blinked at him, but his smile was warm and sincere. "Thank you, my lord. I shall send someone 'round with the money tomorrow," she said, and wondered what she could sell to make up the missing money. "May I ask how much I owe you?"

His eyes slid away from hers, as if he were embarrassed to be speaking to a lady about anything so crass as money.

"I gave the headmistress five hundred pounds."

Evelyn felt herself blanch. Lord Creighton put his hand on her arm again to steady her, and her skin crawled at his touch. She stepped back, pulled away, and his brows rose.

"Was that not enough?"

Evelyn's heart pounded in her throat. "Yes, of course," she murmured. She curtsied quickly, her knees shaking. "Will you excuse me, my lord? It has been many months since I've danced, and I'm afraid I'm out of practice."

She crossed the room toward Marianne, uncertain where else to go. She kept her pace slow, sedate, as if nothing in the world was wrong. Anyone who looked at her would think she was calm and unconcerned. How wrong they were!

Marianne caught her arm as she reached her, her smile fading. "Evelyn, you are white as paper!" she said in concern. "Is something amiss?"

Evelyn forced a bright smile as she shook her head. "I'm not used to dancing," she said, repeating the excuse.

Marianne held something up. "Someone handed me a note for you while you were out on the floor. Perhaps it's another invitation to dance!"

Evelyn stared at the unfamiliar scrawl. She recalled Eloisa's plans to find her a lover. What if this note contained an invitation to a tryst? Her sisters were not subtle creatures, and when they did what they thought best for her, disaster was always the result.

She blinked at her name, written brazenly across the face of the letter in violet ink.

"You must tell me what it says, especially if it's from a new admirer," Marianne said. "It's been quite an evening for notes and *billet doux*. Adam received one earlier."

Fear raised the hairs on the back of her neck and turned her knees to water.

"Aren't you going to open it?" Marianne asked.

Evelyn swallowed. She was being silly. She took the letter from Marianne's hand and opened it, scanning the single line that slanted across the page.

How charming you look in green. With the compliments of P.R., Chevalier, comte d'Elenoire.

Philip's initials, his French title, earned through treachery. She looked around the room in a panic, searching every dark corner, every alcove. *Philip wouldn't dare to come here, of all places. But she held his note in her hand.* The writing blurred before her eyes, became his familiar scrawl.

Her skin crawled, as if his eyes were on her, his hands. As if he were standing beside her. It was merely a cruel trick, surely, but she felt dizzy, sick with fear.

"Marianne, who gave this to you?"

Marianne frowned. "One of Somerson's servants. Why? What does it say?"

But Evelyn crumpled the note in her hand. "Which man? Can you point him out?"

Marianne looked around. "I don't see him now. Perhaps he's returned to the kitchen."

Images of the Frenchman in the park flashed through Evelyn's mind.

"There he is!" Marianne pointed to a liveried servant

carrying a tray of champagne. "No, perhaps not. All Charlotte's footmen look alike."

Evelyn felt her gorge rise. What if he was watching her now, the Frenchman, or Philip, waiting for her to panic?

She would not give anyone that satisfaction.

She looked around the room with a bright, mocking smile, letting her tormentors know they had failed. She turned to Marianne, who was still waiting for an explanation.

"There's a problem at home. My maid is ill," she said. "I shall have to leave at once."

She was afraid to go home, feared Philip was waiting for her.

Sam was outside, also waiting. He'd keep her safe. Somehow she knew it as an unshakable truth. It gave her the courage to walk across the room with an insouciant smile on her face when she wanted to run.

Outside, the cool night air touched her hot cheeks. Shadows loomed everywhere. She hesitated on the step, paralyzed.

Someone stepped out of the dark and paused at the bottom of the steps, waiting for her, and her heart caught in her throat.

Sam. The lean strength of his silhouette stood against the darkness and whatever lurked there.

With a sob, Evelyn ran down the steps and tumbled into his arms.

Chapter 18

Sinjon opened his arms and caught her.

She didn't have her cloak, and her face was as pale as milk against the purple shadows.

She cried out as he folded his arms around her, and he remembered d'Agramant's wife making the same small noise as she crumpled in her husband's embrace, her bravery gone as Creighton fled. Her blood and tears had soaked the front of his tunic, and her husband held her tight for a long moment before he lifted her face to his, examining her cuts and bruises, running gentle hands over each hurt she'd endured at Creighton's hands.

Shaken by the memory, Sinjon put a finger under Evelyn's chin and gazed into her face, but her face was perfect, her only injuries the pain and fear in her eyes. He pulled her close again, cradling her against his chest, holding her safe, letting her cling to him.

"I'm all right," she murmured, just as d'Agramant's wife had, but she didn't move from the haven of his arms. He felt a shudder pass through her.

"No, you're not."

He looked around, searching for the danger she feared, but other than a few coachmen watching them with fascinated interest, there wasn't anything to fear. His stomach clenched. Curious servants were danger enough. He imagined tomorrow's gossip.

He stepped back at once, ignoring her bereft little gasp as he took her arm and led her to the coach.

Her coachman saw them coming and immediately scrambled up to his perch and picked up the reins, jerking his chin at Sinjon in silent inquiry.

Sinjon ignored him and helped Evelyn into the coach. She sat on the edge of her seat and stared at him, her green eyes wet pools of misery.

He hovered in the open doorway. A footman would have shut the door and taken his place on the back of the vehicle, given her privacy, pretended he hadn't seen her tears, didn't care.

But he did care.

He glanced up at the coachman. "Home," he ordered.

Then he climbed into the coach.

She didn't object as he settled himself next to her, pulling her back into his arms.

The vehicle jolted forward, and he heard her sniffle in the dark. He pressed his handkerchief into her gloved palm and closed her fingers over it, as if she were a child.

He glanced out the window, scanning the sidewalk as the coach pulled away. No one watched them go.

The attack in the park hadn't brought tears, but a London ball was a far more dangerous venue. Ladies were the cruelest creatures on earth, and the higher the pedigree, the more vicious the cat. He'd seen other ladies leave balls in tears, the attacker smirking in triumph at the lethal sharpness of her tongue.

Who would make a better target for insults than Philip Renshaw's wife? Despite her strong, quiet confidence,

Evelyn was as likely to be hurt by a harsh word as any other woman. More so, perhaps, given all that she'd endured since her husband's treason.

"Tell me what happened," he murmured against the softness of her hair. He could smell the subtle violet drift of her perfume. He breathed her in.

She didn't answer for a long moment, and Sinjon wondered if she'd decided to bear her injuries in brave silence.

"My husband sent me a note. Or someone did, signed with his name," she said at last.

Sinjon's brows shot up.

"It wasn't his hand, but the message was personal, a comment about my gown. What if he was there, in my sister's ballroom, watching me?" He heard her struggle to keep her voice even.

"Or perhaps it was someone's idea of a joke, to see how you'd react," Sinjon replied, wondering who could be that cruel.

For some reason, Westlake sprang to mind. Perhaps the earl was trying to draw Evelyn out, make her panic, reveal what she knew, give up her husband's hiding place by running to him at the drop of a note. He felt a sharp prod of guilt. Wasn't that exactly what he'd been sent to Renshaw House to do?

"Did you see him?" he asked.

"No. But the Frenchman, that day in the park—" She shifted on the seat, and the silk of her dress gave a hiss of . . . what? Warning, fear? Sinjon doubted the French agent's face had healed enough for him to appear unnoticed at a society ball. Still, there were any number of suspicious characters watching Evelyn.

Including him.

Doubt lodged in his throat, niggled there, and he coughed.

"Your attacker wanted a flag, I seem to remember," he prompted, hoping her emotional state would make her less cautious.

"I remember," she said tightly. "If you hadn't come along, hadn't—" He heard renewed tears in her voice, though she fought them. "I am tired, so very tired, of being afraid all the time!"

She was shivering, and Sinjon pulled her closer to the heat of his body. Marielle d'Agramant had stood at attention during her ordeal, her eyes grim, her jaw tight, refusing to show Creighton any fear. She'd worn her dignity like a cloak, the way Evelyn had for weeks. She had not broken under the terrifying odds against her. But unlike Madame d'Agramant, there was no one to comfort Evelyn.

Except him.

He tightened his arms around her, resting his chin on the top of her head. She sank into him with a sigh, burying her face in his shoulder, letting her tears flow.

She felt good in his arms, right. He felt desire stir, and he swore silently. He was offering a kind shoulder, as a brother or a father might, he told himself, but the mental warning had no effect at all on the part of his body that wanted her. Evelyn wasn't his sister. She was an extremely desirable woman. He willed his erection away, but it refused to obey.

It didn't help that they fit together perfectly, as if this was an old and familiar habit between them. Evelyn had stopped crying and simply rested in his arms, completely unaware of what she was doing to him. She began drawing absent circles on his chest with the tip of her fingernail. It tickled, and it was damned arousing. He gritted his teeth, tried to shift away, open some space between them, but she wriggled nearer, fitting herself closer still.

He gave in to temptation. How could he not? It seemed

the most natural thing in the world to lift her face and lower his mouth to hers. He kissed her gently, carefully, giving her time to object, a chance to pull away. Her lips were silken, salty with tears, and shaped themselves to his, her response sweet. He held back lust that raged like a battle charge.

Her hands crept up to touch his face, to curl around his neck and draw him closer. With a sigh she kissed him back, laying gentle, butterfly kisses on his mouth.

Hungrily, he licked the seam of her lips, angling to kiss her more deeply. She gasped, her lips parting, and he plunged in, seeking her tongue with his own. She drew back in shock, and he frowned. It was an oddly virginal response for a married woman.

But he wasn't ready to stop kissing her. He trailed his mouth along the delicate bones of her jaw, nibbled at the frantic pulse point at her throat, and lapped at the delicate jut of her collarbones.

"Oh," she sighed, seeming almost surprised. "Oh, my." She let her head fall back, giving him access to the delicate spot under her ear, baring the upper slopes of her breasts to his eyes and his hands. He could hear her little pants of desire, and it drove his own need higher. He captured her mouth again, nipping at her lips until she opened, let him in, let his tongue meet hers and tangle. She tasted of champagne. How long had it been since he'd had either wine or woman?

He could have her, he thought. She was willing, certainly, and it wouldn't be the first time he'd taken a woman in a moving coach. He pressed his erection against her hip, slid his hands up the sweet curves of her waist.

He paused, his hand stopping an inch beneath the swell of her breast. He could feel the heat of her body through the thin silk of her gown. She was looking up at him, the faint light of the city shining on her face. She opened her mouth in anticipation of another kiss. When he hesitated, she clutched his shoulders, tugging, urging him on.

He gazed at her. She was beautiful, desirable, and he wondered at his hesitation. He'd never refused an invitation like this before. He was a master of seduction, and he was hard, ready for her, and she wanted him too. But it was wrong.

He shut his eyes, swore silently. She was feeling shock, or fear, or both. Her desire was merely the turmoil of her wounded emotions. He could not take advantage of her in this state. She needed a warm bath, a glass of sherry, and a good night's sleep.

She moaned and moved restively against him, a sinuous undulating swirl of her hips that almost undid his resolve. "Sweetheart," he murmured, desperately trying to think of a good excuse, a reason to stop that wouldn't drive her into another flood of tears.

The coach jolted, driving her against his erection. He groaned and kissed her again, but the coach had stopped. He lifted his head and looked out the window.

They'd arrived at Renshaw House, and Starling was coming down the front steps.

Evelyn was still nuzzling his cheek, kissing his neck, driving him wild, but he shook her gently.

"We're home, Evelyn."

He pointed at Starling, and she gasped and stiffened at once, pulling away from him. He moved to the other seat, across from her, and she fussed with her dress, her hair, touched trembling fingers to her lips.

Starling opened the door.

The butler looked stunned to see Sinjon inside, and his white brows rose skyward like twin moths in silent question. Sinjon smiled wryly, keeping his legs crossed, the evidence of his arousal hidden. If the coach had taken a few more minutes to arrive, or Starling had opened the door a few seconds faster, the poor man would have found Lady Evelyn Renshaw kissing her footman. Or worse.

"Lady Evelyn felt ill, and wished to return home earlier than expected," Sinjon explained.

"Just a headache," Evelyn said, her voice still smoky with desire. She swallowed, the white length of her throat working, and strove for a brighter tone for Starling's sake. "Too much champagne, perhaps."

The butler relaxed and smiled fondly, obviously glad to see that her ladyship had enjoyed the dreaded party after all, Sinjon thought.

"Shall I have Mary prepare you a headache powder?" he asked, handing her out of the coach.

Sinjon watched her climb the steps. She did not look back at him. He peered out at the coachman, who regarded him curiously.

"Well?" the man said. "I've never ridden inside this rig. What's it like?"

Sinjon almost laughed. Was that all he wanted to know?

"Lovely, my friend. Warm and soft and comfortable. Ride me 'round to the stables, if you will. I want to enjoy the pleasure a little longer."

He glanced up, saw light flare in Evelyn's bedroom as the candles were lit. He shut his eyes, still smelling her perfume in the dark coach, still feeling the imprint of her lips on his, still tasting her. Desire stirred again, and he clenched his fists, willing it away, but it would not go.

He growled out the darkest soldier's curse he knew.

He was on dangerous ground.

Chapter 19

Evelyn paced her bedroom until noon the next day, afraid to leave for fear of seeing Sam at breakfast, or in the hallway. What would she say?

She'd kissed her footman.

She'd fallen into his arms like a strumpet, pressed her body to his, and she hadn't wanted to stop.

How far would it have gone? She pressed a hand to her lips to still the telltale tingle, and felt a blush heat her body from her toes to her hairline.

Yet again, he'd been there to make her feel safe. In his arms, kissing him, she'd forgotten the note and the debt she owed Lord Creighton. She didn't want to think about them even now. She couldn't get her thoughts off Sam, and how different she'd felt with him.

Kissing him made her feel wild and out-of-control, *burning* with desire. It hadn't been like that with Philip. Her husband was not a man of passion, at least not with her. She supposed it had been different with his mistresses, and the scores of actresses and whores he took to his bed.

Philip had handled bedding his wife like he dealt with his business affairs—quickly, decisively, and completely to his own advantage. He gave her no pleasure and barely seemed to derive any from their brief, infrequent matings. His unwelcome attentions were visited upon her as punishment, discipline.

She had never kissed anyone the way she'd kissed Sam, with open mouths, tongues touching. The only kiss Philip had ever bestowed upon her was a dry brush of his lips on hers to seal their marriage vows.

She relived the taste of Sam's tongue, the intimate sensation of having a part of his body inside hers. She recognized the similarity to the sex act, of course, but it had been the most exquisite sensation she'd ever known.

And it must never happen again.

She crossed the room and rang for Mary. She couldn't hide in her room all day. It was only a kiss, and he'd probably forgotten it by now. He wasn't hiding, she was certain of that. He had work to do, and was getting on with his day.

She chose a simple morning gown, and when Mary finished pulling her hair into a sensible bun, went downstairs to the library, her sanctuary, and closed the door behind her and leaned on it. Her heart was still pounding out her fear of meeting Sam in the hall, and in disappointment at not seeing him.

Sitting down on the settee, she remembered the day he'd brought her the tarts, watched her eat them. She'd wanted to kiss him then, and he resisted.

She frowned, running her fingertip over her mouth again. Had he been the one to initiate the kiss last night, or was it her? Had it been the same desire that overwhelmed her that afternoon in this room, or it was born of the spark of awareness she felt when she first saw him in the park?

Whatever it was, she had never meant to act upon her feelings.

She had been grateful when he climbed into the coach.

It had also been shocking, of course. He was a servant, separated from her by the unbridgeable gulf of class and the strict rules of proper behavior. Servants did not ride inside a coach with their mistress, and even a gentleman would not be so bold as to sit beside a lady. Those trifling rules of etiquette hardly mattered when she'd broken the strictest rule of all.

Ladies did not kiss their servants.

She shut her eyes. What devil's spell was she under? She had always prided herself on being immune to the temptations of a handsome face, a rogue's grin, a clever wit.

Perhaps she was indeed as silly as her sisters, every bit as wanton, vain, and gluttonous. She wanted more of Sam's kisses, more of him. There was no other way to describe it. Even in the cold light of day, when good sense should have taken over, her mouth watered, her body craved him. She pressed her fist against the sharp ache of longing in her belly. Was this what lust felt like? She knew what it *looked* like.

She crossed to the bookshelf at the back of the library and climbed the ladder to the top shelf. Philip kept a collection of books for his private delight, believing that she knew nothing about them. She'd found them while looking for a book of poetry her father had given her. She'd been shocked, of course, but curious as well. The erotic drawings were intriguing and forbidden, especially to a well-bred lady. She suspected Philip's books were valuable, if only to someone with similarly debauched tastes to his own, but it would be impossible for her, a lady, to sell them.

She took one of the heavy volumes from the shelf now. The leather cover warmed instantly at her touch.

She propped it against the top rung of the ladder and opened it, holding her breath.

The drawings inside were of a man and a woman, naked, entwined. She had looked at the woman's face before, thought her a lewd and unnatural creature. Now she recognized her arched back, closed eyes, her slack mouth, as desire, and pleasure.

She'd felt it in Sam's arms.

She shivered, feeling it now.

In the drawing, the man's face was buried in his lover's neck, his hair dark, like Sam's, his naked back lean and strong. One of his hands cupped a lush breast, and the other was buried between her thighs.

How would it feel to be touched like this by Sam? She pictured his hands, long-fingered and tanned, imagined them touching, caressing, squeezing. A small, needy little noise escaped from her, half gasp, half sigh. Her body felt liquid, feverish.

"My lady?"

She almost fell off the ladder. She looked down to find Starling staring up at her. She snapped the book shut and shoved it back on the shelf.

"I didn't mean to startle you. I did knock, but when you didn't answer I became concerned."

"Just looking for a book," she murmured.

He held the ladder as she descended. "If you wish to have books brought down from the high shelves, I can ask Sam to do it for you. It's a long way up, and dangerous. Is there a particular volume you'd like him to fetch?"

She felt her cheeks heat at the mention of Sam's name. "That won't be necessary," she said, smoothing a hand over her skirt. "What did you wish to see me about?"

He looked contrite as he delivered the news. "Your sisters have arrived, my lady."

"Sisters?" she parroted. "More than one?"

"Yes, my lady, all three, and all in yellow. I asked Sam to show them into the salon."

She felt herself turn a sickly shade of the same color. She was in for a long, blistering lecture.

She should have worn yellow last night, she told herself again, and she should not have left without a word of goodnight. Actually, she should have stayed home, out of harm's way. There would have been no note, no upsetting encounter with Lord Creighton, and no forbidden, stolen kisses in the velvety darkness of her coach.

She took a bracing breath. "Thank you, Starling. Please have cook send up tea, and plenty of cakes. Charlotte prefers cream cakes, and Eloisa eats only plain biscuits. Lucy will want strawberries, and probably champagne, if there is any."

He bowed and withdrew, and Evelyn crossed to the mirror. Did she look wanton? She brushed her hand over her hot cheeks, tried to suck the color out of her lips, still pink from Sam's rough skin. Her eyes looked different, she thought. Glowing, as if there was a banked fire inside her, ready to rage out of control at the slightest breeze. Would her sisters notice?

She checked her gown. It was a sprigged muslin, but even if some of the tiny flowers that adorned it were yellow, the ribbon trim was green, and sure to remind Eloisa of last night's fashion faux pas. It couldn't be helped. She didn't have time to go upstairs and change. Her sisters would not wait patiently for her. They'd follow her up and confront her in her room, and that was to be avoided at all costs, since it would take Eloisa straight to the wardrobe, where she'd spend the rest of the afternoon explaining why each and every garment she owned was *wrong*.

She pictured her sisters kidnapping her and dragging her

off to the nearest modiste to be refitted from head to toe in cheddar, or porridge, or roast goose.

Before she even reached the closed door of the salon, she could hear the squawk of conversation. It sounded like birds fighting over a particularly tasty morsel. Probably her. The only variable was whether they were discussing her fortune, her clothing, or who would move in and play chaperone next.

Evelyn paused outside the door, her hand on the latch, her stomach knotted, gathering the courage to enter the fray.

The latch moved under her hand, and the door opened. Sam almost ran into her. He put a hand under her elbow to steady her, and she felt heat race up her arm.

She looked up at him, saw the answering flare in his eyes.

"I was sent to see what was taking you so long," he said apologetically, giving her a rueful smile.

He didn't let go immediately, and she couldn't seem to look away from him. She stood breathing him in, gazing into the depths of his gray eyes. Her knees wobbled.

"Evie! There you are at last!" Charlotte cried. "We've been here almost ten minutes."

Sam stepped aside at once, let her precede him into the room, and took his place inside the door, standing at attention.

"Ooh, Evie, you have a new footman!" Lucy gushed, eyeing Sam. "How delicious!"

"Down, Lucy," Evelyn said, bristling. "Don't you have footmen of your own to molest?"

Lucy sniffed. "I never dally with the help. That's Frayne's peccadillo, not mine." Her eyes lit. "Speaking of ladies and servants, I heard the most delicious bit of scandal this morning from my maid."

"Oh, I love gossip!" Charlotte said as she leaned in to

help herself to a cream cake. Eloisa was regarding Evelyn's gown, her lips pinched in disapproval. Evelyn resisted the urge to fold her arms over her bodice, and sent her sister a sweet smile instead.

"Well, I heard—" Lucy began, only to be interrupted as the door opened.

"More callers, my lady," Starling announced. "The Marchioness of Blackwood and Countess Westlake have arrived."

Evelyn almost sagged with relief. Reinforcements had arrived in the nick of time. With Isobel and Marianne by her side, she wouldn't be overrun and trampled by her sisters today. She smiled and sent up a prayer that neither lady was wearing yellow and could be held up as a shining golden example for her to follow.

"Show them in, Starling, and fetch more cups," she said.

"I thought you didn't have any visitors," Charlotte said, clearly annoyed at the interruption to Lucy's *on dit*.

"I still have friends," Evelyn said.

"And we are two of her closest and dearest," Isobel, the Marchioness of Blackwood, said, and she swept into the room with Marianne. Isobel was wearing a soft shade of azure blue, and Marianne's gown was leaf green. They kissed Evelyn's cheek and took their places on either side of her, facing the three sisters on the opposite settee. Evelyn hid a smile. They looked like opposing armies. Eloisa regarded the three of them with dismay, but refrained from comment, other than dramatically smoothing her hand over her lemon yellow skirt.

"Lucy had a shocking *on dit* from her maid this morning, and I am dying to hear it," Charlotte said, looking at Marianne and Isobel. "What were you going to tell us, Lucy?"

"Isobel's news first," Marianne said, holding up a hand

to still the sisters. She grinned like a conspirator. "Go on, Isobel, tell them."

Isobel blushed scarlet, but her eyes glowed. "I hadn't expected to announce it to *everyone*." She touched a hand to her stomach and smiled. "I am expecting a child."

Lucy's jaw dropped. "Blackwood's?" she asked. Marianne bristled.

Isobel's eyes burned into Lucy's. "Of course!"

Lucy shrugged. "Well, I had to ask. He's such an incorrigible rake. Worse than Frayne, and I always find if it's good for the gander, why shouldn't the goose enjoy it too?"

"*Was* incorrigible," Isobel murmured. "He has reformed."

"Phineas is utterly and completely devoted to his *wife*," Marianne said pointedly, glaring at Lucy. She looked at Evelyn. "We had to come to visit today. Blackwood is insisting on taking Isobel home to the country at once. He won't let her out of his sight, and he wants her to eat plenty of cream and good country butter."

"And strawberries. I have the most powerful yearning for strawberries," Isobel said. "And cherries."

Charlotte sniffed. "Do forgive me, Isobel, it's good news, I'm sure, but I have five children. News of a married lady in an interesting condition is, well, hardly interesting at all. Go on, Lucy. Tell us what you heard."

Evelyn sent Isobel a smile. Her friend was glowing, utterly in love with her husband, obviously filled with such joy that not even Charlotte could dampen her spirits.

Evelyn had wished for a child. Before her marriage she'd also wished for a husband who would adore her. She got neither. She toyed with the wedding ring on her finger, wanting to tear it off and throw it into the fireplace.

"Well, my maid told me that she heard it from one of our footmen, who heard it from Lady Carstairs's groom. *He* said that he saw a *lady* kissing a *footman* on the very steps of Somerson House last night."

Evelyn's heart stopped beating.

The collective gasp filled the room like a windstorm. She looked up at Sam in surprise. He looked back at her, his expression unreadable. There was no guilt, no regret, and no apology in his eyes. She wondered if he'd even heard Lucy's comment.

"At my ball?" Charlotte warbled, her hand on her chest. "Oh, fetch the hartshorn—I think I'm going to faint!"

Eloisa poked her. "You will not! Lucy, does your maid know who the lady was?"

Lucy giggled. "No. She had her face buried in the footman's coat, and his arms were around her nice and tight. I'd guess it was Alice Cox. She has a penchant for the lower orders, likes her men rough and ready."

Marianne shook her head. "No, Alice was dancing with Lord Melrose's youngest son all evening. That was enough of a scandal. They stood up for *four* dances, and she knows the limit is three."

Eloisa made a face. "Whoever she was, how dreadful to engage in an *amour* with a mere footman! He certainly couldn't afford to buy her the kind of jewelry and little delights a lady is entitled to."

"There are other rewards," Lucy said pointedly.

Evelyn dared to glance at Sam again. Her cheeks were on fire. Any moment someone would remember she left early, or notice Sam in the corner. His gaze was heavy-lidded, careful.

Charlotte gave an exasperated sigh. "Why is it acceptable for a lord to diddle every maid on his staff, while a lady must keep to her own class? No one thinks any less of Somerson for having an occasional liaison with the upstairs maid."

"Only *one* of the maids?" Lucy asked. Charlotte glared daggers at her sister.

"Who would be more discreet than a servant?" Marianne asked, her eyes glowing with mischief. "Not that I would ever consider straying from Westlake, but just think. He'd be afraid of losing his post if he didn't please his lady, so he'd work extra hard at both jobs."

No, it wasn't like that, Evelyn told Sam with her eyes.

"Who would be more dangerous?" Isobel countered. "Servants see everything, know the most intimate details. One indiscreet comment and things have a habit of spreading through the kitchen, out the back door, and all over London. Just look at the poor lady who dared to embrace her footman in the dark. What if she simply tripped, or lost her slipper?"

Or fell.

Sam's expression didn't change. She couldn't imagine him bragging of his conquest to Starling or the footmen next door. He was steadfast and honorable, and she had nothing to fear from him.

Or did she? She squirmed.

"Still, it would be very convenient, wouldn't it?" Charlotte said. "It could all take place behind closed doors in your own home. Who'd know?"

The ladies all nodded in agreement. Evelyn swallowed, imagining Sam in her bed.

Eloisa smiled archly. "Well, whoever she was, *everyone* knows now, since she was indiscreet enough to be caught a-kissing her servant in broad daylight—"

"I thought you said it was too dark to see her clearly," Evelyn croaked.

Eloisa waved a dismissive hand that sparkled with yellow diamonds. "Of course it was dark. It doesn't make any difference. It's only a matter of hours before her identity is winkled out and her reputation is ruined." She lifted her chin. "You needn't look so shocked, Evie. The one lady in all England we can most certainly rule out is *you*."

She didn't dare look at Sam now. She felt a blush creep up from her ankles.

"Of course it wasn't Evelyn! She is a lady to her fingertips," Marianne defended her.

"Might loosen her up," Lucy said. "Especially now that Philip isn't here to play stud."

"Lucy!" Evelyn protested, but Eloisa opened her reticule and waved a piece of paper.

Evelyn's heart skipped a beat. Had her sister somehow gotten hold of last night's note?

"You know we adore you, Evelyn, but Lucy is quite right. You are our baby sister, even if you do behave more like an elderly spinster." Evelyn swallowed the lump of indignation and the sharp retort that filled her throat. "As I promised, I have compiled a list of potential lovers for you to consider," Eloisa went on. "You simply need to choose one and Wilton will make the introduction. I will arrange everything else."

With a squeal of delight Lucy snatched the list. "Oh, how delicious! And to think I was dreading this afternoon would be a bore." She squinted. "Oh, not Lord Morton! He's exceedingly dull."

"She wouldn't have to talk to him!" Eloisa argued.

"I wasn't suggesting it was his *conversation* that was dull!" Lucy shot back, and Eloisa's mouth shut with a snap.

Marianne squeezed Evelyn's arm. "I had no idea you were looking for a lover."

"I'm not," Evelyn replied through clenched teeth, furious with her sisters, but they were too busy haggling over the merits of the gentlemen on the list to pay attention to her.

Her eyes strayed to Sam again, somewhat desperate for a teasing grin, a reassuring nod, but there was ice in his gray eyes now. He was positively glaring at her. Her breath caught in her throat. Did he think she was actually considering Eloisa's ridiculous scheme? She blushed and looked away. She didn't want a lover. She could not imagine any other man in her arms, in her bed, but him.

"Viscount Hazlett won't do either. He's just taken that wretched little yellow-haired actress as his mistress, and she's bedded *everyone*," Lucy said. She looked at Evelyn. "She was with Philip for nearly four months."

Evelyn blushed anew.

"You see, Evelyn?" Eloisa crowed. "I told you yellow was the color of fashion!"

"What about Lord Elkins?" Charlotte suggested.

"No," Lucy said. "He's getting married and going to Scotland on his wedding trip. He won't be back for several months. Still, if Evie could wait that long, he might do."

"No," Evelyn said.

Lucy mistook her meaning. "Well then, fetch me something to write with and a fresh sheet of paper. There are at least a dozen other men I can think of who are available now." She looked at Isobel. "Are you quite certain Blackwood has given up other women?"

Isobel scowled at her. "Most certain, Countess."

Lucy was hardly deterred. "*Quelle dommage!* Blackwood was the most skilled lover in London."

"How would you know, Lucy? He never bedded *you*," Charlotte said. "Remember how you tried and tried to get him to—"

Lucy raised her chin. "I remember!" she snapped. Isobel smiled coldly at her.

"Anyway," Eloisa said, "unless you can think of someone else, we're down to second sons and Scotsmen."

"Wait," Marianne said. "I was introduced to a very pleasant gentleman last night, Lord William Rutherford, Viscount Mears. He's in London for the Season, and then he'll return home to the country. What could be better? A few weeks pleasure, and then he'll go, leaving no entanglements."

Sam coughed. In fact, he appeared to be choking. Every lady's eye shot across the room to him.

"Are you well, Sam?" Evelyn asked in concern.

"May I be excused, my lady?" he asked in a dark voice, his eyes flat, his face carefully devoid of any expression at all.

She nodded, relieved to have him out of the room for the rest of the embarrassing discussion. She waited until he shut the door behind him.

"What about Lord—" Charlotte began again, but Evelyn raised her chin.

"No," she said firmly. "I have no intention of heaping further scandal upon myself by taking a lover. I am not interested."

"But I hear Lord Downing has made a study of *eastern techniques*!" Charlotte protested. She waggled her eyebrows. "He knows a dozen ways to make a lady—"

"Stop!" Evelyn insisted.

A fleeting memory of Philip's collection of erotic art and books passed through her mind, but the face she pictured was Sam's, not Lord Downing's. She blushed, her nerves at the breaking point.

"You are welcome to finish your tea, but we will discuss another topic, if you please. I am done with this one."

"We could talk about your wardrobe," Eloisa said dryly.

"Not that topic either," Evelyn said sharply. "What about the weather, or where the best strawberries are grown, or the latest news of the war? I hear Lord Wellington has had several recent victories."

"War?" Charlotte gasped. "Ladies do not discuss war! It is our duty to admire the gentlemen in their scarlet officers' tunics and wave them off to battle with tears in our eyes, but what they do after that is their affair!"

Sam slipped into the room and resumed his post. He did not meet her eye, but fixed his gaze on the wall behind her, his expression cold and correct.

"Speaking of affairs, did you see how dashing Major Lord Creighton looked last night?" Lucy said.

"He's quite a hero, I understand," Isobel added.

"Indeed he is," Lucy said. "I saw you dancing with him, Evelyn. Are you considering him for the, um, *position*?" she asked.

Evelyn sent her sister a quelling look and didn't bother to answer.

Eloisa sighed. "Obviously you're going to be stubborn again today. I will arrange to have my modiste send you the latest pattern books and some samples of silk. I think a walking gown in egg yolk and perhaps a bonnet in mulligatawny would suit you very well. Even you could not object to a shade as lovely as mulligatawny."

Isobel wrinkled her nose. "What is mulligatawny?"

"It's soup," Marianne answered. "One of Westlake's ships brought a recipe back from India. It's quite delicious, but the only way I'd wear it is if I spilled it on my gown."

Eloisa sniffed. "I think it's time we left, since we can't be of any further assistance here." She held up her gloves before putting them on. "Mulligatawny."

Charlotte rose as well. "By the way, Evie, I have been so

busy with invitations since the ball that I shan't be able to devote myself to staying here in the house with you. Eloisa and Lucy assure me they are also busy.

"Then I shall be content on my own," Evelyn said quickly.

"Certainly not! My maid shall come and stay," Charlotte said. "She will make a perfect companion. If you do not wish to have her, then you will have to come and stay with me or Eloisa."

Evelyn's heart sank. It was hardly a choice at all. Charlotte's maid was a spy and a busybody. Still, it would be worse staying with her sisters. She pictured a guest room done over in a dozen shades of yellow, just for her.

Her sisters marched toward the door, but Lucy lingered to finish her champagne, fishing the strawberry out of the empty glass.

"Come on, Lucy," Eloisa said impatiently.

Lucy sauntered across the room and linked arms with Charlotte. "Tell me more about Lord Downing's eastern practices."

Marianne and Isobel rose as well. And Evelyn smiled at Isobel. "You look lovely," she said. "And happy."

Isobel grinned as she leaned in to whisper, "That's because everything they say about Blackwood is quite true. A lover can truly make the unbearable situations of life bearable, Evelyn. Do consider it."

Evelyn studied her hands and didn't reply.

Marianne chimed in. "I don't often agree with your sisters, but you deserve some pleasure, and some happiness, and—"

"Thank you both for coming. We shall have to visit soon," Evelyn said, ending the conversation yet again.

She watched as Sam opened the door for her guests and led them down the hall without so much as a glance at her.

He did not return to the salon afterward, and she stared at the spot where he'd been standing for a long time.

Pleasure and happiness. How long had it been since she'd had either? Never in a man's arms. At least not until Sam. She shivered, and wondered if she should ring for a shawl.

But she wasn't cold. She was desperate and restless and she wanted the one thing she couldn't, shouldn't, want.

She wanted Sam.

Chapter 20

William, his own brother, Evelyn's lover?

As her servant, he would probably be expected to tuck them in at night and serve them breakfast in the morning. He couldn't do it. He wouldn't.

Sinjon lengthened his stride, walked faster. He didn't have permission to leave his post, but he didn't care. He had no intention of going back. He was on his way to tell Westlake he quit.

Had the earl sent his wife to goad him? Why else would Marianne have suggested that *William* would make Evelyn a perfect bedmate? Had she been watching for his reaction, ready to report to her husband?

He'd do his own reporting.

Evelyn's sisters reminded him of his father's hunting dogs, loud, mannerless, and deadly. But these bitches had powerful husbands, and the pack of them was circling, scenting blood. The Crown would be lucky if there was a single farthing or a scrap of flesh left once Evelyn's family finished with her.

She *needed* a protector. He stopped walking and looked back along the street toward Renshaw House.

Of course he'd think so—he'd been brought up to care

for women. Whether they needed his help to carry parcels, to fight off rapists in Spain, or to defend against French assailants in Hyde Park, he served with a smile.

In bed too. He was a considerate, passionate lover. He made sure the lady's pleasure equaled his own.

He tried to remember a woman he desired with the intensity he felt for Evelyn, but it simply hadn't happened. The idea did nothing to soothe his rage. There had to be a reason why he wanted her so badly. He leaned against an iron railing and considered.

Perhaps it was the mystery that surrounded Evelyn, and his own disguise, that added spice to the situation.

Or was it the lady herself? She had made it clear enough that she wanted him as well, but Evelyn Renshaw would never act on her desire for a mere footman.

That was a good thing—if he was her lover, he'd want to protect her from Westlake, not entrap her for the wily earl. It wouldn't matter if she was guilty or not, and that was treason of the most foolish kind.

"You there!" someone called, and Sinjon turned to find a sour-faced butler glaring at him from the doorway of the house he was standing in front of. "What do you think you're doing?"

"Is this no longer a free country?" Sinjon demanded. If the man wanted to fight, then he would happily oblige. It would feel good to punch someone.

"Are you here to see Countess Lucy or Lord Frayne?" the man demanded, and Sinjon looked up and realized he was loitering in front of Frayne House. "If you have a note, I'll take it now, but next time use the back door."

Sinjon could imagine the kind of a *billet doux* Lucy received—invitations to secret assignations filled with saucy innuendos and wicked suggestions.

The kind of letters Evelyn would soon be receiving from her own lover.

He gritted his teeth and cursed Evelyn's sisters again. He felt helpless, and that was a feeling he'd endured long enough.

"No, there's no note, just a message. Tell Countess Lucy that the gentleman in possession of her locket wishes to return it at her earliest convenience."

There. That should give Lewd Lucy something to worry about other than Evelyn's love life. Let her look over her shoulder, and wonder if Philip was coming for *her.*

The butler frowned. "But what does it mean? Who is the message from?"

"She'll know," Sinjon said, and walked on.

De Courcey House was only a few blocks farther on. He wondered exactly what he was going to say when he confronted Westlake.

He could hardly tell him he was giving up his post because he desired Evelyn Renshaw.

Nor could he punch that superior expression off the earl's face and tell him he did not appreciate Marianne playing procurer for his older brother.

Westlake would laugh, if he was capable of such a thing, and then he'd snap his fingers and the burly sailors would drag him to the closest gallows.

He stared up at the magnificent facade of the earl's London home. It glared back, warning him away.

He wished his jealousy and resentment were enough to topple the elegant granite columns that flanked the front door. As a servant, he wasn't worthy to walk through that door. But bloody William could, as an earl's son.

The thought struck him like a body blow. If he was standing here as Sinjon instead of Sam, as a nobleman's son, a gentleman with an army commission, a hero instead of an outlaw, then it would be *his* name, not William's, that topped the damned lover's list. Under his false footman's livery, his pedigree was as good as Evelyn's, his blood every bit as blue.

And he knew Evelyn would choose him over William, heir to an earldom, or even above Lord Downing and his eastern techniques. It put a smile on his face.

Then he remembered how she'd turned to flame in his arms, and groaned, wishing he hadn't thought of it at all.

There was no place to hide, not from Westlake, and not from his own desires.

An hour later he was back at Renshaw House, and this time he entered through the front door.

Chapter 21

"Would you send Sam to me?" Evelyn asked Starling. He looked at her sharply, and she felt herself blush. Did he know?

"Is it about his absence yesterday afternoon, my lady? I hope you won't be too harsh with him. He was only gone for a few hours, and he did explain that it was just to return a glove that Countess Westlake had dropped as she got into her coach," he said.

Of course Sam had walked all the way to De Courcey House to return a lost glove. It was chivalrous, and one of the qualities she liked best about him. He'd probably taken a few moments to slay a dragon threatening a damsel in Grosvenor Square on his way back.

"I simply wished to thank him on the countess's behalf," she lied, and to her relief, Starling beamed.

"I'm sure he'll be delighted."

Would he? Evelyn had no intention of thanking Sam. She wanted to see him for another reason entirely.

Her sisters were right. She needed a lover.

But not Lord Downing, or Elkins, or Creighton.

She wanted Sam.

Gentlemen took mistresses all time, women from outside their own class. Why couldn't she?

She'd spent the night pacing, thinking her decision through, considering how to word her unusual request.

It was past midnight when she gathered the courage to creep downstairs to his room. She thought it might be easier in the dark, when he couldn't see her face. But Starling slept in the room next to Sam's, and Mrs. Cooper was nearby as well. She lost her nerve at the top of the kitchen steps and retreated back upstairs, unsure all over again.

It should have ended there, but she *wanted* this man.

She'd spent her life as a moral, dignified, socially up-standing lady, an earl's daughter, a baron's wife. She'd avoided untidy emotions, sidestepped pain and longing and loneliness. She'd refused to be tempted by desires of any kind. And what had proper behavior gained her? A husband who detested her, and the scorn of society.

In the dark, her feelings for Sam had rushed in on her, left her breathless with longing. It was becoming impos-sible to hide her desires.

Now, in the soft light of day, primly dressed as usual, sipping tea, she was a bundle of nerves. Any moment Sam would answer her summons. She was eager to see him, and dreading the encounter.

She had decided to meet with him in the library, a formal, dignified room, though her request was born of unruly, desperate passion. It was the kind of interview that should take place in the dark, a whispered request in his ear, just before— She swallowed.

She'd practiced what she would say. "I want you to be my lover" made her blush when she said it aloud. "I would like you to take on a new duty" was too cold.

Perhaps she'd look him straight in the eye and inform

him, "Lords take mistresses all the time. Why shouldn't a lady have her pleasures?" She bit her lip. Too forward.

What if he laughed, or refused, or both? She didn't think she could stand the humiliation of that. She crumbled a shortbread biscuit between nervous fingers.

She had to try. Sam had awakened a hunger in her that she'd not even known she was capable of. Not just a hunger—a realization that she was *starving*.

Should she offer him extra pay? She squirmed. That was the most mortifying thought of all. Still, there had to be rules.

She would insist he keep their liaison secret. Wagging tongues all over London were still speculating about the identity of the lady in the footman's arms. If the *ton*'s gossips saw Sam, there wasn't a woman among them who wouldn't understand her infatuation.

She sighed, and absently poured more tea. The amber liquid flowed over the rim and swam across the desk. Evelyn leapt to her feet and dabbed at the mess with a napkin.

She had already decided where they would meet for their trysts. Charlotte's maid had moved into the attic bedroom above her rooms, serving as chaperone and guard dog, and she snored like one. With such a dreadful noise coming through the ceiling, who'd blame her for taking refuge in the spare bedroom at the opposite end of the hall? It would explain the rumpled sheets when Sal discovered the bed had been slept in.

That bedroom was the most private room in the house. Sam could slip up the back stairs and— Evelyn drew a shaky breath as a cascade of shivers raced through her. Distracted, she wrung the sodden napkin back into the cup and took a sip.

How would it feel to lie in the dark and wait for him, anticipating his arrival, yearning for his hands on her body?

She'd dreaded Philip's footsteps outside her door. She had learned to shut her mind, to think of other things until he finished. She bit her lip. What if it was like that with Sam, a cold, unfeeling duty?

She raised her chin and smiled. If he wasn't to her liking she would simply end the affair and send him away.

The knock on the door made her jump.

Should she be sitting or standing when he entered?

She sat.

Then she got to her feet.

She moved to stand behind the settee, facing the door.

"Come," she croaked, and cleared the frog from her throat.

Her breath caught as he entered the room. He filled the space, just like he had that first day. He looked solemn now, not roguish or teasing. His expression was closed, unreadable.

She swallowed. Perhaps he was indeed expecting a reprimand for his absence. She stifled a hysterical giggle. He was in for a shock, then, wasn't he? She clasped her hands together in front of her. He put his behind his back and stood at attention, like a soldier.

Her soldier. *Her lover.*

The frog leapt back into her gullet.

"You wished to see me, my lady?" he asked as the silence stretched, and his deep voice rumbled over every nerve in her body. Oh, where was her legendary calm now?

"Yes," she said, and hesitated. Should she invite him to sit? It wasn't usual, but given the nature of this conversation, perhaps she should.

She decided against it, afraid he would refuse, and it would lead him to refuse *everything* she asked. What if he *did* say no? Or was angry at her audacity?

"I trust you are well?' she said, stalling.

"Of course," he said.

She ran her eyes over him. Surely no other soldier, no footman, no gentleman, was as handsome as Sam Carr. He was tall, his legs so long, so deliciously lean in the tight breeches of his livery. Those powerful legs would be wrapped around her as he made love to her, his fingers exploring and caressing every inch of her. She drew a ragged breath, tried to concentrate. He was watching her soberly, with no idea what wicked thoughts were rushing through her mind.

Everything about him exuded confidence. He made her feel safe, sure he could handle any problem, overcome any setback, rescue her from any peril, and make her tingle as she thanked him.

Would she thank him, after? Should she, given the nature of the arrangement?

She realized he was still waiting for her to speak, to say something sensible and succinct, to tell him what she wanted.

Her throat closed again. She put a hand to her collar, as if she could squeeze the words out.

"I wished to ask, that is, I hoped you would consider—" She took a deep breath and let it out along with the words, "There's an extra service I wish you to perform."

Something sparked in those clear gray eyes of his. Interest, perhaps, or humor. "Would this be *on top* of my usual duties?" he asked.

The way he said "on top" made her quiver.

"Um, yes. It is a service of a personal nature, but it's not necessarily a duty, or a dull job," she babbled, and stopped. What if it *was* dull to him?

She watched his eyebrows rise at her hesitation. The faint

shadow of the dimple on his cheek appeared, as if he was suppressing a smile. Did he know what she meant, what she wanted?

It would make it so much easier if she didn't have to say the words.

Be my lover, my bedmate. Take me!

She waited for him to give a clearer indication that he understood, but he remained silent, his expression enigmatic, smug. She felt a rush of frustration. How on earth did men like Frayne or Somerson arrange *amours* with the females they seduced?

Did they simply pounce on them? She came out from behind the settee and took a step toward Sam, hoping he would make the first pounce, but he stayed where he was, still standing at attention. At least he was looking at her, his eyes fixed on hers. She couldn't look away.

"I want, that is, I—" Again she hesitated, and fought with the frog. Sam was watching her expectantly. "I want to thank you for returning Countess Westlake's glove to her," the frog croaked, obviously realizing she had lost her nerve.

He smiled, and tilted his head in disbelief. "Truly? Is that what you wished to see me about? Returning a glove hardly qualifies as a service of a personal nature."

She felt her skin heat. "No, perhaps not, but you were kind to do so, and—" She sighed, and looked away. She could not look at him without wanting to kiss him. "About the night of the ball . . ." she started again.

"Are you worried I won't be discreet about what happened between us?" he asked, and her eyes shot to his, read the knowing look, the memory of the intimacy they'd shared in the coach.

"I wasn't thinking that at all!" she protested, then hesitated. "You are discreet, aren't you? I mean you *will* be discreet about . . . ?" She let her voice trail off, and realized she was making a mess of everything.

"A footman could dine out for a month on a tale like that," he drawled. "If, of course, anyone cared to invite a mere servant to dinner."

"Dinner?" she parroted.

"Yes," he said, taking a step toward her. "Footmen eat." He took another step. "We sleep. We even—" He was toe-to-toe with her now, and she had to tip her head back to hold his gaze. She felt dizzy, and her body burned. She clenched her hands against her skirts to keep from touching him.

"Kiss?" she finished breathlessly, hopefully.

For a long moment he stood very still, staring down at her, his jaw tight, his own arms at his sides, a frown pleating the tanned skin between his brows, as if he were calculating a complex problem in his head.

She waited for his mouth to descend on hers. It seemed to take forever for him to decide.

Finally, he swore softly, and she was in his arms, with her own wrapped around his neck. She knocked off his wig as she stood on her toes, trying to get closer, to devour him. He'd taught her well in the coach, and she opened her mouth at once this time, wanting the taste of him, needing him to ease the hunger.

He broke the kiss far too soon. "Evelyn," he murmured, nuzzling her ear, and she sighed with frustration, tried to capture his mouth again, but he reached up, gently unwound her arms from his neck and stepped back.

"Yes," he growled.

"Yes?" she asked.

"I'll be your lover."

She stared at him in surprise, unable to reply. He looked amused as he reached out to brush a lock of her hair out of her eyes.

"You will?" she breathed.

"Isn't that what you were going to ask?"

She felt her stomach clench. Her first instinct, the lady-like, dignified part of her, urged her to deny it. But every womanly, feminine fiber of her body refused to give him up. She managed to nod, not trusting her voice.

He gave her a wicked, seductive smile, the understanding clear in his eyes at last, along with the flattering gleam of desire for her.

Her heart flipped in her chest.

"You will," she sighed, and reached for him, but he shook his head, stepped out of reach.

"Not here."

"What?" she asked, not understanding. She was on fire, and wanted him to fuel the blaze, not put it out.

"You asked me to be discreet, didn't you? It's hardly discreet to make love on the settee in the middle of the day," he said.

She shut her eyes. He was right, of course. She should have thought of that herself. Anyone might walk in. Starling, or Charlotte, or Eloisa.

She raised her chin, striving for a little of her usual dignity. "Tonight, then," she said, giving it an edge of command.

He folded his arms, leaned back against the table, completely at his ease. "If we do this, Evelyn, then I have some rules."

Her stomach knotted. Now he would ask for money.

"In this room, in the dining room, in the coach, I am your servant." His eyes heated, and she felt her own temperature rise in response. "In bed, we are equals. Do you agree?"

She hadn't thought of that. Had she intended or expected anything else? She didn't know. She had no idea what to expect. She had not been Philip's equal in bed. "Yes," she said.

"And I insist that our arrangement is exclusive for the duration of our time together."

"Exclusive?" she asked.

He stepped toward her, grasped her shoulders, his eyes smoldering coals that burned into hers. "I don't care about the list your sisters compiled, or whose name is on it. While we are together, until one of us decides that it's over, I will be the only man sharing your bed, is that clear?"

A flare of anger filled her. "Do you honestly believe I do this often?"

He didn't reply.

She felt her skin flush. He did not know her well enough to say, but surely his suspicion was more embarrassing than being asked for money, or being refused outright. A protest formed on her lips, denial that she would *ever*— She swallowed it. Her husband was still alive, and this was adultery, and a forbidden liaison between a lady and her servant.

"Exclusive," she murmured in agreement.

He put a hand under her chin and kissed her forehead gently before he stepped away again. She felt the tingle between her eyes. It shot to her knees, stopping to torment every inch in between.

He bent and picked up his wig, replacing it on his head as he moved toward the door. She stood where she was, watching him, her legs shaking.

He turned and bowed.

"Until tonight, my lady," he said formally, her footman again.

When he was gone, Evelyn sank onto the settee and brushed a hand over her mouth.

She'd done it. She'd gotten her heart's desire for the first time in her life. It was an incredible feeling, a mixture of anticipation, power, and happiness. She bit her lip. And trepidation. And doubt.

What on earth had she set in motion?

She couldn't wait to find out.

Chapter 22

Sinjon expected Evelyn to be waiting for him. She'd specified the room, and the time of their first encounter, but the bedroom was empty when he arrived at midnight.

He'd been tormented all afternoon, picturing her here, waiting for him in bed, naked. Her lips would part as she sat up eagerly, reaching for him, the sheets falling away to reveal—

He set the candle down beside the empty bed, his disappointment as cold as the untouched linens.

The room reminded him of Evelyn herself—tidy, and correct, and elegant. It was hard to imagine this room as a romantic hideaway, but that's exactly what it was about to become.

He pictured the room—and the lady—after they'd made love. The pristine bedclothes would be rumpled and sweat-stained, the pillows crushed. The room would be perfumed with the scent of sex. Evelyn's hair would be loose, love-tangled, her cheeks flushed, her eyes glowing with the particular joy of a well-loved woman. She was passionate under her aloof exterior. He'd seen it, tasted it.

Tonight, here in this plain little room, he'd strip away

every social grace, every genteel artifice that hid her deepest desires, and lay her bare to his hands, his lips, his body.

He wanted to see her face as he made love to her, drove her wild again and again, gave her pleasure and took his own.

He unbuttoned his shirt, tossed it aside, and lay down on the bed, wearing only his breeches.

He still marveled at her boldness. The words may have stuck in her throat, but her desire had been clear enough in her eyes. It had been flattering and arousing, knowing that she'd chosen him over any of the names on the list.

It also surprised him. Evelyn was discreet and dignified, bound by etiquette in everything she did. It was a risk, choosing to bed her footman. He grinned, then frowned. What would she say if she knew *his* secret?

The traitor's wife, bedding the outlaw.

It hardly mattered. He'd be gone before she found out his true identity. He'd leave her with fond memories. When she took other lovers in the future, she'd remember him, and find every other man lacking.

He groaned, erotic images of what he was going to do to her making him hard again. He shifted, frowning up at the ceiling, wondering how long she meant to keep him waiting.

Perhaps she'd decided not to come at all.

His ears pricked at the creak of the floorboards outside the door. He leaned up on his elbow and held his breath, waiting for her to decide. She'd most likely walk away. It was the sensible thing to do, but he fervently hoped she'd choose passion over good sense.

The door opened, and he let his breath out slowly, anticipation and desire surging.

The soft glow of her candle preceded her into the room. She entered without even glancing at him, her expression crisp and businesslike, and turned away to shut the door. She stood with her back to him, a wraith in a white nightgown, her hand clenching the latch.

"Are you intending to stay?"

She turned to look at him, and her eyes flicked over his naked chest. He watched them widen, saw her jaw drop, heard her soft exhalation of breath.

He kept still and stared at her in return. She was beautiful in the candlelight, though she wore a prim high-necked nightgown. Her lips were soft and moist, parted slightly. The flame of her candle reflected in her eyes, and her nervous blush was visible even in the low light. The candlestick shook in her hand, and wax dripped onto her wrist where it lay exposed by the lace sleeve of her gown. She gasped, and set the candle down.

He held out his hand in wordless invitation.

She came forward and he turned her palm in his, examined the slight burn, and gently peeled away the wax. Then he put her hand to his lips and kissed the red mark. He tried to draw her to the bed, to sit beside him, but she pulled back.

He raised his eyebrows and waited. Was she going to play the virgin bride? He'd hoped for better from her.

"I must tell you—I suppose I should have said it earlier, but—" She shut her eyes. "I haven't—" The ivory column of her throat moved in the candlelight as she swallowed. "I haven't a great deal of experience, or expertise. You will need to show me how best to please you."

"You want to please *me*?" he asked. Surely that wasn't the usual reason ladies took lovers.

"Of course," she said, her eyes meeting his at last. "Did you think I only meant for you to—" She blushed deeply.

"We'll learn what pleases us both, I expect. Come here," he said. She sat, her hip against his, and he turned on his side, curled his body around hers and watched a slow flush rise over her cheekbones at the intimacy. This time she didn't pull away. He touched her cheek, stroked her skin to see if her face was as warm and soft as it looked.

She tilted her head, fitting her chin into his palm, her eyes drifting shut, her lips parting.

She hardly looked virginal or reticent now. If such a simple touch could so obviously affect her, then she was as eager as he. His desire surged higher.

He drew her forward and kissed her, a mere brush of his lips on hers, since he was still half afraid she'd change her mind. She stayed, her lips a hair's breadth from his, waiting for the next kiss.

"Do you like how I kiss you?" he asked.

"Yes." She sighed the word against his mouth. "More," she ordered, and he smiled.

So she was going to take charge, was she? He felt the demands of his own body, and wanted nothing more than to pull her beneath him and give her what she craved, but there'd be greater pleasure, better pleasure, if he went slowly.

He was, after all, the one with experience on his side.

He frowned. He hardly felt experienced. Why was it that everything he did with Evelyn felt new, as if he'd never truly known what it felt like to make love to a woman? Evelyn was shy, she was wanton, she was passionate, beautiful, and completely unique.

And she was the aggressor now, pressing him back, kissing him, teaching him how a kiss should be, if it were perfect. It was, with her. He couldn't get enough of her lips, her tongue, the taste of her, the fragrance of her perfume, the way her eyes drifted shut and her lashes lay on flushed cheeks. He'd never noticed these things before with other bedmates. He'd given pleasure, taken his own, and it had been enough, but this was new, different.

He forced himself to concentrate. This was supposed to take hours. He fully intended to pleasure every inch of her luscious body, but the struggle to hold back his own need only drove it higher and harder. He wasn't in charge, wasn't the teacher. He gulped for air, pulled back even as she pressed forward, pursuing his mouth with hers, edging closer.

The candlelight behind her shone through the fine lawn fabric of her gown, outlined pert breasts and the slim curve of her waist. The heat of her body was hypnotic, and he felt a bead of sweat trickle between his shoulders and groaned. What else could he do but let the tide sweep him away?

Evelyn had never been drunk, but Sam's kisses made her feel tipsy, restless, excited, the way champagne did. She wanted to laugh at the sheer joy of kissing him. She could kiss him forever. She met him nip for nip, lick for lick, learning, practicing, *daring*. Her body was on fire, moving of its own accord, knowing what was wanted, what they both needed.

She laid her palms on his naked chest and leaned over him, pressing him backward. His skin was warm and soft, the muscles hard. She could feel his heart beating. She curled her hands inward, her nails scraping gently, and he gasped.

"Should I stop?" she asked, not wanting to. She slid her fingers upward over his remarkable body.

"God, no, don't stop!" He lay back and let her explore, and she ran her fingers over his skin, tracing the scars that crossed his ribs, following the faint white lines upward to a deeper wound at his throat.

She frowned as she touched the puckered roughness of it.

He caught her hand, his eyes wary, mistaking her expression. "War leaves marks, Evelyn. Do my scars disgust you?"

She was surprised he might think so. "No." She leaned forward to kiss the mark. "It is the cause of them that upsets me. Is this the reason why you came home?"

"In part," he said cryptically, his voice hard-edged. He shifted out of her reach, sitting up, turning the scarred side of his body into the shadows. "Would you prefer to put out the candles?"

She imagined making love to him in the dark, unable to see him. It was how Philip— She pushed him out of her mind. He had no place here.

"No, I want the light."

He relaxed and lay back on the bed, his hands under his head, feet crossed, at his ease while she still perched on the edge of the mattress like a nervous bird. His gaze roamed over her, his eyes heavy lidded, sensual.

"Undo your hair."

She reached to unplait it for him, her fingers clumsy. The golden brown waves fell over her shoulders, brushed her cheeks, and she saw flame ignite in his eyes. He picked up a long lock and stroked the length of it through his fingers. Desire pooled, hot and sweet, in her belly.

"Beautiful," he murmured.

He plunged his hands into her hair, stroked it, drawing her down, kissing her with a new hunger, a need she suspected he'd held in check before now. Could hair do that, or was it something more, something deeper? She didn't care. She didn't want to think now. She kissed him back, meeting his tongue, sparring, running her hands over the muscles of his back, his shoulders, his arms.

He was touching her as well, his hands sliding over the

slippery fabric of her nightgown, warming the flesh beneath. The garment felt at once too heavy and too thin. She wanted it off, wanted to feel the sensation of his skin against hers.

She had never been fully naked in bed, never wanted to be, until now.

She untied the satin ribbons at her collar and reached for the top button, fumbling with it. He kissed each exposed inch of flesh as the fastenings opened. She was gasping by the time he ran his tongue over the pulse point at the base of her throat, was mad with need as he trailed kisses across her collarbones. He slid his mouth down the slope of her breast with agonizing slowness.

And there the buttons ended. She moaned with frustration.

He wasn't deterred in the least. He cupped the fullness of her breast and lowered his mouth to her nipple, suckling her through the fabric. She arched her back, cupped his dark head in her hands, holding him to her, moaning. She wanted his mouth, his hands, his tongue, everywhere at once.

He was caressing her body, her hips, her thighs, sliding her nightgown up by inches, baring her flesh.

For an instant she panicked, remembering how Philip had shoved her gown out of his way, his hands cold.

But Sam's hands were warm, his touch gentle and arousing. He caressed her upper thighs, her hips, her buttocks, and she shifted restlessly, wanting this.

He drew the garment over her head, tossing it aside. For an instant she was tempted to cross her arms over her breasts and hide, but the look in his eyes stopped her.

"God, Evelyn, you're beautiful," he said, his voice thick.

"Touch me," she pleaded.

"Where?" he tormented her.

"Everywhere."

"Tell me what you want." He kissed her neck, frustrating, teasing, tormenting little pecks. She wanted his hands on her breasts, his mouth there too. She wanted him to lay her down and take her. He was going slowly and carefully, when she wanted wild abandon, passion, and fireworks.

"I want everything," she said, not knowing what to demand first. She pushed him back onto the bed and straddled his hips, gazing at him boldly. His erection pulsed against her, straining the fabric of his breeches. She began to undo the buttons, and he gritted his teeth, his hands fisted in the sheets as she opened his flies and wrapped her hand around the hard length of him.

He groaned as she caressed him, explored his body. It gave her pleasure to touch him, to watch his reaction to what she was doing to him. The muscles in his neck were corded, and she leaned forward, pressing the naked length of her body against him, and nipped his throat. She tasted clean sweat, inhaled the spicy male scent of his body. She rubbed against him, marveling at the feel of his skin on hers, and felt her nipples harden and chafe against the raised pebbles of his own. She could feel the heat of his erection against her belly, pulsing and eager.

She had hated this part of marriage, dreaded it, but not now, not with Sam.

He was muttering, growling in her ear as his hands roamed over every inch of her. She gasped as his fingers dipped between her thighs, found the swollen lips of her sex, and slid inside.

"Sam!" she cried, and for a moment he stilled, stiffened beneath her.

"Sin," he murmured. "Sin."

She didn't understand. How could anything so heavenly

be a sin? She didn't care. His hands moved, his fingers teasing, coaxing, urging. She pressed herself into his hand, moaning, begging, rubbing against him like a cat in heat.

Her climax surprised her when it came. She had heard of such things, of course. She was a married woman with a very experienced, talkative sister. She had not known that it was the finest pleasure on earth.

He lifted her as her body still pulsated, positioning her. With a groan he filled her in one quick thrust, making her cry out anew. He was so hot, so powerful, so delicious. She shifted her hips, wanting friction and heat, and he obliged, driving into her with a growl of male satisfaction.

She felt the rush of pleasure rise again, and she moved with him, matching his rhythm. She never wanted it to end, never wanted him to stop. She cried out as another rush of heat claimed her, felt him thrust into her one last time, his body arching as he found his own release, a wave that surged on forever.

She fell onto his chest and clung to him. He pulled the hair back from her damp face, stroked her, held her close. She could feel his heart pounding under hers. She smiled, and her toes curled. He made her feel safe, protected, even here. He made her feel things she had not even known existed.

She objected with a husky little mewl when he gently lifted her off his chest. He slipped off the bed, and she frowned, her skin cold where his body had warmed hers. She had forgotten he was still wearing his breeches until he peeled them off.

He stood naked before her for a moment, his body golden in the candlelight. He was more magnificent than an Italian sculpture, handsomer and more desirable than the men drawn in Philip's books.

"Oh," she sighed. "Oh, my."

Under her gaze, he hardened again, his erection rising. She reached out to caress him, and he drew a sharp breath. On impulse, she leaned forward and kissed the tip. The musky scent of sex thrilled her. She looked up at him, saw desire darken his eyes. A thrill went through her, and she smiled, feeling wanton, powerful, a goddess with her god. She lay back and opened her arms, and he tumbled into her embrace.

She looked into his eyes as he entered her again with exquisite, maddening slowness, an inch at a time. She clasped her legs around his hips and shut her eyes.

If this was sin, then she could never, ever have enough.

Chapter 23

Lucy Frayne paced her bedroom. She'd drawn the drapes, ordered the doors locked, and still she didn't feel safe.

Philip Renshaw was watching her.

The man was so slippery, she wouldn't be surprised if he popped out from under her bed. Horrified, perhaps, but not surprised.

She'd received his message, a cryptic, garbled thing, delivered by a stranger at the front door, conveyed to her in an embarrassed whisper by her butler. She'd dropped her teacup in terror. Actually, she threw it across the room, as furious as she was frightened.

The butler had merely stepped out of the way, since he'd long ago ceased to be shocked by anything the Fraynes did. He summoned a maid to clean up the mess while he poured Lucy a tot of brandy to calm her nerves.

She'd swallowed the brandy in a single gulp and retreated to her bedroom. Now, she peeked through the curtains at the street below, scanning the sidewalk and shadowed doorways for any sign of Philip. She wouldn't see him, of course. He'd simply appear, like an unwelcome shade rising from hell to claim her soul. Shivering, Lucy stepped away from the window.

She wasn't willing to admit this was her own fault. Her brief affair with Philip had been born from a fit of pique. Frayne had commented that Evelyn was a beauty and would be a delight in any man's bed.

She'd taken his comment as an insult and a challenge.

Her sister was as cold as uncooked bacon, while Philip had a reputation as hot as a sizzling sausage.

She'd thought seducing Philip would be an easy victory. She and Frayne had been trying to outdo each other for years. She was sure such a bold act would shock her roving husband, but she'd been curious as well. Philip had a string of beautiful mistresses. He held wicked parties at country estates. Women stood in line for their turn in his bed, and surely a man that popular must have *something* special. Her sister seemed to be the only woman in the world who did not see Philip Renshaw's sensual appeal.

Lucy shut her eyes, feeling a rare blush heating her cheeks. It wasn't a ladylike flush of mild surprise, or a response to a titillating memory. It was the hard burn of shame.

It turned out the only charm Philip possessed was the size of his fortune. He gave his lovers lavish gifts to make up for the fact that he was a selfish bully in bed.

She wished she hadn't taken the magnificent emerald bracelet he'd given her, but it was worth more than half a year's allowance, even for a countess.

She opened her jewelry box and stared down at the green stones. She'd worn them only once, to taunt Frayne, and he hadn't even noticed. She slammed the lid shut, still angry.

A bead of sweat slid between her breasts, and she turned to look behind her, searching the shadowed corners of her boudoir. There was no one there, but that meant nothing.

Philip Renshaw was watching her.

She opened the jewelry box again and took the bracelet out. The stones glittered coldly, like his reptilian eyes.

She had to find him, had to return the bracelet and demand her locket back. It was the only thing that tied her to him, the only proof that she'd ever meant anything to him aside from being his sister-in-law. Her stomach tightened. What would Evelyn say if she knew?

New heat warmed her face at the thought of confessing to her sister, but she had no other choice. She needed Evelyn's help. She'd *make* Evelyn tell her where Philip was. It was a matter of life and death. Well, salvation and scandal, perhaps.

She crossed to ring the bell, and then threw open the wardrobe. By the time her maid appeared, Lucy had selected three of her most demure yellow walking gowns and tossed them on the bed, afraid none of them was quite demure enough.

"Go down and order the coach, then come and get me dressed."

She crammed the emeralds into her bodice, and they chilled the skin between her breasts, just like Philip's touch.

God knew what Philip might tell the authorities about her if they found him before she did. She had been stupid enough to think his ramblings were some odd kind of foreplay, or just an indiscreet jest to impress her with his family connections. He was a mere baron, bedding a countess, after all. Of course, he had to level the playing field, so to speak.

"Did you know that my mother was a member of the French royal family?" he'd whispered in her ear as he undressed her. "Louis XVI was my cousin. His brother, the duc d'Orleans, was next in line for the throne after they guillotined Louis, and the little dauphin died in prison. Orleans was too weak to take the crown, so he ran away, to England, seeking asylum and help from our king to put him on his throne. Did you know he's here, even now, hiding on an estate in Buckinghamshire?"

Lucy hadn't known, of course. Nor had she cared. She was a creature of love, pleasure, and comfort, and she didn't give a fig about French kings. She'd lifted her breasts, licked her lips, hoping to distract him from his diatribe. She expected him to be impressed by the sight of her lush body, a body most men drooled over, but she was disappointed. He just kept talking. She'd grown bored, drank more champagne while Philip rattled on.

She knew now she should have listened more closely, should have told Frayne, or Somerson. But then she would have had to admit where she'd heard such a tale.

Philip's face had been a bitter mask as he paced the bedroom. "I prepared everything for the duc's arrival. I spent a fortune making over my estate in Dorset for him. No expense was spared." He grabbed a pillow off the bed, tore it open and pulled out a handful of feathers. "I even had geese brought from France and plucked for his pillows. I made him a palace, filled with all the luxuries and comforts he was accustomed to in France."

Philip's eyes burned like the windows of hell, and it had given her shivers, turned her lust to ashes, as the feathers from plain English geese filled the room like snow.

"When my exalted cousin landed, did he come to me, greet me as family the way he should have done?"

He seemed to be waiting for her to answer, so she shrugged, and toyed with the lace edge of the sheet.

"No, he did not. He walked past me as if I were nothing. *Nothing!*"

Lucy had been irritated. She'd driven an hour into the

countryside to this secluded house for their tryst, and he had done nothing but drink and rant like a madman.

"He got into another coach, a plain, ramshackle vehicle belonging to the Marquess of Buckingham. He snubbed me, madam, because Buckingham has a pretty wife and pretty daughters. He went to Buckingham's estate at Stowe. *Stowe!*" He spat the word as if the place were diseased.

Lucy recalled spending a delightful fortnight at Stowe with Buckingham and his marchioness. She hardly blamed the French king for choosing Buckingham over Philip. She wished she had herself. He'd offered enough times.

She'd bitten her lip. He was still whispering as he mounted and took her roughly, as if he blamed her for his troubles.

"Napoleon," he'd grunted in her ear. "*He's* the future of France. Louis is nothing. He will never take the French throne, and I will make him regret his treatment of me."

She'd stopped listening. She'd striven to get some pleasure out of bedding her sister's husband, but there was none to be had.

She cringed inwardly now, recalling how he'd smiled afterward, a cold and superior twist of his thin lips that made her feel like the lowest whore as he dropped the bracelet on the bed between her thighs.

She'd been wrong about bedding him.

She couldn't afford to be wrong about Philip Renshaw again.

Chapter 24

Sinjon's breath caught at the sight of Evelyn, though he had promised himself it wouldn't. She was sitting at her desk, the morning sun on her hair, as he entered the library. He was instantly, desperately, aroused, though they'd both been well sated when they parted at dawn. Had it been only a few hours since he kissed her before slipping out the door of the little bedroom?

He tried to concentrate on his task, which was delivering the morning mail on a silver tray. "The post has arrived, my lady," he said, playing the perfect footman, aloof and courteous.

"Sam," she said on a sigh, half rising from her chair. A blush washed over her cheekbones, and he swallowed a groan. It was going to be harder than he thought to keep their affair secret.

Evelyn looked like a woman who had been well bedded, loved an uncountable number of times, kissed senseless. Obviously, it hadn't been enough for either of them. He had an erection that could knock the desk over, and she was looking at him like she wanted to devour him.

Her fingertips brushed his as he held out the letters to her, and the simple touch ran straight to his groin. He wanted to toss the damned silver tray aside and take her on the desk, or the settee, or even the floor, right here and now, and let propriety and discretion be damned. But that was impossible.

"Are you well this morning, my lady?" he asked.

She smiled wickedly. "Perfectly. And you?"

"I'm finding it difficult not to touch you."

She came around the desk, and kept coming until the toes of her slippers stopped against his buckled shoes. "Then touch me," she whispered against his mouth.

He didn't need a second invitation. He stroked her face, felt the hectic pulse at her throat. He'd kissed her there last night, felt that throb under his mouth. Hell, he'd kissed every single inch of her delicious body.

He slid his hand downward, cupping her breast, remembering the way her nipples hardened in response to his touch. They peaked now under the crisp muslin bodice of her prim gown. He wanted to tear her dress off with his teeth.

But it was day, and he was still holding the tray of letters in one hand. He kissed her once, hard, and stepped back. "I'm supposed to be working. Anyone could walk in and—"

The door burst open.

They sprang apart, and the tray dropped to the floor between them with a clang. The letters swirled like leaves in the wind.

Lucy Frayne didn't notice. Her eyes were on Evelyn as she crossed the room in quick steps, instead of her usual sassy saunter. Her sultry smirk was absent too, and her face was blotchy and unpowdered. Her high-necked gown was almost virginal.

Trouble. Sinjon's stomach tightened.

She did not even spare him a glance, though he was the

only male in the room and would ordinarily have drawn her attention at once.

He bent to retrieve the letters.

"Lucy, what's the matter?" Evelyn cried, taking her sister's hands. "Come and sit down."

She led her to the settee, and Lucy drew a handkerchief out of her reticule, dabbed her eyes, and twisted it between nervous fingers.

Evelyn cast a sideways glance at him, begging for privacy, perhaps. He ignored her plea and concentrated on picking up the spilled letters, reading the addresses as he did.

The first envelope bore the crest of the Marchioness of Blackwood. Another was obviously an invitation, the only one she'd received in days. He picked up the third, and felt his skin heat.

Creighton.

He'd held enough vowels from the man to know his hand. He also recognized the family crest. He stared at the scrawled address, Evelyn's name, and felt rage boil through him. He was tempted to pocket the letter, read it later. Wasn't that why he was here, to spy on Evelyn, open her mail?

Did last night change the rules? Guilt tasted bitter in his mouth. Could he make love to her and spy on her at the same time?

"But you must know!" Lucy's shrill cry drew his attention. She was on her feet now, staring down at Evelyn. He didn't move, just stayed where he was, listening. "Evelyn, how could you *not know* where your own husband is?"

The door opened again, and Starling stood there with Marianne Westlake. Sinjon frowned, irritated at the interruption of what looked like a very interesting conversation. It appeared Lucy had received his message. He felt another pang of guilt. If he'd known Lucy would be so frightened, he would never have played such a cruel trick.

"Countess Westlake," Starling announced from the open doorway. Neither Evelyn nor Lucy noticed. Marianne's eyes kindled with interest at the conversation, and still the sisters failed to look up. They looked like two cats circling before a fight. Evelyn's face was flushed and her eyes glittered dangerously, though her expression remained flat.

"I was of the opinion that no one knows where Philip is, Lucy," Evelyn said, her chin rising along with her color. "There are rumors that he's dead."

Starling's brows shot up as he met Sinjon's eyes. "My lady, if you please, Countess Westlake is—"

"Don't be a fool! We both know he's not dead!" Lucy cried, oblivious to anyone else in the room in her desperation.

Starling started toward Evelyn, but Marianne caught his arm, listening with keen fascination. Sinjon's stomach curled. Westlake would know every detail of this conversation before the day was out. What would *he* make of it?

Sinjon cleared his throat, expecting Evelyn to look at him, but her eyes remained on Lucy, her expression fierce and guarded. His gut tensed. Was she protecting Philip or herself?

"Why do you want to know where he is, Lucy? Do you need more fuel to feed the gossip? Do what Eloisa does and make something up if it pleases you," Evelyn snapped.

Lucy drew a shaky breath. "Oh, Evie, it's not for gossip!"

"Why, then?" Evelyn demanded, her back as stiff as a musket barrel as she braced for her sister's explanation. She was holding herself together so tightly a tap on the shoulder would shatter her. Sinjon was as eager as everyone else in the room to hear Lucy's response. How could she possibly explain such a sin against her sister?

A fat tear rolled down Lucy's face. "He left something with me. Something I cannot keep any longer. I must return it at once."

"What is it?" Evelyn asked.

Sinjon stopped breathing.

The Gonfalon of Charlemagne, perhaps?

But Lucy shook her head miserably and didn't reply, the tears falling faster now. She turned pleading eyes on her sister. "Just tell him, Evelyn, I beg you. If you have any way to get a message to him, then tell him."

"My lady, if you please, we have another guest—" Starling tried again, but Marianne stepped on his toe to silence him. Sinjon winced as the butler let out a most improper grunt of pain.

Lucy caught sight of Marianne at last, and her eyes widened. For a moment no one moved, then Lucy made a strangled sound and left the room as quickly as she'd entered, brushing past Marianne Westlake without a word.

"Countess Westlake has arrived, my lady," Starling said pointlessly as Lucy passed him. Sinjon watched Marianne's sharp gaze follow Lucy out.

Marianne glowed with curiosity. "Whatever was *that* about?"

Evelyn rose to her feet, her cheeks flushing anew with surprise. Her smile did not touch the ice in her eyes. "My sisters are emotional creatures," she said. "Tea, please, Starling."

Marianne wasn't deterred. "It sounded quite serious. What on earth could Lucy have to say to Philip, and what does she have to return to him?"

Evelyn looked down at her hands, now clasped calmly in her lap, and pursed her lips, making it clear she had nothing further to say on the matter.

"You must admit her interest is most intriguing!" Marianne prodded. "Evelyn, *do* you know where Philip is?"

Sinjon held his breath as he waited for her reply.

"Oh, Marianne, not you too! Haven't enough people asked me already? I am tired of the gossip, and the scandal. I have no idea where my husband is. I trust you will not ask me that again," she added stiffly

Westlake's wife fell silent, but her eyes roamed over Evelyn's flushed face, as if trying to read her mind. She would hurry home and report Lucy's odd visit to Westlake, and Sinjon wondered what the earl would do then. Probably search the Fraynes' town house, including Lucy in the scandal, and it would be his own fault.

He placed the letters on the desk, including the one from Creighton, and stood at attention, the perfect footman, without ears or eyes or tongue. The conversation turned dull and ordinary, but he saw Evelyn suppress a shiver even as she discussed the warmth of the weather with her friend. She drew her shawl up over her shoulders.

She was afraid again, because of him. He clenched his fist. He could protect her, or destroy her.

Who knew treason could be so seductive?

Chapter 25

Evelyn went down the hall eagerly that night to meet her lover. Sam was waiting for her in bed, his body half covered with the sheet. The shadow of his erection leapt against the linen as she entered the room, and she felt an answering need surge in her own body.

She untied the satin belt of her robe, pushed it off her shoulders and let it fall. She was naked beneath, and his sharp intake of breath was gratifying, titillating.

"Come here," he said, but she hardly needed encouragement. She was already falling into his arms, her mouth on his, pulling aside the sheet so she could touch him.

She had waited for this all day. She'd been tempted to summon her footman to the nearest broom closet, but Miss Trask, Charlotte's sharp-eyed companion, had decided to spend the afternoon sitting with her in the library. Evelyn pretended to read, almost swooning with lust. Miss Trask feared she was fevered and suggested a tisane of feverfew and willow bark. Evelyn tossed it into a plant when Miss Trask wasn't looking.

She had a number of reasons to want her wits about her—Lucy's troubling words for one thing.

What could Philip have given to her sister, and why? The answer was ugly, and she forced it out of her mind.

She couldn't wait to get to her lover, to find pleasure and forgetfulness in his arms. Feverfew and willow bark be damned—this was the cure for what ailed her, at least for a little while.

She lay in the warm circle of Sam's arms in the afterglow of their lovemaking, breathing in the scent of his skin, feeling safe for the first time that day. She was drowsy, wanted to fall asleep with him and wake up and make love again before dawn separated them.

She wasn't afraid of the dark, not with Sam. It was day that terrified her, brought forth her worst fears—Philip, Lord Creighton, Lucy. . .

She swallowed a sob of desperation that this moment could not last forever, and curled her fingers against the heat of his chest. He caught her hand in his, stroked it. "Is something wrong?" His voice rumbled through her breast.

The words hovered on her lips, but she shook her head.

He pushed a pillow behind his head and met her eyes.

"Is it about Lu—Countess Frayne's visit?" he asked. She shut her eyes.

Not now, not here. Not him too.

"Can't my sister pay a perfectly congenial visit without questions being asked?"

"It hardly seemed congenial."

She shifted away from him. "Lucy is a passionate woman," she said, as if it excused her. The slight twitch of his eyebrows told her he already knew all about Lucy's reputation. Sam wasn't stupid. Perhaps he suspected the same thing she did, that Lucy and Philip had been—

Her stomach churned, and she got up from the bed, reaching for her robe, suddenly cold.

He leaned up on his elbow, watching her, his eyes in shadow. "Evelyn, *do* you know where Philip is?" he asked.

She sent a haughty glare over her shoulder, but his eyes narrowed, glittered.

"Don't give me that look, my lady. In this room, we are equals, remember?"

She raised her chin as she tied to sash on her robe. "Not so equal that you may ask impertinent questions."

He rose and began to pull on his breeches. "I see I've found the boundary line."

"Am I not entitled to privacy?" she demanded.

He crossed to touch her cheek, his eyes soft, sympathetic, and she let him, trying not to swoon against his palm, wanting to fight the rest of the world, but not him.

He lowered his mouth to hers, began to undo her robe again, following the descent of the silk with his lips.

He had no right to ask, she thought. He was her lover, and that was all. Or was it? She trusted this man as she had never trusted another. He kept her safe, made her forget her worries. Still, her husband was alive, and this was adultery.

Just like Lucy.

She pulled away, suddenly feeling ill.

"Evelyn?" He set his hands on his hips and frowned.

"My husband is still alive, Sam. I am a married woman. I have no right to be here with you. I am no better than—"

He laid a finger against her lips. "*Do* you know where Philip is?" he asked again, softly.

"He could be outside this door for all I know. He might walk in here and kill us both. Aren't you afraid?"

He didn't look afraid in the least. In fact, he looked

amused. "Who could blame him? You're beautiful," he quipped, insouciant in the face of danger.

"Not to Philip. I am a possession, property, nothing more." She let him pull her back against his chest. "There was no love, no pleasure between us. If he comes back for me, it will be because he has no one and nothing else. He'll want someone to punish for that. Lucy's message was proof of that."

"And what exactly does that mean?" he asked, his voice husky, his mouth trailing over her shoulder.

Was he daft? She shoved away from him. "What does it 'mean'?" she demanded angrily. "He contacted Lucy as a warning to me. He knew she'd come to me. She's afraid, and I cannot let him hurt her."

His expression was almost stricken, and her fury soared higher. She didn't want his pity. She held his eyes ferociously, refusing to give in to tears, or fear.

He sat on the edge of the bed. "So what did Philip leave with Lucy?" he asked.

She paced the small room. "I don't know. The Frenchman thought I had some kind of French treasure. Perhaps he left it with Lucy instead." Philip had not even left *her* a note of farewell.

"A treasure?" Sam prompted.

"There isn't any treasure," she said bitterly.

"But Philip Renshaw was—is—one of the richest men in England."

"He took it with him, then," she snapped. "He left nothing worth coming back for."

He got off the bed and came toward her. "There's you," he said gallantly, and pulled her into his arms.

Her heart swelled and began to beat again. In the brief years of their marriage, Philip had never offered her a compliment of any kind. Nor had her father been a man of effusive praise. There were, of course, men who offered insincere platitudes to ladies like her at balls and parties. They didn't mean a word of it. Sam did. She could see that in his eyes, feel it in the way he touched her.

Like a treasure.

"Do you want to end this?" he asked. "Would it be easier?"

She shut her eyes against the wave of desire that forced the air from her lungs. "No," she whispered. "I want everything else to be over, but not this."

"Then come back to bed."

He stepped behind her, lifted her hair and kissed her neck, stripping away her robe entirely, letting it fall. He ran his tongue along her spine, leaving a wet tingle on her skin. Rage and fear melted like liquid honey.

"In the morning . . ." He dropped to his knee and kissed the smooth skin of her buttocks. " . . . we will think of what to do."

She turned in his arms. Still kneeling, he laid his head on her belly, and she stroked his hair. "You want to help me? A knight in shining armor?"

He looked up at her, his brow furrowing. "My armor is a little tarnished, I'm afraid, but I will do anything I can to help you."

He had marvelous eyes. She felt like she could read him, detect truth or lies just by looking into their gray depths. Something in her chest softened, opened, and she sobbed. He got to his feet and picked her up, carrying her back to the bed. Their bed, their sanctuary.

He made love to her with slow, exquisite care. Fear ebbed, hope surged.

For the first time in her life she was not alone.

She had Sam.

Chapter 26

"**N**ot that one," Evelyn directed the next morning. "The one to the left. The blue book with the silver lettering."

Sam was up on the library ladder, searching the top shelves, and she watched the flex and play of his muscles as he reached for the book she indicated. He was made to perfection, she decided, enjoying the view. She let her gaze roam over his firm buttocks—was it just last night that she'd caressed the naked flesh?

Her mouth watered as he pulled the book off the shelf, tucked it under his arm, and climbed down the ladder with lithe grace.

She didn't take the book from him, but pointed to the table, and he set it down there. She stood across the polished surface from him, biting her lip. Could she really dare to do this? It meant trusting Sam, and hoping that her husband would not return and want this particular book. Judging by the richness of the painted illustrations, and the lavish embossing on the cover, it was probably the most costly book in Philip's naughty little collection.

"What is it?" Sam asked, and she held her breath as he opened the cover, and waited for his reaction. Shock? Titillation? She watched as he turned a few pages, saw his fingers still when he reached the first illustration. He glanced up at her.

On the page, the lovers were entwined, and the man was about to enter his partner, rudely erect, ready to impale her. The lady's eyes were closed, her expression languid with anticipation. Her hips were tilted to meet her lover's first thrust, her sex on display. For the first time, Evelyn understood the passion the illustrations showed, knew the sense of expectation. Her body throbbed as she met Sinjon eyes.

He was regarding her curiously, waiting for an explanation. "It's Philip's," she said, her voice husky. "Part of a private collection. Treason was just one of his wicked predilections."

"Why are you showing me this?" he asked, his voice low, his tone suggesting he already had an idea why she'd asked him to fetch it from its hiding place.

Unfortunately, it was the wrong idea entirely. She swallowed. This was business, not play. "I need to sell it. I need a large sum of money, and I can hardly take such a thing to a dealer myself."

His eyes widened. "You want me to do it?"

"Y-Yes. There are more as well. I thought someone with similar tastes to Philip's might pay dearly for it."

Sam looked around the library, scanning the shelves as if she'd told him there were bats hiding among the books, waiting to attack. He regarded her shrewdly. "How dearly?"

She raised her chin. "I need five hundred pounds."

His eyebrows shot up at the enormity of the sum. "Why?"

It was an impertinent question from a servant, and she considered not replying, but this was no ordinary request, and Sam was no ordinary servant. She looked away, feeling her cheeks heat. "I owe a gentleman a sum of money. I asked him to deliver a letter for me. It appears the funds I enclosed with my note disappeared. Not knowing the amount, he overpaid on my behalf. I must now reimburse him for his troubles."

Sam's jaw tightened. He didn't look surprised or amused. He looked angry. He leaned forward, his fists on either side of the book, as if he were fighting to control his rage. She gasped and stepped toward him. Did he imagine she meant to give him the book, or the money? Perhaps he thought it was payment for—now her whole body heated in mortification.

"I need to sell it, Sam," she said sharply. "I hoped I could trust you with this. You said last night you would do anything to help. Will you help me with this? You could go today, to Ackerman's perhaps, or one of the gentlemen's clubs."

He looked up at her, his expression dubious, and she felt her stomach tense in desperation.

"I cannot do this myself. Nor is there anyone else I can ask, for obvious reasons."

He studied her face, and the anger in his face and body eased, like a tight rope suddenly released, though he was still frowning. "It will have to be wrapped."

Relief flooded over her. "Best do it yourself. If Starling saw it—"

He looked down at the drawing again, and touched the painted face on the page. "She looks like you, just before you—"

She laid her hand over his, covering the lovers. "Stop. The time passes slowly enough without the torment of wanting you all day long."

His gaze turned playful. He caressed her hand, lifted it, kissed her fingertips until she sighed. Then his grip tightened and he grinned. "Come behind the bookshelf," he said, tugging her toward the back corner of the room where tall shelves made a secluded nook.

Evelyn didn't need a second invitation. She knew exactly what he meant to do, what he wanted. She wanted it as well, was breathless in anticipation. She crossed the library at an undignified run.

He pulled her against him as soon as they were behind the shelf, his mouth on hers, his hands everywhere at once, driving her mad. He tugged up her skirts and entered her in one smooth stroke as she leaned back against the shelf.

She tried to be silent as he thrust into her, but his name and unstoppable cries of delight burst from her.

Sin, and more sin, never enough. She wrapped her legs around his hips and urged him on, harder, faster, wanting instant pleasure, yet never wanting it to end.

Books shook themselves loose and fell around them like rain in the few delicious minutes it took to find their release. Her final cry echoed off the high ceiling as he drove into her one last time.

For a long moment neither of them moved, too overcome, too tangled in the disarray of their clothing.

Had she ever felt this good, this happy? "Oh," she breathed, her body tingling, feeling as if the meaning of the universe had been revealed to her. He chuckled, withdrawing from her as he gently set her feet on the floor.

"Perhaps we should meet here tonight," he muttered, kissing her neck.

"Anywhere," she breathed.

She stepped away to straighten her skirts and run a shaking hand over her hair. He buttoned his flies and grinned at her. "Midnight?" he asked, and she kissed him by way of reply.

"My lady, are you in here?" They froze as Miss Trask's reedy voice echoed over the shelves.

Evelyn shut her eyes. She had sent Charlotte's watchdog to consult with Mrs. Cooper on the meals for the day so she could speak to Sam about the book. Miss Trask was obviously quick and efficient. Or suspicious.

Evelyn walked out from behind the shelf just as the woman was reaching for the book on the table, her eyes sharp. Evelyn quickly picked it up.

"Ah, Miss Trask. There you are at last," she said, surprised her voice sounded almost normal, as if she hadn't just been—

Miss Trask's forehead wrinkled in confusion as Evelyn gave her a brilliant smile.

"Sam was helping me collect up some books," she said. Surely Sam must be right behind her, since the woman was staring at something over Evelyn's shoulder, her frown deepening.

Evelyn turned, holding her breath, but his wig was straight, his flies correctly fastened, and he was holding two other books in his hands, as if he had indeed been assisting her with nothing more exciting than selecting a few dusty books.

She felt another blush race up from her toes as she added the blue book to the top of the pile, her eyes meeting his.

Her co-conspirator. Her lover.

She suppressed the sigh that threatened to bubble out of her.

"Be sure to wrap them properly and deliver them right away," she ordered. "That will be all."

He bowed, his expression flat, bored, and perfectly correct. She watched him walk away, and felt a warm trickle caress the inside of her thigh. She glanced at the clock.

How many hours until midnight?

Chapter 27

Sinjon dropped the books on Westlake's desk. "I need five hundred pounds."

The earl looked at the titles. " *'Mrs. Elgin's Book of Mutton Pies . . . A Treatise on Ethics and Moral Behavior for Well Bred English Ladies,'* " he muttered.

The third book had no title, and Sinjon watched the earl open the blue cover. His brows rose. He shut the book at once and laid it beside the others. "I trust there's an explanation?"

Sinjon could have sworn the man was blushing. "I wish to sell that book," he pointed at it, "for five hundred pounds."

"Where on earth did you get it?" Westlake asked.

"From Evelyn Renshaw's library."

"The quietest ladies keep the deepest secrets. It's hard to judge a book by the cover, as they say. Why do you think I can help you with such a thing?"

Sinjon tilted his head. "You seem to have your finger in more than one mutton pie, my lord."

Westlake smiled, looking pleased at the description. "Yes, but why do you need such a huge sum of money? Do you need to bribe someone? Philip Renshaw, perhaps?"

"Creighton," Sinjon admitted through clenched teeth. Westlake didn't even twitch.

"Have you decided to pay him to tell you where O'Neill is?"

"If he knew, then O'Neill would be dead," Sinjon said. "It's another matter."

"Something to do with Countess Frayne, perhaps? I understand she paid her sister a visit the other day."

"Your wife told you," Sinjon said. "Some ladies keep no secrets at all, it seems." Did no one respect Evelyn's privacy? His own guilt made him shift in his chair.

"Marianne has a keen ear for intriguing morsels of gossip. Apparently Lucy has dealings with Philip, and is holding something she wishes to return to him," Westlake said.

"I believe I mentioned she had an affair with him."

Westlake smirked. "Who hasn't slept with Lucy? Aside from the two of us, of course, and I am merely guessing you haven't had that dubious pleasure. Still, it is most intriguing that she has something that belongs to her sister's husband. Do you suppose it's a keepsake, a *billet doux*? A French battle flag, perhaps?"

Sinjon pictured Lucy wrapped in the sacred Gonfalon of Charlemagne, wearing nothing but a sultry smile, and he remembered her in Evelyn's salon, frightened. His conscience prodded him again.

"She didn't say what she had," Sinjon said. "Now about the money—"

"What would a man like Philip leave with his sister-in-law?" Westlake mused. "I've discovered that if a woman has a secret, it is almost impossible to get her to reveal it unless she wishes to, and in that case the whole world knows."

Was that a hint—or a threat—that Westlake's wife was a spy? Perhaps he'd sent her to keep an eye on *him* while he watched Evelyn.

"Have you had success coaxing information out of ladies in the past?" Sinjon asked.

"In part," Westlake said cryptically. "As I said, some ladies do not give up their secrets easily. I'm sure you've discovered that yourself. What man hasn't, and what man would want a lady without a touch of mystery to her? I do understand how the process works. Every woman wants something. Have you discovered yet what Evelyn wants?"

Him.

Sinjon kept his expression carefully blank, tried to think of anything but Evelyn in bed, the soft sounds she made as he made love to her, the way she'd looked this morning in the library as he—

"Evelyn plays her cards close to her chest, doesn't she?" Westlake said. "It might be simpler to find out what Countess Lucy has. Finding Philip and the gonfalon has become quite urgent. Napoleon's invasion of Russia is going badly. Our sources say he blames Philip. He has sent more spies to look for the flag, and Renshaw." He leaned across the desk. "If Lucy or Evelyn have the gonfalon, they are in a great deal of danger. If Philip has the flag, he could buy half of France by selling it back to Napoleon. We need to know."

Sinjon recalled the panic on Evelyn's face the first morning he'd met her in the park, the ferocity in the Frenchman's eyes as he twisted her arm, taking pleasure in her pain. He swallowed. "And you suspect that's why he contacted Lucy?" Guilt twisted in his gut. His little joke was like quicksand, ready to swallow the unwary who walked into this game.

"I find it odd he would contact her if his wife had the gonfalon, yes. Not to be unkind, but Lucy Frayne is hardly the kind of lady a man returns to. But Evelyn . . ." He let the rest of the question stand in his eyes.

He wanted to know if Evelyn had heard from her husband. Sinjon hesitated. He had not actually seen the note she received at the ball, and Evelyn had said it was not in Philip's hand. It simply complimented her gown and was signed with his name. He'd decided it was just a cruel joke, like the one he'd played on Lucy. But what if he was wrong? He was quickly learning that jokes had ways of twisting themselves into trouble.

"What if Renshaw does come home?" he asked.

"Then you'd better have a pistol handy. But don't kill him. Just shoot him in the leg, so he can't get away." Westlake leaned across the desk. "*Has* she seen him, heard from him?"

"She told Lucy she hasn't. I've searched the house, watched Evelyn closely, and I've found no evidence that she's heard from Philip, or is doing anything treasonous."

Her only secret *was* him, wasn't it? He hadn't actually seen the note she received at the ball, and her answers to his questions about her husband last night had been unenlightening.

"And her involvement with Creighton?" Westlake asked.

"He's trying to cheat her out of her husband's fortune."

The earl's eyebrows headed for his hairline. "Have you proof of this?"

Sinjon felt heat rise under his collar. "Do you imagine I would make up something like this to be rid of the man?" He should have kept Evelyn's letter to the charity, and the envelope addressed to Creighton, brought it to Westlake at once. Instead, he'd taken the money out, hidden it in the library, waiting to see where it might lead. Had it been another mistake? He wanted proof that Creighton was stealing from Evelyn, cheating her as he'd cheated so many others. Or did he just want evidence that Evelyn was innocent? It was a dangerous path, paved with suppositions and false assumptions.

And just what would the spymaster do with the information? Would Evelyn be arrested, questioned, *tortured*?

"He does have the power to see you hanged, and if he were dead—"

"I want him to die for the sins he's actually committed, Westlake, not a lie."

"Of course. This is a matter of honor for you, isn't it? Revenge isn't enough. You must be exonerated as well."

Sinjon held the earl's gaze. Evelyn's future had become as important as his own to him. He couldn't allow Creighton to get away with either sin.

"You're distracted, Captain. You have come to further your cause against Creighton, even demanding money to do so, but you were sent to Renshaw House to find the gonfalon, and evidence against Evelyn Renshaw."

"How will that help exonerate me?" Sinjon demanded.

"Are you so sure that Lord Creighton is not involved more deeply with Lady Evelyn? Are they lovers, perhaps? Is he blackmailing her? Perhaps *he* has the gonfalon."

That was impossible. Evelyn was *his* lover. Still, instinct warned him to move carefully. He felt like a mouse in the sights of a hungry snake. One false move, one careless admission, and Westlake would have him for luncheon. He wondered if the earl had notches in the hilt of his sword to mark his unwary victims.

"Creighton needs money," Sinjon said. "He gambles and usually loses. In Spain, the men who held his vowels had an unfortunate tendency to die in battle, even when they weren't in the front lines. Evelyn entrusted him with the delivery of a letter containing a hundred pounds. The money was missing when he delivered the letter, and he claims he replaced it with five hundred pounds from his own pocket. He now expects Evelyn—"

"Do you have the note?"

Sinjon shook his head.

"Then how do you know the money was missing?"

"Because I took it out of the envelope to see what would happen," he admitted. "This morning Evelyn asked me to sell that book to pay a debt. I assume she needs money to pay the gentleman who delivered the letter, and it was addressed to Creighton," he said, skating carefully around his own involvement with Evelyn. "If you want hard proof, check with the school the donation was meant for. See if they ever received Evelyn's letter, or have heard of Creighton. I'm sure they have not."

Westlake looked inordinately pleased with Sinjon's logic. "Given the fact that the major has vowels all over town, and is selling off family heirlooms to cover them, it certainly makes sense. But why should *I* pay the five hundred pounds?"

"Consider it an investment."

"And what exactly am I investing in?" Westlake asked.

"Capturing Creighton. Righting a wrong."

Saving a lady's honor. Wasn't that what had gotten him into trouble in the first place?

Sinjon could have sworn he saw a forked tongue flick over Westlake's lips. "For your sake, or for Evelyn's?"

"Both."

Westlake didn't react. "Calling it an investment suggests I'll see the money back. How do you intend to make that happen? I doubt a footman's pay will cover the debt."

Sinjon smiled. "The first place Creighton will go with five hundred pounds is to the nearest gaming hell. We will win the money back."

Westlake blinked. "We? If he sees you, he'll kill you, and there are any number of deep players at Crockford's or White's who might take the money off him."

"It's just as easy to lose a fortune at a private party. Here at De Courcey House, for example," Sinjon said. "I assume you gamble, my lord?"

Westlake's lips twisted. "Never. That's not to say I haven't made a study of how to win at cards."

"And your lady wife?" Sinjon asked. Westlake's lips pursed.

"She cheats," he said. "But not for money."

"Then we will find someone who will cheat for money. Someone he won't expect to win."

"Who?" Westlake asked.

Sinjon grinned. "Evelyn Renshaw. I've made my own study of how to win at cards. We can teach her if she doesn't play, show her how Creighton will cheat."

Westlake sat back. "Dishonest, but effective. It won't prove anything, of course, but he won't profit from taking my—her—money. Marianne could show Evelyn how to play for high stakes."

And he would add a few lessons of his own, Sinjon thought, knowing Creighton's particular tricks. He was a master of distraction and charm, for one thing. "I will tell Evelyn it will take a few days to get the money. You can send the invitation to coincide with his receipt of the funds."

A shrewd look crept over Westlake's face. "It's an excellent plan, but if I agree to it, then I need something in return." Westlake met Sinjon's eyes across the desk. "I need you to seduce Lucy Frayne."

Horror raced up Sinjon's spine.

"Me? But I'm Evelyn's—" He stumbled over the word. "—footman."

"Pay Lucy a visit on your half day. Charm her. Find a way to get into her bedroom, coax the information out of her between kisses."

"No."

He couldn't betray Evelyn that way. He had no interest in bedding her sister. He was not Philip Renshaw.

"May I remind you there's a hangman waiting for you?"

"I said no. Find someone else to do it. Surely you have other men beholden to you. Lucy likes men with money, the kind who can buy her expensive gifts. Would you rather I used the five hundred pounds for that?"

He let the earl read the determination in his eyes. West-lake looked away first. He picked up his pen and made out a draft. "I'll have this cashed, and hold it for a fortnight."

"What about the book?" Sinjon asked, and Westlake gave the pile of books a disdainful glance.

"I hate mutton pie, despair of the morality of well-bred English ladies, and would not sully my reputation with any kind of association with the last book."

Sinjon's mouth twitched. "And yet your lady wife was in Evelyn's drawing room, playing procurer the other day."

Westlake frowned. "She calls it matchmaking."

"She suggested my brother would make a perfect lover for Lady Evelyn."

"And he wouldn't?"

Sinjon clenched his fists in his lap. "I had no idea William was even in London."

"I believe Viscount Mears is in Town for the Season, looking for a wife, and probably sowing a few wild oats before he weds."

That bit of family news surprised Sinjon. His father had been pressing William for years to wed the rich and titled daughter of a friend. Apparently the match hadn't been made.

Westlake crossed to a side table that held a decanter of whisky and poured two glasses of the amber liquid. He held one out to Sinjon, who shook his head.

"Footmen aren't allowed to drink on duty. This is an official visit, my lord."

Westlake set both glasses down untouched. "Of course. How are you finding life belowstairs?"

Sinjon imagined making love to Evelyn behind the bookshelves, felt his body stir. He glanced at the clock, habit now whenever he thought of her. How long until he could touch her again?

"The work is light enough, since there is only her ladyship to see to," he said. Heaven help him if she was any more demanding.

"And her companion."

"Yes, Miss Trask," Sinjon agreed.

"Did you realize that her first name is Penance? Westlake asked.

He hadn't known. "It suits her."

"Yes, and it strikes me as very amusing. The traitor's wife, surrounded by Sin and Penance! She is bedeviled indeed."

Sinjon rolled his eyes at the unfortunate jest. Evelyn was indeed beset from all sides by spies, traitors, and French assassins. The only place she had peace was in bed, in his arms. Yet he was one of the spies watching her. He'd thought perhaps Miss Trask was spying for Somerson, but perhaps he was wrong. "Is Penance Trask your—"

The door opened. "I had no idea you had a visitor," Marianne Westlake said as she entered. "Aren't you Lady Evelyn's footman? I recognize the livery."

Sinjon bowed, and Westlake kissed his wife's cheek.

"Ah, my dear. Home at last. Are Isobel and Phineas safely away, then?" he asked.

"Yes," she said distractedly, still looking at Sinjon. "What is the reason for this special visit? I assume there's something wrong, since you are in my husband's library instead of waiting at the kitchen door. Is Lady Evelyn ill?"

"She'd have sent me for a doctor if she was, Countess," Sinjon said.

"He came to deliver a book, my dear. A gift for you, from Evelyn," Westlake said, and held out the mutton cookbook. Sinjon noted the other two books had quietly disappeared from view.

Marianne looked baffled. "Recipes for mutton pies?" she asked. "Why would she send me this?"

"Lady Evelyn especially recommends page thirty-six," Sinjon said quickly, hoping that page didn't contain instructions for disemboweling a sheep or boiling the head.

Marianne flipped through the book. "Mutton pies with apples, chicken, and sausage," she read, frowning. "Well, it might be palatable, I suppose, if you left out the mutton."

Then a slow smile spread over her face. She blinked at him. Then she laughed.

"Is there something amusing about mutton I've failed to see?" Westlake asked.

"Of course there is!" Marianne giggled. "It's Evelyn's way of making a joke. Yellow. Her sisters named this Season's most fashionable colors after yellow foods. We were laughing about it over tea last week. I assume this a continuation of the jest." She looked at Sinjon. "Is that it?"

Sinjon wondered how much time and energy Evelyn would need to come up with such an elaborate jab at her sisters. "Exactly, my lady," he said, grinning charmingly.

"Who could have imagined Evelyn was so witty?" Westlake asked, and Marianne sent him a sharp glare.

"Of course she is! She's a lady, Adam, but she's also a woman."

Sinjon agreed. In the salon, in the library, and especially in bed, Evelyn was the most incredible woman on earth. His woman.

Marianne shut the book and clasped it to her bosom. "I must think of a suitable jest to send back in reply. Wait, if you please."

Westlake resumed his seat as the door closed behind her. "You have the potential to be an excellent spy, Captain Rutherford. You think quickly. It is not easy to best my wife. I feared you were in for a hard grilling, and would end the afternoon a broken man without a single secret left to you."

He tapped the cover of the blue book, which had miraculously reappeared. "Now if you were to find Philip Renshaw, I would know you were as good a spy as—" He stopped without saying the name of Sinjon's predecessor. "You can wait in the hall for Marianne's reply," Westlake said, dismissing him. "I'll expect to hear from you very soon with further news."

Sinjon sat in the hall and sighed. He had work to do, righting all the wrongs in London, it seemed. He was Westlake's spy, Evelyn's lover, Creighton's nemesis, and everyone's servant, and one mistake in any of his roles could end in disaster. Was he Sam or Sinjon?

He hardly knew anymore. He was playing a dangerous game, and one wrong move would see him hanged. He had no choice but to play it through to whatever conclusion fate brought him. He hoped luck—and Evelyn—were the ladies he thought they were.

Chapter 28

Starling opened the door to announce Charlotte's arrival, but she bowled past him before he could speak and hurried into the salon. Evelyn rose, her heart clenching when she saw her second sister's anxious face.

But Charlotte turned to Miss Trask first. "Penance, dear, do go down to the kitchen and have the cook make some cream buns. I am simply starved."

She looked around the room. "Where is your footman? Has another servant quit your employ?"

Evelyn sank back onto the settee. "My footman is merely out running an errand for me." She glanced at the clock. He'd be back shortly, but there would still be eight hours to wait until midnight. Her breath caught in her throat in anticipation. "To what do I owe the honor of today's visit, Charlotte?"

"Can't I pay my sister a visit without facing an inquisition?" Charlotte asked.

Evelyn raised her brows and waited.

"Actually, I've come for two reasons, other than to see how you are. I am simply beset, and I need your help *desperately*. But first of all I must ask you what you did to upset poor Lucy so. She is considering leaving London for the country, *now,* in the middle of the Season! She asked me if I'd heard from Philip, as if he'd dare write to me! Lucy hasn't been out of her house in days, and she's positively languishing without the nourishing light of male attention."

"It has nothing at all to do with me," Evelyn said calmly. "I have no idea where Philip is. Perhaps Lucy wishes to enjoy some time outdoors. The weather is lovely in the countryside now."

Charlotte snorted. "Lucy detests weather of any kind, fair or foul, and other than plowmen and country bumpkins, there's no one at all in the country at this time of year. She says she *must* see Philip. Are you sure you don't—"

Evelyn raised her chin. "Very sure, Charlotte."

Charlotte sighed like an ill wind. "Actually, despite Lucy's ennui, I am glad to hear it. I dread Philip's return, if he returns at all. Somerson says the betting book at White's has been revised again. Most gentlemen are now wagering Philip is dead, and even you must admit it would be better for all of us if he were—"

"Was that all you needed my help with so desperately?" Evelyn interrupted. Would her sisters expect her to wear black or yellow for mourning? She touched the lace collar of the pink muslin she was wearing. Sam said he liked pink. It reminded him of her—

She suppressed a smile as that part of her grew warm, and snuck another glance at the clock. She'd get there first tonight, be naked, waiting for him.

"Pay attention, Evie. I have a favor to ask." Charlotte's tone indicated it was going to be more of a command than a plea.

"Oh?" Evelyn said hopefully. Perhaps her sister needed Miss Trask to return to Somerson House. Penance had set herself the task of saving the soul of the traitor's wife, but

Evelyn had found her own salvation. She had Sam. If Penance had been a moment quicker this morning, she would have caught her in the corner of the library with her legs wrapped around Sam's hips. The punishment her sisters would visit upon her for that sin would be far worse than just Penance. The longer the woman stayed, the greater the chance she'd catch them.

"Somerson's half sister is coming to Town," Charlotte said, as if announcing that the plague was coming back and likely to kill everyone.

"I had no idea he had a half sister."

Charlotte sniffed. "We rarely mention her. Her mother was the late earl's second wife, and Somerson was grown by the time his father married her. He did not approve, since the lady was barely older than Somerson himself, and a mere miss without a title. As a matter of wifely devotion, I could not like her either. After his father died, Somerson banished his half sister and her mama to the most distant of his estates. It was a kindness, and we were all happier for it, to be sure, but the dowager has decided to inconvenience us by dying."

"Oh," Evelyn said, unable to think of anything more appropriate under the circumstances.

"The girl has been staying with *neighbors* since her mother's death, and they have decided to bring Caroline to London to be thrust upon *us*. They seemed to think we were joking when Somerson suggested they could keep her. It is his responsibility to see her married off. It's too soon to give her a full Season, since she is still in mourning, but *something* must be arranged."

Evelyn bit her lip, remembering the heartless way Eloisa's husband had arranged her own marriage to Philip. Poor Caroline. As the half sister of a wealthy earl, there would be a bidding war for her hand, but she would have no say at all in her brother's choice, since Somerson was a bully, and Charlotte was worse.

"What is it you wish me to do?" Evelyn asked. Surely Charlotte didn't expect the girl to come and live with her, did she? The only bedroom she could offer would be the one she shared with Sam. She pursed her lips on the premature refusal that threatened to burst out.

Charlotte sighed. "As you know, I am busy with my daughter's debut. I have no time to amuse dull little Caroline now. Somerson insists he requires a few weeks to find her a suitable husband. I can hardly let her languish in the meantime. I have obtained suitable reading material for her—books on cookery, housekeeping, proper behavior in good society, and even pattern books so she can sew her own clothing. I understand country ladies enjoy those activities, since there is so little else for them to do."

Charlotte paused eagerly as the door opened and Starling entered with the tea tray, which included a heaping plate of cream buns. Charlotte licked her lips, momentarily distracted. She helped herself to a cake, and devoured it in two huge bites.

"Anyway, I must do something to keep the girl busy. I am counting on the charity of my sisters." She batted her eyes in entreaty. "Would you be so kind as to host a small dinner party for her? It would get Caroline out of the house for an evening, without making too much of her in public."

"Here?" Evelyn asked. She imagined the country-bred young lady's shock when Caroline heard of her scandal.

"It will just be little Caroline and her friends from the North, a viscount something-or-other and his mother. As country peers, they won't know it isn't a truly elegant evening. Oh, sorry," she added when Evelyn frowned at the barb.

She had once been the *ton*'s most envied hostess. Her parties had been famous, her invitations coveted. Her sister seemed to have forgotten that, along with the rest of society.

"What I *meant* is that they're not likely to have heard of your difficulties, and by the time they do, the girl will be wedded, bedded, and packed off back to the country where she belongs." Charlotte plopped three cream buns on her plate, one each for "wedded," "bedded," and "packed off." She settled back to enjoy them as if the tasks were already accomplished.

"How efficient," Evelyn murmured.

"I'm glad you agree," Charlotte said around a mouthful of cream. Yellow custard ringed her lips, making her look like a rabid fox. "She is arriving within the week. I suppose she'll need a few days to settle in. Shall we say a fortnight from today?" She picked up another bun, and swallowed it whole in her excitement. Evelyn watched it slide down her gullet. "It needn't be a bother for you. I shall ask Penance Trask to arrange everything."

Evelyn dug her nails into her knee and forced herself to smile. "I'll see to it myself."

Charlotte shrugged. "Well, I suppose since you have nothing else to do—are you going to eat that last bun?"

"Please, enjoy it. You are a *guest* in my home," Evelyn said pointedly, but Charlotte didn't notice. When the cakes were gone, she rose to leave.

"I cannot tarry. I must go and pay a comforting call on poor Lucy, and visit my modiste. I believe my maid washed several of my best gowns incorrectly and shrank the lot of them. None of them fit the way they did a few weeks ago. I cannot tell you how I long to have Miss Trask back with me again, but she is, of course, now indispensable to you."

"I'm sure she would be glad to return to Somserson House. Her talents are going to waste here, " Evelyn hinted.

But Charlotte had already set sail toward the door, full of cream cakes and empty of further conversation.

"Do send me a copy of the menu for dinner, Evelyn. I shall advise you if it is lacking in any way."

"I believe I can assure you that the evening will go off without the slightest misstep, Charlotte."

"I do hope so. Somerson's half sister has been raised in strict seclusion in the country. She has no knowledge of treason, sin, or fancy dishes. Plain fare and dull conversation are what's wanted."

Evelyn forced a smile. How could it be dull, with the traitor's wife entertaining a viscount, a countess, and an unwanted girl who had just lost her mother, all strangers to her?

Fortunately, Sam would be there, helping to serve the meal, teasing her with secret glances, waiting as eagerly as she for the tedious evening to be over so they could go upstairs. The strictures of a formal dinner party would only heighten their desire.

Evelyn smiled. She would gladly put up with a dozen dull country viscounts for dinner if she could have Sam for dessert.

Chapter 29

Sinjon was trimming the wicks of a dozen lamps and packing up baskets of candles to be distributed to each room. The rich fragrance of beeswax, a luxury that Evelyn insisted upon, reminded him of the scent of the bedroom they shared, the honey sweetness of the wax mixing with her perfume and the deeper odors of sex. He glanced at the clock and tried to think of something else.

"Her ladyship has been in a very fine mood of late," Mary said. "She gave me a dozen yellow ribbons this morning, and she was smiling as she did so!" She patted the golden band around her bodice. "I hear every lady at the Somerson ball was dressed in yellow. Who could be melancholy dancing the night away in such a happy color? That ball did Lady Evelyn a great deal of good, if you ask me. I've never seen her as happy as she's been lately."

Sinjon hid a smile.

Mrs. Cooper, aware that Charlotte was upstairs, piled more cream buns on a plate, making ready in case a second helping was needed. "I agree. Her ladyship is looking lovely of late, but it's good, wholesome food, not dancing. My strawberry tarts are what's put the roses back in her cheeks, and there's nothing like fresh eggs, butter, and beef to put meat on her bones and a smile on her face."

Sinjon looked at the cream buns, imagined other, more daring uses for whipped cream that would make Evelyn smile.

Annie looked up from peeling a turnip. "It's certainly not turnips. Or beet roots."

Penance Trask entered the kitchen. "Countess Charlotte will not require any more buns. She has left for today."

Mrs. Cooper blew out a sigh of relief and set the plate down amid the servants. "Well, then, we mustn't let these go to waste. Sal, put the kettle on."

"We were discussing how happy Lady Evelyn is looking, Miss Trask," Mary said, trying to ingratiate herself with the companion. "What is your opinion of the reason for it?"

Penance preened. "I believe the credit belongs entirely to me. I read to her every day from improving books. They fortify the mind, and do the soul a world of good. Inner strength shows upon the face. I have improved her thoughts, and therefore, her countenance is also improved."

Sinjon's lips rippled. If Penance Trask had any idea of the direction of Evelyn's thoughts, her own countenance would be as purple as Annie's beets.

Sal set the kettle on the fire. "If you ask me, there's only one thing that makes a woman sparkle like that," she said. "And that's a man."

Sinjon nearly lopped off his finger instead of the charred end of the lamp wick.

Shocked silence fell over the kitchen for a moment, then laughter erupted. Mrs. Cooper chortled. Annie giggled. Mary snickered. Penance Trask snorted.

"A man! She hasn't been out of this house for a week, and her only visitors are ladies!" Miss Trask said. She took a small notebook out of her pocket. "Countess Westlake and Viscountess Frayne were here on Monday last. Countess Eloisa has called twice, and of course my own mistress Countess Charlotte was here this morning. *Her* visits are sure to have a salubrious effect on Lady Evelyn. She is a lady who knows how to enjoy the simple pleasures of life—"

"Like a pound of butter and two pints of cream," Mrs. Cooper muttered.

Penance ignored her. "In fact, I have a treatise on the value of feminine companionship I think I shall read to Lady Evelyn this afternoon—"

"What do you think, Sam?" Sal interrupted, and every female eye in the room turned on him. "Have you got any idea why Lady Evelyn has been so much happier lately?"

Sin.

His chest tightened as he looked at each woman, but there was no suspicion in anyone's eyes, just simple curiosity.

If he told them the truth, they'd swoon like a pack of overfed dowagers in undersized corsets. Or they'd call him a liar. Who'd believe a lady like Evelyn would keep a secret like *him*?

"We've been enjoying excellent weather," he said. "Her ladyship has been able to ride in the park nearly every morning."

And at night, she was enjoying an entirely different kind of ride.

His body twitched at the memory of Evelyn, naked in his arms, urging him to go faster.

"But it could be the morning chocolate you make for her, Mrs. Cooper. I have heard that chocolate is very beneficial to a lady's nerves."

He served her a pot of steaming chocolate this morning, and had stolen a kiss, right there in the breakfast room, tasting the rich sweetness on her lips, her tongue, and in her sigh of longing.

"I make it with cinnamon and a touch of sweet cream," Mrs. Cooper said, blushing at the praise.

Sinjon smiled at Mary next. "Dancing *is* a pleasant pastime. There's nothing lovelier than a country lass, flushed pink and pretty from dancing at a country fete or a harvest ball. More ladies should take up vigorous dancing."

Making love to Evelyn was a kind of dance. In a few short weeks together, they'd learned the steps that best pleased them both, enhanced them. Every night was different, thrilling, an exhilarating waltz.

He looked at Sal. She was waiting for him to confirm that only a man could make a woman feel the way Evelyn looked—radiant and beautiful. *Loved.*

He felt a jolt of surprise.

Loved? Surely there was a better, lesser word to describe what he felt for Evelyn, but his tongue tied itself in a knot. Admired, perhaps? Esteemed? Neither of those polite descriptions captured it.

Starling's arrival saved him from the need to reply. "I have wonderful news," he said with a broad smile. "We're to have a dinner party here at Renshaw House!"

Mrs. Cooper squealed, and was suddenly radiant herself. Her face bloomed like a garden, pink, then fuchsia, then red, then purple with pleasure. "When?" the cook cried. "How many guests?"

She lovingly stroked the scrubbed surface of the kitchen table, as if it was an artist's canvas awaiting inspiration. "It has been over a year since our last dinner party. I must go to the butcher's and bespeak a leg of lamb at once! It's Lady Evelyn's favorite. We'll need spices, and I'll need to send to the country for fresh fruit, and partridges. How fast can we get a Scottish salmon?"

"Six days if he walks fast," Sinjon quipped, but no one heard him.

"I was not informed that there was anything to celebrate," Miss Trask sniffed. "Is there an occasion?"

"Indeed. Countess Charlotte has relatives coming to visit. Lady Evelyn has graciously agreed to host a dinner to welcome them to London," Starling explained.

Graciously agreed, or was coerced? Sinjon wondered.

"Will there be dancing?" Mary asked.

"What about gentlemen?" Sal put in. "They always bring coachmen and footmen with them."

"I understand there is to be no more than six people for dinner," Starling said.

Mrs. Cooper deflated. "Such a small gathering! I can recall when fifty made an intimate party in this house."

Miss Trask tucked her notebook back into her pocket. "I'd better go upstairs at once. Lady Evelyn will want me to write the invitations. I have perfect penmanship."

"That will have to wait until tomorrow, Miss Trask," Starling said. "Her ladyship is going out. It is her day to deliver things to the Foundling Hospital. Sam, you will accompany her, carry the bundles."

Sinjon wiped the lamp oil off his fingers, still wondering what had convinced Evelyn to entertain, and who her guests might be. Dull aunts or cousins probably, foisted on her by her sisters, as one of their "good works" on Evelyn's behalf.

He went out to order the coach prepared for her errand.

However boring the evening might be, it would end upstairs, in bed, tangled in the sheets.

Sinjon frowned. Thinking about making love to Evelyn had become an obsession. It was almost impossible not to touch her or kiss her when he saw her during the day.

Even now, standing in the yard waiting for the coach, he was sporting an extremely inconvenient erection. He seemed to be permanently in that state, every time he thought of her, or heard her voice, or caught the scent of her perfume in an empty room, or served her breakfast. A hundred ordinary activities, all made erotic by the secret they shared.

By the time they met at night, he was like a starving man who had been awaiting a banquet. Making love a dozen times a night wasn't enough.

He glanced up at the window of the little bedroom, their secret love nest. How long could it last? He had been with Evelyn longer than any woman. Weeks. Soon, they would tire of each other. There would be fewer and fewer nights together, until there were none at all.

Would she find another man? That idea bothered him more as the days went on.

He climbed on the back of the coach and rode around to the front door to wait for her.

He wasn't possessive or jealous. In fact, he usually grew bored with his bedmates once the conquest was made. He couldn't leave them fast enough.

With Evelyn, he was content to watch her sleep, and he actually liked her conversation. He wondered what she was thinking, tried to read each fleeting, fascinating expression that crossed her face.

It was damned uncomfortable, and dangerous, to feel this way for any woman, especially the wife of a traitor.

The front door opened and Evelyn descended the steps, peeping at him from under her bonnet, trying not to smile, and all he could think was how beautiful she was, and how much he wanted her.

Chapter 30

Evelyn tried not to look at Sam as he held the door of the coach for her, but she was aware of his eyes on her, and it made her melt with desire. She could smell the fine wool of his livery, and she longed to bury her nose in his shoulder, to smell his skin, feel his arms around her. If she looked at him now, she'd be lost.

The touch of their gloved hands was proper and impersonal, an ordinary exchange between a footman and lady, but even that slight contact made her breathless. She couldn't help but glance up at him, wanting to see the desire in his eyes, but except for the slightly suggestive lift of one eyebrow, it was as if there was no such thing as Evelyn and Sam.

She felt the cold steel of disappointment, let it give her the strength to let go of his hand and climb into the coach.

Evelyn felt the vehicle tilt as he climbed onto the back, just the way the bed shifted as he joined her there, or rose to leave her in the pale light of dawn.

A gasp of longing caught in her throat. Could she ever have enough of him? She hesitated a moment before knocking on the roof, half considering inviting Sam to ride inside where she could touch him. But their intimacy belonged in the dark, behind locked doors, secret and forbidden.

She signaled the coachman, and the vehicle jerked forward.

She looked at the bundle of linens, shirts, and cast-off gowns that Sal and Mary had helped her sort. She had picked the monograms out of the cuffs of Philip's shirts herself, taking wicked pleasure in every stitch she unraveled, knowing that a poor man or even a beggar might wear her husband's expensive shirts. How Philip would hate that. She wished she could snip away the threads that tied her to Philip as easily, undo her marriage as if it had never been.

A quiet fantasy had filled her mind of late, a dream of a cottage by the sea with a little plot of land, or a thatched house by a rushing stream in a country village. She'd live the rest of her life there with Sam, a peaceful, simple existence. As long as she had him in her bed at night and at her side during the day, she would be happy.

She looked at the heavy gold wedding band on her left hand, Philip's brand upon her, the shackle that bound them together. Taking it off, she let the sun glint through it, was surprised at how light and free she felt without it.

She pushed it into her pocket instead of replacing it on her finger.

Sinjon handed Evelyn out of the coach at the Foundling Hospital, trying not to notice how she caught her lip between her teeth when he touched her, how his body responded.

A short, ruffled gentleman raced down the steps to meet the coach, pulling on his russet coat and babbling his delight at Evelyn's visit. Children stared at them from the windows of the brick building, wide-eyed and white-faced.

Sinjon wished he had a pocket full of coins or sweets to share with them. He grinned at them, and they scattered like leaves in the wind.

He took the heavy bundle out of the coach.

"How generous, Lady Evelyn!" the russet gnome gushed. He glanced at Sinjon and pointed. "Take it 'round the side, if you please." He offered his arm and led Evelyn up the steps to the front door.

Sinjon carried Evelyn's donation around to a door that stood open to catch the breeze.

Inside, a girl was sweeping the floor. She looked at him and his burden without much interest and set the broom aside.

"This way," she said dully, as if she fully expected the parcel to contain what it did, shirts and old linens, when she wanted sweets and lace gowns.

He followed her down the ill-lit passageway, listening to the sounds of children's voices and shuffling footsteps. There was no laughter or singing. This place was childhood's antithesis, despite the fact that the children were fed, dressed, and housed. He supposed there was some comfort in that, but he remembered his own boyhood, spent outdoors, fishing or swimming or running through the woods on late spring days like this one, and he regretted that these children would never know that freedom.

"In here," the girl said, and swept back a curtain for him, exposing the shelves and baskets of a small storage room. The tattered threads of the concealing drapery dragged over his cheek as he passed through and caught on the wool of his coat, begging for notice. Was everything in this place so needy?

He glanced up impatiently and saw the shimmer of old silk, faded and fraying at the edges. It was a fancy curtain for such a place. He wondered what service it had seen before it was forced to give way to modern times and new styles, and ended up here.

Most *ton* matrons redecorated annually if the budget allowed, or every other year if it did not. It was an unwritten but strictly held female law that a lady's drawing room curtains must be every bit *au courant* as her gowns, and she would certainly not be seen in the same dress more than twice.

The girl opened the bundle with work-reddened hands and began sorting the contents. The white linen was stark in the gray shadows of the little storeroom. Sinjon stood where he was in the doorway.

He glanced again at the curtain, noting the careful embroidery upon it and the once colorful fringe. Wrinkles and small handprints marked the places where it had recently seen service as a handkerchief or a napkin. There were letters stitched on it in gold thread, and he ran his finger over them.

His gut clenched.

He'd seen this curtain before. He unfastened it, let it fall, and stepped back to look at it.

"Hey!" the girl croaked, left in the dark.

Sinjon barely heard her.

An army of avenging angels and ivory doves flew above a fierce knight in shining silver armor. His sword was raised high over his head, radiating the embroidered Latin words Purity, Courage, and Victory.

Sinjon swallowed, his knees weakening. He'd seen this flag before, met this knight, faced him across the field of battle. In his mind he heard the sound of drumbeats, felt the bone deep thunder of enemy troops approaching. The deafening crash of musket and artillery fire mingled with the screams of the dying.

He licked his teeth, expecting to taste the acrid dust of a Spanish battlefield, but this was London, not Spain. He rubbed a hand across his eyes, but it was true.

He was staring at the Gonfalon of Charlemagne.

Chapter 31

"**L**ady Evelyn!" a familiar voice called as Evelyn finished her visit. She turned and saw Anne O'Neill hurrying toward her.

"Miss O'Neill, how lovely to see you."

"I was delivering some sewing for the littlest ones," Anne said, pointing to the empty basket on her arm. She looked careworn and tired.

"Have you had news of your brother?" Evelyn asked, concerned.

Anne's face crumpled. "No, not a word, but I've had other news that has distressed me greatly."

Evelyn took her arm. "Come, let me take you home in my carriage. You can tell me what's happened." She led the way to the coach, and Sam opened the door and handed both ladies in, then closed it behind them.

Evelyn watched him walk toward the back of the vehicle. "My footman was a soldier like your brother. He said that some men take longer to come home because they are afraid we will be shocked by the changes in them."

Anne blinked back tears. "It's not that. I know Patrick was wounded. Major Lord Creighton told me he was, and I am prepared for scars. But the major came to see me again yesterday."

Evelyn took her friend's hand. "Is there bad news?"

"There's someone else looking for Patrick, someone the major fears means him harm," Anne said in a fear-pinched whisper. "The man is a traitor, and Patrick can give testimony against him. He wants Patrick dead to save his own life. The major warned me I must take every precaution if the man comes to see me. He believes he will try to force me to tell him where Patrick is. Lord Creighton offered to fetch Patrick, to keep him safe until this wicked traitor can be apprehended." She dissolved into fresh tears. "But I truly don't know where he is!"

Evelyn pressed a handkerchief into Anne's hand.

"The major told me to try and think of where Patrick might go, a friend he might visit, but I cannot think of anything at all. I am overcome with worry, both for my brother and now for myself."

"Surely the authorities are looking for this man," Evelyn said. The hunt for traitors was becoming a national pastime. Just how many men like Philip were lurking in the shadows, waiting to jump out at ladies like Anne, or Lucy, or herself? She shivered. "*Has* he tried to contact you?"

Anne shook her head. "No, but I live in terror for my life. Major Creighton told me this soldier was caught selling secrets to the French, the kind of secrets that might have gotten thousands of men killed if Patrick—and Major Creighton—had not put a stop to his treachery. He ravished a woman, and killed a patrol of a dozen men to try to cover his crime!" She shuddered, and twisted the handkerchief in her gloved hands. "He was the one who wounded Patrick, tried to kill him."

Evelyn's skin crawled. "Have you male servants to watch over you?" she asked.

"Major Lord Creighton left a man with me." Anne's voice quavered. "I do not wish to seem ungrateful, but Mr. Bassett scares me almost as badly as the traitorous officer."

Evelyn understood too well how Anne felt. She dreaded Philip's return, but Sam gave her the courage to face whatever might come.

"I'm sure Mr. Bassett means you no harm, Anne. Major Creighton would never allow that."

They reached Anne's modest home and pulled up to the curb.

"Anne, what is the name of the man Lord Creighton warned you about?"

"Captain Sinjon Rutherford," Anne said, shuddering. "I shall pray that he never comes your way, Lady Evelyn."

The door opened and Sam handed her guest out of the coach. Evelyn watched her hurry up the steps to her door, glancing anxiously over her shoulder.

She sent up a prayer for her friend's safety, and thanked heaven again for Sam.

He'd found the legendary Gonfalon of Charlemagne.

He'd touched it, held it in his hand. Sinjon stared at the back of the coach as they drove through the streets of London, but he saw nothing but the gonfalon in his fevered brain. Evelyn must have unwittingly donated it to the Foundling Hospital, probably months ago.

He'd return tomorrow, on his half day, and buy it back.

And then what?

He had Westlake's price in his hands. He was free.

He helped Evelyn's friend out of the coach and bowed

distractedly. Evelyn smiled at him, and his heart turned over.

He could walk away from her now, this very moment.

Instead, he climbed back onto his perch and the coach lurched forward.

Salvation could not have come at a less welcome moment.

Chapter 32

He kept her waiting for half an hour, and then he arrived in the bedroom with a deck of playing cards in his hands.

Evelyn held out her arms, but he gave her a devil's grin and stayed where he was, standing beside the bed.

"Let's play cards."

She leveled her best lady-of-the-manor look at him. "I don't wish to play cards, Sam. I want—" He laid a finger over her lips and sent her a smoldering look that trumped hers.

"You'll have to win what you want," he whispered, holding up the Queen and Knave of Hearts.

"I don't play cards."

He tilted his head and smiled, and her heart tripped on the rush of desire that raced through her. "Not even whist? Every lady plays whist."

He was just out of easy reach, and she was certainly not going to wrestle him into bed. She raised her chin. "Fine. I'll admit I've played whist. Is that what you wish to do?" She made a great show of searching the shadows. "Of course, we'll need two more players. Shall we wake Starling and Mrs. Cooper and ask them to join us?" She ran a fingertip over her naked shoulder. "Of course, they may be somewhat abashed by the dress required for the game."

He ignored her jest, probably because *he* was still fully clothed, though his shirt was open at the collar, revealing a vee of skin that made her mouth water. She was stark naked under the sheet. Was he even aware of that? She let the cover drop, exposing one breast.

She watched his eyes fall on her, feast, and his throat bobbed as he swallowed. A thrill coursed through her veins. A few short weeks ago she wouldn't have dared such a bawdy trick. How expert she was becoming at seduction. She arched her shoulders, offering herself to him. His breathing grew ragged and his hands tightened on the cards. They began to bend under the strain. In a moment, she thought, they'd flutter to the floor, forgotten.

But he shut his eyes and his grip relaxed. She felt a fizzle of disappointment, both in him and her fledgling wiles.

"Are you any good?" he asked. "At whist, I mean."

His voice was husky, thick with desire, and he avoided looking at her. She smiled. Refusing to be tempted, was he? She took it as a challenge, and let the sheet fall away from her other breast and pool at her hips. She raised her arms above her head, lifted the thick silk of her hair and let it fall. He stifled a groan.

"I've only ever played for pennies," she said, picking up a lock of hair, trailing the end of it over her collarbone and down the slope of her breast, teasing them both. "But I won almost three pounds in an afternoon once."

He was looking at her now, and he was sweating, his eyes dark with need.

"Come here," she said. "And I'll give you the whole sum."

He didn't need a second invitation. With a groan, he knelt

on the bed, pulled her close and kissed her, his tongue finding hers. She gasped as he filled his hands with her lovely breasts, caressed them until the nipples peaked. That was much better. She sighed and began to undo the buttons of his shirt, wanting him naked.

"Evelyn," he said against her neck, a mild warning, but she ignored it and tilted her head to give him better access. She slid her hand into his open shirt, caressing the hard planes of his chest. His heart was pounding under her palm, and she felt a thrill that she could excite this man, drive him as wild as he drove her. She reached for the top button of his flies, but he caught her hand before she could open it, stopping her busy fingers,

"Evelyn," he murmured again, and pulled back.

"Yes?" she said a trifle sharply.

"What about faro?"

So Sam taught her how to play faro, and she won the first three hands easily. Of course, they played for kisses and caresses, so she had a vested interest in winning.

Then it got more difficult. He challenged her, tricked her, battled wit for wit for every point. It quickly became a thrilling contest, with only the barest acknowledgment of the rules.

She blatantly cheated, slipping a card under the sheet when he wasn't looking. It was not that she approved of cheating, of course. It's just that she wanted Sam, and Sam seemed to be obsessed with playing games. She wondered if he truly did not notice her clumsy sleight of hand, or if he was letting her cheat, knowing that no matter who won, it meant pleasure for both of them. She quickly became an excellent player, which seemed to give him tremendous delight.

Two nights later he taught her to play piquet for even higher stakes. Not so much as a chaste peck on the cheek unless she won three hands in a row. He was as skilled as a cardsharp. If they'd been playing for money, he'd no doubt own the house, the lady, and her coach and four, lock, stock, and boudoir.

Three days after that she found herself arriving in the bedroom looking forward to playing cards with Sam. It challenged her mind, added spice to their coupling.

"I wish to add a new rule to the game," she said as he dealt by candlelight.

He raised a lazy eyebrow. "Oh? And what might that be?"

She smiled. "Secrets. If you win, then you may ask me to reveal a secret. If I win, you must answer my queries."

His mouth tightened. "I think that would be a very dangerous game indeed."

"Ah, so there are dark secrets you cannot reveal, is that it?" she teased. "What could it be? Another lover, perhaps, or a wife and five children? Or are they blacker sins than that?" She leaned forward and tiptoed her fingers up his chest playfully.

She didn't believe he had any sins at all. She knew the kind of men who were wicked at heart, and Sam wasn't one of them. She simply wanted to hear tales of his childhood, stories about his time in Spain. She carried him inside her skin, part of her, and she wanted to be part of him as well.

He grabbed her hand, plucked it off his chest, squeezed it. "Stop it," he said. Something flashed through the gray depths of his eyes, and she frowned. Torment, perhaps? Guilt? He turned away before she could name it.

Doubt bit deep, with sharp teeth. "Is there truly something you cannot tell me?"

"Everyone has a private side, Evelyn."

She picked up the cards and held them out to him. Her hand trembled slightly, but she had to know. "And you fear revealing yours?" she asked. "Deal, Sam."

He recoiled, his refusal clear in his eyes. She forced herself to hold his gaze, determined. They had broken down all the physical barriers between them, knew each other's bodies as well as their own, but she wanted more. Surely there was more, wasn't there?

She waited, sure he would give in, pull her into his arms, take away the uncertainty.

For a moment he stared at her, seemed about to speak. She held her breath, for whatever admission was coming, but he shook his head and cursed under his breath. He got up from the bed and began to dress.

"What are you doing? Are you leaving?" she asked, breathless. Her heart dropped into the pit of her stomach, afraid that everything between them came down to sex, a mere physical release. She did not touch his heart as he touched hers.

This fear was blacker, more painful than any she'd faced in the past months.

She watched in frozen horror as he buttoned his shirt and walked to the door. "You can't win this game, Evelyn. The stakes are too high. Worry about your own conscience, sweetheart, not mine. No doubt there's someone in the park who'll gladly hear your confession. Maybe they even know where your husband is."

She stared at him, her heart shriveling. His face was cold, his mouth cruel. He turned away. "Your dinner party is tomorrow night, and it will be a busy day. I think it might be best if we both got some sleep."

Evelyn's tongue glued itself to the roof of her mouth. She wanted to stop him, call him back, make light of her foolish game, but something stopped her. Terror? No, worse. Confusion.

She had never been in love. She hadn't even realized she was until that instant. Raw pain rendered her dumb, paralyzed her limbs.

He shut the door behind him without another word, leaving her alone. She listened to his soft footfalls fading away until there was only silence.

She huddled in the scant ring of the candlelight that illuminated the bed. The sheets where he'd lain were cooling already. A sob caught in her throat, tore free. She buried her face in the pillow, inhaling the scent of him.

She'd fallen in love with a man she could not have, a lover who saw their affair as a moment's pleasure. She was no better than Lucy, or Philip, for that matter. Cold shame washed over her.

Would this be the pattern of her life from now on, a string of lovers, each taken in a desperate hope that she'd find love, *feel* something as breathtaking and wonderful as this?

Evelyn wiped her tears away and rose, finding her dressing gown on the floor. She put it on, carefully fastening the dozens of tiny pearl buttons and tying the ribbons in a precise, ladylike bow under her chin, putting the cold, correct, untouchable Evelyn Renshaw back into her place as the lady of the manor.

She stared at the door, dreading leaving this room. Tomorrow Somerson's half sister was coming to dinner, and there were a hundred things to see to before she arrived, but she couldn't think of that now. There were too many terrible things that might happen before then. Sam might hand her his resignation in the morning. Or he might stay, but end their affair.

He might leave without a word, and she'd never see him again.

She squeezed her eyes shut, tears threatening. She loved him.

What a fool she was. She shut the door firmly behind her.

For a moment she stood at the top of the back stairs, wondering if he hovered there, might still come back, but there was only empty darkness, and nothing to do but return to her own lonely room.

Sinjon returned to the coldness of his own bed in the servants' quarters. How many nights had it been since he'd slept here? He'd grown used to the feel of Evelyn's sweet body next to him at night.

But she wanted secrets. His were blacker than she could even imagine. He could not lie to her. He'd done enough of that. Nor could he tell her the truth.

He sat on the bed, his head in his hands. If he had any sense, he'd leave now, tonight, before she found out the truth.

But he couldn't.

He peeled back the top blanket on his bed, exposing the Gonfalon of Charlemagne, hidden between cover and sheet where no one would ever think to look.

He could have taken it to Westlake, but had hesitated. What if he could buy Evelyn's freedom with it, bribe Philip to leave her alone for good?

He'd come close to telling her the truth tonight. "I'm the Earl of Halliwell's son," he might have said, but he wasn't. His father had disowned him. "I'm Captain the Honorable

Sinjon Rutherford." But that wasn't true either. He was neither honorable nor captain. He was an outlaw with a price on his head, and only Westlake stood between him and the hangman.

He stared at the gonfalon, and the angels glared back, resentful of their lowly quarters.

"I'm a fool," he whispered to them, but could not bring himself to admit how far he'd fallen, how much he wanted a life and a future with a woman he could not have. He was living a lie, loving her, spying on her.

Perhaps the best thing he could do was use the gonfalon to buy his own freedom. He could trade it to Westlake for his sword and return to war. He could join the Spanish army, or serve with the Prussians.

And if he died?

At least it would be an honorable death, and not a fool's end, hanging at the end of a rope for something he didn't do.

He wondered if Evelyn would mourn him.

Chapter 33

The servants flew around the house, happily preparing for the dinner party.

Evelyn stared down at the elegant table, set with costly dinner plates that bore Philip's initials in gold, and was tempted to throw them against the wall, one by one.

Instead, she clasped her hands at her waist and smiled and murmured praise to her devoted staff.

She didn't see Sam, but there was work to be done belowstairs. She wondered if he was thinking about her. If she went back to the room tonight, would he come to her, beg forgiveness? She doubted he was the kind of man who begged for anything.

Nor did ladies apologize to their footmen.

So where did that leave things?

Charlotte had claimed Miss Trask back again after all, having fired her own maid. Evelyn paid little attention to Mary's choice of gown. It wasn't until she was fastening the buttons on the back that she realized she was wearing yellow. She had no idea which shade it might be. Dry stick or old hen would fit her mood.

"You look beautiful," Mary assured her.

Did she? Evelyn hardly knew, didn't care. She felt like a

lump of lead, or perhaps fool's gold was a better comparison, given the yards of insipid yellow satin that covered her.

She pasted a smile on her face, but her stomach trembled at the possibility of meeting Sam in the hall. What if she made a fool of herself by bursting into tears? She pursed her lips. She hadn't let a single teardrop fall all day, and there wasn't time to feel sorry for herself now. Her guests would be here in a few minutes. She didn't have time to think of what might happen when the clock struck midnight in the little bedroom.

Evelyn drew a fortifying breath, straightened her spine, and left the false sanctuary of her bedroom.

"It's going to be a very exciting evening!" Countess Elizabeth said as the coach set off from Somerson House. "I'll admit I'm looking forward to getting a look at Evelyn Renshaw, so I can go home and tell everyone I actually dined with the notorious traitor's wife!"

Caroline Forrester glanced at her friend in the darkness, dreading the evening already.

"I hope you won't ask her embarrassing questions, Mother," Lord William said, shifting in his seat. "I can't see why you're so excited. There are a dozen more pleasant ways to spend an evening in London, and that list includes suffering the attentions of pickpockets and predatory *ton* mamas looking to wed their daughters to any man with a title, so long as he's breathing and has a thousand a year to his credit."

"You aren't enjoying London?" Elizabeth asked her son.

"No," William said sourly. "Too many parties and inedible dinners."

"And no wife," Caroline said sympathetically. "Poor Will."

William sighed. "I wonder if it will be too late to go to Somerson's club after dinner?"

Elizabeth swatted her son playfully. "You are our escort tonight, and a poor one at that. You have not even told Caroline how lovely she looks. Did you notice she's put off mourning?"

Caroline resisted the urge to touch the yellow ribbon that adorned the pale cream-colored gown. Charlotte had insisted she wear color in hopes she'd quickly find a husband.

Despite the prompt, William remained stubbornly silent.

"Did you know I have been given rules for tonight?" Caroline asked, and patted her reticule. "Charlotte wrote them down for me."

"Truly?" William asked, looking at her at last. "Are we expected to observe them as well?"

"I suppose not, or she would have given you a copy," Caroline said.

"What are they?" William asked.

"I'm not to mention Lord Philip's name, for one."

"Then what are we to discuss over dinner?" Elizabeth objected. "The weather will not even take us through the soup course!"

Caroline shrugged, then remembered not to. No country manners was the second rule, and that included smiling with teeth showing, tapping her feet, and laughing out loud. "I doubt it will be a problem, since the third rule warns against chattering needlessly."

"You? Talk too much? No one can get a spare word out of you, Caro," William interrupted. "How unfortunate you didn't bring a book tonight."

Caroline ignored the jibe.

"What other rules did she give you?" he demanded.

"No singing, even if invited, but if I am invited, I am to

limit myself to one of three songs. Charlotte wrote down the titles."

"Does Lady Evelyn have a pianoforte?" Elizabeth asked.

"Apparently she does, but according to Charlotte it is unlikely the instrument has been tuned since 'the incident that cannot be named.'"

"The incident that cannot be named?" William asked.

"The *treason*, dear. It is how Lady Charlotte refers to it," Elizabeth explained.

"I'm not supposed to know anything about it," Caroline whispered, giving William a warm smile, though it was probably too dark in the coach for him to get the full effect.

"I understand there is a vast collection of art at Renshaw House. May we mention that?" Lady Elizabeth asked. "I hope it is not too extensive. I have been charged with committing every detail of her house to memory, so I can give my friends accurate details."

"I wonder what notorious ladies serve for dinner?" William mused.

"The heart of an innocent?" Caroline suggested. "Sacrificial lamb, perhaps?"

William missed the joke.

"So long as it's cooked properly," he muttered.

"You are always thinking of your stomach, William!" Lady Elizabeth said. "It reminds me of the time your brother hid in the pantry and devoured half a roast beef we were intending to serve for dinner! He felt so guilty, he fed the rest to the dogs to hide his crime. The cook feared we'd been robbed. I shall never forget your father's face when she burst into the dining room in front of the Duke and Duchess of Welford, shrieking her dismay . . ." Her voice faded away into sorrow.

"We should have seen it then. We might have nipped it

in the bud. Now Sinjon is as much a traitor as Renshaw," William said bitterly. "I know you only came to London to look for him, but I advise you to forget him. Father and I have put him out of our lives. He has caused this family too much embarrassment."

Caroline bit her lip. It would be quite impossible to forget Sinjon, the dashing, charming Rutherford who had run away to war rather than marry her as their families expected. She missed him as much as his mother did. She shuddered at William's harsh expression, and wondered how a man could hate his own brother, no matter what he was guilty of. She reached out to squeeze the countess's hand.

"Sinjon is my son," the countess said. "He cannot possibly have done the things they say he did. I know it in my heart, William."

"They say he ravished a woman, betrayed his men, sold secret battle plans to the French. This is not some childish prank that deserves a lecture and bed without supper. He's a grown man. He has not even written to us to tell us his side of it."

"How would we know? Your father would have burned his letter, unopened."

"Rightfully so. Sinjon's been disowned."

"Not by me, William. Never by me."

Caroline hid a smile. Nor by her. They would not marry, but she still loved him as a brother. Or a brother-in-law. She slid hopeful eyes to William.

But he was staring out at Renshaw House as if he expected the traitor to pop out of an upstairs window. "I see we've arrived."

Elizabeth took out her handkerchief and carefully dabbed her eyes. "No more gloomy chatter. I suppose there is a danger in not guarding your tongue after all."

"Let's think of half a dozen witty things to discuss as we walk up the front steps," Caroline suggested. "That way we'll be fully prepared if the soup is not praiseworthy."

"A fine idea," William said sarcastically. "What would most interest a traitor's wife?"

"I imagine she wonders where he is, and worries," Elizabeth murmured.

Adam Westlake settled back against the plush squabs of his coach. For a change he was looking forward to going to a dinner party, since this one was at Renshaw House, and he would be present to overhear any slips of the tongue the lady might make with regards to her husband's whereabouts. Not that such an occurrence was likely. Evelyn Renshaw was as discreet and careful as he was.

"I'm surprised you agreed so readily to come to Evelyn's for dinner," Marianne said.

"Why? I remember Evelyn as a fine hostess with an excellent table. Surely the evening won't be as dreadful as that."

"No, it won't be dreadful. None of her sisters are going to be there. Imagine what an evening it would be listening to them chatter without ceasing."

"You wouldn't be able to get a word in," Adam teased.

Marianne glared daggers at him.

"Has Evelyn heard anything more from Lucy, or from Philip, perhaps?" he asked.

Marianne sniffed. "You know I am not interested in gossip, Adam."

Which meant she wasn't willing to admit that she hadn't heard a word since Lucy's emotional scene in Evelyn's salon.

"Yet I predict that by the end of this evening, you will

have winkled out every available detail about the lives of Evelyn's other guests," he said. "Who is coming, anyway? You merely said they were kin to Somerson."

"The dinner is for his half sister, Lady Caroline Forrester. She's coming with the traveling companion who brought her to London, a Countess Halliwell, and her son."

Adam's cravat was suddenly choking him.

"Did you say Halliwell?" he croaked.

"Yes, why?"

Sinjon Rutherford's family was coming to dinner?

Disaster loomed, fangs bared.

Adam wondered if Rutherford knew, and why he hadn't said something, sent a warning. He made a strangled sound. Marianne crossed to his side as he began to cough and thumped him on the back.

"Whatever's the matter? Shall I have the coachman return home?"

He gripped her elbow. "I'll be fine if you stop pounding on me, Marianne."

He straightened his coat, took firm control of his body and his emotions once again, and gave his wide-eyed wife a bland smile.

It didn't convince her in the least.

"Why should the Countess Halliwell's name shock you so?" Marianne asked. "Or is it her son, Viscount Mears, that surprised you? Do you know something about them?"

"I've never met them," Adam replied quickly. "Mears was at several of the parties we've attended in the past months, but we have not been introduced."

"I've heard his brother stands accused of treason."

The cravat tightened its grip anew. "That has not yet been proven. Or so I understand."

Marianne snorted. "Nor has Philip come to trial, but we

both know *he's* guilty, don't we? D'you suppose Evelyn invited the countess tonight to commiserate?"

Did Evelyn suspect Sam Carr was the infamous Captain Rutherford? Adam's tongue glued itself to his tonsils.

"Perhaps it's a club, like a sewing circle, for the relations of traitors," Marianne suggested.

"You know Evelyn better than I, but I would have thought her too discreet for such an enterprise."

"It was a jest, Adam. Of course she is. I can only imagine everyone will find themselves most surprised if the conversation turns to the topic of traitors lurking in family trees. How awkward that we haven't got one to speak of."

Even more awkward if one of the named traitors was helping to serve dinner, Adam thought. What would the countess say when she set eyes on her son? He hoped Rutherford had the good sense to absent himself for the evening if he knew. Would a lady tell her servants who was included on her guest list?

"It's going to be a very interesting dinner indeed," he said, not realizing he'd spoken aloud until Marianne agreed with him. She fell silent again.

"What are you thinking about?" he asked.

"I'm making a list of safe and interesting topics to discuss, just in case the conversation lapses, or turns to something embarrassing."

Adam shut his eyes.

It was going to be a disaster.

Chapter 34

Evelyn reached the salon without meeting Sam. She wouldn't see him until their eyes met across the dining room. Would she know at a glance how he felt, what he was thinking? She went to the sideboard to check the supply of sherry and port.

The sherry was for the ladies, the port for the gentlemen. Philip preferred brandy, the drink of traitors.

Evelyn refused to serve the French spirit now that he was gone.

The door opened, and her fingers tightened nervously on the decanter as Sam entered.

She hoped he was here on an errand from the kitchen, sent to ask a question about the wine, or sauce or flowers, but the look in his eyes, dark and earnest, told her that this had nothing to do with dinner. Hope pushed the breath out of her lungs as he strode toward her. She put the decanter back in place and made ready for whatever was about to come.

"I wanted to see you before your guests arrived. I have something to tell you." He looked down at her yellow gown. "What the devil are you wearing?"

"Don't you like it?" She couldn't seem to think of anything more intelligent to say. "It was a gift from my sister, and it is styli—"

He kissed her quickly, his mouth firm and cool against hers, rendering further speech impossible. Hope rose with desire, curled like smoke through her limbs. Weak with relief, she gripped his forearms for strength.

"Can you meet me upstairs?"

"Now?" she gasped. "My guests will be here any minute!" She wanted to go with him. Oh, how she wanted to let the whole world wait. Her body turned to molten liquid at the thought.

"Just to talk." There wasn't a hint of passion in his voice. Dread skittered over her raw nerves. This was serious, then, not a reconciliation. He was going to leave her. Her blood turned to ice and she shut her eyes.

"Evelyn, please. What I have to say cannot wait."

She slid her hands off his sleeves and turned away, hiding her dismay. "I—can't." She could see his reflection in the glass doors of the cabinet. He looked frustrated, annoyed. She couldn't help that. She was holding her own emotions together with fraying threads.

Philip had left her without a word. She had simply woken up one morning to find him gone. There'd been no parting and no ugly words. She couldn't bear a scene now, not with Sam. She clasped her fingers at her waist, wanting to turn and plead with him to stay, but dignity and fear kept her silent.

"Evelyn, please. You wanted to know about my past—" He stopped, swallowed and glanced at the door.

"Is it as bad as that?" she asked, turning to face him, keeping her voice even.

He looked down at her without answering, his hands at his sides, clenched into fists. His expression was guarded, carefully free of any emotion that might give her a clue. Her heart sank. She was staring at a stranger.

A stranger she'd foolishly fallen in love with. She could list everything she knew about him on the fingers of one butter-yellow glove. Soldier, knight errant, lover, footman and— She tightened her fist so hard the satin squeaked in protest.

She knew nothing else about him.

There was a soft tap at the door, and Sam quickly stepped away from her as Starling entered. She resisted the urge to hug her arms around her body.

"Your first guests are arriving, my lady. The Earl and Countess of Westlake. Sam, Mrs. Cooper needs help with the large soup tureen. You'd best go down and see to it for her," he instructed.

Dark blood filled Sam's face. He hadn't taken his eyes off her, even to acknowledge Starling's order. Wordlessly, he pleaded with her to spare him a moment, but how could she now, when she had guests? How could she bear to hear the words he'd say as he took his leave of her for good? She shook her head, almost imperceptibly, and looked away.

His jaw tightened, but he bowed with crisp precision and left the room. Evelyn shut her eyes, unable to watch him go. Her stomach was a jumble of emotions, her nerves in knots. How was she going to eat or make pleasant conversation?

Marianne swept into the room, resplendent in violet silk, with her husband behind her in pristine black and white.

"Good heavens, Evelyn, what are you wearing?" Marianne parroted Sam. "Is it meant as part of a joke?"

She forced a brilliant smile. "Yes, of course. It's to match Mrs. Cooper's third course, which is, um, chicken trifle." She hoped it would turn out to be chicken. She couldn't remember anything about the menu just now.

Sam was going to leave.

Marianne grinned. "It would have been even funnier if you jumped out of the dish itself."

"But rather messy, and likely to render it inedible," Westlake said, bending over Evelyn's hand.

"I would have worn yellow as well if you'd told me. Possibly a ridiculous hat, with canary feathers and a riot of ribbons."

"If there's truly such a bonnet lurking about the house, I will order Northcott to shoot it on sight," Adam said.

Marianne sent him a look. "Of course there isn't, but I would have obtained one if Evelyn had told me her plans."

Lord Westlake smiled distractedly. Evelyn watched his eyes scan the room restlessly, poking into the shadowy corners beyond the candlelight as if he were looking for someone. Philip, perhaps?

"Would you care for a drink, my lord?" she asked. She turned to Sam, to ask him to serve sherry, but he wasn't at his usual post by the door. Starling was. Sam was downstairs carrying soup tureens, deciding how to tell her he was leaving.

Evelyn felt utterly alone in the company of her friends.

"Countess Halliwell, Viscount Mears, and Lady Caroline Forrester," Starling announced, his tone plummy, his posture stiff with the pleasure of welcoming guests to Renshaw House once more.

The countess's gray eyes darted around the room like nervous sparrows before coming to perch at last on her.

Viscount Mears was fair-haired like his mother. He reminded her of someone, she thought. Perhaps it was something about his manner as he came forward and bowed, his expression guarded.

grace and good fortune, Caroline Forrester looked

nothing at all like Somerson, and her beauty spoke volumes as to why Charlotte disliked her.

"How kind of you to invite us, Lady Evelyn," Countess Elizabeth said as they exchanged curtsies, and Evelyn felt a twinge of anxiety at the undisguised curiosity in the countess's eyes. She obviously knew she was dining with the most infamous woman in London. It seemed she was doomed to go through the rest of her life with Philip's shame standing behind her like a ghost. She forced a gracious, welcoming smile.

"It is my pleasure." She turned away from the countess's stare. "Lady Caroline, are you enjoying your visit to Somerson House?"

Caroline colored and her pleasant expression set itself in stone. "Very much, thank you," she said dutifully, and Evelyn wondered what Charlotte had done now.

"We have been quite busy since our arrival, seeing all the sights of London," Countess Elizabeth put in. She turned to Marianne. "Perhaps you could suggest amusements we might seek out while we are in Town, Countess Westlake."

Marianne's eyes lit up. "Nothing would please me more! Tell me, will Viscount Mears be escorting you? I'm sure Westlake would be delighted to—" A glance at Westlake's subtle frown stopped her. "Or I would be pleased to accompany you."

"William says he's already seen everything. He's been in London since the start of the Season," Caroline said.

"Dinner is served," Starling announced, his voice a full octave lower than usual.

They proceeded into the dining room rather awkwardly since there was a very uneven number of gentlemen to ladies. Everyone else Evelyn had invited, including her own sisters, had refused her invitation, pleading prior engagements. With only six people, the evening promised to be intimate.

Evelyn smiled as everyone took their seats. Marianne was chattering with the countess, she realized, and no one else needed to make an effort at all.

Evelyn nodded to Starling, who was waiting to serve the first course.

The evening was successfully under way, she thought. Everything was perfect.

She couldn't wait for it to end.

Chapter 35

Sinjon held the tureen as Mrs. Cooper filled it with turtle soup. There was also cream of cauliflower for those who were sick of turtle, since it was served at most *ton* dinners.

"Lady Evelyn must feed her guests in popular style," Mrs. Cooper explained. "It's as important as what she's wearing. Everyone will be watching, and sniffing and tasting. Her guests will go home and tell their maids and valets what they ate, and they'll rush down to the kitchen to report to the cook. By tea time tomorrow the details of tonight's menu will be all over London."

Since there was no other news of the Renshaws to serve with tea, Mrs. Cooper might be right, Sinjon thought. He climbed the stairs with Annie and Sal at his heels, carrying the second tureen. Starling stood anxiously outside the door to the dining room.

"Sam and I will serve," he informed the maids, and pushed open the door.

"May I ask what shade of yellow you are wearing?" Marianne Westlake was asking someone, and Sinjon rolled his eyes.

"My cousin Lottie called it 'honey.'"

Sinjon stopped in his tracks, recognizing the lady's voice. He nearly dropped the tureen.

Caroline Forrester—*his* Caroline Forrester—was sitting on Evelyn's left. Her head started to turn at the clatter of the crockery, and he held his breath. In a moment her eyes would meet his and—

"Lady Caroline, have you been to see the Tower menagerie since your arrival in London?" Westlake asked, drawing her attention instantly. She cast her smile on *him*, instead, and Sinjon was saved. At least for the moment.

"Why yes, I went with Countess Elizabeth last week."

Countess Elizabeth? Not his mother! Sinjon's eyes shot to her placid profile. She was wearing the Halliwell rubies. He stopped in his tracks and stared, but she didn't even look up. She rarely acknowledged servants, he recalled, unless they did something wrong.

He took a better grip on the tureen and burned his hand. His eyes watered and the lid rattled like chattering teeth. Starling scowled a warning and nudged him toward the table.

"Honey is a delicious name for a color," Marianne Westlake continued. "Evelyn is wearing 'chicken soup.'"

"Trifle," Adam corrected.

"A lady's attire is never a trifle, my lord," Sinjon's mother said, the gentle tone of her rebuke as familiar as the rubies. He could smell her rose perfume as he served her soup.

He looked around the room. His brother was here as well, seated next to Marianne, looking as dull and pompous as ever. Sinjon met the question in Westlake's eyes and answered it with the barest shake of his head.

He glanced at Evelyn, but she avoided his eyes, kept her expression placid, holding her place as hostess with her usual unshakable elegance.

She had no idea that she was dining with his family.

He set a plate of soup before her, cleared his throat quietly, but she didn't look up. Frustration flared. He resisted the urge to shake her. He'd tried to tell her the truth, but she refused to listen. Now it was too late. This wasn't the way he wanted to introduce himself.

The shock would kill her.

He thanked the stars his father wasn't here as well.

His brother held up his wineglass. "More hock, if you please," he said, looking straight at Sinjon without the slightest hint of recognition.

Had he changed so remarkably that his own family didn't know him? A mixture of pain and relief surged through him as Starling stepped in to refill the glass when Sinjon hesitated. With a crisp nod, he sent Sam to his place by the door to wait until the soup was finished.

Sinjon stood in the shadows and watched his mother eat. How many years had it been since she last visited London? His father couldn't abide what he called "the false powdered fools of the *ton*," which showed *he* hadn't been to Town since powdered wigs went out of fashion. William was drinking too much, and trying to draw Westlake into a conversation about hunting.

Sinjon smirked. If Will knew the kind of hunting Westlake did, he'd run and hide under the nearest bed.

Westlake was skillfully diverting every glance away from Sinjon's direction, his face red with the effort of such animated conversation. Had *he* known? Sinjon wondered. Damn him if he did, or if Westlake thought he could use his family to ensure his cooperation.

He let his eyes fall on Caroline. Her gaze was fixed on William, soft and bemused, exactly the way she used to look at him. He looked at her hand, expecting to see the family betrothal ring, but her fingers were bare. He glanced at Evelyn, and knew he would never have been happy with Caroline. His guilt at deserting her faded, and he wished her well of William.

He cleared the soup plates, passing the dishes to Annie outside the door, who hustled them down the kitchen stairs as Starling carried up the next course, a magnificent poached salmon, displayed on a bed of oysters.

Sinjon skipped his mother as he served, knowing that she did not like fish, and felt the room go quiet at his faux pas. If he hadn't been holding a heavy platter, he might have kicked himself. Caroline glanced up at him, and he felt his skin heat.

"Lady Caroline! Do you like the theater?" Westlake cried out.

"I prefer the opera myself," William interrupted. He grinned at Evelyn, who smiled back warmly. Sinjon bristled, tempted to drop an oyster down his brother's back, or Evelyn's. He wanted her eyes on him, and only him. She hadn't looked at him all evening.

He served the oysters onto her plate instead, coming close enough that he could smell her perfume, feel the brush of her hair on his cheek as he bent.

He blew in her ear. Her hand tightened on the stem of her wineglass, and he knew she was aware of him.

He wondered how the conversation would go between them now. He'd been prepared to tell her who he was and why he was in disgrace, leaving out his connection to Westlake.

The conversation was going to be even more difficult now, after he'd served his family dinner as Evelyn's anonymous footman without saying a word. But what *could* he say?

The third course arrived, a succulent dish of chicken, rabbit, and ham, and Marianne grinned. "The sauce matches your gown perfectly, Evelyn! How clever you are!"

Caroline and his mother glanced at each other as if they were quite mystified by London customs.

Westlake sighed. "I do hope that ladies tire of fashions named for food very soon. What do you suppose next year's theme will be? Birds? Animals? What names might they give those items?"

"Ladies already wear fur and feathers," William pointed out dully. "What about vegetables?"

"Vegetables are still food," Westlake murmured, and the topic fizzled.

Sinjon served the French dishes, doling out asparagus, cauliflower in sauce, potatoes, and minted peas, unnoticed.

Starling sent him down to the kitchen a dozen times to fetch more wine, more plates, or the next dish. He was tempted to linger in the wine cellar, take a fortifying swig of something potent. Instead he climbed the stairs, kept his face blank, tried to catch Evelyn's stubborn eye, and did his job. No one even glanced at him.

He remembered the footmen at his father's estate. He'd grinned at them when they gave him a choice bit of beef, or an extra potato, and they'd winked back. His mother would probably faint if he winked at her, he thought, putting extra asparagus on her plate, since it was her favorite.

Mrs. Cooper accosted him between each course. "Well? Did they like it? What did they say?" He hardly knew. He embellished his reports with every superlative he could think of, and his confidence grew with each course. Once Evelyn's guests had left, he would find a way to explain. Fortunately it looked like she'd be spared the embarrassment of a surprise family reunion.

He carried up a towering plate of cakes, almost whistling. Apricot tart was one of William's favorites, and Caroline would be delighted to see the croquembouche and charlotte russe.

"I wonder if you might have any connections at Horse Guards who might help me, Lord Westlake," his mother was saying as he entered the room. "I came to London to find news of my youngest son. He's serving with Lord Wellington in Spain, but it has been some time since I have had word from him—"

Sinjon's heart stopped in his chest, and he looked at his mother in surprise, staring at her, reading the concern in her eyes. The grand entrance of dessert was missed in the earnest conversation.

"Go out and come in again," Starling instructed. Sinjon couldn't move. The sorrow in his mother's eyes held him rooted to the floor.

"Sam!" Starling hissed, and tugged his sleeve.

The plate slipped. The charlotte russe toppled into the lap of the Earl of Westlake with a creamy plop.

For an instant there was shocked silence. Then everything happened at once.

Caroline looked up at him, and Sinjon watched recognition bloom in her eyes. "Sin!" she cried.

Marianne Westlake was scooping whipped cream out of her husband's lap. "Oh, no, not a *sin,* Lady Caroline, merely an accident. Adam has an excellent valet, and he should have no trouble cleaning—"

Sinjon's mother gasped and rose to her feet, pointing, her mouth moving without sound. Sinjon pressed the empty tray into Starling's hands and caught her as she fainted.

William grabbed his arm. "What the devil are you doing?

Unhand my mother at once!" he ordered. "What kind of servant would dare —"

Sinjon glared at him, and saw William start as he recognized him at last.

"Good God, Sinjon, you're a servant? A mere *footman*? Haven't you heaped enough shame upon this family?" William's shocked gaze roamed over Sinjon's livery.

Sinjon looked at Evelyn. She was the only one looking at him as if she'd never seen him before. He supposed she hadn't. Her face was as white as the whipped cream in Westlake's lap. Confusion and hurt filled her eyes before she looked away, schooling her features to placid nothingness.

"Carry the countess through to the sitting room, if you please, Sam," Starling ordered.

"Sam?" Caroline parroted. Sinjon glared at her, trying to silence her. "Sinjon, what's this about?" she asked. He could feel Evelyn's eyes on him now. *Sinjon.* She mouthed his name, and her jaw dropped in realization of who he was, and what he stood accused of.

She looked around at each member of his family and back at him, noting the family resemblance. Her green eyes darkened with accusation. He sent her a pleading look, but she turned away.

"Take the countess upstairs to recover. Starling, have Mary bring the hartshorn and a warmed blanket," she instructed, taking charge of everything, hiding behind the necessities of the moment.

Sinjon lifted his prostrate mother, but Westlake stepped forward. "She's likely to faint again if she wakes up and sees you," he murmured. "Lord William? Perhaps you'd see to your mother?"

William was still staring at Sinjon as he took her. "We thought you were in Spain."

"I was," Sinjon replied. For now, explanations would have to wait, though every face in the room demanded one.

Except Evelyn's. There was no curiosity on her face.

Only betrayal.

Chapter 36

"How could you let this happen?" Westlake demanded.

They were closeted in the library, while everyone else hovered over Countess Elizabeth upstairs. Sinjon had no idea what was being said in the kitchen.

Sinjon stared at Adam. "Me? I had no idea my family was coming to dinner. *You* should have warned me."

Westlake straightened his stained coat. "I was not party to the guest list until we were on our way over here and my wife informed me—"

Sinjon laughed. "She knows more than you do, my lord."

Westlake colored. "How could you not know?"

Sinjon glowered at him. "I am—was—a footman. Do you consult with your footmen about who to include on your guest lists? I was told Somerson's sister-in-law was coming. I had no idea she meant Caroline."

"Well, you're not a servant anymore. You've been dismissed. I heard Lady Evelyn tell Starling to see that you left at once."

Sinjon shut his eyes. "I need to speak to her before I go anywhere," he insisted.

Westlake crossed to a side table, lifted the stopper on the

decanter and made a face. "Sherry." He replaced the lid. "Wait for a day or two. We'll come up with a logical story and you'll apologize. I'll need to find another footman to—"

Sinjon got to his feet. "No."

Westlake raised a haughty eyebrow. Anger flared in Sinjon, and he curled his hand into a fist.

"Leave her alone, Westlake, or I'll knock your teeth down your throat!"

Westlake's expression didn't change. "I still need information and—"

"I know where the damned gonfalon is!"

The silence that filled the room was deafening.

"Do you intend to give me details?" Westlake asked at last. "Were you going to tell me at all?"

The door opened before he could reply, and William strode into the room. "What the devil do you think you're playing at, Sinjon? Look what you've done to Mother, to say nothing of how upset Caroline is! I should call you out and shoot you."

"Dueling is illegal, my lord," Westlake murmured. "And he *is* your brother."

"My father disowned him," William snapped. "I want you gone before Mother wakes, Sinjon. I'll tell her it was a dream, or bad fish. If you don't leave at once, I'll have you arrested for treason."

"The situation is not as it appears, Lord Mears," Westlake warned.

"Does that mean he's *not* guilty?" William spluttered.

"You sound disappointed," Sinjon said.

"Mother said there'd be an explanation."

"And Father?"

"Never wants to see you again. He's forbidden anyone to mention your name."

Starling entered the room. "Your pardon, my lords. Countess Halliwell is asking to see her son."

Sinjon stepped forward, but William grabbed his arm. "Oh, no—you've caused enough harm for one night. I'm taking her home. You can call tomorrow." He left without bothering to say good-night.

"Shall I pack your things, *sir*?" Starling asked stiffly.

"No, Mr. Starling, I'll do it myself. Where is Lady Evelyn?"

Starling's lips pursed. "She won't see you, and I have orders to escort you out if necessary." Evelyn's small elderly butler looked ready to try, Sinjon thought.

"I'll go and gather my belongings," he said. "Can you find some whisky for Lord Westlake?"

Instead of going downstairs, Sinjon climbed the stairs two at a time.

In a day or two all of London would know this story, and that included Creighton. He had to see Evelyn now.

He paused as he came to the door to the small bedroom. There wasn't a sound from inside, nor any light coming from under the door, but he knew she was there.

He hesitated. Perhaps he should walk away, leave her in peace, but guilt gnawed at him, kept him standing outside the door, his hand on the latch.

He owed her an explanation.

And a warning.

Chapter 37

Evelyn knew who it was before the door opened.

There was the telltale creak of the floorboard in the hall, the sound she'd listened for, anticipated, for so many nights. Tonight she dreaded it.

He entered and shut the door behind him. He wasn't wearing his wig or the coat to his uniform, and she felt her heart turn to stone. They were no longer lovers or equals. He was an officer, not a soldier, a gentleman instead of a servant. An earl's son.

And a traitor.

He stood waiting for her to speak first, his expression bland. Did he expect her to scream or cry? She would never give him that satisfaction. She wondered how she had the misfortune to end up with a traitor a second time. "Did Philip send you?" she asked.

He winced. "No. God, Evelyn, no." He took a step toward her, and she got off the bed, sent him a look that dared him to touch her now. He stopped short, a scant few feet in front of her. The familiar wave of longing rose, and she squelched it.

"I would have told you the truth before dinner, if you'd allowed me the chance."

He sounded as angry as she was, and he hadn't the right. She narrowed her eyes. "What truth? The only truth is that you lied. You are, I take it, *the* Sinjon Rutherford?" The name swirled over her tongue, thick and bitter.

"Yes. Countess Elizabeth is my mother and Mears is my brother."

She raised her eyebrows. "And you are a traitor, don't forget that part, and a rapist, and a liar. Lord Creighton already warned me about you," she said.

"He lied," he said flatly. "Evelyn, I—"

But she didn't let him finish. "You dare to accuse someone else of *lying*? Sin is a good name for you. Your soul is every bit as black and ugly as—" She couldn't say her husband's name, not in this room, even now. "I should have left this room locked."

"Don't be a hypocrite, Evelyn! You didn't care who I was," he accused.

But she did care. She'd chosen him, hadn't wanted anyone else, ever. Just him. Her limbs shook with anger, or remorse, or loss, she didn't know what to call the dreadful sensation that threatened to overwhelm her.

"You chose me because I was your servant, close at hand and oh-so-convenient, so one would know that the high and mighty Lady Evelyn Renshaw has needs and passions and a heart."

Would he ever stop talking? Every word was a knife wound.

"My heart was not involved," she lied boldly. "*You* meant nothing. My sisters take lovers. Why shouldn't I? You were a pleasant distraction. I thank you for that at least. Shall I offer you a shilling before I dismiss you?"

His eyes narrowed, and she read something in his expression that stopped her breath. Hurt, perhaps. She'd touched a nerve, gotten a taste of revenge. It had a bitter aftertaste, though.

"I didn't come up here to argue. I came to warn you, Evelyn. Philip is dangerous, and he's got enemies who will do what's necessary to get what they want."

"Ah, yes, the Frenchman in the park. How long ago was that?" she asked sarcastically. "Do you dare to imagine I can't live without your protection?" She drew breath to dismiss him, but he stepped closer. She breathed him in, the fragrance of wool, sugar, and his own body. She'd fallen in love with that scent. Her mouth dried to ashes and she forgot what she was going to say.

He put his hand on her shoulder, and his touch shot through her like lightning. She shook him off, backed up a step and glared him into submission.

He let his hands fall to his sides, trying, she supposed, to look harmless, innocent.

But he wasn't.

"Evelyn, I swear I will tell you everything, but not tonight. I'll leave, and come and see you tomorrow."

"No. I do not wish to see you again, Mr. Rutherford. Or is it captain? I do not even know what to call you."

"Call me Sinjon."

She raised her chin. "I think not."

"I'll come in few days, then. Evelyn, after all that's passed between us, I deserve the chance to explain."

How did he dare to speak of their affair as if it meant something to him? She glared at him, furious, but there was no pride in his eyes, no sense of conquest. He looked as honest and reliable as he always did.

She felt the edge of the iceberg in her chest melt a little. He must have sensed it.

"Look, you can send me a note when the time is right. I will be at—" He paused as if he didn't know.

"I don't want to know. I don't care. I will not be duped or betrayed again." She turned away, giving him the scorn of her back. "Go. I don't care where you go from here. Prison, or hell, I hope."

He stood behind her for a long moment, but she refused to turn. She counted the seconds, her limbs trembling. If he hesitated a moment more, she'd burst into tears. She could feel them threatening behind her lashes, and she fought them with all her strength.

He left at last, shutting the door quietly, and she waited until his footsteps faded down the staircase.

She dashed away a single teardrop with the back of her hand and lay down on the bed. The scandal would swell with tonight's tales to tell. The traitor's wife, guilty of new sins. With fresh fuel the gossip would burn forever. She couldn't bear to hear the mocking laughter as the name of yet another traitor was linked with hers.

She had to leave London. The spies could chase her all the way to Linwood if they wished.

There was no reason to wait, no lover coming to claim her. She had nothing left here.

She was alone again, and the wolves were circling.

Chapter 38

She was the most stubborn, difficult woman he'd ever met, Sinjon thought bitterly as he packed the few belongings in his small room.

And she was the most vulnerable. The thought that Evelyn might be facing danger made his gut tighten and ache.

He took the gonfalon out of its hiding place. It didn't belong here any more than he did.

He shrugged off his livery coat and folded the flag, tucking it under the lining. He put it back on and gathered the rest of his belongings. He had little to pack—just his boots, a few clean shirts, some handkerchiefs. He left the hated footman's wig on the bed.

The whispering stopped as he entered the kitchen, and the staff stared at him. Starling looked angry, Sal bemused. Annie seemed confused, and Mary's brown eyes were narrowed in speculation. Mrs. Cooper was in tears, her marvelous dinner forgotten amid the shocking events of the evening. He wondered what Starling had told them.

"Should we bow?" Mary asked the butler.

Starling pursed his lips. "No, I don't think so. Here in this kitchen, he's still one of us. He's not one of them until he leaves."

Sinjon bowed to them instead. "It has been an honor to know each of you."

"I'll escort you out the front door, milord," Starling said. "In keeping with who you really are."

"Did you—" Annie began, stopping Sinjon at the kitchen door.

He turned to look at her.

"Did you really murder a woman in Spain?" she asked in a rush.

He shook his head. "No, Annie. I would never hurt any woman. I was just a soldier."

She let out the breath she was holding and nodded.

He led the way up the kitchen stairs for the last time with Starling at his heels. "Mr. Starling, you once asked me to protect Lady Evelyn."

"What of it?" the butler growled.

"She still needs to be protected. If she needs me, then send for me."

Starling puffed like an indignant pigeon, but Sinjon held his gaze. Finally the butler looked away, but his jaw tightened mutinously in wordless refusal.

William and Caroline and his mother had gone, but Westlake was waiting in the front hall.

"I suppose you'd better come to De Courcey House since you have nowhere else to go at present," he said stiffly. "I'll warn you now that my wife is waiting in the coach, since she refused to allow me to send her home ahead of us."

Sinjon smiled wryly. "Am I to be grilled or roasted as the evening's final course?"

Westlake colored slightly. "Everyone who was here tonight has questions, Rutherford. Some of those questions have dangerous answers."

Sinjon turned to meet the butler's eyes. "There, Starling.

You have my direction if you need me. I'll be at De Courcey House, a guest of the earl."

"We won't need you," the butler said stiffly, and bowed. "Good night, my lords." He shut the door, and left Sinjon on the unfriendly darkness of Evelyn's doorstep.

Chapter 39

"I must thank you, Captain Rutherford, for the most entertaining dinner party I've been to in a very long time," Marianne Westlake said as the coach pulled away from Renshaw House. "The service was flawless, by the way, right up until you dropped the cake in Adam's lap."

"Thank you, Countess," Sinjon said.

"I mean, I'm sure Adam would be hard pressed to serve a cake or even a plate of biscuits and not slip up." She paused for only a moment before pouncing. "So tell me, is everything I've heard about you true?"

"Marianne, most of what's printed in the scandal sheets are lies," Adam admonished.

"Then let him tell me the truth himself," Marianne objected. "You cannot expect me to take a reputed rapist and traitor into my home and not ask questions."

Sinjon winced at the description, and Adam sighed in exasperation.

"Since he is to be *our* guest, perhaps you might offer him some modicum of privacy and decorum, and the benefit of the doubt."

"I shall be pleased to tell you truth of the matter, Countess, since I am innocent of the charges," Sinjon said.

"I do hope you'll tell a version suitable for a lady's ears, Captain," Westlake warned him.

"Then you already know the tale, do you, Adam? Including the 'unsuitable' version?" she asked.

Sinjon felt his temperature rise, but Westlake didn't answer.

"I do hope whichever version you tell me, it will include an explanation of how an officer and a nobleman's son came to be working as Evelyn Renshaw's footman."

"Is he not to be allowed any privacy at all?" Westlake objected.

"Not under the circumstances! Never mind my husband, Captain. I am an excellent listener, and may be able to offer some helpful advice."

"And since you are an excellent hostess as well as a good listener, you won't forget that Captain Rutherford worked all day, and would probably prefer a good night's rest to a long interrogation."

The coach pulled up at the front door of De Courcey House, and a footman immediately sprang forward to open the door. Sinjon looked carefully at him, wondering what secrets Westlake's servants kept under *their* livery. This one might number skills as a trained assassin or a code breaker among his daily duties.

"I shall wait until morning to hear your side of things, Captain," the countess said. "Adam can tell me what he knows tonight. We breakfast at nine. Do you prefer coffee or tea?"

"Coffee, thank you, Countess," Sinjon murmured. Marianne Westlake would probably come and drag him out of bed personally if he did not appear at her table.

"Good. I shall inform Northcott at once, and remind him that you are no longer a footman, but an honored guest under the benefit of the doubt until breakfast. Good night."

Sinjon bowed, and he and Adam watched her climb the steps. "My wife will be discreet regarding your presence here. I assume you'll take care what you tell her?"

"I won't lie," Sinjon said tiredly. He'd done too much of that already.

"Need I remind you that my wife has no idea what I do for the Crown?"

"Then I shall leave you out of it entirely."

They entered the vast foyer, and Northcott bowed to both gentlemen, showing no sign of surprise at Sinjon's new status. Adam handed the butler his coat and turned to Sinjon. "A drink before going up?" he asked.

"If you don't mind, my lord, it has been a very busy day. I'll say good-night." As he climbed the stairs with Northcott leading the way, Sinjon felt Adam Westlake's eyes on his back, knew he was weighing the small valise, wondering if the gonfalon was inside. He straightened his coat and kept walking.

He was here because he had something Westlake wanted. The butler opened the door on a comfortable, handsome room, and Sinjon nodded his thanks.

Still, a prison was a prison, even if it included a feather bed hung with velvet curtains.

Chapter 40

Philip hated being without his luxurious traveling coach. It offered incredible comfort on long journeys, unlike the squalid chaise he found himself in. He'd bought it for the housekeeper's use at the estate he furbished for his royal French cousin, but when Napoleon's agents arrived unannounced, he'd been forced to escape in the plain vehicle, or not escape at all.

After five almost unendurable days of travel, he'd managed to lose his pursuers. He had no doubt they'd find him again, and when they did, he'd need the gonfalon.

He reached for the silver flask on the seat beside him and grimaced at the sour odor of the ordinary wine it contained. It had been the best the last coaching inn had to offer, and it was still worse than swill. He didn't bother pouring it into the crystal glass he usually used. It wasn't worthy of such consideration. He swallowed, and swore at the thin bitterness. Water would have been better, and no one drank water.

He'd been hiding in Dorset for months, every since his plot to kidnap and execute the French king in exile had failed and he became a wanted man. No one had thought to look for him in such an obvious place, and he enjoyed the life of luxury he'd prepared for his French cousin.

Napoleon's agents had found him first, bursting in to skewer his butler and shoot his valet in the knee, demanding in French to know where Philip Renshaw was and where the gonfalon was hidden. Philip smiled coldly now. His servants didn't speak a word of French, nor did they have any idea who Renshaw was or what a gonfalon might be. To them, he was Lord Elenoire.

Philip was not a man to be captured easily. He'd escaped better men than these, last time with a pistol ball buried in his shoulder. This time he slipped out through the tunnels he'd had constructed under the house, and was gone before the servants' screams subsided.

Philip had imagined he was being clever, stealing the gonfalon. It had offered security. If he was double-crossed by Napoleon, then the French would never see their holy battle flag again. He'd promised the Emperor two things, and had failed to give him either. Louis XVIII remained in comfortable exile here in England, with his head still firmly fixed to his shoulders, and his existence remained a threat to Napoleon's grip on the French throne. Philip had promised the Emperor his undying loyalty in exchange for his grandfather's defunct title, and then betrayed him by stealing the Gonfalon of Charlemagne.

He poured the rest of the wine out of the window. He didn't trust Napoleon any more than the Emperor trusted him. They were both ruthless men interested only in their own glory. Patriotism was for lesser men.

He arrived in London just after dark, directing his carriage down the broad avenues of the West End first, past the grand homes of marquesses and earls, where he had once been a welcome guest. It was the height of the Season, and the cream of London society was dancing the night away. He wondered if they were still talking about him, or if his star had fallen to a fresher scandal.

"Stop here," he commanded, knocking on the roof. He sat well back in the shadows and stared at the dark facade of his own house. No parties here, then. The only light was in Evelyn's bedroom, the wan flicker of a single candle. Did she sleep with the light on out of fear or hope of his return?

He waited another half hour for her light to go out. It didn't. He got out of the coach impatiently. "Wait for me here, and don't speak to anyone," he ordered his driver.

He entered through the front door. It was his house, after all. He smiled. Maybe he'd sell it without telling Evelyn. That would shake the insipid calm off her face.

His nostrils flared as he opened the door. The house smelled of Evelyn's perfume. It had become her house since he left. He entered the salon and moved through the dark toward the brandy decanter near the window.

He tripped over something and fell.

When his eyes grew accustomed to the darkness, he swore under his breath. She'd rearranged the furniture. He'd fallen over a small chair that should not have been there. He picked it up and put it back where it used to be, against the wall.

Philip poured a brimming glass of brandy and took it at a swallow.

He choked. "Sherry," he growled, and hurled the glass against the wall. In the faint light from outside, the glistening liquor crawled down the striped wallpaper like blood.

He took the precaution of lighting a candle when he went into the library. She would not dare change this room, he thought smugly, and looked around. First, he wanted the painting above the fireplace. The portrait of the famous actress was legendary among the connoisseurs of the *ton*. He'd once been offered a small fortune for it. Now, with his own notoriety, it would fetch much more.

He held the candle up, his mouth watering at the prospect of seeing his mistress's incomparable breasts once again.

The sober face of the late Earl of Tilby, Evelyn's father, glared down at him instead. Philip recoiled. The late earl's high and mighty frown matched Evelyn's perfectly. He was tempted to tear the portrait off the wall, but the noise would wake the servants. He wondered if Starling was still here, still as loyal. He might enlist the butler to carry his belongings out to the carriage when he was done here.

He checked the shelves, looking for the most valuable books in his collection. He found the first, a book of Venetian prints. He ran his hand over the painted breasts of the lush prostitutes and glanced at the execrable poetry that accompanied each salacious drawing. It was one of his favorite possessions. Placing it on the desk, he went in search of the others under Tilby's disapproving eye.

The rest of the books weren't in the usual place.

He scanned the shelves, looking for the familiar spines of his treasures, but there was no sign of them.

"The bitch," he muttered. She would not dare dispose of them. More likely she'd hidden them away so no decent person would find them. He climbed the stairs. The art on the walls had changed, or disappeared. Evelyn had redecorated him out of his own house, tried to eradicate every sign of him.

He paused at the top of the steps, tempted to go to her room first, grab her by the hair and force her out of bed, make her show him where she'd put his prized possessions, and prove to her he was still the master of this house.

Instead, he went into his own bedchamber and breathed a sigh of relief. Nothing had been moved here, at least. It looked as if he'd left only yesterday. His coats still hung in the wardrobe, his shirts and handkerchiefs lay ready in his bureau drawers.

He went into his dressing room. His dressing gown no longer hung behind the door, and there were no linens laid out for his bath. Even the scented soap he favored was missing.

He opened the cupboard, and his heart leapt into his mouth.

Every sheet, every towel, was gone. The bare shelves mocked him. He reached a hand in, felt only the painted wood, cold and empty under his palm.

It wasn't here.

He moaned, and looked around the room again, searching. He went back into his bedroom and tore the drawers apart, scattering everything.

It was one thing to move a few paintings, or to change his brandy for sherry, but this was a matter of life and death. Fury rose. He grabbed a discarded shirt and tore it in half, and the fine linen shrieked.

Damn her! She had no right to move anything. She was his wife, *his property*. He would have to remind her who was in charge here.

Philip Renshaw left his room and stalked down the hall toward Evelyn's bedchamber.

Her door was unlocked, and he pushed it open. He'd never worn a path in the carpet coming here at night, but he'd done the minimum to try and get himself an heir, and to keep Evelyn in line. She hated his visits to her bed, and that was the only pleasure he got in this room. He grabbed the bed curtains with pulled them back violently.

She didn't leap up in terror as he'd hoped. The bed was empty, and he stared down at the smooth white counterpane in surprise.

"She's not here, my lord," said a familiar voice, and he turned. Starling, his faithful butler, was standing behind him.

Well, perhaps not so faithful after all, since he was pointing one of Philip's own dueling pistols at his master's chest.

"I can see that, Starling. Give me the gun at once and tell me where she is."

Starling shifted, obviously uneasy about disobeying a direct order. "There are men outside, my lord, watching the house."

Philip felt his stomach clench. He'd taken too great a risk in coming here, and hadn't expected to find disobedience and mayhem threatening him in his own household. He forced himself to sneer at the threat.

"Should I ask them where my wife is?"

"She's out. Gone to a party," Starling replied stiffly. "If you don't leave, I will summon the watch."

Philip chuckled and took a step toward the spindly butler. He snatched the gun from Starling's hand before the servant could even react, and gripped his throat. "How will you summon them? With your last breath?"

He felt the butler swallow. To his surprise, Starling pulled a massive kitchen knife out from somewhere. He put it against his chest. Philip could feel the point through his waistcoat. By the light of the single candle, he read hatred in Starling's eyes. "All I have to do is cry out, my lord. The window's open. They'll come running, but they won't reach this room before you're dead."

Philip let the butler go, giving him a shove that knocked him off balance, and strode past him toward the door.

"My wife has something I want, Starling. A banner. Do you know where it is?"

He shook his head, still holding the knife.

"Then you may tell her I'll be back."

Starling sagged against the banister as the front door slammed. He crossed to the bedroom window and watched Philip Renshaw leave in a plain coach. He scanned the darkness, wondering if there truly were men out there. He'd been bluffing, and now that it was over, he realized he was shaking. He tucked Mrs. Cooper's knife back into his waistband.

Picking up the candle he walked along the upper hall. He put his ear to the door of the back bedroom. There wasn't a sound inside. Lady Evelyn was asleep. He let go a sigh of relief.

Starling wasn't surprised she was in this room. She had slept here for weeks, and he was well aware she hadn't been alone. At first he'd been shocked, but Sam was a good man, discreet and dependable, and he made everyone feel safe while he was here. Starling touched the handle of the knife, realized his hand was still shaking. He was too old for this kind of thing.

Philip Renshaw would be back.

Starling had never known a more ruthless man. He shivered, and sat down in the hall outside the door, placing the knife beside him on the floor, settling himself for the night.

Much as he hated to admit it, Lady Evelyn needed Sam Carr more than ever.

They all did.

Chapter 41

"**L**ord Westlake explained why it wasn't possible for you to come and visit me, Sinjon. Dreadful charges, and not a one of them true," Countess Elizabeth said to her son in Westlake's drawing room. Marianne had shown the countess in, and then withdrawn to give mother and son privacy. He had no idea what Westlake had told his wife, but she'd been the perfect hostess.

"You look well," his mother said. "Even Caroline said so."

"I am pleased to see that you have recovered from the shock I gave you."

She waved the apology away. "I am glad to see you alive, Sinjon. I've missed you, feared you were dead. I have been in London for weeks, hoping for news of you, and you were scarcely a mile away. You might have written to me, or sent word to Caroline."

"Father disowned me. He sent a man to London before I sailed for Spain to tell me not to come home again. I thought you knew."

"Of course I knew, but *I* did not disown you, Sinjon. You are still my son, and your father will come to his senses." She blinked away maternal tears and he gave her his handkerchief.

"I have a letter for you. Your father received it some months ago. He tried to burn it, the stubborn old fool, but I rescued it from the grate. I had to have news of you, you see."

Sinjon's skin prickled. "Who sent it?" Would Creighton dare to write to his mother?

"It was badly singed, I'm afraid, but I believe it's from someone you knew in Spain. Do you owe him money, perchance?" she asked. "I can lend you some, if it will help. There was another letter enclosed as well, in a feminine hand, written in French. I thought you had come to an understanding with Caroline before you left."

Sinjon stared at her. "Who wrote the letter, Mother? Was his name O'Neill?"

"I don't know his last name, Sinjon. That part was burned away." She opened her reticule. "Here, see for yourself. I have carried this for weeks, my only connection to my youngest son."

He looked at the charred envelope in his mother's hand. The melted wax seal was like blood, and the blackened edges looked like battle scars. He took it, his stomach tightening.

The scrawl on the front, what could be read, was unfamiliar. It was not from Creighton, then. He opened it. The first sheet bore the same hand.

> —afraid for my life. I barely escaped alive from Major C, who has proven himself an enemy to both of us. I wish to make amends for my sins, and be of assistance to you in the matter that has seen you brought low under false charges. I will gladly do what I can to make this right for you. You are as fine an officer as I—

The rest of the text was burned away, but part of the signature was visible: *Sergeant Patr—* Sinjon stared at it, his heart in his throat.

"Who is the lady who wrote you?" his mother asked, looking over his shoulder at the second note. "That's obviously a woman's hand."

Sinjon rose and crossed to the window to read it, pretending he needed better light to make out the words, but in truth wanting a moment's privacy.

I am sending this to your family home in hopes it will find you. The soldier who wrote the letter enclosed came to me in fear of his life. He asked me to help him, and to help you. I have not forgotten your kindness to me, and to protect your friend I have brought him here to my farm in Normandy. He is afraid to return to England. If you can find a way to come to us, you will be most welcome, treated as a friend and a guest.

It was signed by Marielle d'Agramant. Sinjon felt a shock run through his veins. Whatever the service he had done her, he was still an enemy to her husband and her country.

"Well?" his mother asked.

"She's a lady I met in Spain, a colonel's wife."

Relief flooded her face. "I see. Then you will marry Caroline?"

Did Caroline truly still expect him to propose? "No," he said, and watched her face fall.

"Is there someone else?"

Evelyn's face filled his mind, but he shook his head.

"Then when can we expect you to come home?" she asked.

"Mother, have you heard the charges against me?"

She sniffed. "Of course! London gossip is full of two topics, and you seem to be part of both. I don't understand how you came to be working as a footman for Lord Renshaw's wife, but I know that you would never commit rape or treason. I would more quickly believe it of your brother than you." She patted his cheek. "Perhaps I should have named you Gabriel, or Angel, so they could never call you Sin."

He felt like a child of six again. He squeezed her hand gently. "I'll come home when I can face Father without these charges hanging over my head."

"Then I suppose I'd better go back to Chelton and prepare him."

"It could take some time."

She smiled with a mother's confidence that he'd have no difficulty proving his innocence. "Do let me know where you are from time to time." She looked pointedly at the letters on the table. "Whatever you plan to do."

He picked up Marielle d'Agramant's letter and looked at the address, smeared by the melted wax. Normandy.

It seemed he'd have to go to France if he wanted to prove he wasn't a traitor, for his parents, for O'Neill, and especially for Evelyn.

Chapter 42

Adam Westlake woke at dawn, when his wife poked him in the ribs.

"Do you recall the Somerson's ball, and the gossip about a lady and a footman embracing on the steps?"

"It's too early for gossip," Adam mumbled. "Can't this wait for breakfast?"

She pulled the covers off him. "No, it can't! Do pay attention."

He unwillingly opened one eye. His wife was beautiful in the morning, with her hair loose, her nightgown lost somewhere on the floor with his. He instantly found himself in a state that ruled out listening. He reached for her, and frowned when she slipped away.

"I think it was Evelyn, Adam. And Captain Rutherford."

"Come back to bed and stop talking nonsense. He's a footman. A lady like Evelyn would never—"

"But he isn't!" Marianne said triumphantly. "I agree, it would be most shocking if he were truly a servant, but he's an earl's son."

"But she didn't know that until last night."

His wife mulled that over for a moment. "Still." She

shrugged. "It's very romantic. Is he innocent?" Adam squirmed inwardly.

"How would I know that?"

Her eyes sparked. "You wouldn't have invited him to stay if he were guilty of rape and treason. I assume you're being noble, and trying to help him prove his innocence."

"Come back to bed, Marianne," he murmured, hoping to distract her, but as she slipped back under the sheet, she grinned that knowing smile of hers, the one that suggested she knew everything and he didn't have any secrets she hadn't already discovered.

He'd hurried to Rutherford's room as soon as his wife had breakfasted and headed upstairs to the nursery, in case she had the same idea and came looking for something to prove that Rutherford and Evelyn were—

"Impossible," he muttered to the footman's coat in Rutherford's closet. Or was it?

Marianne's theory offered one reason for Rutherford to keep the gonfalon. Love made men do ridiculous things. There were a number of ways the flag could benefit the good captain.

He could sell it back to the French for a fortune. He needed money. He might also sell it to Philip Renshaw for the same reason.

He could be using it to blackmail Evelyn into sleeping with him. How much, Adam wondered, did he truly know about the man's honor?

Rutherford might simply surrender himself and the gonfalon to Horse Guards, bypassing him entirely, in return for exoneration of the charges against him. The army would do almost anything to own their enemy's prize possession.

None of these ideas pleased Adam. He looked around the room, at the few personal items it contained. Sinjon Rutherford was a man without a home or a family. All he had was trouble.

And the gonfalon.

He shut the closet and left his guest's room. He had no choice but to trust that Sinjon Rutherford was indeed an honorable man. And if he turned out to be as craven as most men, well, Rutherford wasn't going anywhere without his permission.

All he had to do was watch him, and wait.

Chapter 43

"Sam! My apologies— I mean *my lord*," Starling said as Sinjon entered the salon. He sketched an awkward bow.

Sinjon looked at the man's haggard face, felt his gut tighten in apprehension. "Is Evelyn all right?"

"Yes, and no," Starling sighed. "Lord Renshaw came to the house last night."

"Did he hurt her?"

"He didn't find her. She was sleeping in the small bedroom at the end of the hall," Starling said. "You know the one."

His meaning was clear in his eyes, and Sinjon swallowed. Did that mean the rest of the staff knew about their affair as well? For a panicked second he wondered if it would help if he denied it, but Starling shook his head.

"I'm not here to judge. All that is between you and the lady, but she *is* married, and her husband is a very unpleasant man. I saw him off, but he said he'll be back."

"What did he want?" Sinjon asked.

"I don't know exactly. A flag, he said, but what would a traitor want with a flag? I can't recall ever seeing a flag around the house."

Sinjon sat down in the nearest chair to prevent himself from running for Renshaw House to see for himself that Evelyn was safe. "Does she know he was there?"

Starling puffed like a bantam cock. "I made sure she didn't, but he's still the master of that house. I left John Coachman sitting in the kitchen armed with one of his lordship's dueling pistols. I doubt he knows how to use it, Sam—er, *sir*. I must get back before he shoots himself in the foot, or wings Mrs. Cooper." He bit his lip. "I know you did not part on good terms with her ladyship, but we—the servants—need your help to keep her safe. I can hide you in the attic. You could keep an eye on things from there."

Sinjon's spine prickled the way it used to before a battle, a warning of bad things to come. Even if she was in danger, Evelyn would not welcome his protection now. If he hid in her attic, he'd be one more of the unseen watchers she loathed. He'd kept enough secrets from her.

"No."

Starling's jaw dropped. "But what if Lord Renshaw returns?"

He pictured Evelyn snatching the pistol from the coachman and using it to defend *him* from Philip.

He got up and paced the room. The safest thing, of course, would be to get her out of Renshaw House, and out of Philip's reach.

"My lord?" Starling prompted after a few minutes of silence.

The butler's face was drawn with worry. He would do anything for Evelyn, regardless of his personal safety. So, Sinjon thought, would he.

"I believe I have an idea, Mr. Starling."

Chapter 44

"I'm going to France."

Adam watched Sinjon Rutherford pace the carpet in his study for a moment before replying. "I can't see how that will be possible. I read your letters, of course. O'Neill may be right across the Channel, but we are at war with the French. It would be a fool's mission. You'd be shot as a spy if you were caught, and you realize, of course, I could not be of assistance."

"I could as easily hang in London, and Creighton would shoot me if he knew where I was. Other than hiding me, you haven't been a lot of assistance here, my lord."

Adam studied him. Rutherford wasn't afraid. He looked like a man who believed he was doing the right thing, the only thing. He wasn't going to be dissuaded by anything less than arrest and imprisonment. Whatever Adam said or did, Sinjon Rutherford intended to go to France. Admiration swelled in Adam's breast.

"How will you get there?" he asked. "Swim?"

"I'll rent a boat. I used to sail when I was a boy."

A small boat on the English Channel. Why were heroes always so rash? Apparently the more honor a man had to his credit, the further he'd risk life and limb to defend it.

"I'll provide the transportation," Adam said, and the captain's eyes narrowed suspiciously.

"Why would you do that?" Rutherford asked softly. "What's your price? You always have a price."

Adam smiled, trying to look easy, friendly, kind. By the frown on Rutherford's face, he knew he'd missed his mark. "I'm simply trying to be helpful. One of my ships is making ready to sail. Later today, in fact, and a discreet stop on the French coast wouldn't be impossible." His ships frequently made the trip to spy on the enemy, but Rutherford didn't need to know that. "Come now, I'm doing you a favor."

If Sinjon Rutherford was a traitor, he was offering him enough rope to hang himself. If not, he might prove worthy of greater trust, more responsibility, a job doing important tasks for the Crown on a regular basis. His men would keep a close eye on Rutherford, report on his activities.

"Is that all you want? Gratitude?" Rutherford asked, as Adam took out his pen and wrote a quick note to the captain of the *Edmond.*

"Not at all. I want the gonfalon as well."

Sinjon's lips pursed.

"Is there a problem, Captain? You did say you have it, didn't you?"

Rutherford looked away. "Did you know that Philip Renshaw came home last night?"

Adam's brows rose. He hadn't known. He wondered where his agents were.

"Starling saw him off, but he's promised to return."

"For Evelyn?" Adam asked. Sinjon shook his head, and Adam's chest tightened. So Renshaw had come for the flag.

"He'll kill her when he discovers the gonfalon isn't where he left it, Westlake."

"I'll set extra men to watch the house, make sure he's caught if he—"

"No," Rutherford growled.

"Then what do you suggest, Captain? Especially since you plan to be out of England for a few critical days."

A crafty, sinister smile bloomed on Sinjon's face, and Adam wondered if he'd missed something, or had played into the captain's plans.

"I want Evelyn out of that house when Renshaw comes back, in fact out of London would be even better. With her absent, you can fill every room with all the agents, spies, and assassins you've got. When Philip comes again, you'll have him."

Adam wished he'd thought of it himself, but he kept his expression bland, since it was his job to point out the flaws. "There are other people watching Evelyn Renshaw, not just you and I. She can't leave London. She'd face immediate arrest, and they'd seize every bit of Renshaw's property. She could stay with her sisters, I suppose. I'm afraid I cannot invite her here with you in residence. It would be improper, given the circumstances." Rutherford colored at the implication, and Adam marveled again at his wife's perception.

"She's coming with me."

"To France? Are you mad?" Adam demanded. "If she cannot leave London, then going abroad is most definitely out of the question. Renshaw has lands in France, a French title. Think how that would look. We'd both hang."

"She won't leave the ship, and no one will know she's even left the house. The servants will pretend Evelyn is at home. She gets very few callers, and Starling can turn her sisters away."

"The dreadful trio? Even Northcott could not deflect those ladies."

Sinjon grinned. "If Lucy calls, Starling will hint that Evelyn is upstairs with a lover. If Charlotte arrives, he will inform her that Evelyn is at the Foundling Hospital. Charlotte would never set foot there. If Eloisa shows up, she'll learn that Evelyn is here, taking tea with Marianne."

"And if Eloisa comes here?" Adam was fascinated.

"Perhaps Northcott would be kind enough to inform her that Evelyn has just left."

The man was a natural spy. Adam's toes curled in his boots.

"Even if there was an intimate connection between yourself and Evelyn Renshaw," he said, "you did not part on the best of terms. How do anticipate getting her to accompany you to France?"

Sinjon smiled. "I'm going to kidnap her."

"Don't you have enough sins accredited to you already?"

"One more for a good cause. I'd be the villain, and Evelyn would be entirely innocent."

There was a knock on the door. "Lady Evelyn Renshaw is here to see Captain Rutherford, my lord," Northcott announced.

Adam looked at Sinjon in surprise. "You receive more callers in my home than I do. Should I expect that the lady has arrived with a case packed, ready to travel?"

Sinjon got to his feet. "She won't need more than a cloak in case the sea wind is cold. I am assuming she'll spend most of the voyage belowdecks, furious."

"You've thought of everything, haven't you?" Adam asked. "At least the *Edmond*'s cook is excellent. Perhaps that will placate her somewhat."

"Just one more thing, my lord. May I ask that you return my sword?"

"I'll send it to the ship." He met Sinjon's eyes. "You are planning to return to England, aren't you, Captain?"

Sinjon's expression was unreadable as he took his leave without answering the question. Adam watched him go. The man wore his honor like armor. He was a man of honor himself, and he knew Rutherford would do what was right first, and what was necessary second.

He'd have to trust the captain for now. There was no other choice.

But if worst came to worst, he'd have his men drag Rutherford back to England to hang.

Chapter 45

Evelyn paced Marianne's salon, waiting for Sam—no, not Sam—Sinjon Rutherford, traitor, rapist, and liar.

His message, relayed by Starling, was cryptic. If she wanted the money from the sale of the book, she would have to come and get it.

The money was the *only* reason why she wanted to see him. He'd give her the sum, and she would leave, never to set eyes on him again.

She turned as the door opened, the sharp rebuke ready on her tongue, but it melted like sugar at the sight of him. He was dressed as a gentleman, without wig or livery. Polished Hessians and buff breeches made his legs long and sinfully lean.

She remembered them naked, wrapped around her body.

His shoulders were broad under his tailored blue coat, shoulders she'd clung to as he—

She gritted her teeth, turning lust into anger. She strode toward him with quick steps and struck him with all the force in her hand. He looked stunned, then hurt, then something more dangerous sparked in the depths of his eyes.

"I want my money," she said.

He touched his lip, and looked at the blood on his fingertip. "I see Starling gave you my message."

"Indeed he did."

He smiled disarmingly, and she had the ridiculous urge to kiss the droplet of blood from his injured mouth.

"How are you?" he asked, as if this were a social call.

How was she? She was lonely, unable to sleep, and she was busy—very busy—planning a future without him.

"I have been waiting for the proceeds from the book," she clipped. "Fetch the money at once." Surely those tight breeches, that formfitting coat, had no room to hold Sinjon Rutherford *and* five hundred pounds.

His mouth twisted ruefully, and her stomach dropped.

"You do have it, don't you? Starling said you did!" She wanted to take the money and sever the last tie between them. It was unbearable to see him and feel pain and temptation. Another minute in his company and she'd—

"Actually, I haven't got it at the moment. The buyer promised to pay me today. I had not thought you would arrive so promptly."

"Where is this gentleman? I shall go and collect the money myself!"

"That would hardly be proper," he said, and she hated the fact that he was right. "I'll go and get the money and bring it to you at Renshaw House, shall I?" he asked in a patronizing tone that set her teeth on edge. "This evening, perhaps, if you have no plans. Or at midnight?"

Midnight. Her body quivered.

She raised her chin. "That won't do at all. I don't trust you, especially not with five hundred pounds. You might use my money to flee the country, and I would lose the chance to watch you hang for your crimes."

He had the nerve to grin at her, as if she'd offered him a

compliment. "Perhaps they'll allow you to pull the lever to open the trapdoor under my feet." He gave the bell a sharp tug, and she winced.

"Would you please inform his lordship that I will be going out on a short errand with Lady Evelyn?" he said when Northcott appeared.

She led the way down the steps to her coach. Sinjon gave John Coachman a jaunty nod like an old friend, and the fool smiled back. He turned away at Evelyn's scowl.

Sinjon gave her a rogue's grin as he climbed into the coach. "If it pleases you, my lady, I shall ride inside, instead of on the back."

It didn't please her at all. He had mischief dancing in his eyes, and she clenched her hands in her lap. How often had she imagined him inside?

She swallowed desire and regret, said nothing as he took the seat opposite hers. She couldn't look at him. She stared out the window, as if the street was the most fascinating thing in the world, though it was the nearness of his body that held her attention. The familiar scent of his skin filled the small space. She could hear him breathing, and their knees almost touched. His eyes were on her, moving over her like a caress, she knew. She fought the desire to stare back.

Once she had discharged her debt to Major Creighton and left London for good, she would forget all about Sinjon Rutherford. She sent up a prayer to make that possible.

"Are you cold?" Sinjon asked, and she snapped her attention to him with a frown. "You shivered."

She pulled the velvet collar of her spencer more tightly around her throat. "I'm warm enough, thank you."

"Then surely you aren't afraid of me, Evelyn, after all we've—"

She sent him a warning glare. "I do not wish to discuss it!"

He shifted, and his knee did press hers now, warm through the thin muslin of her dress. "What don't you wish to discuss? The fact that we were lovers, or that you think I betrayed you?"

His bluntness surprised her. She scanned his face, looking for smug masculine pride, triumph, but it wasn't there. She read a twinge of guilt behind his rueful smile. Her mouth dried. Would he apologize now, explain? And then what? She looked down at her gloves as a surge of longing passed through her and she fought to deny it.

"You lied to me!"

"Never in bed." His voice was silky, soothing on her raw nerves. She wanted to believe him, but she didn't dare.

"*Did* Philip send you to spy on me? Is that why you were there, in my house, pretending to be a footman? What other reason could there be?"

"You've heard the charges against me, Evelyn. I needed a place to hide, and a job."

"You could have gone home. You have family."

"My father disowned me before I left for Spain. He wanted me to become a clergyman."

Her mouth twisted. "You? A man of the cloth?"

He wasn't insulted. "I agree. I am not suited to that kind of life. I was a good soldier, though. I needed to remain in London to prove my innocence. It means a great deal to me. I don't mind dying for a cause, but not for something I didn't do."

Evelyn swallowed. She understood. How could she not? Philip had taken everything material from her, and society had stripped her of the rest—dignity, regard, and privacy. Pride was all she had left.

"You might have at least told me your name," she said.

"Ah, but I did, Evelyn. Sin."

His quip stung, made her remember what they'd shared, what she'd live without. "Sin. An excellent description. Did that sobriquet come before the rape or after?"

His mouth tightened as he looked away. He wasn't going to apologize for deceiving her, for invading her home, her bed, and her heart.

"Damn you to hell," she said.

The rank smell of the Thames invaded the coach, an evil miasma of the city's worst sins. "We're at the docks!" she said in surprise.

"The gentleman who purchased the book is taking ship for Spain. He asked me to meet him before he sailed this evening."

"A soldier friend?" she asked scornfully. "One with tastes like yours?"

"You're my taste, Evelyn," he said mildly, letting her make what she wished of the comment as he got out. "Will you wait here?"

She looked around at the rough faces, the dirty streets, heard angry cries and bawdy singing. "No, I'll come," she said quickly, and caught his smirk. She raised her chin. "I told you I don't trust you."

He held out a hand to her, and she took it without thinking. She was almost grateful when he tucked her hand under his arm to lead her up the narrow gangplank, though she was careful not to let it show. Her heart was pounding by the time she reached the deck, and she wondered if it was his touch that did it or the small adventure of boarding a ship.

He summoned a cabin boy. "I'll turn you over to this likely lad while I find my friend," he said.

The lad sketched a bow, regarding her with cheeky curiosity from under a curling lock of blond hair. "Would you like to see the ship, my lady?" he asked.

He reminded her of the boys at the Foundling Hospital, but he was well fed, his skin bronzed by the sun. His eyes held pride and hope. It made her smile.

"I would, if you please," she said, and followed him through a narrow door that led down a set of steep stairs into a shadowed corridor that smelled of lamp oil and polish.

He opened a set of doors at the end of the narrow corridor, revealing a well-appointed cabin with wide windows.

"You can see the whole harbor from here," the lad chirped.

She crossed to look. A hundred ships lay at anchor, men of war, merchantmen, and fishing boats. Some were making ready to sail, others arriving. Cutters filled with passengers, boxes, and bundles butted across the open water, sails billowing, wet oars shining in the afternoon sun.

Evelyn turned to ask the lad a question, but he was gone, and she was alone in the room. She crossed to the door.

It was locked.

His wife had matured into a beauty in his absence, Philip thought as he watched her emerge from De Courcey House with a gentleman he didn't know.

"Follow them," he commanded his driver as her coach set off. He remembered Evelyn as pale and dull, with plain brown hair and eyes devoid of emotion. Had he missed something?

The mouse he'd known would not have dared to remove his belongings or rearrange his furniture. This Evelyn had fire in her eyes, sensual elegance in every lithe line of her figure.

The hard edge of lust made Philip smirk. Their reunion would take place with the lights on.

He held a lace handkerchief to his nose as they reached the docks. Evelyn and her escort boarded a ship called the *Edmond*. The man was handsome, well-built, and confident, and Philip's lip curled, noting the familiar way he handled his wife, his hand easily spanning her waist as she navigated the narrow gangplank, the trusting way she leaned against him.

Long minutes ticked by and they failed to emerge. "What the devil are you doing?" he muttered, growing suspicious as the shadows stretched and the ship made ready to sail.

"Give me your coat," he demanded of his driver. He made a face as he put the plain work-worn garment over his own.

Hoisting a bundle from the dock to his shoulder, he followed other similarly burdened men onto the ship. In the hold, he crouched in the shadows.

Wherever Evelyn was going, he'd find her.

And when he did, she'd pay for all the sins she'd committed in his absence.

Chapter 46

Evelyn heard footsteps on the deck above her and heavy thumps coming from the hold beneath, but no one answered when she called out, and the door remained locked, no matter how persistently she tugged on the latch.

She looked around for another means of escape, but the windows were weather tight, except for narrow panels that opened an inch or two to admit a gasp of stale London air. The door was solid oak and the furniture was bolted securely to the floor.

There was nothing to do but wait, and waiting was the last thing she wanted to do.

Hours passed, and as the afternoon turned to evening, the ship slipped away from the dock. She waved frantically at the passing ships, but aside from a few friendly nods, no one made any move to help her.

Was Sinjon working for Philip after all? There were rumors that Philip was living in France, in a luxurious chateau once owned by his royal ancestors. She imagined such a place would have deep dungeons in which to hide an inconvenient wife. She would simply disappear.

Or, she thought, as the ship skipped over the waves and

glistening foam sprayed the windows, he might intend to throw her over the side. Her heart lodged in her throat.

Would Sinjon, her lover, her protector, be capable of such a thing?

She shut her eyes. He stood accused of other heinous crimes. So did Philip. What would one more sin matter?

Evelyn clenched her teeth. She would not go quietly. She searched for a weapon, settled on a lantern that hung from a hook above the desk. Taking it down, she held onto it, her eyes on the door, ready for the moment they'd come for her.

She wasn't ready at all when the door swung open. She leapt to her feet, dropping the lantern with a clatter. It wasn't Philip who entered, or Sinjon, but a smiling sailor bearing a tray, followed by the cabin boy who'd locked her in earlier.

"Evening, milady. I've brought you food, and some water for a wash," the sailor said, and set the heavy tray on the table. The boy opened a cupboard and poured steaming water into a basin securely mounted there, then laid thick towels on the bed.

"Where is Sinjon Rutherford?" she demanded, not moving.

"With the captain, I believe, my lady, but he'll be down to dine with you shortly," he said calmly. There was nothing sinister in his eyes, she noted.

"I'd like a word with the captain myself," she said. "You may take me to him at once."

The man's smile faltered. "I'm afraid I haven't got orders for that, ma'am."

"Then I'll go myself," she said, and strode toward the door.

She walked straight into a black wall in the doorway. Sinjon caught her against his chest.

She pulled away from him, stepped back. He was dressed in black from head to toe. He looked dangerous, and handsome. She drew a shaky breath.

"Is there any point in asking where you're taking me?" she asked. "Or in demanding that you turn this ship back to England at once?"

He nodded to the sailors, dismissing them.

"I'll serve the lady's dinner," he said. She'd almost forgotten he'd been her footman. He looked like what he was, a gentleman's son, an army officer, a man used to command.

"You were a terrible footman," she muttered.

He raised his eyebrows.

"What do you intend to do with me?" she asked, suddenly breathless, aware that they were alone in a cabin with a massive bed.

"You've nothing to fear, Evelyn, I promise. The captain will make you as comfortable as possible for a day or two, and then you can return home."

Anger flared. "Is this supposed to be a pleasure trip, then, like a ride in the park?" she demanded.

He lifted the cover on the first dish, and the tantalizing aroma of beef stew filled the room. He smiled at her, as if he were serving dinner at Renshaw House.

"Would you like to sit down while I pour the wine?" It sparkled in the glass, ruby in the light of the lantern the sailor had picked up, lit, and put back on the hook.

"I would not. I want an explanation."

"I have business to attend to in France, and you'll be safer here than in London at present."

"Safer here than in my own home?"

His eyes were in shadow. "Starling told me Philip paid you a visit in the middle of the night."

Evelyn felt her skin blanch. Starling hadn't told *her*. Was everyone she knew spying on her, reporting on her private life?

"I believe I fired you, Captain. Mr. Starling had no right to tell you anything. I don't allow my staff to gossip with outsiders. It's one of the strictest rules in my household, if you'll recall."

He grinned, a dazzling flash in the dark. "I'm not a footman anymore, and it was a plea for help, not gossip. Do you honestly expect your sixty-year-old butler and four maidservants to protect you? They'd try, though."

Her heart turned in her chest. Philip was a big man, violent. "Turn the boat around immediately—*please*," she begged, her throat closing on fear for her servants.

"It's a ship, Evelyn, and I can't do that. The captain has his orders. You have nothing to fear. I have been ordered to return you to England unharmed, or the owner of this ship will hang me twice."

He looked around the cabin, at the wide bed made up with fine linens, at the embroidered draperies that framed the windows. "I should've known it would be a floating palace," he muttered.

Her skin prickled. Philip created a palace for his last victim. She drew back, afraid. "What does that mean?" she asked.

"It means that you'll be extremely comfortable while you're on board. There's a trap being laid for Philip. When he returns to Renshaw House, they'll arrest him. By the time you return home in a few days, it will be over."

Evelyn swallowed. "And then what?"

He concentrated on ladling stew onto a plate for her. "You'll be free. You can leave London and do whatever you want."

She sat down heavily and stared at a chunk of carrot in glossy gravy.

"And you? What will happen to you?" she asked.

He placed a bit of warm bread on a plate, using tongs as if he was still her footman. "This trip should sort things out for me."

"And after?" she persisted.

He took his seat across from her, his smile roguish but not quite meeting his eyes. "I never plan that far ahead."

In other circumstances the meal would have been intimate and romantic, but they ate in tense silence, and she wondered if the future felt as bleak and friendless to him as it did to her. She couldn't guess his thoughts by reading his face. They might have been sharing supper at a ball, or a last meal before his hanging.

"How will this trip exonerate you?" she asked.

He smiled, and she wondered if he'd fob off her question with a glib half-truth or another blatant lie. She held his eyes. "I deserve the truth, Sinjon. You said that much yourself."

He put his spoon down. "I'm going to France to find a British soldier who can tell the truth of what happened on the road in Spain that day. A court-martial is hardly likely to take the word of the French colonel who was there, or his wife."

"Patrick O'Neill," she muttered.

"Now how did you know that?" he asked in surprise.

"Lord Creighton warned his sister you'd come looking for Patrick. She said you wanted to kill him so he couldn't give evidence against you." She read the indignation in his eyes, the anger at the false accusation. "How is Creighton involved? Why would he make such terrible accusations if they aren't true?"

He didn't answer. He got to his feet, tossed his napkin on the chair and crossed to the window, his back to her. His black silhouette was outlined by starlight.

"Isn't it dangerous, going to France?" Evelyn asked. "We're at war. If Major Creighton is mistaken, then surely you could speak to him—"

He turned to look at her, his eyes icy, freezing the words on her lips. "It shouldn't take me more than a day or two to find O'Neill. You'll be safe here. The captain has orders to get you home if anything goes wrong. But whatever happens to me, Evelyn, stay away from Creighton."

"If anything goes wrong?" she repeated, ignoring the rest, trying not to picture him dead, his sightless eyes open, blood spilling from a final, fatal wound. She'd seen the scars on his body, knew he'd faced danger before. This time there was someone to care if he lived or died. Her throat closed. The corners of the cabin were in shadow, and they shared the ring of yellow lantern light, a safe haven against the darkness that was closing in on him.

He'd tricked her and lied to her. He'd kept her safe, made her feel loved.

He'd kidnapped her. To protect her from Philip.

Her heart opened like a rusty music box.

"Do you even speak French?" she asked.

He frowned. *"Un peu,"* he said. "A little. Why?"

He came back and sat down, and she watched him swallow another spoonful of stew.

"I speak fluent French," she said.

"Do you?"

"Indeed. Shouldn't you have someone with you who speaks proper French?" she asked, her eyes on his. "Just in case?"

She watched understanding kindle in his eyes. He dropped the spoon with a clatter.

"Oh, no. You're staying here, on this boat, where it's safe, Evelyn. This isn't a game."

She leaned toward him. "Ship," she corrected. "And we've

been playing a very elaborate game from the first moment I saw you. You pretended to be a footman. You played hide and seek with the authorities under my roof. You pretended to be my lover, and now you are playing a deadly version of blind man's buff with Philip. I'm one of the major players, and you still owe me five hundred pounds, if nothing else. I must insist on going with you when you leave this ship."

"I never pretended when I was your lover," he said, trying to distract her. "That was honest."

She forced a smile, as if it meant nothing to her. "Only the names were wrong," she quipped. "Well, yours was." She swiftly changed the subject back to the matter at hand. "Since the French are our enemies, I will do the talking if we are stopped. I can answer in French. You will play the role of my servant, so no one will expect you to say a word."

She read the bemused refusal on his face and refused to accept it. "I am still the comtesse d'Elenoire while Philip keeps breathing. A *French* comtesse. No one will question a noblewoman traveling with a servant boy."

His brows rose at the rude description. "No one will question a single man riding fast either."

"Do you have a horse?" she asked.

He looked away. "I planned to borrow one."

"You mean *steal* one."

He didn't reply. Nor did he look ashamed.

"We'll rent a coach and four. Where are we going? Is it far?" She leaned forward, excited now. For the first time in months, years, she was free, and she meant to make the most of it.

"Evelyn, you can't—"

"Have you got French coins?"

There was a knock on the door. *"Entrez,"* she said in lilting, perfect French, and grinned at Sinjon.

"No," he said.

"I insist," she replied.

The captain entered and swept off his hat, bowing over Evelyn's hand before turning to Sinjon. "We'll be off the coast of Normandy within the hour. Are you ready?"

Sinjon nodded.

"We'll row you in and leave you on the beach. If there's any sign of trouble, we're leaving immediately. I have orders to send a man in if necessary to bring you back alive, but I'm confident you won't make me risk the life of one of my men on a fool's errand. Is that clear?"

"Perfectly. Thank you, Captain," Sinjon said. "I'll meet you on deck shortly."

"Captain? I'll be going as well," Evelyn informed him, looking past Sinjon's shoulder.

The man's eyes popped and he glanced at Sinjon. Evelyn pinched him.

"I suspect the lady will swim to shore if we do not give her room in the boat," Sinjon said.

The captain sighed. "His lordship said to be ready for trouble. Now I can see why. Still, knowing Countess Marianne, I've learned not to dispute a determined woman. I only hope she'll make you more careful and I'll not have to rescue both of you. She's in your care, then. Best of luck. I suspect you'll need it."

Philip took his place in the launch with the rowers, a cap pulled low over his forehead, the collar of his coat standing high around his chin.

He watched as Rutherford tossed a bundle into the bottom of the boat.

His mouth twisted as Rutherford positioned himself behind his wife on the ladder, protecting her. Evelyn's bottom swayed against Rutherford's hips, and Philip let his hand stray to the pistol hidden in his coat. As soon as he had her in his clutches, he'd make her watch as he put a ball between her lover's eyes.

He wondered if Rutherford was one of Westlake's agents, since this was Westlake's ship. If this was a mission, how did it involve Evelyn—how could it? She wasn't a spy. She was stiff and dignified, and the dullest woman alive.

But here she was, landing in the dead of night on the unfriendly shores of enemy France.

Philip studied Evelyn's profile in the darkness. Even now, her dress was prim and tidy, and she didn't have a hair out of place. She settled herself on the narrow seat, close to Rutherford. Philip bristled as she leaned even closer to whisper in his ear.

A hard elbow jarred him back to the moment. "Row, damn you!" the sailor next to him hissed, and Philip gripped the oar and put his back into the cover of the task.

His hands were blistered and his shoulders burned long before the bottom of the boat finally scraped gravel. He leapt over the side with the others, and the icy water soaked him to the waist. Rutherford lifted Evelyn as if she weighed nothing and carried her to shore on his shoulder.

Philip reached into the boat and slung the bundle at him, just so Rutherford would be forced to unhand his wife. He caught it easily.

Philip fingered the gun again. It would be easy to shoot her now, but he was curious, and he wanted answers to some very important questions before Evelyn died. He slipped into the shadows, his eyes burning into Rutherford's back as he watched the launch retreat.

Chapter 47

"**W**hat's in the bundle?" Evelyn asked him as they walked up the beach toward a small inn. He glanced at her, noted her flushed cheeks, the shine in her eyes. She still imagined this was just an adventure. He swept the dark beach for signs of the local militia, but aside from the man following them, they were alone.

Probably a sailor, assigned to keep an eye on him. He damned Westlake and his spies, but if anything happened to him, the sailor would see Evelyn safely home.

He knelt and untied the pack, answering her question by showing her. "My sword, a purse, and my livery."

"You kept it?"

He let her imagine he was sentimental. "You did say you wished me to play your servant, did you not?" He took her elbow to help her up over a lip of wet pebbles, and realized her skin was icy under her fashionable spencer.

"Put this on," he said, holding out the livery coat.

"You're supposed to be the servant, not me," she objected, though her teeth were chattering.

Sinjon hesitated. He could let her shiver, wait until they reached the inn and purchase a blanket, or he could take another risk entirely. He withdrew his knife and slit open the lining of the coat. He draped the gonfalon over her shoulders like a shawl.

"Where on earth did you get this?" she asked, fingering the silk.

"Just don't lose it." He started walking again. "Are you warmer?"

"Yes, thank you," she said crisply, her half boots slipping on the pebbles. "You're very resourceful, aren't you? You seem to have a plan for everything. Escaping, hiding, and subterfuge seem to be your greatest talents. Were you a spy in Spain? Is that why you refused to tell me about your past?"

"I was just a soldier," he said. "I ran into a little trouble and needed to get myself out of it, so I left."

"Rape is hardly a 'little trouble.' I'm surprised they didn't hang you on the spot."

"If they want to hang me, they'll have to catch me."

"Is that why you came to France? To escape?

"I come to France annually for the wine," he quipped. "If you hurry along, I'll buy you a cup."

"To keep me quiet? I could simply go into the inn and tell them you kidnapped me, that you're a wanted man," she threatened.

He laughed. "You asked to come ashore, Evelyn, remember? Before you denounce me, remember you're an English lady in France, and as much an enemy here as I am."

She sniffed. "You should be grateful for my company. You said yourself your French is atrocious."

"Poor, not atrocious," he muttered.

"Bad enough that you'd do well to hold your tongue and let me do the talking!"

There was laughter in her voice. She was enjoying this. He wondered if she realized that this little excursion could get them both killed. But then, a ride in the park had nearly gotten her killed in London. He gripped the sword in his hand. He'd protected her then, and he'd keep her safe now.

There was no point in telling her that he was in command. Once again he was her servant.

"We need directions to Louviers," he instructed her as they neared an inn.

"Why are we going there?"

"We aren't, but it's in the right direction. Tell them you're going to visit your sister, if they ask."

"And what should I say her name is?"

He gritted his teeth. "Evelyn, you won't need to tell them a long story. Hand them a coin for the coach, buy some provisions, and we'll be on our way."

She stopped. "I have three sisters, Sinjon. They are *always* curious. If the innkeeper has a wife, she'll ask questions. The less we say, the more she'll wish to know. One does not simply walk in out of the night and rent a coach."

There was a certain logic in that. "Tell the innkeeper's wife that yours broke down on the road and you are in a hurry." He shrugged. "A damaged wheel, perhaps? Your coachman is fixing it, but you cannot wait."

"Because my sister is ill, near to death, and I must get to her at Louviers," she finished happily.

Frustration nudged him. It would have been so much easier to steal a horse. He'd be halfway to Agramant by now. Instead, he was facing a long conversation about an imaginary sister. Given the sisters Evelyn already had, he was surprised she'd *want* to invent another one.

He shrugged out of his own coat and into the livery. "Why can't I play the role of your husband instead of your servant?"

She looked at him as if he were the village idiot. "Because my husband would speak for me, while my servant wouldn't dare, *compris?*"

She didn't wait for a reply, but took a breath and opened the door of the inn.

Sinjon's gut clenched as the conversation inside stopped. He felt for the pistol hidden under his livery, and prayed no one noticed that Evelyn was wearing the sacred Gonfalon of Charlemagne as a shawl.

Evelyn waved her supposed footman to a halt by the door as she approached the sleepy innkeeper, but he ignored the command, as stubborn now as he had been in her service in London. He stood behind her, ready to get her out of harm's way if he had to.

She sent him a glare of warning, but he stood his ground, his gaze as stubborn as hers.

Giving up the battle, she turned to smile at the innkeeper. The man's wife also rose from her chair, set her knitting aside, and glared at Evelyn suspiciously.

Evelyn took a breath and began her performance. She fixed her eyes on the proprietress and described the inconveniences and terrors of her imaginary carriage accident with vivid detail. By the time she described her poor sister's desperate illness and her haste to reach her side, the inn wife had tears in her eyes. Even the innkeeper turned away to ply his rumpled handkerchief.

The sympathetic couple sprang into action, and within the hour Evelyn was safely ensconced in a carriage, with a basket of bread, cheese, and wine by her side, and a small gift of strawberry preserves for her ailing sister.

She gave Sinjon a bright smile as he closed the door of the coach, her mission accomplished.

* * *

Sinjon climbed up on the driver's seat and nodded farewell to the innkeeper's wife, who tearfully waved her handkerchief and wished them luck. He didn't need luck. He had Evelyn. It couldn't have gone better, he thought with a swell of admiration. He was tempted to pull off the road, climb inside and kiss Evelyn senseless, make love to her until they were both sated and breathless, but there wasn't time.

She continued to surprise him, even when he thought he could not be more in awe of her, more in love.

Perhaps when he had O'Neill's confession in his hand, and they were safely back in London, laughing over the perils of this adventure, he'd tell her. Westlake would have Philip in custody by then, and Evelyn would be free.

Sinjon frowned. She hadn't forgiven him, and he was a long way from free himself.

Chapter 48

Evelyn stared at the magnificent chateau as Sinjon drove through the wrought-iron gates. Fragrant lilacs and roses, heavy with early morning dew, flanked the long driveway beside the coach, escorting them to the front door.

A lady was waiting when they pulled up. She smiled warmly at Sinjon and kissed his cheeks. Evelyn felt her skin heat, and she ran a hand over her hair. She untied the tattered silk shawl and straightened her bonnet and her spencer. There was no hope for her wrinkled muslin gown.

Sinjon seemed to be explaining who she was. The woman turned to look at her in surprise as she stepped out of the coach.

"Lady Evelyn Renshaw, may I introduce Madame Marielle d'Agramant?" Sinjon said, as if they were meeting at a garden tea, and their countries weren't at war. The Frenchwoman assessed her boldly as they made their curtsies, and Evelyn wondered how Sinjon had explained her presence. She looked at him quickly, but his eyes were on the Frenchwoman.

"The captain tells me you came as an interpreter," Madame d'Agramant said as she led the way to the house. An interpreter. It was not as bad as being described as a traitor's wife, nor so possessive as being called his lover. It was polite, cool, and tidy.

Her stomach tightened and she clasped her hands together, stilling the desire to reach for Sinjon, cling to his arm, and feel the reassurance of his eyes on her.

"My husband is in the study, Captain Rutherford. He will be pleased to see you immediately. I'll take Lady Renshaw upstairs so she may bathe before luncheon."

Sinjon bowed and turned to follow a manservant down the corridor.

Marielle d'Agramant showed Evelyn to a comfortable bedroom. She rang for her maid and ordered a bath and fresh clothing.

"I hope you'll forgive my curiosity, but are you related to Philip Renshaw, the comte d'Elenoire?" Marielle asked, and Evelyn's stomach dropped to her ankles. Would the colonel arrest her in Philip's place? She pictured being dragged through the streets to the guillotine like Marie Antoinette.

And what would happen to Sinjon?

Marielle's bright blue eyes demanded an answer. "Lord Philip is my husband, but I have not seen him in many months. In fact, there are rumors that he is dead."

Marielle looked dubious. "Since you are not wearing a wedding ring, I assume you believe those rumors. Or you have stopped thinking of yourself as his wife." Evelyn blushed, and Marielle laughed. "Oh, I have no objection. He is a traitor to both our countries, a wanted man here as well as in England. I was simply surprised to see you here, since Elenoire is nearby."

"Was he here in France, all these months?" Evelyn asked, breathless. He was in England now, wasn't he? She swallowed, but she had nothing to fear. He had no idea where she was.

"No one has lived at Elenoire for many years. It is a ruin." She took Evelyn's hand. "I can also see that you fear what I will do, but I assure you, you are quite safe. Or is it your husband that you are afraid of?"

Evelyn bit her lip, and Marielle sighed.

"I know the feeling of fear. I was with my husband, at war, in Spain. You could not have a better champion than Captain Rutherford. If all men had such honor as he, this war would not exist."

Evelyn looked at her in surprise. "Are you the colonel's wife he stands accused of raping?"

Before Marielle could reply, there was a knock at the door. A parade of servants carried steaming buckets to the copper tub, and Marielle opened a jar and sprinkled dried lavender into the water. The fragrance filled the room. The maid set a screen around the tub for privacy, and took her leave.

"I suppose you'd like to know what happened," Marielle said from the other side of the screen as Evelyn slipped into the delicious hot water. Was it an imposition to want to know? She'd asked Sinjon to reveal his secrets and he had refused.

"I do," she said.

"My coach broke down in the Spanish hills. I had been to a local church, and thought I would be safe without an escort, which was foolish. Only my maid and my coachman were with me."

Evelyn's heart climbed into her throat as she listened. She heard the floorboards creaking as Marielle paced. "A British patrol found us, and still I thought I might be safe, counting that the officer was a gentleman and would not harm a lady alone. But I was wrong. I'd sent my coachman for help, but he had not yet returned. The officer gave my maid to his men, and saved me for his own pleasure."

Evelyn shut her eyes. Sinjon could not have been that man, surely. He would never harm a woman.

"Captain Rutherford arrived then. I feared the worst, but he rescued me, an enemy, from his own kind. He stood alone against a superior officer and a dozen British soldiers. He covered me with his coat, protected me. The officer ordered his men to shoot Captain Rutherford, and I believe they would have if my husband had not arrived. There was shooting, and the British soldiers were killed, all but two of them. The officer escaped, and the last man was wounded. Captain Rutherford would not allow my husband's men to kill him, though they wanted to. My maid was dead, you see, and I was covered in blood. Mostly Captain Rutherford's blood."

Evelyn rose from the bath and wrapped a towel around her body. She came out from behind the screen. Marielle d'Agramant had tears streaming down her cheeks.

"The soldier was Sergeant O'Neill, wasn't it?" she asked, her heart pounding.

"Yes."

Evelyn gripped the towel tightly. "And the officer?" she asked, breathless. "What was his name?"

Marielle d'Agramant's face twisted. "His name was Creighton."

How could she have been so wrong about Major Lord Creighton? He was famous in London as a hero who had captured a traitor, a rapist, a liar. She had thought that he somehow made a mistake, arrested the wrong man, but had not even considered he might be guilty of the crime himself.

She shuddered in the bright sunlight of Marielle's rose garden, and paced along the path, needing solitude, time to think.

It was another secret Sinjon had kept from her. He'd
told her he was innocent of the charges, but not that it was
Creighton, the *ton*'s favorite hero, who had committed the
brutal crime.

A dozen soldiers and a maid had died. If Sinjon had not
been there—

Her whole body shook. She recalled the scars that covered his body, and his reluctance to speak of how the injuries had happened.

Marielle had told her that Creighton tried to kill Sergeant O'Neill as well, and the sergeant made his way to
the French camp, surrendered himself, and begged Colonel d'Agramant for help, both for himself and for Sinjon.
There was nothing the French officer could do, but Marielle
had insisted that O'Neill accompany her home to France in
hopes they'd find a way to help Sinjon eventually by saving
the last witness to Creighton's crime.

Evelyn let out a sob of disgust. She had danced with
Creighton, trusted him.

She owed him money!

More than anything else, she owed Sinjon an apology.

"How picturesque—an English rose among the French,"
a familiar voice drawled, and Evelyn spun in horror.

Philip stood on the path behind her. He looked older, his
skin sallow, as if he'd spent too much time indoors, hiding.
His eyes were the same, though, filled with pride and icy
hatred.

She backed up until she bumped into a bench and could
go no farther. How was it possible he was here? He was supposed to be in England, being arrested and hanged. Sinjon
had promised she would never see the traitor again.

Desperation made her angry, incautious. "And there's a
snake among the blossoms too," she dared.

His eyes narrowed. "How bold you've become, Evelyn. You used to be such a mouse. Come here. It's been quite some time since I've seen you."

She held her ground, her mouth filled with bitterness. "I'm done with you, Philip. Go away."

His eyes flashed fury, and she flinched instinctively. He stepped forward, grabbed her by the hair and jabbed a pistol under her breast. She could smell the familiar heavy cologne he favored. Nausea rose in her gut.

"We're going to leave in the coach you came in, and you'll do it without making a sound, is that clear, *wife*?" He spat the last word in her ear, made it an insult.

She felt the chill of the gun on her skin as he dragged her toward the coach. This was Philip, the traitor, the man who had terrorized her for four years of marriage. She could not speak, or scream. She could only stumble forward at his command. She prayed they did not meet anyone on the path who Philip might harm, yet hoped someone would see and run for help, fetch Sinjon.

Disappointment bloomed in her chest as they came around the corner of the house. The courtyard was empty. Philip shoved her onto the driver's perch and climbed up beside her. He whipped the horses to a hard gallop.

"Where are you taking me?" she asked. The pistol lay in his lap, and she wondered if she could grab it, stop him, but the look in his eyes froze her with fear.

"You're the comtesse d'Elenoire. It's time you started acting like it."

She cast a desperate glance over her shoulder at Chateau Agramant, silently bid Sinjon farewell, and prepared herself to die.

Chapter 49

"I need another favor," Sinjon said.

"Oh?" d'Agramant asked, pouring more apple brandy into Sinjon's glass. "Surely Sergeant O'Neill's written statement will assist you, but he refuses to return to England until Creighton is in prison or dead."

"I'm hoping it will. You have my thanks for keeping him safe, but I've brought something with me." Sinjon unfolded the gonfalon. The colonel stared at it.

"*Mon Dieu*, Rutherford, where did you get this? Our troops believe it was lost, and think that is why they are losing every battle." He spread it over the surface of his desk and regarded Sinjon with a bemused frown. "Why return it to me? Surely your own army could make use of it, if only to frighten the French."

"I believe that's what some in England have in mind. Philip Renshaw stole it. I found it."

D'Agramant shook his head. "I am not a superstitious man, but this is a holy relic, touched by Charlemagne, and Jeanne d'Arc. It belongs in Reims Cathedral, not in battle. Thank you for returning it to France. Once again I owe you my thanks. I think I can promise the flag won't be used in this war again."

"Where is Sergeant O'Neill?" Sinjon asked, rising. "I'd like to thank him."

D'Agramant smiled. "In the orchard, I believe. He is learning the secrets of making apple brandy. He still fears French troops will arrest him, or Creighton will find out he's here and murder him. I will send someone to fetch him."

The sound of feet on the steps brought both gentlemen to their feet. Sinjon found himself anxious to see Evelyn, anticipating the sight of her, but only Marielle entered the room.

"Where's Evelyn?" he asked.

"She said she wished to go for a walk in the garden. She was quite upset when I told her—"

A man limped in, and Sinjon recognized Patrick O'Neill, even with the grievous scar across his throat and lower jaw. "Colonel, there is trouble, I think," he said, his eyes wide. "A man and a woman just left in a coach. The man had a gun!"

"Was it Creighton?" the Colonel demanded.

O'Neill shook his head painfully. "I'd recognize him. This man was older, mean looking."

"Renshaw," Sinjon growled as he ran for the door. The coach he'd arrived in with Evelyn was gone.

D'Agramant was right behind him, issuing orders. "If it is Renshaw, he may head for the Chateau Elenoire. It's only a few miles away. I'll call out the militia."

"I'll go on ahead, try to stop the coach," Sinjon insisted as a groom came around the side of the house, leading the colonel's saddled horse. "Colonel, I need the gonfalon back again. Forgive me for bringing it back and taking it away again, but it may help stop Renshaw and save Evelyn's life."

"I cannot allow it to come to harm, Captain. It is a holy object. There must be another way,"

Marielle laid her hand on her husband's sleeve. "Jean-Pierre, give it to him. He saved me for you, and you must help him rescue the woman he loves. It's time the gonfalon served love instead of war."

"It's not like that," Sinjon objected. "She's in danger, and Renshaw is a dangerous man."

Marielle smiled. "I can see it in your eyes, Captain, and in hers. It's very much like that. Take the gonfalon, and go and save her."

Sinjon didn't argue. He tucked the flag under his coat and set off on the wildest, most desperate charge of his life.

Chapter 50

If Chateau d'Agramant was a jewel in the French countryside, Chateau d'Elenoire was a bunion. It crouched in ugly decay, the crumbling yellow stone sallow and sickly in the hot sun.

Evelyn watched Philip glower at his ancestral home. He'd spent a fortune in England to prepare a palace fit for a king in exile, and this, a hovel not fit for a beggar, was all that he had left.

"Is this what you betrayed your country for?" she asked.

He puffed like an adder. "The servants will answer for this. I hired twenty gardeners, a full household staff—" He stopped, and his face reddened dangerously as he read her expression. "Don't you dare pity me!"

He dragged her off the coach and frog-marched her up the broken stone steps. She wondered if he'd set her to work, sweeping and scrubbing.

The front door stood open, and inside was worse than out. A startled flock of birds took flight through a glassless window, and Philip swung the gun in surprise.

Evelyn snatched herself out of his grip, tried to run, but he caught her easily. He slapped her for her audacity, and she felt her lip break against her teeth, tasted blood.

"I will make Elenoire a palace to rival Versailles or Fontainebleau," he snarled, pushing her against the wall, holding her there. "Do you doubt me? I am the comte d'Elenoire, kin to royalty. I will not be disobeyed or mocked, especially not by you."

He held her against the wall and squeezed her throat. She shut her eyes against the pain, refusing to scream or panic. Philip enjoyed causing suffering.

She let her face go blank, the way she used to, but it wasn't enough. He curled his fingers around her jaw, digging in until it hurt. Tears filled her eyes, blurred his hate-filled face. She ground her fingernails into the crumbling plaster of the wall behind her and bore it silently.

"Where is the gonfalon, Evelyn?" he demanded. "What did you do with it?"

The pain he was inflicting weakened her knees, made her eyes water, reminded her of her terror when the French spy demanded the same thing in Hyde Park. Sinjon had found her that day, rescued her. She glanced at the empty doorway, but now she was on her own. "I have no idea what you're talking about," she said.

He shook her so hard her head banged against the wall and she saw stars. "I left it in *my* house, the house you despoiled. It's a flag, made of silk, very old. It was in my *private* dressing room."

"I don't know," she gasped. She wondered if Philip would kill her now. She shut her eyes against the pain, prayed for strength, but he grabbed her chin again, made her open her eyes and look at him. His eyes were red-rimmed hollows of fury. She wondered when he'd last slept or eaten. The cruel, cold, aristocrat had been replaced by a madman, ruined, driven by desperation.

"No? Then where are my paintings, my clothes, my books? Do you know where they are, *wife*?"

"Sold." She choked out the word, not bothering to lie. There was no point. She clawed at Philip's hand as the pressure on her throat increased and the pain burned white hot in her head.

"You had no right," he growled. "You are my wife!" He flung Evelyn away so suddenly that she fell to the floor. Putting a hand to her bruised face, she felt the cuts and welts he'd left. She let the sharp sting fuel fury instead of fear.

"I had no choice, Philip. You left me without any money, and the Crown froze your assets."

"Why? What did you tell them? Did you play the loyal wife and swear I was innocent?"

Her eyes burned into his. "They did not even ask me. There is no doubt in anyone's mind of your guilt. Even the French are hunting you. They'll come here, Philip, find you, and you'll hang."

Mirth lit in his eyes for a moment as he grabbed her by the shoulders and hauled her upright. "You know nothing! I am a friend of the Emperor's!"

"And an enemy of the king!" She had never dared to fight back, to rebuke him, but if he was going to kill her, she would not die silently.

"Where is the gonfalon?" he demanded again, sounding desperate. He slapped her, making her head ring. "You must have seen it. It was silk, embroidered with angels, Evelyn."

Angels.

She remembered angels on the shawl Sinjon had put around her shoulders. It couldn't be— She looked away, but not in time. Philip let out a long breath, a hiss from hell.

"Ah, so you know something after all."

She shook her head, but it was too late.

"That man with you, Rutherford, who is he?"

"N-No one," she said. "A footman."

"A footman," he mocked her. "Handsome, young, virile. He doesn't look like a servant. What else is he to you, wife? Why did you come to France? Did you come looking for me, bring him here to kill me for you?" He pushed his face into hers, pressing her to the wall with the weight of his body. "I'm alive, Evelyn, and I intend to stay that way."

A wave of revulsion swept through her. "Get off me!" she said, and shoved him. He caught her, pulled her, laughing.

"You are my wife, Evelyn. My property. I can do as I like. Has your footman taught you anything new? I'm surprised. You never liked sex." He curled his hand around her breast, a painful, ugly parody of Sinjon's caresses, and squeezed. She felt a scream gather itself in her throat. She wanted to fight, but he held her against the wall, unable to move or even breathe. Tears stung her eyes. She went limp, and he chuckled in her ear, and ground his erection against her hip.

"That's better. You can fight if you want to. It won't change a thing. Do you remember what it was like, in your bed, my hands on you? Fight me, Evelyn, I dare you." He grabbed her skirts in his fist, yanked the delicate muslin upward as he forced his knee between her legs.

Rage filled her. No, she thought. She knew what love felt like, what kindness and honor looked like. She kicked him, her knee connecting with his crotch. He grunted a curse and slapped her, but he did not let go. She raised her hand, tore at his face with her nails, but he grabbed her wrist, twisted her arm behind her and tugged. The pain was excruciating. A moan of agony escaped from her lips.

"There, that's better," he hissed. "Moan for it, Evelyn." He twisted her arm again, and the room blurred. As he reached down to undo his flies, she kicked him again, harder this time, with every ounce of fear and determination she possessed. He dropped to his knee, and she ran.

* * *

Sinjon didn't give the horse a chance to slow as he dismounted at the front steps of Chateau d'Elenoire. The coach was there, proof enough that Evelyn was inside.

He took the steps two at a time. A single scream ended abruptly, and he followed the sound down the corridor, peering into each ruined room he passed, but they were all empty.

Evelyn burst out of a doorway on his right. Running blindly down the hall, straight toward him.

"Evelyn!" Relief surged as he opened his arms to catch her.

The roar of a pistol drowned her reply. He felt the ball punch into him, saw her eyes widen, watched her lips peel back in a scream as the breath left his body and he fell. Philip stood behind her, the gun still clutched in his hand. The pain was instant and white hot, burning like the Spanish sun. Philip dragged Evelyn backward, away from him.

"Sinjon!" Evelyn screamed, trying to reach him, her white hand outstretched, but Philip struck her with the butt of the pistol.

"Renshaw!" Sinjon's voice echoed back at him through the empty rooms. "I have something you want." He pulled the gonfalon out from under his coat, ignoring the pain. "A trade, Evelyn for the flag."

Renshaw stared at the gonfalon as he came forward, holding Evelyn by the arm. Her mouth was bleeding, her face was bruised, and her eyes were pools of hell. Sinjon grinned at her, but she sobbed, not trusting he'd be able to rescue her this time. Renshaw snatched the gonfalon from Sinjon's numb fingers and stepped back.

"How very convenient," he said. "But I'll take both, I believe." He pointed a second pistol at Sinjon.

"No!" Evelyn screamed, careening against her husband. The shot went wide, hit the wall beside Sinjon's head. Shards of plaster stung his cheek.

"The French are coming, Renshaw." He was surprised at the calm in his tone, and by the effort it took to speak at all. He wasn't sure Philip heard him, but Evelyn gasped, either from pain or surprise as Renshaw dragged her away. Sinjon fought the urge to sink into blackness. The room wavered around him, and he put his hand inside his coat, feeling the wet heat of blood. He had no idea how bad it was. Chest wounds were always fatal in Spain, but he couldn't die yet.

Evelyn needed him.

Chapter 51

Philip forced her up a steep set of circular stairs, and she wondered if he knew where he was going. The steps ended abruptly, and she stumbled out into bright sunlight at the top of an ancient tower.

The chateau's crumbling battlements framed a magnificent view of fields and woods. He forced her to the edge and pushed her between the thick blocks of yellow stone until she dangled over the drop.

"Everything you can see is my land, wife, my kingdom. You might have lived like a queen here."

All Evelyn could see was a sixty-foot drop. She shut her eyes, feeling dizzy, waiting for the final push that would send her over the parapet. Sinjon was hurt, perhaps dying. She had so much to say to him. She said it in her mind like a prayer and stared at the horizon.

A movement in the distance caught her eye, a plume of dust coiling in the air behind a column of riders.

"The French are coming!" she croaked. She willed Sinjon to hang on, to let someone rescue him for a change.

Philip let her go and began reloading the pistols. He didn't even glance at the advancing soldiers. "It doesn't matter. I have the gonfalon."

"I'm afraid I didn't make myself clear downstairs, Renshaw. You can have the gonfalon, but Evelyn comes with me."

Evelyn turned. Sinjon was leaning against the doorpost. He was pale and sweating, and blood dripped from his sleeve to patter on the thirsty stone, but he had his sword in his hand, and he was glaring at Philip like one of the avenging angels on the flag. Evelyn's breath caught in her throat, half in fear, half in love. He looked magnificent.

Philip raised his pistol and cocked it.

Evelyn leapt between Philip's pistol and the man she loved. "Sinjon, the army is coming. Go back down and wait for them, if you please," she ordered, lady of the manor again. "You're bleeding."

"Did you hear that, Renshaw? The French are coming for you," Sinjon said, ignoring her. Philip sighed. "God, how I hate heroes! You are all so tiresome, and predictable. You won't leave her, will you? It's some ridiculous code you live by. You'll stand there and let me shoot you before you'd even *think* of abandoning her. I have the flag, Rutherford. I'm invincible. You, however, will still die, and you won't have saved anyone."

Evelyn could hear the pounding of hooves now, and the shouts of men below. Philip jerked the pistol toward the stairs. "Evelyn, go and see what's happening, or I'll shoot him between the eyes."

She didn't move.

Sinjon smirked. "Let me describe what's happening. The officer is Colonel Jean-Pierre d'Agramant, Renshaw. He has orders to shoot you on sight. He commands a unit of crack shots, personally chosen by Napoleon for their skill."

A bead of sweat rolled down Philip's cheek, but he threw back his head and laughed.

"Napoleon? I'm emperor here!" He unfurled the gonfalon and wrapped it around his shoulders like a royal robe. "When they see the gonfalon, those crack shots will kneel to me. They will not shoot me, or dare to raise a hand against this blessed scrap of cloth."

Evelyn's ears pricked at the sound of boots on the stone steps. Sinjon kept his eyes on Philip, who drew himself up to full height and waited, the gonfalon billowing around him, gleaming in the sun.

The first soldier appeared in the doorway. He stopped and stared at the flag for a moment before he dropped to one knee and crossed himself. His fellows followed, and Philip laughed.

"You see, Rutherford? As I said, they are kneeling to me."

"Not to you, Renshaw. Never to you," Sinjon growled.

D'Agramant arrived and stood behind his men, regarding the situation.

"Order them to fight!" Evelyn cried desperately. "He's a traitor! Will they allow such a man to hold such a holy object?"

"Return the gonfalon, Lord Renshaw, and you may walk away," d'Agramant bargained.

Philip smiled. "You aren't kneeling, Colonel. Are you not a believer? I could walk through fire unscathed, wrapped in this flag. Ask your men. Order them to shoot. They won't do it. I *will* leave, but the gonfalon comes with me. I'll ride through the streets of Paris with it around my shoulders and shame Napoleon before God and man." He held out his hand. "Come, Evelyn, we're leaving."

She hesitated.

"You didn't think I'd leave you here with *him*, did you? Winner takes all, my dear. The loser gets nothing."

Evelyn looked at Sinjon. He would die if his wounds weren't tended. With Philip gone, the colonel could bandage him, get him safely home to England. She told him with her eyes that she loved him, and took a step toward her husband.

Sinjon caught her hand with more strength than she thought he had left. "No. If you go, Renshaw, you will relinquish your claim on Evelyn. You will swear never to come near her again."

Philip tilted his head, amused. "Are you in love with my wife, Rutherford?"

Evelyn held her breath, but Sinjon didn't reply.

"Apparently not. Poor Evelyn," Philip mocked. "Do you love him, or was he just a roll in the hay to satisfy the itch in my absence?"

"I did not miss you at all," she said. "I wished you were—" Sinjon's grip tightened on her hand before she could say the word.

"Indeed." Philip frowned. "With such tender feelings involved, it will be all the more amusing to kill you, Rutherford." He waved a hand at the kneeling soldiers. "There's not a man here who'd stop me. Not because of the gonfalon, but because adultery is a sin."

He let his eyes bore into Sinjon's. "Imagine this man with *your* wives, *mes amis*, and I'm sure you'll agree to kill him for me. You!" He pointed to the first man. "In the name of the holy Gonfalon de Charlemagne, I order you to kill my wife's defiler."

Evelyn watched in disbelief as the soldier crossed himself and reached for his sword.

"You see, Evelyn? With this flag, I can do anything. Now watch your lover die."

Behind her, Sinjon's breathing was ragged. He would not survive a long fight.

"Put down your weapon," Colonel d'Agramant ordered the soldier, but the man shook his head and crossed himself again.

"Evelyn, move," Sinjon said. He pushed her aside and raised his sword, facing his attacker. Philip was smiling, smug, sure of the situation. He wouldn't stop. He'd kill them all for his amusement.

"Stop!" she pleaded as Sinjon parried the first thrust. On the second, his opponent knocked his sword from his hand, and Sinjon swayed.

Only Evelyn was watching Philip, saw him raise his pistol and point it at Sinjon, his finger curling on the trigger.

She grabbed for Sinjon's sword and lunged at her husband with a cry of rage as the gun fired.

The shot went wide, and Philip screamed as the sword sank into his flesh. Evelyn felt it press home, shudder in her hand. She let go, her shock mirrored in Philip's eyes. He clutched the blade, staring at her in horrified surprise. He backed away and hit the edge of the parapet. For a moment he cartwheeled in space, trying to save himself. The gonfalon floated free, caught by the wind, unfurling over the rooftop to hover above the fray. Philip's eyes were fixed on the flag as he toppled backward.

Sinjon reached for her, tore the sword from her hand and gathered her to his chest, trying to keep her from seeing Philip's death, protecting her even from that.

"I'm all right," she said, her voice quivering.

He touched her cheek. "No you're not," he said, but his eyes rolled back as she watched, and his body sagged.

"Colonel!" she screamed, holding her lover, and d'Agramant caught Sinjon and lowered him gently.

Evelyn dropped to her knees beside him and tore open his coat and his blood-soaked shirt.

"Retrieve the gonfalon," the colonel ordered his men, then came to Evelyn's side. "How bad is it?"

"Flesh wound," Sinjon muttered through clenched teeth.

But d'Agramant drew a sharp breath. "We'll need to get him back to my home," he said.

Sinjon shook his head and began to get up, grunting at the pain. "There's a ship waiting, and they'll hang me if I'm not on it. I must get Evelyn home."

The colonel regarded her soberly. "The coast is four hours from here. My home is only two."

"Home," Sinjon insisted weakly.

"I'll see to him," Evelyn said quickly.

D'Agramant indicated that several of his men should carry Sinjon down to the coach. Then he bent and picked up Sinjon's sword, looking down at it for a moment. "I gave this sword to Captain Renshaw for rescuing my wife," he said to Evelyn. "It has been in my family for many generations. It has always been used honorably, and I thank you for what you did here today. It can't have been easy."

"I couldn't let him die," Evelyn murmured, staring at the bloody blade.

"You are a remarkably brave woman, a woman worthy of a man like Captain Rutherford." He bowed and held out the sword to her. "Will you return this to him with my thanks?" She took it gingerly, and nodded.

The colonel's men poured brandy over Sinjon's wound, and a good deal down his throat to dull the pain. They found clean bandages, and warned her again that the injury would need stitching as soon as possible.

Sinjon looked at her with glazed eyes. "You're free, Evelyn," he murmured before he fell asleep in her arms.

She was free. Just what did that mean?

Chapter 52

Sinjon awoke to the sound of the waves slapping against the hull of the ship. Evelyn was close to him. He could smell the faint sweetness of her skin before he'd even opened his eyes. He felt the tickle of her hair against his chest.

Was he naked?

He opened his eyes as something sharp stabbed him.

"Ow!" he protested.

She didn't flinch. "Hold still."

"What the devil are you doing?"

She looked up at him, her green eyes luminous in the lamplight. "Stitching your wound. It should have been done hours ago."

"Stitching—" He gasped as she jabbed him again. "Have you ever done this before? Isn't there a ship's surgeon?"

She raised her brows. "I have embroidered all my life. I have even sewn for soldiers."

"But never *on* soldiers!"

She sent him a quelling look. "I'm almost done. If you lie still, I'll finish all the faster. Surely you've had worse wounds than this. Like this one." She ran a gentle finger over the scar that crossed his collarbone. It was a light, intimate caress, but she ruined the moment with another stitch.

"How bad is it?" he asked, gritting his teeth.

"The bullet nicked a rib and grazed your flesh. It didn't hit anything vital."

"Are you a doctor as well as a tailor?" he asked. The light from the swinging lantern turned her hair a dozen shades of copper and gold.

She sent him another speaking look. "The surgeon told me."

"Then there is a ship's surgeon?"

She grinned. "No, the colonel insisted a doctor examine you before he'd let you leave. He didn't want France's newest hero dying of a flesh wound."

Sinjon frowned. "You make it sound so inconsequential."

She met his eyes again. "Inconsequential? No, never that. You saved my life, and the gonfalon, and Philip is dead. You're a hero in two countries. It's not inconsequential at all."

"Evelyn," he said, touching her face, seeing the tears glittering like molten gold in her eyes. She hadn't mentioned her role in Philip's death. She pulled away, rejecting comfort.

"Let me finish this," she said, and pushed the needle into his skin again. He lay very still and watched her. Her face was bruised and scratched, and there were shadows on her throat where Philip had held her. His stomach clenched. She should be curled in a corner, sobbing, but she was clear-eyed, sewing his wounds, tending to him.

"Evelyn, how badly are you hurt? Did the surgeon see to you as well?"

She got up to fetch a bundle of white cloth without answering. She tore it into bandages with a deft ferocity.

"You'll need to sit up so I can bandage you," she said crisply, no hint of sorrow or weakness in her eyes.

He let her help him, feeling weak as a child. He leaned

on her, buried his face in her neck as she wrapped his ribs tightly.

"Evelyn, I'm sorry."

She looked up at him in surprise. "Do you think I regret that Philip is dead?"

"Do you?" he asked, touching her face, running his fingers carefully over the cuts and scrapes. She let her cheek rest in his palm for a moment, let her eyes drift shut.

"Perhaps it should matter more to me."

"It may be shock. You'll feel it later."

She looked at him, bereft and afraid. "I don't want to feel it or think about it. I just want it to be over."

He wanted to drag her into bed beside him, comfort her, but she stood apart from him, her expression unreadable, and he didn't have the strength to reach for her.

She was brave, beautiful, and everything he'd ever imagined in a lover. He wanted to keep her safe, love her, honor her and keep her.

Except he didn't have a penny to his name. Or a home. Or a family. He was still a wanted man, a traitor, despite the letter O'Neill had given him.

And she was a new widow, a woman who had endured kidnapping, lies, brutality, and had killed her husband to save him. Was he worthy of such a sacrifice?

She began to wind the bandages around him again.

"So what will you do now?" she asked. "Where will you go?" He saw tears in her eyes, but she refused to let them fall. He read the hope there too.

The words hovered on his tongue, but he had no right to say them.

Instead he grinned at her, the most roguish, devil-may-care smile he could manage.

"I never plan that far ahead."

Chapter 53

Evelyn hovered as the sailors carried Sinjon off the ship. She had let him sleep once she bandaged him. She sat beside him, watching his face, memorizing it. He'd woken as they reached London, found her lying beside him, touched her face. She'd burrowed carefully against his side until the captain knocked on the door to tell her they'd arrived. She rose from the bed, and he clutched at her hand, squeezing it, thanking her wordlessly. For what? Bandaging him? He pulled her against him in the coach, which conveniently awaited them at the pier, held her. Dawn was breaking over the city as they drove through the empty streets.

Sinjon lifted her chin gently, careful of her bruises, and kissed her. His lips clung to hers, roamed over every scratch and bruise, a blessing.

Or farewell.

He kissed away her tears too, but didn't ask why she was crying. Perhaps he assumed it was shock at last. She kissed him back, silently, letting her touch speak for her, knowing if she spoke now, she'd beg him to stay with her, embarrass them both. He didn't want a future with her. For him, their affair was over. She ran her fingers through the silk of his hair, over the stubble of his jaw, breathed him in, memorizing him, because for her there would never be anyone else.

Her heart was breaking as they pulled up at Renshaw House. He'd given the coachman orders to bring her home before taking him to De Courcey House. He wasn't staying. She moved out of his arms, suddenly chilled without his warmth.

"Evelyn, would you come and see me tomorrow?" he asked. "There's something I need to tell you."

She swallowed. "What more can there be to say?" She did not want to hear any more admissions. If he had a wife, a fiancée, a good reason why they could never be together, she didn't want to know.

He winced as he sat up, and she feared he'd open the wound. "You'll tear the stitches!" she said. He let her press him back against the squabs, gasping at the pain.

"Tomorrow," he murmured. "I'll tell you everything tomorrow."

Her heart clenched in her chest.

"But I want—" She paused. What did she want? She wanted him to get out of this coach and walk up the steps with her. She wanted to sleep beside him, and wake up knowing they were both alive and Philip was gone forever.

The door of the vehicle swung open.

"Welcome home, my lady, I trust all is well?" Starling asked, offering his hand as if Evelyn had merely been out dancing the night away at a ball, or visiting a friend for tea, instead of kidnapped and taken to France where her life had changed forever.

Philip is dead, she longed to say, *there is nothing more to fear*, but the coach jerked forward, pulling away, taking Sinjon with it, and she couldn't speak a word.

"It's late, Starling. We'll talk in the morning. Lock up and go to bed," she said instead. He bowed and watched her climb the stairs. She heard the bolt on the front door slide home. The sound of safety.

Starling didn't comment on the cuts and bruises on her face. In fact, he'd been careful not to notice them at all. Evelyn entered her room and looked in the mirror. Was that how it would be from now on? She would simply continue on, a notorious widow in an empty house, her staff polite and protective, never mentioning Philip or treason again. She shut her eyes and turned away from the glass.

Evelyn undressed slowly, crawled into bed and blew out the candle. She could see Sinjon's face in the curling smoke. She reached out a hand across the cold linen of the sheets, and considered going to sleep in the other room. Their room.

But that was over.

Chapter 54

Evelyn paced Marianne's sitting room as she waited for Sinjon to appear. She wore a demure gown of plain blue and a veil to hide the marks on her face. She had considered wearing black, but she could not mourn Philip. She supposed once it was known that he was dead, she might be expected to wear black then. How hypocritical that would be, considering how he died. She fidgeted with the satin strings of her reticule and hoped she would be gone from London by then and no one would see or care what she wore.

Sinjon entered at last. He was elegantly dressed, every inch a gentleman, but he moved stiffly, and she winced, picturing his body bandaged and scarred under his fine clothes.

Because of her.

He'd rescued her again, and had nearly been killed doing it. It was the last time. Today they would say civil good-byes and go back to separate, ordinary lives.

He sat down across from her and smiled, and she wondered if there was anything ordinary about him at all.

"I have had another letter from Creighton," she said. "It was waiting for me when I got home. Marielle told me the truth, Sinjon."

He didn't reply, just looked at her as if he were drinking

her in. Butterflies flitted across her ragged nerves. "Are you well?" he asked, ignoring her comment. "You've had quite an ordeal."

"I'd be better if I knew what to do about Lord Creighton. Can I have him arrested?" she demanded.

Adam Westlake entered the room. "On what charge?" he asked.

"For attempted rape. For false accusation. For—" She shut her mouth with a snap. Creighton hadn't done any of those things to *her*.

"You owe him money, Evelyn. If you make accusations against him, it will look as if you're trying to get out of paying the debt," Adam said.

"Without proof, he'd smile that charming smile, laugh disarmingly, and everyone would believe him," Sinjon added, his mouth twisting in disgust.

"I can't just pay him!" Evelyn said.

"You can't do anything else," Adam said calmly. His eyes roved over her face, taking stock of her injuries. "Shall I order tea?" he asked.

She didn't want tea, or pity. She leapt to her feet, began to pace. "But you could have him arrested, couldn't you?" she asked Sinjon.

"I have a price on my head, Evelyn. If I walked in to Horse Guards now, they'd hang me on sight. Creighton has spread his poison well."

"But you have O'Neill's letter!"

"It still may not be enough."

"We need O'Neill in person," Adam explained, "and he refuses to return to England until he can be sure we can keep him safe."

"Perhaps I can accuse Creighton of fraud," Evelyn suggested. "I only meant to enclose a hundred pounds with the letter I gave him, and he had the gall to spend five hundred in my name."

Sinjon smiled grimly. "You didn't forget to include the money, and Creighton didn't pay anyone a single farthing. I doubt he's ever even been to Lincolnshire."

She blinked at him. "How could you know that?"

"I saw your letter, knew he was meant to carry it for you. I opened it. I had my suspicions that he would keep the money for himself rather than delivering it as you wished, so I took it out and waited to see what would happen."

"Servants are fired for stealing!" she blurted.

Sinjon laughed.

"What's so funny?" she demanded.

"I didn't actually steal it. I left it in a book in your library. I *did* take it later, but only to buy back the gonfalon from the Foundling Hospital."

"Creighton will receive his money today, Evelyn. Five hundred pounds, paid in your name," Adam said.

She stared at him. "Did *you* buy the book, Lord West-lake?" she asked. He turned pale, then purple.

"I most assuredly did not, my lady. I paid the sum as part of an investment. I wish to see justice done, and fully expect to be reimbursed."

"Thank you, but I can't afford to repay you," she said. "Once the Crown knows Philip is dead, they'll take everything. I will not ask my sisters for money to live on or to pay a man like Creighton." An idea struck her. She turned to Sinjon. "Challenge him to a duel!"

He raised a lazy eyebrow, and glanced at Westlake, who looked irritatingly amused at the suggestion. "I am in no condition to fight anyone right now, Evelyn."

"Nor is dueling legal," Adam put in.

"I have a better idea, something that will hurt Creighton

even more than a sword thrust," Sinjon said. Evelyn swallowed, and he winced, realizing what he'd said.

"So what will you do?" She subsided back onto the settee. He sat beside her, taking her hand in his. She savored that little touch, memorized it, storing it away like a squirrel for the cold, loveless months ahead.

"I can't do anything, Evelyn, but you can. If Creighton sees me, he'll shoot me on sight, or have me arrested and hanged before I can say a word in my own defense. He isn't safe while I'm alive. He needs me dead."

Fear prickled along her spine. She'd danced with Creighton, trusted him, liked him. She remembered Marielle's face as she told the story of her encounter with him in Spain. The Frenchwoman still bore a small silver scar on her cheek that would remind her of Creighton every time she looked in the mirror.

"What can I do?" Evelyn asked. "I'll do anything."

Sinjon looked at her with that slow seductive smile that turned her heart inside out and made her feel like the most beautiful, desirable woman on earth.

"Do you remember how I taught you to play cards?" he asked.

She blushed, and nodded. "Every detail." She looked at him, breathless, and saw the answering heat in his eyes.

"We'll host a card party, here, Thursday evening. Creighton will be on the guest list," Adam was saying, but she was barely listening. She was fighting the desire to throw herself into Sinjon's arms. She stared at his mouth, wanting a kiss.

"Evelyn?" he asked, his lips moving, his voice husky, plucking her nerves, rubbing over her desire.

"Yes?"

"Do you still remember how to cheat?"

Chapter 55

The Westlake invitation to an evening of cards came as a very pleasant surprise.

Creighton hadn't even had time to make arrangements to cash Evelyn's recently arrived draft, or to decide how to spend it, when his aunt's sour-faced butler brought him the earl's gilt-edged card. He briefly regretted that there wasn't even a salver under the envelope, since he'd already pawned it, and such a precious, golden invitation deserved a silver tray.

He might have gone to Crockford's, or possibly White's, to wager the five hundred pounds, but there were many men in those establishments who refused to gamble with him, since he had not paid off his losses in some weeks. He could probably paper the walls of this town house with the number of vowels he'd written lately.

A lower class of gaming hell was a possibility, but a house party, especially one held by the esteemed and fabulously wealthy Earl and Countess of Westlake, was a magnificent opportunity. There would be ladies in attendance, ready to be fleeced of their quarterly allowance, ladies who could be flirted with until they were too bemused to notice he was cheating.

And the kind of gentlemen who gambled at house parties were not the deep, knowledgeable players one found in the gaming hells. They were rich snobs who thought themselves morally superior to men like him. None of them knew the intricacies of gambling or cheating the way he did, and none of these lords would go hungry for the loss of a few thousand pounds.

Creighton looked at the draft again, and his mouth watered. It was only five hundred pounds. It would scarcely cover a tenth of his debts. But if he wagered it and won, he could see to his expenses for the whole of the next year.

"Here," he said, scrawling a note and handing it to the waiting butler. "Send my acceptance to Countess Westlake at once."

Sinjon stood in a curtained alcove of Westlake's salon and watched the guests arrive. The room was set up with a dozen tables for whist, faro, vingt-et-un, piquet, and loo. It was a veritable banquet for a hardened gambler like Creighton. Everything he could want was laid out for him—rich widows, young lords flush with cash, ladies sagging under the weight of their jewels.

Footmen circled among the players offering champagne to refresh them. At midnight a light supper would be served, and the games would continue, if necessary, until dawn. Sinjon hoped it would be over long before then.

Evelyn knew her role, but Sinjon's hands sweated. He shifted in his seat impatiently. Westlake didn't expect trouble or need him here but knew he would want to watch. He had strict instructions not to react, no matter what happened, even if Evelyn lost.

He watched Creighton arrive, making a grand entrance in a scarlet uniform adorned with expensive gold braid. The ladies cast admiring glances at him, and he charmed them with a toothy smile and tossed out compliments that made each lady blush with delight.

The major turned as Evelyn entered. She was dressed in her green silk gown, but tonight was adorned with enough pearls and emeralds to tempt any gambler. Her eyes sparkled, darted around the room, but Sinjon noted the way the pulse at her throat hammered against the jewels like a caged bird as she turned her smile on Creighton, a dove dazzling a wolf.

Sinjon clenched his fists as Creighton took her hand, turned it and kissed the flesh above her glove intimately, as if he had the right to do so.

Evelyn plucked her hand out of his and said something witty, her eyes flashing, and Creighton laughed. Sinjon bristled as he watched the man's gaze ooze over her body, coming to rest on the emerald that nestled between her breasts.

He recalled the terror in Marielle d'Agramant's eyes as Creighton pawed her body and tore her gown, and he wiped away a bead of sweat. There was no fear in Evelyn's eyes as she flirted outrageously, sending Creighton a smoldering glance, the exact look that always turned him hard as stone. She simpered, and laid her hand on the major's sleeve, let him escort her to a table.

It was exactly what she was supposed to do, but his stomach was tight with nerves. He'd never been jealous, but the desire to punch Creighton for the sin of merely touching Evelyn's hand was almost overwhelming. He paced in the tight confines of his hiding place.

He looked again, unable to keep his eyes off Evelyn. Creighton was staring at her, his eyes glazed with lust, and pride warred with fury in Sinjon's breast. Good girl—

she had him. She'd charmed Creighton, made him dizzy, distracted him. He wouldn't be able to concentrate on the cards, not with her seated across from him.

At least he hoped so.

Or was it simply her jewels that fascinated Creighton? Was he calculating their worth, planning how best to cheat her out them? The man was a master at this game, and Evelyn had learned to play for mere kisses.

"Good evening, Rutherford," Westlake said, invading his hiding space for a moment. "We're ready to begin. Can we count on Evelyn to win?"

She laughed at something Creighton said. "The game has already begun," Sinjon murmured.

"He's a wily opponent, used to besting hardened gamblers. Did you not say he has a habit of killing the men he owes money to? A man as ruthless as that isn't going to politely let a woman win, no matter how charming she is." He stepped in front of Sinjon, blocking his view of Evelyn. "Whatever happens tonight, Rutherford, the lady is not yet free of the taint of scandal, nor are you. I'll remind you again that you must allow the events of this evening to unfold without interference."

"You expect me to allow Creighton to walk out of here free and rich if Evelyn loses?"

Westlake's expression was as hard and unfeeling as marble. "A good rat catcher knows many ways to catch a rat. We may have to wait for O'Neill's return."

Sinjon felt frustration bite at him, pent up and caged too long.

Westlake stepped away to peer out at the room. "Ah, they've taken their places, I see. I trust Evelyn plays vingt-et-un?"

Sinjon's heart skipped in his chest. Vignt-et-un was the

one game he hadn't taught her. Faro was Creighton's preferred game. He had taught Evelyn everything about faro—how to win, how to cheat, how to bid to draw Creighton into the kind of deep play that made a gambler overeager and careless.

He watched a nervous blush rise over Evelyn's cheeks as she took her seat, and his stomach sank to his boots. What disturbed him most was the look on Creighton's face. He smiled at her, the all-too-familiar wolf's grin he had seen him give other players in other places when Creighton knew he couldn't lose.

He was going to cheat. That was a truth that could not be avoided. But could Evelyn beat the bastard at his own game? Cards riffled and the deal was made. It was up to luck now.

And Evelyn.

Evelyn felt butterflies cascading through her stomach in anxious loops as the next hand was dealt. She was losing.

Creighton's smile had grown progressively wider as his winnings grew. Lady Wilburn desperately tossed her earrings, heirloom diamonds, into the center of the table. Viscount Stanford added a ruby ring. Mr. Ellerby scrawled a hasty vowel on a scrap of paper and set it atop the glittering pile.

Now it was her turn to wager. Creighton smiled at her expectantly, a cat hoping his prey would try to squirm out from under his paw.

"I notice you are not wearing your wedding ring, Lady Evelyn," he said lightly. The others at the table gasped and sat forward, intrigued.

Evelyn forced herself to smile, but she did not reply. Instead she slid the gold bracelet from her arm and watched it sparkle on the top of the heap.

Creighton was cheating. She was sure of it but she could not quite see how. He'd been a perfect gentleman all evening, making elderly Mrs. Ellersby blush under his compliments and sending the young viscount into fits of laughter at his jokes. He was exceptionally talented, incredibly wily, and Evelyn could see why others had been gulled by him. Men like Patrick O'Neill, who had trusted Creighton with their lives. Women like Marielle d'Agramant, who thought the dazzling uniform meant the man inside was honorable.

She focused on her cards, felt anger make her sweat. The hand went around, and he won again. He won the next hand as well, taking Lady Wilburn's tiara and another vowel from Mr. Ellersby.

"Champagne!" Creighton called, snapping his fingers, and a footman came over with a tray. Everyone took a glass, and Evelyn watched Creighton. He slipped a pair of cards off the table, dropping them into his pocket, unobserved by anyone but her. He met her eyes, and she forced herself to smile sweetly.

Lady Wilburn dropped out after the next hand, stripped of her jewelry, and Viscount Stanford lost his allowance for the year and left the table to commiserate with other gentlemen who found themselves with lighter purses.

"Well, my lady?" Creighton asked. "Would you like to continue to play? You still have your necklace."

"A family heirloom," Evelyn simpered. "Would you let me win just once?"

His smile was broad, his eyes hard. "You may wager other things, my lady. I will take your vowel, for example."

"Indeed? How kind of you."

He leaned closer. "Or you wager yourself, and agree to become my mistress if I win."

His smile wasn't charming now. It was a ruthless leer.

She tilted her head, hiding her anger behind a teasing smile, but that gambit only made him bolder.

He reached out and traced the pearls, following them down to the emerald between her breasts, grazing her skin. "When I win, I will allow you to keep your necklace. Will you make the wager?"

Evelyn gritted her teeth and forced herself not to flinch at his touch. "For such high stakes, my lord, I must insist on a new deck of cards."

She watched the smugness in his eyes falter slightly, and he hesitated a moment before he waved a footman over and made the request.

Lord Westlake brought the new deck himself. He sat down to watch the game, his expression bland.

Evelyn won the hand. She took back Lady Wilburn's jewelry. Creighton's face reddened, but he smiled graciously enough and dealt again.

His hands shook. "I believe you dropped a card, my lord," Evelyn said sweetly.

Around Creighton, the crowd murmured. Beads of sweat broke out on his forehead, and he mopped them away with his handkerchief and hid an ace in the linen folds.

"What will you wager now, my lord?" she asked.

He tried another cheat. "We are still playing for your favors, my lady. If I win this hand, the game ends, and you become my mistress."

Her stomach quaked. *Never.* "And if I win?"

"I will marry you, if you wish."

She smiled at him, genuinely amused by his gall, barely resisting the urge to laugh.

"My husband may object to that arrangement," she bluffed. "But I have something else to wager, my lord." She took O'Neill's letter out of her reticule. Westlake stiffened almost imperceptibly, then frowned. Creighton smiled indulgently as he took the letter, scanned it.

He turned ashen and the grin slid off his face. "Where the devil did you get this?"

Now, she thought triumphantly, he looked like what he was, craven, greedy, and evil. A rapist, a liar, and a cheat.

"Mind your language in front of the ladies, Creighton," Westlake admonished. He reached for the letter. "I'll hold the lady's wager, and since the stakes are so high, I'll deal."

A crowd had gathered around them, most of them eager to witness her disgrace at the hands of their favorite hero, Evelyn realized. Ladies smirked and chattered behind fans and gloved palms, delighted that Evelyn Renshaw was about to sink to becoming a courtesan. Others speculated about the contents of the letter.

Creighton was sweating, regarding her with new eyes. He ran a finger under his collar. He could not flee—the crowd was too dense, and fascinated by the deep play between the dashing major and the traitor's wife.

The cards lay facedown. Creighton turned the first one over. The Jack of Spades smirked at Evelyn. The crowd sighed, and the whispers ascended to the ceiling. "A wager on Lord Creighton!" someone cried.

Evelyn's heart pounded as she turned her card over. The Queen of Hearts smiled benignly, as if she had no idea what was at stake. The crowd shifted again, and the buzz of voices fell silent. Only the flutter of anxious fans could be heard.

Creighton mopped his face again, and turned over his second card. The Ace of Hearts throbbed. His smile was slow, spreading over his face, lighting his eyes with malice. "I win, I believe."

"Lady Evelyn still has another card to play, my lord," Westlake warned.

Evelyn's fingers shook as she touched the edge of the card, felt the thin edge slip under her fingernail. There was a lump in her throat as she lifted it, her eyes on the card.

She stared, stunned. Another Ace of Hearts lay beside the queen.

The crowd hissed, and the accusation rose to a howl. "Cheating! Renshaw's wife is cheating!" Angry faces loomed over her, fingers pointing. She recoiled in horror.

"Check the major's pockets." The whisper was so quiet she barely heard it, but the people nearest to Lord Westlake picked it up, spread it, amplified it until it became a roar of suspicion and disbelief. Creighton was on his feet, fighting off the hands that snatched at his magnificent tunic, slapping at the fingers that plunged into his pockets. Lady Wilburn screamed when the Queen of Diamonds was pulled from his coat. Viscount Stanford held up another ace, wrapped in yet another handkerchief. Mr. Ellersby hit the major in the jaw.

"Arrest him!" Westlake called, his voice cutting a thin path of sanity through the mayhem.

"For cheating?" someone asked.

Westlake held up O'Neill's letter. "For treason and false accusation."

Westlake found a face in the crowd, a colonel in the dark tunic of a prestigious guards regiment. "Perhaps you would do the honors, Colonel?" he asked, holding out the letter. "You'll find this concerns accusations made against Captain the Honorable Sinjon Rutherford."

The colonel took the message with a frown.

"Rutherford?" Creighton croaked, his face reddening. *"Rutherford did this?"* He stared at Evelyn in horror, and she let him read the answer in her eyes.

"Are there traitors everywhere?" a lady warbled in terror.

Evelyn took her arm. "Calm yourself, dear madam. The honorable gentlemen among us far outnumber the traitors."

The colonel scanned the letter and looked up at Creighton in grim surprise.

"It's not true! It's a lie, and a forgery!" Creighton tried, struggling against his captors, but they held him tightly, not wanting to let the newest scandal slip away.

"It's enough to start an inquiry," the colonel said. "These charges are serious. If they prove to be true, then you'll hang, Creighton."

"I demand Sergeant O'Neill be produced in person!" Creighton screamed.

"He was delayed in his return to England due to grievous wounds, but has recovered enough to come home at last," Westlake said calmly. "And there are a number of others willing to testify on the captain's behalf as well, I believe."

The colonel drew the dress sword at his hip. He advanced on Creighton, who cowered back against his captors. The colonel sliced off the emblems of regiment and rank and glared at Creighton.

"You are a dishonor to that uniform, sir! Take him away."

Evelyn scooped the rest of the jewels and vowels off the table and returned them to their rightful owners with Marianne's help.

When the last necklace had been returned, Evelyn caught Westlake's sleeve. "Where's Sinjon?"

He glanced toward the alcove without replying, and she picked up her skirts and crossed the room, skirting the crowd unnoticed as they gossiped about Creighton's crime, her own scandal forgotten at last.

She ducked through the drapery, ready to fall into Sinjon's arms.

But the closet was empty.

Chapter 56

"**A**re you sure it's Renshaw?" Lord Blakely asked Adam, wrapping his cloak more tightly around himself as the traitor's body was uncovered.

The two gentlemen stood in the light of a single lantern in Westlake's dockside warehouse. The damp, fetid odor of the river competed with the stench of the remains on the table between them.

The Prince Regent's majordomo blanched as Renshaw's dead gray face was revealed, and he raised his handkerchief to his lips. Even in death Philip's face was harsh. He looked as if he were already suffering the torments of hell for his sins.

"My men brought him back from France," Adam said. "They had to buy him. The French wanted to parade the body through the streets of Paris."

Blakely chuckled coldly. "Even dead, he's worth money, eh? What of his wife? Has your investigation turned up anything to implicate her?"

"I believe Lady Evelyn has more than proven her loyalty to England, my lord. She was . . . instrumental . . . in Renshaw's demise."

"Hmmph," Blakely muttered, missing the hint. "Has she asked for anything?"

"She wishes to leave London. She has a dower estate in Wiltshire—Linwood Park."

"I suppose we can be magnanimous, then. We'll seize the rest of Renshaw's fortune. Allowing her to stay at her estate as a ward of the Crown should be a fitting enough gesture of thanks for her assistance," Blakely said.

Adam pursed his lips. "I think, my lord, that a fitting gesture would be to allow the lady to *keep* her estate, and to grant her a generous reward for her service," he said firmly. "She has been helpful in a number of sensitive matters. The Creighton case for one, and she did put an end to Renshaw for another."

Blakely's rheumy eyes widened. "You don't mean *she* killed Renshaw *herself*?"

"She did indeed," Adam said proudly.

"And are you suggesting we reward ladies who kill their husbands?" Blakely asked in horror.

"I'm sure you'll agree that Renshaw needed killing. She saved the life of one of my best agents in doing so. The cause was just."

Blakely shuddered. "Still, we don't want to be seen encouraging the weaker sex to take the law into their own hands. What husband would sleep soundly in his bed?"

Adam kept his expression flat, and Blakely sighed. "I shall speak to the Prince Regent and see what can be done to quietly recognize her assistance to the Crown. Are you certain the tale is true, that she dispatched the traitor herself?"

Adam smiled grimly. "The French are comparing her to Joan of Arc. Colonel d'Agramant has petitioned the Emperor to give her a medal, a title, and a fortune. She did what no man in the colonel's company was willing to do. We have, of course, refused on her behalf, since we are still at war."

Blakely's eyes lit. "Ah yes, Renshaw had the Gonfalon of Charlemagne, didn't he? I read that in your report. You didn't say what became of the flag, though. I hope it wasn't recaptured by the French. His Highness would be most displeased if it were to reappear at the head of a French army."

"I understand that things are continuing to go badly for Napoleon in Russia," Adam said. "The losses are terrible, and many still blame the army's continuing ill-fortune on the absence of the gonfalon. The grumblings against the Emperor are turning to demands for his abdication."

"Then the flag is in the right hands, *British* hands," Blakely enthused.

Adam merely smiled, and let Blakely think what he would. According to Sinjon Rutherford, the Gonfalon de Charlemagne was now in the care of a holy order of nuns, being lovingly cleaned and repaired. The process would take many months, and the flag would not reappear before a French army again.

Blakely flicked the shroud back over Renshaw's face. "I think we have proof enough that this matter is closed. You may announce Renshaw's death. Best say *we* captured him and leave the French and his wife out of it. Make up some heroic tale to tell. Start the process of securing Renshaw's lands and fortune, and give Lady Evelyn permission to travel. I shall see that she receives a generous reward for her rather gruesome service to her country."

He tucked his handkerchief away and began pulling on his gloves, turning away from the body, dismissing Renshaw. "Have we covered everything?" he asked when Adam hesitated.

"All but the body, my lord. What shall we do with it?"

Blakely shrugged. "Do as you will, I suppose. You can throw it in the Thames for all I care, or give it back to the

French. In my opinion, he's not worthy even of a pauper's burial. Offer him to a medical school, if you wish to be noble."

"Is that the word of the Crown, my lord?" Adam asked.

"Indeed. Thank you, Westlake. Excellent work as usual."

With that, he left the warehouse and hurried out to his carriage.

Adam blew out the lantern and followed.

Chapter 57

Evelyn settled into a peaceful routine at Linwood. In the morning, she wrote letters, read, or sewed. In the afternoon, she walked out over the hills and fields, or visited tenants. In the evenings, she played the piano.

It was dull in the extreme.

She had hoped that once she left London, she would forget Sinjon Rutherford, and learn to enjoy the quiet life of a respectable widow, but she saw him everywhere. She woke in the night craving his touch. She looked up, expecting him, every time the door to the sitting room opened.

She did not allow the London newspapers in the house. She didn't want to know what gossip was firing the over-active imaginations of the *ton* now that she was gone. She did not want to hear that Sinjon had been exonerated and returned to war, or was planning to wed, or was being feted by London hostesses who could not resist a hero, be he false like Creighton or a true knight like Sinjon.

He had not written to her in the three months she'd been closeted in the country. She had received several letters from Charlotte, begging her to return to London, having heard the announcement that Philip had been captured and killed while trying to flee to France. It was a suitable tale, she supposed. It did not mention her name or Sinjon's.

The government had generously allowed her to keep Linwood Park and all the plate, art, and jewels from Philip's principal estate. The treasure palace in Dorset, so painstakingly crafted for the comfort of the French king, was seized by the English one. Tales of the magnificence of the architecture and the furnishings had reached even Evelyn's unwilling ears. Philip had spent his entire fortune on it, gambling everything he had on a vague family connection, and losing.

She took long rides through the woods, enjoying the crisp autumn weather. In London she'd been afraid to ride alone, but Sinjon had taught her that courage was the key to living life to the fullest. She was no longer the frightened wife of a traitor. If the French agent from Hyde Park were to accost her now, he'd get a very different welcome. Her hands tightened the reins and she kicked the mare to a gallop. It was the same kind of misty morning, silver and shining, and she shivered as she remembered the details of the attack. If not for Sinjon's timely appearance, the encounter might have ended very differently. He'd saved her life, and made her feel alive for the first time. She shut her eyes against the familiar wave of longing.

Something clutched at her, snatched her hat from her head, and she cried out in surprise and turned to face her attacker. The hat dangled from a low tree branch that hung over the path.

"Foolish," she murmured, staring at the bonnet.

The sudden drum of hoofbeats echoed through the fog. Her heart stilled in her chest. Was someone following her? But this was Wiltshire, not Hyde Park, and Philip was dead. Surely it was only her imagination.

She pulled the horse to the side of the track. She had

a small pistol tucked in her saddle, a gift from Marianne, and she reached for it now. All she had to do was cock it, aim, and wait. She raised her arm, rested the pistol upon her sleeve and waited for the intruder to ride out of the fog.

The hoofbeats slowed, then stopped. She still couldn't see him through the swirling mist, but could hear the harsh breathing of the winded horse. Good sense urged her to set her heels to the mare and flee, but she didn't move. Evelyn closed one eye and cocked the pistol. She wasn't going to run this time, or give in to fear. She didn't move.

The horse came forward slowly.

She saw the blaze of a scarlet tunic, sharp as blood against the milk white fog. The rider stared up at the blue velvet hat that hung from the tree like an injured bird.

Her limbs turned to water. She shut her eyes, ran a hand across them. He was still there when she looked again.

"Sinjon," she whispered, the word sibilant and breathless.

He reached up and plucked her hat free. "Starling told me you ride this way often." He looked at the pistol. "I didn't mean to frighten you."

She put the weapon away. "You didn't. I have learned to be—prepared."

He grinned and held out her hat to her. She took it, her hand brushing his, the touch still electric, even after so many months apart.

She stared at her bonnet. "You're still coming to my rescue," she murmured.

He shook his head. "I came in hopes that you'd rescue me, Evelyn. Or release me." She met his eyes, and the intensity of his gaze took her breath away.

He dismounted and drew his sword, planting it in the earth in front of him. Then he knelt before her, like a knight before a lady.

"What are you doing?" she asked, unable to move.

"I've been exonerated of the charges against me, and promoted to the rank of major. I have a command waiting for me in Spain if I want it."

She drew a sharp breath, pressed a hand to her heart.

"I must tell you how I feel, Evelyn. I can't leave—or stay—until I have. I came to propose to you."

Her heart began beating again for the first time in months. She stared at him, her tongue glued to her teeth.

"I have no fortune, but I have my army commission to sell, if you accept me."

"I—" she began, but he held up his hand.

"Hear me out before you give me your answer."

He looked into her eyes, everything that mattered written there. He didn't have to say another word, but she waited.

"I love you, Evelyn. If you agree to be my wife, I swear I will love you and keep you safe for the rest of your life. There will be no secrets, no need to hide, and only honesty between us."

"I will," she said.

"I will understand if you refuse me, and I will return to my regiment at once and not trouble you again."

"Yes," she said. His jaw dropped and he stopped talking at last, and met her eyes. She smiled. "Yes," she said again. "I will marry you, Sinjon."

He got to his feet and lifted her out of the saddle. She wrapped her arms around him and slid down the length of his body, breathing him in. She held his face in her hands and he looked into her eyes.

"I love you," she said. She kissed his chin, and his neck, and his eyelids. Then she let her mouth find his.

He broke the kiss "Thank you. I haven't had a clear thought or a decent night's sleep for weeks. All I've thought of is you, and this moment. We'd best go back to Linwood. My father came with me today."

"Your father?" she asked.

He helped her mount. "He wanted to meet the woman I love. My mother insisted upon it. She likes you, Evelyn. She sent my father to assure you that he had forgiven me, taken me back as his son. She wanted my proposal to be honorable. She knows what it means to have a traitor in the family, and was afraid you might not be willing to marry me without my family's approval."

He was right, she realized. But she would have refused for his sake, not her own. She would forever remain tainted by Philip's scandal, but Sinjon was a hero.

The Earl of Halliwell was seated in the salon when they arrived back at the house, sipping tea. He rose as she entered on Sinjon's arm, and looked at his son, the question clear in his eyes.

"Evelyn, may I present my father, the Earl of Halliwell? Father, this is Lady Evelyn Renshaw, my fiancée."

The earl smiled at her, his grin identical to his son's, his gray eyes the same.

He bowed over her hand. "Good morning, my lady. I am pleased that my son has won your acceptance. Welcome to our family. I have warned him that I will thrash him first and disown him a second time if he fails to make you a good husband." He looked at his son. "Your mother wished me to give you this when the moment came." He withdrew a velvet box from his coat and handed it to Sinjon.

"It was my grandmother's betrothal ring," Sinjon said, sliding the emerald onto her finger. He squeezed her hand as he gazed at it.

"You and Sinjon have both suffered under false accusations," Halliwell said as he stepped forward to buss Evelyn's cheek. He clasped her hand and kissed it. "I hope you'll both be very happy."

There was a quiet sound, and Evelyn turned. Starling stood behind her with the rest of the staff. The butler had tears in his eyes. The rest of the staff hovered behind him, waiting to hear the news. "May we offer you our congratulations, my lady? He's a fine man, and I've never known a better footman."

"Thank you, Starling," she said.

"You'll need a new gown, my lady," Mary said. "Something suitable for a wedding."

"And there's the cake to be considered! And the wedding breakfast!" Mrs. Cooper added.

"And flowers," Annie said. "A bride must have flowers."

Sinjon blinked at them. "How long will all these arrangements take?"

"A gown could take a month or more," Mary mused. "We'll have to send to London for patterns and sufficient lace, ribbons, and silk."

"There's invitations to be sent out," Starling said.

"And the best of the flowers are done for the year. We'll have to wait for spring," Annie said.

"There's lists to be made, and menus to plan, and we need a proper Scottish salmon," Mrs. Cooper said. "I can't see a wedding being possible for at least a month. A good fruit cake needs some time longer than that to be right for the celebrations."

Sinjon shook his head. "I'm afraid that won't do." He turned to Evelyn. "We've waited long enough. I don't want to wait another month, or another week, or even another day."

"My coach is outside," Halliwell offered. "And you

brought a special license with you, Sinjon. There is a church in the village. It seems to me that today would be a fine day for a wedding."

And so it was.

Evelyn wore the green silk. Starling picked the last of the late roses and tied them with the last of Charlotte's yellow ribbons for the bouquet.

Mary, Mrs. Cooper, Sal, and Annie rode with Evelyn in Lord Halliwell's coach, all crying a flood of joyful tears, which didn't seem to worry the earl in the least.

"You've never looked more beautiful," Sinjon said as he led her to the altar. The vicar opened his book and began to speak, but Evelyn hardly heard him. She held Sinjon's eyes with her own, read the sincerity of his pledge of love in the way he gazed at her. She let her own love shine in her eyes, and promised to love him forever.

The villagers showered them with rose petals as they left the church, and the local fiddler played a merry tune. After a turn about the village green, Sinjon led her to his horse.

"We'd better hurry," Evelyn said as he mounted the horse and lifted her into his lap.

"We won't be going back to Linwood today," he said firmly.

"We won't?" she asked. She felt her body heat at the look in his eye.

"It's our wedding night."

"But it's broad daylight!" she teased.

He kicked the horse to an exhilarating gallop and rode over the stubbled fields with her. The wind kissed her cheeks, and she hung onto him for dear life. He paused on the top of a hill and pointed down the valley. She could see Linwood Park in the distance. "There." He pointed to a whitewashed cottage by a river.

"Who lives there?" she asked.

"We do," he said. "For tonight, it's our honeymoon cottage. I bought the farm that borders Linwood. I thought we might turn it into a school, or a foundling home, or anything you'd like, but for now it contains a bottle of cider to toast our happiness, some cheese, jam, and bread, and a large, comfortable bed."

Sinjon slid out of the saddle with her—was she really his wife?—in his arms. His mouth descended on hers as he carried her up the path. He didn't even pause. He kicked the door open and carried her up the stairs.

The cider was entirely forgotten.

Chapter 58

"**T**he Honorable Sinjon and Mrs. Rutherford!" Charlotte's butler announced as they entered the Somerson ballroom. Every eye in the room turned to watch as they made their way down the steps. Evelyn's heart lodged in her throat, but this time she wasn't alone.

"I suppose that marks the first time you've been officially announced as Mrs. Rutherford," Sinjon murmured as he scanned the faces below them. "Do you suppose that's what's shocked them?"

"I suppose we'd better enjoy the attention. It will be the last time we make so grand an entrance for quite some time to come." Evelyn sighed, pleased by the thought.

"We could still change our plans," Sinjon said. "If you wish to keep Renshaw House, we could spend time in Town. I can still accept Westlake's offer of the position at Horse Guards."

"I thought you were content to sell your commission and live in the country!"

He squeezed her hand. "I would live anywhere with you, Evelyn, and be very happy."

He let go of her arm just long enough to bow to the

Somersons. Evelyn dipped a curtsy, and kissed her sister on the cheek.

"I suppose congratulations are in order, Rutherford," Somerson said dryly. "I hear your court-martial was concluded in your favor."

"The marriage," Charlotte hissed, elbowing her husband.

"Yes, and that." The earl frowned. "You really should have come and asked permission of Evelyn's family. There has been enough scandal surrounding her name without this hasty, slapped-up marriage. You should have allowed a proper period of mourning."

Evelyn frowned. "I was apart from Philip for over a year. I saw no need to wait any longer to continue with my life."

Somerson looked pained. "There's little we can do now but wish you a happy life together. You should thank me. It was only my tireless effort on your behalf that ensured you were allowed to keep Linwood, Evelyn."

"Then I thank you, my lord," Evelyn said, curtsying again, though everyone present knew it had little to do with Somerson.

"Tell them." Charlotte elbowed Somerson again.

"Since your brother is marrying my daughter, Rutherford, we will be bound rather tightly by blood on both sides. Since you are selling Renshaw House, you will need a place to stay when you come to Town. You will be welcome here at Somerson House."

"We won't be coming to Town at all for some time," Evelyn said, and Charlotte's jaw dropped into her chins.

"But you'll want to come for the Season in the spring!"

Evelyn leaned in and whispered in Charlotte's ear. Charlotte staggered backward in surprise. Somerson caught her.

"Can you be sure?" Charlotte croaked. "It's only been a

month since your wedding! You were married to Philip for years and did not conceive!"

"I'm very sure," Evelyn said proudly.

"Well, if you won't come to London, we shall certainly come to Linwood," Charlotte said.

"I'm afraid that will be impossible," Sinjon said firmly. "We'll be enjoying an extended honeymoon for some time to come."

"How long?" Charlotte sputtered.

Sinjon smiled at Evelyn, his eyes so full of love that her heart flipped in her chest.

"About twenty years should suffice." He bowed and they took their leave of the Somersons.

Marianne and Adam Westlake approached them. "Congratulations!" Marianne gushed, kissing Evelyn. "I told Adam you were in love, but he thought it was something else entirely. He doesn't know love in others when he sees it, I'm afraid. It is up to me to see that he does not miss the finer points of life!"

Adam bowed over Evelyn's hand. "Congratulations, my lady. Rutherford, is there any way I can convince you to take the post at Horse Guards? There is an important matter at hand you could assist with."

Evelyn watched Sinjon shake his head. "You have my thanks for your assistance in proving my innocence, among other things."

"What other things?" Marianne pounced.

"Nothing at all, my dear," Adam said blandly. "Why is it that women always assume a man is involved in something sinister?"

"I know for a fact you have a romantic soul, Adam. I suppose you will never admit you were instrumental in bringing Evelyn and Sinjon together, or tell me the tale."

Westlake took her arm. "Come, Marianne, there's a waltz starting," he said, and led his wife away.

Lady Caroline Forrester watched her cousin Lottie dance with her fiancé. She had seen William Rutherford's coach pull up at Somerson house a week ago. She'd sat in her room and waited to be summoned to her half brother's study to be told that Viscount Mears had asked for her hand in marriage. Instead, Lottie had burst into her room and told Caroline that William had offered for *her*.

Caroline had done her best to be happy for her cousin. Now Sinjon, her first love, the man she had once dreamed of marrying, was also married to someone else.

She watched him whirl Evelyn Renshaw—Evelyn Rutherford—around the dance floor, looking at her with so much love that Caroline thought her own heart would burst. Sinjon had certainly never looked at her like that. She supposed it was a case of growing up too close to the Rutherford family. They saw her more as a sister than a wife.

"Will you dance, Lady Caroline?" It was Lord Arthur Peavey, Viscount Kingsland. He was dull, doughy, and definitely interested in a family connection to the Earl of Somerson, despite the fact that he had received no encouragement from Caroline at all. Still, there was no way to refuse him graciously. She forced a smile and let him lead her out.

Evelyn watched her sisters descend upon her like a flock of yellow birds of prey. "We've been desperately waiting for you to come back to Town!" Eloisa said, slipping her arm through Evelyn's. "Is it true what they're saying about Philip? Oh, to die in such a way!"

"What have you heard?" Evelyn asked.

"They say he appeared at Renshaw House in the dark

of night, and was apprehended by members of the Prince Regent's own Life Guards! You must have been terrified!" Charlotte cried.

Evelyn opened her mouth to reply, but Eloisa answered first.

"Yes, but according to my dear friend Lady Penshurst, he was followed there by *French agents,* men sent by the Emperor himself!"

Lucy's eyes were like saucers. "Truly, Evie? What did Philip say to you?"

"Well—" Evelyn began, but Charlotte laid a hand on her chest.

"It was that footman of hers, the one we said she should fire. He drove them out of the house with a fireplace poker, and chased them all the way to the docks. Philip was shot dead and the Frenchmen were captured." She tilted her head and looked at Evelyn. "Whatever happened to that footman?"

All three of her sisters stared at her, Charlotte's eyes narrowed in speculation, Lucy's wide with curiosity, Eloisa's shiny with pleasure at the gossip.

Over her sisters' shoulders, Evelyn saw Sinjon approaching, and her breath caught in her throat. "I'm afraid I fired him after all."

Her sisters gasped. "You fired such a hero?"

Evelyn's eyes were on Sinjon, her body warm at the unspoken message that he conveyed with just a smile. She couldn't wait for the party to end.

"He was a soldier, and he wasn't suited to the post," she explained, and stepped between her siblings to take her husband's hand.

*   *   *

Evelyn's sisters watched her leave. "Well! I wonder if there are any heroes among my staff?" Charlotte mused, and looked around at the liveried lads serving champagne and standing at attention around the room.

"I doubt it," Eloisa said. "They all look as dull as wood pigeons."

"You never know," Lucy said. "Things are not always what they seem, and under their livery—"

"Under their livery?" Charlotte spluttered, and plied her fan. "What a dreadful thought!"

Eloisa frowned. "Wasn't there a story going around about a lady and her footman?"

"See? Dreadful!" Charlotte croaked again.

"Maybe not," Lucy murmured, her eyes on Evelyn and Sinjon. "Perhaps the best secrets are hidden in plain sight, if you know where to look." She gave her sisters an arch smile and sauntered away.

"Whatever did that mean?" Eloisa squawked.

Charlotte shook her head, equally baffled. They watched as Evelyn swept past, laughing up at her handsome new husband.

"He hasn't even got a title!" Charlotte moaned.

"And imagine marrying for love. How ridiculous!" Eloisa replied.

Sinjon leaned close to his wife's ear, and Evelyn laughed again, blushing an intimate and very becoming shade of pink. "She's never looked prettier," Eloisa said.

"Or happier," Charlotte replied. "And she's not even wearing yellow."

They sighed in unison.

Perhaps marrying for love wasn't so ridiculous after all.

Next month, don't miss these exciting new love stories only from Avon Books

All Things Wicked by Karina Cooper
After Caleb Leigh betrayed their coven, Juliet knew she'd never forgive him, no matter what they once meant to each other. Caleb can't hide from the demons of his past, but he will stop at nothing to fulfill a promise he made long ago: protect Juliet, no matter the cost.

A Town Called Valentine by Emma Cane
When Emily Murphy returns to her mother's hometown in the Colorado Mountains looking for a fresh start, a steamy encounter with handsome rancher Nate Thalberg is not exactly the new beginning she had in mind.

A Devil Named Desire by Terri Garey
Hope will do anything to find her missing sister, even make a deal with the Devil. Archangel Gabriel will stop at nothing to keep an ancient promise, even become mortal. With the fate of the world hanging in the balance, Hope and Gabriel learn that desire can be a devil that's impossible to control.

A Secret In Her Kiss by Anna Randol
A near brush with death convinces Mari Sinclair it's time to end her career as a British spy. But when her superiors send in Major Bennett Prestwood to see that she completes her final mission, passion and desire change all the rules.

978-0-06-184132-3

978-0-06-202719-1

978-0-06-206932-0

978-0-06-204515-7

978-0-06-207998-5

978-0-06-178209-1

At Avon Books, we know your passion for romance — once you finish one of our novels, you find yourself wanting more.

May we tempt you with . . .

- **Excerpts** from our upcoming releases.

- Entertaining **extras**, including authors' personal photo albums and book lists.

- Behind-the-scenes **scoop** on your favorite characters and series.

- **Sweepstakes** for the chance to win free books, romantic getaways, and other fun prizes.

- Writing **tips** from our authors and editors.

- **Blog** with our authors and find out why they love to write romance.

- **Exclusive content** that's not contained within the pages of our novels.

Join us at
www.avonbooks.com

AVON

An Imprint of HarperCollins*Publishers*
www.avonromance.com

Available wherever books are sold or please call 1-800-331-3761 to order.

FTH 0708